NEVER FALL FOR THE FAKE BOYFRIEND

LAUREN LANDISH

EDITED BY
VALORIE CLIFTON

EDITED BY
STACI ETHERIDGE

ALSO BY LAUREN LANDISH

CHAPTER 1
JANEY

"ALRIGHT, that's it for me, Mrs. Michaelson," I tell the woman lying peacefully in the bed as I tuck the blankets around her frail body. She's been a resident here for years, and her children rarely come anymore. They're all too busy with their own lives and have already grieved the loss of their once-vibrant matriarch. But though they've moved on, she's still here, and it's my job as her nurse to make sure she's well-cared for, something I take seriously.

I pause as though she's going to respond and then answer accordingly in a bright, happy voice. "Of course, I'll be careful and have fun. And if I survive the time with my family, I'll tell you all about the wedding when I get back. It's going to be straight off a telenovela—drama, catfights, and fake tears, oh, my!" I throw an overexaggerated wink her way, comfortable being my weird self with my patients, mostly because they're a captive audience who appreciate the conversation.

Or at least I like to think they do. They don't share their opinions with me often.

Still, I imagine Mrs. Michaelson clucking her tongue fussily at the unflattering depiction of my family. I'm not sure that was her nature when she was herself, but in my imagination, she's a very proper, ladylike, and slightly judgmental woman.

Glancing out the small window that gives the room some

natural light, I sigh. The next week is bound to be the literal live-action remake of Dickens's 'the best of times . . . the worst of times.' Guaranteed.

First, I have days of peace in a cabin well outside the city with my boyfriend, Henry, where our plans are to read, relax, take a few nature walks, and soak in the hot tub. It'll be our first big vacation together, and I'm both excited and nervous, especially since now he's stuck at work for a few more days and is meeting me there . . .

"You seriously have to work? We scheduled this months ago."

"Sorry, babe. Duty calls. You know they can't do it without me, and the deadline's coming up quick." He sounds distracted, like he's reading a computer screen while he tells me that he can't go with me for the entire time.

"How about I wait for you?" I suggest hopefully. *"That way, we can still go together and enjoy the obscene amounts of junk food and off-key singalongs of the road trip."* It's a good idea even if it'll waste a few nights of our reservation. But I don't care. I want Henry.

Henry, though, apparently feels differently. *"Pass on that. You know you can't sing."*

I never claimed to be a red-headed Kelly Clarkson, but it sounds worse when he says I can't sing. I agree anyway because my lack of pitch is not the issue. The demise of our couple-cation is. *"Hence, why I said off-key."*

"Huh? Oh, yeah, good one. Listen, I've gotta go. The guys are looking to me to crack the whip. But you should go ahead without me. You need the peace and quiet. I'll meet you there when I'm done, 'kay?"

It sounds like I don't have a choice, and I don't want to start our time off with an argument, so I force a smile into my voice. *"Okay. I've never vacationed alone, and I'm not entirely sure I'll know what to do with myself, but I guess I'll figure it out. When do you think—"*

"Good girl. I'll be in touch. Bye, babe."

The line goes dead.

Yeah, so that's the *best of times* part.

And then, after the forced solitary relaxation and a happy reunion with Henry, the *worst of times* kicks in.

My cousin Paisley's nuptials, which are next weekend, have been destined to be my own personal hell since we were children. In a family that wanted to spend loads of time together, watching the kids play while the adults sipped hard lemonades and gossiped about everyone, Paisley has always been my built-in, ever-present bully.

Of course, no adults ever saw her tormenting me. They would turn the other cheek as she'd knock down my building blocks, clap as she cast me as the monster in family skits, and laugh when she called me 'Plainy Janey', a blunt commentary on my late-to-arrive and none-too-friendly experience with puberty. Because of course, she grew up well and is everything I'm not.

Paisley is tall and lithe, built like a fairytale princess. I'm short and curvy. Her hair is naturally caramel-blonde-brown and falls in a sheet down her back. Mine is bright red-orange, and the curls stand out from my head like I stuck a finger in a live light socket. She's got the perfect dentist office ad smile, while my smile is too wide and shows off the chipped tooth I was too chicken shit to get fixed because I didn't want to tell the dentist that I got it walking into a door while gawking at a cute guy.

And then there's our personalities. While Paisley is a bitch to me, to everyone else, she's charming, and people fall in love with her in seconds. I'm an odd mix of quiet mouse and filter-less mouth, always rambling to myself but never really saying much, not that it matters because people don't listen to me anyway. Then again, my hope and dream is to be as invisible as possible so I don't become someone else's target the way I was Paisley's for all my life.

Not that I'm holding grudges, exactly, but I'm also not looking forward to seeing certain family members. Like the bride. Unless she's tripping down the aisle, ripping her dress, and tearfully admitting that she doesn't deserve Max, her fiancé.

Okay, I don't want that to happen. Not really. Much.

I wish I could skip the wedding, but that would kick off a whole new spin-off series of family drama, so slapping on a fake smile (closed lips, of course—damned chip), attending, suffering through, and scurrying away before anyone deigns to look my way is my best option. My only option.

"I know, I shouldn't be like that about my family, but you don't know them like I do," I tell Mrs. Michaelson, imagining her maternal disappointment in me. But she doesn't have flashbacks of peeing herself at sleepovers because someone stuck her hand in warm water. I do. And I wasn't a kid. I was fifteen, which made it *so* much worse. Especially when the teasing turned from 'ew, did you wet the bed?' to 'maybe she's a squirter' and jokes about my 'wet dreams', and I didn't know what that meant, which led to a whole new round of taunts. Yeah, super funny.

So yeah, excuse me if I'm dreading seeing Paisley all dolled up, everyone fawning over her and her new hubby, and my family asking whether I have any prospects. And then laughing at the very idea.

Shit. I'm holding grudges.

They're warranted, though. I think. Probably.

On the bright side, at least I have a date for the wedding. I can't imagine what Paisley would say if I showed up to her wedding solo. I'm sure it'd be lots of 'poor, pitiful, Plainy Janey' couched as actual concern and sorrow while she not-so-subtly grinned at my misfortune and laughed behind my back. Or straight to my face.

Checking my watch, I realize how late it's gotten. "Oops, I've gotta go. Mason'll be taking over for the evening shift," I say, changing the name on the whiteboard Mrs. Michaelson has never looked at. "Oh, and don't forget to give Mason a hard time about his porn-stache. He needs to grow his beard back out, STAT," I stage whisper to the woman.

"Hey!" Mason complains from the door, where he's peeking around the corner. "I know your true issue with my 'stache. You're lusting after the Chris Evans villain-era look." He wipes his hand over his mouth, needlessly and dramatically smoothing the wiry hair down and then grinning as his hand transforms into a finger gun. "Oh, yeah," he rumbles, nodding as if that show was the epitome of sexy-cool.

Mason is my best friend at work, and beyond, too. He's a great guy, and I've worked with him for years at the care center, helping him go from newbie nurse to confident caregiver. In return, he's my personal hype guy, cheering me on, boosting me up, and telling everyone else at the center 'move, bitch' when my polite and too-quiet 'pardon me' isn't enough. Along the way, we've gotten to know each other, and he's one of the few people I feel comfortable joking around with.

I knew he was listening, which is the entire reason I mentioned his facial hair, so I grin back. "I'm right and you know it. Your chinny-chin-chin hairs are epic, and you've proclaimed an annoyingly high number of times that the ladies love your beard," I tease. "Hell, we joked about taking a cue from LL Cool J and calling you LL Hairy M, but that has a completely different vibe, so . . . ew."

His natural confidence melts, and he ducks his nearly naked chin with a shy shrug that is the antithesis of his usual swagger. "Greta wasn't a fan."

"Then we're not a fan of Greta," I counter with a raised brow and a fire I wouldn't typically express, but Mason's situation calls for it. When he doesn't seem any surer, I propose, "If you told her that you prefer blondes, with even the barest hint of a suggestion that she color her hair, she would rightfully burn you in effigy. And all of womankind, myself included, would cheer her on and offer a lighter. Why should your beard be any different? If you like it, rock it."

Ever heard the expression, *Those who can, do. Those who can't, teach*? Yeah, I'm teaching hard right now because Mason reminds me, "Aren't you the same girl who got a professional blow-out that took three whole hours and several hundred dollars because Henry thought your hair should look less wild for the company Christmas party?"

"*Well*, yes," I agree. "But that doesn't make it right. And my hair is crazy. Your beard is like an ad out of a lumberjack magazine. Don't waste it."

"You're right," he allows, but I don't think he actually agrees. Hopefully, the seed's been planted, though, because he deserves someone who appreciates his sly humor, good looks, and heart of gold. If that's Greta, great. If not, Mason could have women lining up down the curb with a look. "You and Henry heading out for some R-and-R-and-R?" he asks, redirecting the conversation away from things he'd rather not examine too closely.

Of course, I let him, not arguing a bit. But I frown, racking my brain for what the third R might be. Rest, relaxation, and . . .?

"Relaxin', romancin', and ridin' 'em, cowgirl," he hoots in the worst fake twang I've ever heard. Twirling an arm overhead, he mimes riding a bull . . . or something else. "Yah, yah!"

The moves become more spanking and less rodeo, and I can't help but laugh. Glancing over my shoulder at Mrs. Michaelson, I scold him through a smile, "You're awful and that's wrong, so wrong. She'd be clutching her pearls and wagging a finger at you, for sure. Mason Bowen Tillman!" I throw my voice high the way I imagine she might sound, using his full government name to give him a talking-to for being crass.

"Probably," he agrees as his pleased grin only grows. I shake my head, still giggling a bit myself. "For real, have fun. You deserve it, Janey."

"I know," I quip as I sign off on the chart.

I deserve this.

I keep saying it to myself, hoping that if I make it into a mantra, I'll start believing it. So far, it's not working. But I keep trying, practice-makes-perfect style.

Despite my judging Mason's relationship, I didn't tell him that Henry bailed on me in favor of work. I know what he'd say, and I don't want another TED talk about how I'm letting Henry walk all over me and giving way more than I'm getting. We've already had that convo a few times, and I stand by my argument that while Henry's not perfect, neither am I, and we're making it work, even taking steps toward a more serious relationship.

Like a vacation together.

And going to a wedding.

Besides, these days, I thank my lucky stars that I have a boyfriend who's gainfully employed, has a car and place of his own, and doesn't drink to excess. Things that should be bare minimum requirements but are all too often a hard find in a single person.

"Hey, Mrs. Michaelson. I'm Mason. You and I are gonna have some fun tonight. We've got a lovely 2023 electrolyte dosage prepared for you this evening," I overhear him say as if he's reading her the wine list.

I wave to the other nurses at the desk, friendly to a fault, and I'm off. My first vacation in years and my first solo vacation ever. Even if it's only for a few days until Henry finishes the McDermott project.

———

I've got my favorite strawberry apricot Red Bull in the cupholder, a smutty audiobook playing, and surrounding the gray strip of two lane road I'm driving down is nothing but dark green forest, making me feel like a million bucks. Miles to go before I sleep? Fuck you, Robert Frost. I'm feeling like I've got miles to go in order to live.

The sun dances through the leaves, creating a dappled effect in front of me, and I feel like with every mile further from the city I go, I can breathe a little deeper. I do deserve this.

"Yes, my Queen. Show me how you need it. I am here to serve." Devon's cock pistons in and out of Veronica's slippery pussy as he bares his neck, inviting her sharp bite. Veronica moves her fingers to dance over and around their connection, finally feeling full and complete. In one way. But in another way, she's still hungry . . . so hungry."

An automated voice interrupts my book, and I startle, feeling my cheeks go hot like I'm the one getting railed and ravished. *"Take the next right onto private drive."*

"Shit," I hiss and then immediately laugh at my overreaction. "Carry on, you two," I say as Devon and Veronica's story starts back up again.

But a moment later, I have to turn it down so I can concentrate. This 'private drive' is more like a trail, with trees encroaching on both sides of Sioux-B, my yellow Crosstrek, and

I have to stay directly centered in the two tire tracks to keep the branches from scratching my paint.

I hope the GPS isn't steering me wrong. I refuse to be one of those people who turns into a river simply because they assume their GPS knows what it's doing, so if I don't start to see cabins soon, I might have to reverse out of here. And while I'm a good driver, reversing through the forest as sunset approaches sounds like a bad plan.

Creeping forward at barely five miles per hour, I keep one eye on the path—I mean, private drive—and one on the trees. I left the main road several minutes ago, and even that was barely a two-lane stretch of rural asphalt that'd seen better days. And now? I'm out in the boonies.

A secret thrill runs through me.

While majorly remote, the forest is already so beautiful, and I have faith that this is going to be a great vacation.

Just Henry and me, alone in the woods, with a private hot tub and a queen-size loft bed all our own. No stress, no work, no plans. Just us.

I'm choosing to ignore the elephant in the plan that is Paisley's wedding. For now, I'm focusing on the good the way I always do. No sense in wallowing in a storm I can't stop from coming, so I'm going to focus on the sunshine.

I crest over a hill and see through the trees to a small clearing, and there it is! The cabin looks exactly like the posting online, with a porch just big enough for a two-seater rocking chair, a chimney, and a rock engraved with a bear paw and the name *Anderson*. I squeal as I dance in my seat a bit, proud that I found it on my own and excited to get inside. I park my car off to the side as instructed and pull my suitcase from the trunk, beelining for the door.

A quick check of my confirmation email gives me the door code, and when the light turns green and I hear the soft snick of the lock turning, I dance again. The tippy-taps of my tennis shoes on the wood porch are the only sound as I open the door . . . into heaven.

Okay, maybe it's not everyone's version of heaven, but it's

mine. The cabin is perfect, like the online pictures were taken this morning, right down to the fresh knife-hand chops in the two matching couch pillows.

The ad called it modern rustic, and I'd agree, with the big wood beams on the ceiling, stark white walls, and minimal décor. There's a fireplace with a fluffy rug in front of it—wait, is that a bearskin? Hopefully, it's fake or at the least, antique. But the thought is whisked away as my eyes scan the rest of the space. The kitchen is small and efficient, with an apartment-sized stove and refrigerator, and the stairs are almost ladder-like, reaching up to an unseeable loft where I know the bed is located, and the windows out the back of the space are unadorned, letting the green of the trees surround you, even when you're inside. Not that you need curtains. There's not another sign of human interference for as far as the eye can see.

I drop my suitcase, running for the back door and throwing open the slider.

The hot tub is here, along with some outside seating. I take a deep breath, letting the smells of fresh forest air and bright sunshine fill my lungs, and then I exhale jaggedly. I can feel the weight of the city falling from my shoulders, the responsibility of my patients floating away, and the excitement of possibilities swirling in to replace them.

I'm here. I deserve this.

It feels a little truer this time. I pull my phone from my back pocket and take a quick selfie. I look happy, pink-cheeked and bright-eyed against the green backdrop. I send the picture to Henry, along with a quick message of *Made it, wish you were here*. I don't expect him to reply. He's got to keep his attention on his work if he's going to come enjoy this place with me, but I want him to know I've safely arrived.

I busy myself with getting set up, pretty quickly deciding that I'm not hauling my suitcase up the ladder to the loft, and instead, I leave it in the bathroom where I can get dressed after showering. It's down a short hallway and is surprisingly large, nearly the same size as the kitchen, with a walk-in shower and a vanity with two sinks.

"Ooh! A rain shower head! I've always wanted to see what one of those was like," I say aloud, not giving a second thought to talking to myself. I do it all the time. I'd like to blame it on my work where I talk to patients, whether they respond or not, but the truth is, I've done it my whole life. I'm missing the switch in your brain that tells your mouth to shut up, and for the most part, people ignore me anyway, so my constant muttering has never mattered. As long as no one tells me any government secrets, it's fine.

Keeping up the running chatter, I ooh and aah over the black matte handrail on the stairs as I climb up and then gasp at the plush comfort the bed offers. "I'm going to curl up and never leave," I vow. The loft is tucked under the roof pitch and has a sharply sloped ceiling. Luckily, I'm short and can stand to my full five-foot-three height with no problem. Henry will have to duck down to avoid conking himself to sleep, but that's okay. Especially when the bed is covered with a fluffy green comforter, a soft plaid blanket, and pillows that I can tell are down feather-filled from feet away. They look that cozy.

The best part? There's a window right over the low-slung headboard that makes it feel like a treehouse.

"Tomorrow's plan—curl up with my morning caffeine hit and watch the birds and squirrels outside," I say to the empty room. "Get my *Snow White* on with the forest critters."

I may never leave this place.

CHAPTER 2
COLE

STAKEOUTS SUCK. That's it. The end.

But more often than not, they're how I spend my days and nights, weeks and weekends. Alone, staring at a mark, flipping through a file of information either mentally or digitally.

Minutes pass, hours pass, sometimes days and weeks pass. My ass barely moves.

Luckily, this gig probably won't take that long. The man I've been hired to watch is already inside his secretly rented unit, pacing around with a glass of scotch in his hand. Liquid courage, perhaps, for what he's about to do? He doesn't seem the type to need it, though.

Mr. Webster is a good-looking man in his late fifties, with salt and pepper hair, a penchant for expensive watches, and apparently, a mistress thirty years his junior. At least that's the suspicion his wife came to me with, and it seems on par with his type —old enough to be at the top of the food chain career-wise, kids out of the house, and after having lived a life of climbing one ladder after another, looking for some sort of excitement and challenge. Or maybe he's just an asshole who's finally getting caught by a wife who's ignored the signs in the past. Either way, or even both, it doesn't matter to me.

Infidelity isn't the type of case I prefer, but unfortunately, it brings people to my door and pays well. Especially with the clientele I serve.

Like Mrs. Webster. She sits on at least three Boards of Directors, two corporate and one non-profit, her perfectly coiffed hair doesn't dare get out of place, and she moves in a social circle of the wealthy elite courtesy of her husband's work. So when she showed up, delicately dabbing at bone-dry eyes and proclaiming that she had concerns about her husband's loyalty, I added an annoyance fee guised as travel costs, and she never batted a glued-on lash.

Because it all comes down to money. It affords people like the Websters the gift of buying their way out of almost any situation without actual consequences. Like an unhappy marriage, for example.

Except for Mr. Webster.

I'm not a simple tool to be aimed at a target and used for someone else's purposes, and as soon as I accepted Mrs. Webster's job, I researched her first. After that came Mr. Webster, his company, her boards, their connections, finances, and preferences on everything from how they take their morning coffee to their favorite extravagances.

What I discovered is that any infidelity from either party triggers a clause in their pre-nup agreement. One Mrs. Webster seems to be particularly interested in activating. How a thirty-year-old prenup clause might hold up in court isn't my area of expertise, so I'll let the lawyers handle that. My job is just to find the proof.

And so here I am, on stakeout again. This time, like an Army sniper, on my belly in the bushes fifty yards from my target.

Silently, I curse the dragonfly that's been buzzing around me, occasionally landing on my ass, but I don't move. My hips ache, my shoulders hurt, I'm out of beef jerky, and I needed to piss three hours ago, but the slightest shift in position might catch my target's eye, so I stay frozen like a statue, lying prone in the dirt with my eyes pressed to the binoculars.

Why the fuck aren't we in some five-star, luxury hotel in town for this meet-n-greet? That'd be the usual MO for guys like

Webster. Half of the reason they get caught is because they're stupid enough to leave a credit card trail or someone catches them on social media.

But for some reason, Webster's rendezvous plan includes a remote cabin in unfriendly woods. It'd make sense if he were doing a clandestine deal with a drug cartel and prioritized an ambush-unfriendly landscape. But that's not what he's up to. He's just getting his dick wet, something he could've done around the corner from his downtown penthouse.

Mr. Webster pulls his phone from his pocket and stares at the screen for a moment before a soft smile dawns, transforming his face. I wish I had a cloning app installed on his device, but this trip was too last-minute to risk getting that close to him. So I watch . . . as he talks, nods, and his smile dissolves. He hangs up a moment later, and after dropping his phone to a nearby table, he scrubs his face with his hands and sighs heavily. Whoever it was, that call aged him ten years.

After a long minute, he grabs the bottle of scotch and pours a healthy two fingers into his nearly empty glass. He stares into its depths and then gulps the majority of it in one swallow.

She's not coming.

That's who was on the phone—his alleged mistress. If she were still coming, he wouldn't be well on his way to a whiskey dick. Maybe she realized what she was doing, or maybe she realized his lies about her being permanent were just that. Or maybe she caught wind that the Missus is sniffing around. Either way, she's a no-show for tonight.

It's late and I'm tired, so it doesn't take much to talk myself into calling off the stakeout. I've got a hot shower and a comfortable bed calling my name, and I can continue surveillance tomorrow.

Quietly and slowly, I extricate myself from the hiding spot I've been in for hours, stashing my camera and binoculars against a tree and covering the waterproof cases with vegetation. That'll be one less thing to haul in tomorrow. I make my way back to my truck, parked on a pathway well away from Mr. Webster's cabin, and drive up the hill to the cabin I'm staying at, which is close enough to make walking over to spy on Webster doable, but far enough away that we won't run into each other. Not that Mr. Webster is the type to go traipsing through the forest.

Still, I park my truck away from the cabin and lock it up, making the short trek to the front door. I put the code into the door lock and step inside, typing an accounting of today's activities on my phone.

18:32—Phone call received. Target appears distressed. Surveillance suspended until am.

I'm in the middle of saving the note to my secure cloud when it happens. That's the only excuse I have for not realizing that I'm no longer alone.

"G-g-get out!" a female voice shouts.

I jerk my eyes up to find a small spitfire of a woman, wrapped in a towel but with water droplets all over her skin, a riot of red curls sprouting from her head in every direction like a halo, and gray eyes that are glaring at me in fear. She's holding a small canister out in front of her like it's her saving grace.

Unaccustomed to someone getting the drop on me, I sputter, "What the—"

I don't step toward her, but I do turn to face her more fully, and she must take that as a threat because she lets loose with a panic-stricken, high-pitched scream and the bear spray she's holding. She's thankfully too far away for the jet stream of burning poison to reach my eyes, and it falls in an arc to the floor, several feet in front of me. She must've gotten some fake shit off Amazon because the range should be better than that.

A dark grin steals my face as I watch it puddle and then spit the last few drops as the canister is spent. It's going to make a cloud that burns like a motherfucker in five minutes, but for now I'm good. When I lift my gaze to the woman's, she's the one frozen now.

She's the first to realize the disadvantage she's at and makes a loud squeaking noise as she turns, bolting down the short hallway toward the bathroom. With her high-kneeing it, the towel drops dangerously low before falling away completely as she decides to save herself rather than her modesty. I get a quick glimpse of a floral tattoo on her left ass cheek, and then the bathroom door slams shut and locks a split-second later.

I could pick the lock in seconds, or take it down with a single kick, but instead, I bang on it. "Hey!" I yell, then demand, "What the fuck are you doing here?"

"I'm a black belt in karate! You should get outta here or I'll kick your ass!" the woman screeches back in a hysterical voice.

A black belt? Does she think that's remotely believable? Because given the way she was shaking and the fear in her eyes, she's no more a karate expert than I'm a plumber.

Though I am fully skilled in laying a particular type of pipe.

Where did that come from? I don't think in stupid double-entendres like that. That's my brother's specialty. Kyle can make anything sound downright filthy, but that's not my style. It must be because of the peek at her bare ass, which was round and perky, bouncing as she ran.

I take a slow breath, calming down from the shock of her 'attack'. "Look, you're safe. I'm not going to hurt you. Are you going to hurt me?" I only ask to be polite. I don't think she could actually hurt a fly even if she wanted to. Not with aim like hers.

"Get out!" she orders again, but it sounds more like a plea. A request. A beg.

"Afraid not. This is my cabin, or my buddy's, at least. He gave me permission, and I'm staying here for a few days."

A horrible thought occurs to me.

Motherfucker, I'm going to kill Anderson with my bare hands. Metaphorically speaking, of course. I don't offer that service. I'm a private investigator, not a hitman, though my family does like to speculate, which I find infinitely amusing and entertaining. Listening to their wild theories about what I do is half the reason I've never told them. The other half is that it's none of their fucking business.

"Did Anderson send you?" I ask carefully.

He's more of an acquaintance than a close friend, given that we met when he hired me to find his daughter who'd gone missing with a sketchy guy. I found Oriana for him and returned her safely, sans abusive boyfriend, of course, who was having difficulty chewing solid food for the next six weeks and subsequently heeded the warning to stay far, far away from Anderson's daughter. I don't think he'd set me up, but the woman's appearance seems a little coincidental, and I'm a firm believer that there's no such thing as coincidence. But if Anderson thinks it's acceptable to stock his cabin with a naked woman when I only asked to borrow it as a base camp for work, we're going to have words that he will not enjoy.

"Anderson?" she echoes. "Like the rock out front?"

"Yes." I keep my eyes on the doorknob, watching for any movement. She won't get the drop on me again.

"That's what my confirmation says—the cabin has a rock out front with *Anderson* engraved on it. This is my cabin. Where I'm staying." Her tone invites zero argument, as though her decree should be more than enough to send me packing. It's cute. And annoying.

I just want a shower, dinner, and to crash until morning, but there's a big obstacle in that plan. Her.

She has a 'confirmation', she said, like a short-term rental booking, I'd guess. Anderson does that with this cabin when he's not using it, but he assured me it was available and it couldn't have been located any better to surveil Mr. Webster, who by some stroke of luck is staying at a cabin less than a mile away through the dense forest. It's perfect, except it's apparently already inhabited.

"Maybe this is a simple mix-up. I'll call Anderson and get it straightened out, see if there's another cabin you can stay in." It seems like a generous offer to me.

The door jerks open.

She's dressed in tight yoga shorts and a T-shirt, as though she might need to have her movements totally unrestrained in order to actually kick my ass. "I'm not going anywhere. This is my vacation, a much-needed one, thank you very much. You go ahead and call your buddy, see if he can get you a place to stay."

She's pointing a short-nailed finger in my face, trying to be tough, but fear is nearly vibrating in the air around her. Instinctively, I catalog everything about her in an instant. Beyond the red curls and gray eyes, she's nearly a foot shorter than me. Her full breasts are pearled up beneath the T-shirt, likely a result of the temperature difference between the steamy bathroom and cool cabin. She smells faintly of sandalwood from Anderson's supplied soap, and there's a dark freckle to the right of her full lips.

Lips which are pressed together in a flat line as she glares at me. At least I think it's supposed to be a glare, but at most, it's a dark look.

I hold my hands out wide, showing that I mean no harm as I placate her. "Sure, let's make that call."

CHAPTER 3
JANEY

STANDING with my ear not-too-subtly turned toward my uninvited guest, I'll admit that I'm eavesdropping. Normally, I'd feel guilty for intruding, but it seems prudent when you're trapped alone in an isolated cabin in the woods with a tall, sexy, blond murderer.

At least he *said* he won't hurt me.

I'd like to believe that, I really would. But when someone dressed head to toe in black shows up, leaves in their hair, and I'm pretty sure a streak of bird poop on one shoulder, I think I'm fully permitted to freak the hell out. Like he's been out there in the woods, becoming one with nature, before breaking in here to kill me. Probably.

I was in the middle of my post-shower routine, slathering body oil on my legs, when I suddenly knew I wasn't alone. I hadn't heard anything, exactly, but after years of caring for patients who are completely silent but still 'present', I've developed a sort of sixth sense about these things. At first, I thought Henry had decided to surprise me and had a flash of excitement, but a quick check of his location in the app we share showed me that he was still in the city at work.

I'd sent up a silent thanks that I'd been lazy and stashed my bag in the bathroom because I quickly and silently dug out the bear spray I'd packed, as had been recommended on the Airbnb ad for this cabin, and stepped out into the hallway, ready to scare off a bear smart enough to come in the front door.

Except it hadn't been a bear.

I think I might've preferred a big, Yogi-smart grizzly at this point. Or even a slashing and clawing one like in that Leonardo DiCaprio movie.

Because this man is angry, which is why I'm listening closely and watching even closer. I tend to see the best in people, but I'm not an idiot, so I'm keeping my position by the front door. Ready to make a run for it, just in case.

"What do you mean there's nothing you can do?" he snarls into the phone. He runs a hand through his hair, finding a leaf which he frowns at as if it personally offends him. He strides to the kitchen, opens a lower cabinet near the sink, and throws the leaf away in the trashcan, obviously familiar with the layout, which gives me pause.

Could he be right? Am I the one who shouldn't be here? But I can virtually picture the confirmation email in my mind, complete with dates, notes on the location, and the door lock code. Not to mention the dozen times I've made lists, checked calendars, and rehashed plans for this vacation. I know I'm right. Probably.

Turning back toward me, he's nodding, but his jaw is clenched tight, not happy with what he's hearing. "Fine. Yeah, I know. Thanks, Anderson." He hangs up, slipping his phone into a back pocket as he meets my questioning gaze. He narrows his eyes, but I can still see the storm raging in their blue depths. "Fuck."

I almost say 'your eyes are pretty' but manage to swallow that not-helpful commentary down for a change. Instead, I ask hopefully, "What'd he say?"

The man sits in the armchair nearest the cold fireplace. "This is a vacation for you?"

"*Yes*," I answer slowly, feeling like he's leading me somewhere, but I'm not going anywhere. I've got a non-refundable reservation to be right here where I am. Non-bear, grumpy, likely-murderers, notwithstanding.

I'm pretty sure *that* has to fall under some refund clause somewhere, right?

Sighing heavily, he explains, "There was a delay when Anderson pulled the availability of the cabin from the short-term rental website. That delay allowed you to book after he'd already told me I could stay here."

I open my mouth to argue. Whatever delay isn't my fault, and I have a confirmed and paid-for stay. The man holds up a hand to stop me, but it's the stony look he flashes that actually makes me clamp my mouth shut.

"Anderson is concerned about his rating or whatever with the website and wants you to stay. I get that, but this is a work situation for me. I need to be in this area." He glances out the window at the forest, which is getting darker by the minute. "I'll be out for the most part and can sleep in my truck, but I'd like to come in for a shower in the evening before bedding down. It'll be a few days at most, and I'll reimburse your whole stay for the inconvenience. Any chance you'd be agreeable to that?"

I'm good at reading people, always have been with a family like mine, and only got better at it when I started working at the care center. I see families, patients, and doctors, sometimes at their best and more often at their worst.

It's those skills that kick in as I evaluate this guy. And the more I see, the more I grow intrigued.

There's a formality to the way he asks to strike some sort of deal, like he's negotiated before. He's dressed in all black, and while there's a tactical vibe to the clothing, it's high-end and expensive. He didn't buy this crap from your average Army-Navy store. He's laid back in the chair casually, but there's an undercurrent of urgency as though every muscle is poised for action. He's dangerous, but I don't feel in danger. The distinction is important.

And if I'm not mistaken, he's offering to pay for my entire stay in exchange for a few showers. If he's not a murderer, it's a pretty sweet deal. For me.

I give myself a moment to think, aware that I have a well-documented weakness for helping people in need at nearly any cost, including my own well-being. But still, I trust my gut. It's (mostly) never steered me wrong.

Plus, I remember that drive in and it's getting late. I can't, in good conscience, turn him out to traverse that in the dark. I'd never forgive myself if something happened.

"What's your name?" He blinks like that's not what he expected me to say. "If I'm sharing the facilities with someone, I'd like to at least know his name," I explain, having mostly made my decision.

He moves slowly like he doesn't want to startle me, and I watch warily as he stands and approaches. At the last minute, he reaches for the closet next to me. Huh, I didn't even notice that door with the eye-catching view out the back windows.

He pulls out a small black duffle and digs in an outside pocket. Holding up a driver's license to show me the picture and name, he says, "Cole Harrington. You?"

I confirm the picture is him and then offer, "Janey Williams."

"Janey," he echoes. One side of his mouth tilts up in the slightest hint of a smile. It makes him look boyish and mischievous, something I sincerely doubt he'd appreciate being told. His whole vibe is serious business in the front, no party in the back.

"Are you here to kill anyone or anything?" I ask bluntly, thinking I might as well get the Question of the Day out of the way.

His blond brows jump up his forehead. "What? No."

He sounds appropriately shocked at the question and not at all murder-y. Probably.

"I'm a photographer. I left my camera in a hide so I didn't have to haul it." He's smart, answering my next question before I could ask it, but if I'd listed the top ten things Cole Harrington does for a living, photography wouldn't have remotely been in consideration.

He's answered my questions, and I'm not seeing any obvious red flags, so I feel eighty-five percent good about my decision to agree to this idea, which is enough for me. "If you're paying for my vacation, the least I can do is let you sleep here. But I want private hot tub time. I have plans for those jets."

I point out the back window toward the currently cold and quiet tub. At the sharp look he gives me, I belatedly realize how sketchy that sounds. Whoops.

"No! I mean, for my back. I had to move Mrs. Michaelson to change her bedding before I left, and we were short-staffed. I'm a nurse, and we're always short-staffed . . . it's an industry-wide problem." I wave a hand dismissively because there's nothing I can do about that. "So I had to do it alone. Mrs. Michaelson is a tiny woman, but she's frail so you have to be extremely careful. And ooh, my back's been aching ever since. I want to sit in the hot tub with a jet aimed at this knot right here." I rub at a spot on my lower back.

Cole blinks . . . and blinks again, looking at me as if I'm speaking a foreign language. "I have no idea what you just said, but you can have full access to the hot tub."

Some sort of deal agreed upon, I hold my hand out. "Good. Nice to meet you, Cole."

He shakes my hand with the slightest chuckle. "I sincerely doubt that's true, but thanks for the polite lie." His palm is a little rough, not callused like he does hard labor, but also not soft and doughy like he's never worked a day. He releases me and picks up the duffel bag from the floor. "Mind if I shower?"

"Yeah, no. That's fine," I say as I move out of his way, though I wasn't in his way to begin with. "I was gonna make dinner. You hungry? I brought groceries and have plenty. I don't mind sharing. Do you like chicken? Or I bought soup. I could heat that up for us and toast some bread. Unless you're vegetarian? If that's the case, all I can offer is a baked potato because I bought those to go with steaks one night for Henry and me. But you don't strike me as the vegetarian type."

Cole is looking at me strangely again, and I realize that I'm rambling.

"Sorry, I talk a lot. Always have. Henry calls me out on it, always wants me to 'shut up for a single fucking minute'." I throw my voice to mimic his annoyance. I continue in my own voice. "But it's hard to keep my thoughts in my head. I talk to patients, like Mrs. Michaelson." I drop her name like they're old friends already. "All day, so it feels natural to provide some narrative to the passing of time, you know? But it's a bad habit, so . . . sorry."

"Dinner would be great. I'm not vegetarian."

He disappears down the hall, and a moment later, the bathroom door closes. I hear the click of the lock, which makes me pause. He's locking *me* out? Like I'm the probably-not-a-murderer in all black.

Laughing under my breath, I go to the kitchen and start pulling out food. I decide to heat up the soup, but if Cole's been outside all day, which seems to be the case, he probably needs more than a light dinner, so instead of the plain bread I'd planned, I toast the bread with cheese and turkey, making stovetop paninis. I only burn one of them a little bit, and they smell pretty damn good if I say so myself, making me rather impressed with my off the cuff creativity.

Right as I'm setting the food on the island, Cole reappears. His hair is damp, the ends flicked up and out like he rubbed a towel willy-nilly over his head. I could never. The frizz would be extreme.

His white T-shirt strains at his chest, where his pecs seem intent on making the cotton give up the ghost, while his biceps do the same to the sleeves, hugging the muscles like a lover. Well-worn jeans are low-slung on his hips, and he walks toward me on bare feet looking like a model right off some grocery store checkout line magazine.

Dayumm!

I give myself a mental high-five for keeping that reaction in my head instead of letting it fall out of my mouth like I usually would. I'm not looking-looking, too loyal to Henry to disrespect him that way, but it's not like Cole's hiding his attractiveness. It's obvious in the same way the sun is blinding in the sky.

"Smells good," he says, eyeing the meal as he pulls out one of the barstools that ring the small island, but he doesn't sit down.

I stand there stupidly until he looks pointedly from me to the seat. Surprised at the gentlemanly gesture, I jump. "Oh! Thank you. Henry isn't big on chivalrous gestures so I'm not used to it, I guess." I laugh at my own awkward confusion.

Cole sits beside me, a respectable distance between us. "You've mentioned him a couple times. Henry?"

Scooping a bite of soup, I explain, "My boyfriend. He's coming up after he finishes a project. He's a software engineer and got stuck fixing a bug his team can't figure out. He's good at working out the nuances of code and how to improve it. We've been together for almost a year, but he works a lot so I should probably adjust for that, in which case, it's been . . . doo-doo-doo-doo . . ." I mimic tapping on an air calculator before concluding, "Twelve weeks." I laugh at the joke, but Cole doesn't so much as crack a smile.

"Harrumph." It's a mere sound, but I feel judged.

"We're going to have a romantic vacation, so it's a good thing you're only going to be here for a few days," I say with a wink. "Then next weekend, I have my cousin's wedding to go to, which is going to be downright painful. Thank God for open bars, amiright?" Another joke, and it falls flat too.

Disappointed, I focus on my soup, and silence reigns while we eat for a few moments.

"People don't surprise me. It's a given. But you . . . I have no idea how, but you do," he says.

He looks at me with clear eyes, seeming anything but confused, but he sounds sincere. Almost like he's complimenting me? It definitely feels deeper than the superficial chatting I've been offering as a way to keep the conversation going one-handed.

"Thanks?"

Not offering more on the topic, he says, "I'll take the couch. You can have the bed."

"Oh, you don't have to do that. If you're paying, the least I can do is give you the bed," I protest. "Besides, I have to warn you, I snore. Not a lot, like I don't need a CPAP." I put a clawed hand over my nose and mouth and make a sound imitating the machines that sounds a lot like *schlooo-chuh* before realizing how weird that sounds, and rush to explain. "But not a little, either, not like a tiny, cute puppy. Somewhere in between, I guess."

His eyes narrow, and I wait for him to skip over my over-share. Instead, he offers, "My brother's dog snores. He drools everywhere, and his paws flop around like he's chasing squirrels in his dreams. All the while, snoring." He's saying ugly things about the animal, but it's with amusement and affection. He even smiles, which completely changes his face. The crack in his straight, pressed lips is like the sun coming out from behind clouds on a stormy day.

I found it! His weak spot is dogs, apparently. I store the infor-mation away for future conversations.

"What's his name?"

"My brother or the dog?" he clarifies.

"Either. Both," I say eagerly. I want to keep him talking. I like listening to his voice. It's deep and rumbly but smooth, like silk and gravel. And even when he's talking about a dog, it feels meaningful.

"Peanut Butter, but we usually call him Nutbuster." I assume he's talking about the dog, not his brother, whose name he doesn't offer. "So, you hurt your back with Mrs. Michaelson?"

I sense that he's directing the conversation away from him, but I let him, telling him more about the woman I've come to care for even though she's never spoken a word to me. But in my mind, she has a sassy personality, cares for her family, and offers great advice.

By the time we finish eating and clean up the kitchen, I've told him all about being a nurse and how much I love it, more about Henry, and a little about the wedding, though I don't want to even think about it yet. He's been an attentive listener but hasn't shared much at all, answering my long rambles with mostly one-word answers and the occasional grunt.

But he reacts to everything if you pay attention. His brows move incrementally when he's surprised, his lips curl when he's amused, and he hums thoughtfully when he's playing something out in his mind. He's quiet, but it's a completely different conversation than the ones I have with the silent people at work.

Or with Henry, a tiny voice whispers.

I don't like to admit it, but it's true.

Henry is a great guy—handsome, smart, and nice—but he also gives me grief for my rambling. To be fair, he's also usually multitasking with his attention divided between me and his phone. I could be chattering away about giant purple people eaters attacking the city and Henry would probably say, 'Wow.'

Cole isn't like that. In fact, I bet I could pop-quiz him on everything I've said tonight and he'd probably be able to quote me verbatim. He's that engaged.

"Good night," Cole says as he walks me to the ladder-like stairs. It vaguely feels like getting walked to the door after a first date, but that's wrong. This is nothing like a date. It's just two people making the best of a difficult situation.

Yep, that's it. Nothing to see here, nothing inappropriate, nothing weird at all.

"Sleep tight, don't let the boogieman bite," I finish suddenly, then explain. "That's how my Grandma always said it. Not good night, sleep tight, don't let the bed bugs bite. Said she wasn't inviting bugs anywhere near her bed so she refused to say it the regular way." I smile as a memory replays in my mind. "One time, I asked her about inviting the boogieman, which, to me, seemed way worse than bed bugs, but she laughed and said that he was too scared of getting her frying pan upside the head to come around so she'd take her chances."

His lips twitch up at the corners, and he repeats, "Don't let the boogieman bite." I decide to take the win and leave on a high note so he doesn't change his mind and kill me in my sleep.

I start to climb, wondering if he's going to stare at my ass as I go up, but a glance behind me shows that he's already turned away and is striding toward the couch. He's being gentlemanly again, but I'd be a liar if I didn't admit that I'm a teeny-tiny bit disappointed.

I shouldn't be. He's being respectful, a rare and unexpected trait.

But in a weird way, tonight was . . . fun. More fun than I've had in a long time. Not once did Cole seem annoyed with me or like he was tuning out our conversation, and I enjoyed pushing to see if I could crack his stoic exterior.

Lying in bed, I stare at the lofted ceiling and listen. I hear Cole spread out a blanket and the creaking of the couch as he lies down. He takes a few deep breaths and then his breathing goes steady and even.

Is that it? That's all it takes for him to go to sleep?

Good for him. In my experience, it takes a quiet head, a clear conscience, and a happy heart to sleep that easily. Or some good medications.

I'm usually a pretty good sleeper too, especially after a long shift. But tonight? With a stranger sleeping below who might hear my snoring and decide to murder me after all just to shut me up? And an entire evening's worth of conversations to replay in my mind and obsess over?

I think I'll toss and turn for a while. Probably.

CHAPTER 4
COLE

I'M up before the sun, which isn't unusual for me on assignment. In the darkness, I can hear Janey snoring away, like even in sleep, she can't be quiet.

There used to be an adage about women having something like ten thousand words a day. Whoever came up with that never met Janey. I think she has ten thousand words per hour. Over dinner, I heard all about her job, her patients, and some guy she works with, Mason, and his facial hair escapades. I heard almost every detail of her daily life.

What I didn't hear as much about is this boyfriend she says is coming to meet her for a romantic getaway, which is odd. But I didn't ask questions. Or at least not about that. I didn't have to. Janey kept a running commentary about everything and nothing.

It was entertaining. It was enjoyable. Those are not things I usually associate with being around other people. People are annoying. They lie, cheat, do things that only serve themselves, and hurt others. I see it every day. Hell, I profit from it.

Janey was different last night. Her litany of verbiage was given with no hint of pretense, no desire for approval or to garner sympathy or throw shade. And for having so many opinions on so many different subjects, most of her commentary was positive, or at least fun to listen to.

I sip my coffee, staring out the back windows of the cabin at the darkness that'll start to turn gray sooner than later. Every once in a while, I see a green glow flash as some animal walks by, senses my presence, and looks into the dark cabin windows. I'll give it fifteen more minutes, then I've got to get back to my hiding spot. I don't expect Webster to be up this early, but experience tells me it's better to get into position for the day before he's moving around at all. Less chance of being spotted that way.

Up in the loft, Janey makes a snorting sound as she moves around in the bed, causing the mattress to creak slightly. I'm dragging out this cup of rocket fuel, I realize. I'm waiting for her to wake up, curious what Morning Janey is like. Is she as talkative, waking up with words falling off her tongue and a smile on her face? Or cranky and growly, in opposition to her later-hour self?

I won't find out today because I've got to go, which is for the best since I'm a little irritated that I want to know more about the beautiful, mouthy, trusting woman upstairs. Seriously, she let me stay in the house? Has she not seen any of a half-million 'true crime' shows?

As a courtesy, I leave the coffee maker on, certain that any respectable nurse will want a caffeine fix first thing, and wash my own mug, leaving it in the dish drainer to dry. Grabbing a small bag of gear for today, mostly water and snacks, I leave out the front door, making sure it locks behind me.

I inhale deeply, expanding my lungs as I stretch my arms overhead, nearly touching the edge of the porch's sloped roof in the process. I feel pretty good considering yesterday's stakeout, but another day of being completely still on the hard ground is going to do a number on my back.

Maybe a soak in the hot tub with Janey would help?

I grit my teeth, not sure where that thought came from. Dinner last night was one thing, and being civil is expected, but that's not what either of us is here for, and she's got a boyfriend. I'm not the type to get in the middle of others' relationships, at least not on a personal level. But professionally? Hell yes, which I need to get to.

I take off at a long, loping pace that eats up the ground while preserving my stamina, burning the energy out of my muscles in preparation. It only takes a few minutes for me to make it to my hiding spot, although I take a few extra in order to approach slowly, careful not to make any extra noise as I get into position. Just as the sun begins to turn the monochromatic gray morning woods into an explosion of green, I take out my gear and finish getting set up.

Peering through my binoculars, I can see that Mr. Webster's cabin is quiet and pitch-black. As I planned, he's still asleep.

Hours later, I wish he were still dead to the world because watching Mr. Webster is boring as fuck. First, he sat on the couch in his boxers and scratched his balls while he stared at his phone, then he drank a pre-made protein drink for breakfast, and now he's disappeared into the bathroom for his morning constitutional. He reappears freshly shaven, his hair slicked, and wearing slacks and a button-down shirt with the sleeves rolled up.

Clearly, his mistress is coming. He wouldn't be dressed like that otherwise. I trade out my binoculars for the camera and take a few shots to document the time and Webster's appearance. A short thirty minutes later, a car pulls up.

Yep, it's showtime.

A woman gets out, heads for the door, and while she waits for Webster to answer, she scans the woods around the cabin. I have zero concern that she'll spot me. I'm a pro and have never been made on a stakeout, not once, so I keep on clicking, shot after shot. Besides, though she's looking into the forest, she doesn't seem to be truly focusing on anything. She's just occupying her eyes while she waits.

She's tall, slim, with blonde, choppy hair that flips out over her shoulders, and with the zoom, I can see that she has deep blue eyes. She reminds me vaguely of my twin sister, Kayla, except this woman is wearing combat boots, shredded wide-legged jeans, and a hot pink tank top that shows her midriff. Her overall vibe is a bit Y2K, whereas my sister would only dress like that for a costume party. Honestly, I can't remember the last time I saw Kayla in anything other than heels and business chic.

Webster opens the door, and the woman smiles stiffly. As she steps inside, there are a solid six inches between the two of them. They're not comfortable with each other the way lovers should be.

Mrs. Webster is positive her husband has been sleeping with another woman. Her entire concern is documenting that fact. But if time were to stop right now, I'd wager that he's not sleeping with this woman. At least not yet.

Maybe she's an escort?

I'll have to do more research. *Click, click, click.*

"Oopsie," a tiny voice hisses behind me.

In a singular swift move, I set the camera down, flip over, and prepare to fight. But all I find is . . . Janey.

She's wearing black yoga pants, a slim-fitting black shirt, and a black ballcap. Her mass of red curls are gathered into a thick puff of a ponytail on the back of her head below the cap. She winces and waves her fingers.

"Sorry!" she whispers too loudly. "You blend in so well that I didn't see you. And I was looking hard. You're good at this hiding thing. Were you a hide-and-seek champion as a kid? I hated that game. I'd hide, and then everyone would stop playing without telling me. I once stayed in a refrigerator box in the garage for three hours thinking I was the best hider ever. But nope—"

"What the fuck are you doing?" I demand as I yank her to the ground beside me.

Her full lips open in surprise, at her sudden change from vertical to horizontal or my tone, I'm not sure which. Maybe both. "I was worried about you. There are bears, you know? Anderson's ad said so, and that was my first thought when you came into the cabin last night—I thought you were a bear. So, knowing there are bears, I wondered if you had spray. Just in case you didn't, I brought you some." She digs in the thigh pocket of her yoga pants and produces a tiny aerosol bottle, which she holds out, presenting it to me like a golden ticket despite the uselessness of the one last night. "I brought several canisters and don't mind sharing for safety. Though if I'd known you had moves like that, I wouldn't have worried. You could probably tackle a bear with your bare hands." She mimics some karate-esque moves that definitely answer the question of whether or not she's truly a black belt.

She's not.

But she has got to shut up and be still or my 'hunting blind' is going to be blown. And that'll fuck up this entire job. I put my palm over her mouth and glare, our noses mere inches apart. "Be quiet," I say through gritted teeth. "And still."

Her eyes narrow sharply, and she does that dark look thing again that I bet she thinks is intimidating. It's not, at all. It's pouty. In fact, it's bordering on cute, not that I'd tell her that. She'd probably take it as a compliment when I mean it as a warning.

Eventually, she nods behind my hand, so I risk letting her free. Still, I hold one finger up threateningly. Immediately, I turn back to my main priority, picking my camera back up to focus on my targets. I'd rather not do this with Janey here, but it can't be helped at this point. I need the shots.

Janey's smart and follows the sightline of my camera easily. "Who's in the cabin?" she whispers. It sounds like she's talking out of the side of her mouth, as though attempting to obey my order to be quiet.

Peeking at her for a moment, I find her squinting at the cabin. But she feels my attention, and when she looks at me, she presses her lips into a flat line and locks them with an invisible key, which she throws away into the forest. Straight-faced, I lift my chin to gesture at the binoculars. "Oh!" she exclaims happily, but thankfully, still quietly. She lifts them to her eyes, adjusts the focus, and peers through them.

Shaking my head, I go back to looking through my camera. *Click, click, click.*

"Are you watching him? Or her? And why?" Her vow of

silence lasted less than ninety seconds. Might be a record for her, though. "You promised you weren't here to kill anyone, but this is pretty sketchy, you gotta admit, and not exactly the photography you made it sound like. I bet there's not a single shot of a flower or a cute squirrel doing his squirrely things."

I feel the smile trying to lift my lips and am glad she can't see how amusing I find her. If she truly thought I was a danger, she'd be running. But she came after me. She's a good judge of character, at least.

Unless she blindly and stupidly trusts everyone, I think.

"I'm a private investigator, hired by the guy's wife to get proof of his affair," I say shortly, and though I never move my concentration from the camera's viewfinder, I'm ready to analyze her reaction to my bomb drop reveal.

Mr. Webster says something, his face earnest as he smiles at the woman. Judging by the openness of her mouth, she squeals in response and jumps toward Mr. Webster, wrapping her arms around his neck in a tight embrace. It takes less than a blink for his surprise to turn to joy and his arms to thread around her waist.

Click, click, click.

I've got him. Or at least this is the start of getting him.

"You said the wife thinks he's having an affair?" Janey asks.

"Mmhmm."

"I don't think he is," she murmurs.

I grunt in reply, not agreeing or disagreeing but curious as to what's led her to that conclusion.

"No, seriously," Janey says quietly. "Look at them. But mostly, look at the way they're touching. It's like they're close, but not intimate, not like lovers who've seen each other nakey and done the nasty."

Her supposition is ridiculous. I've done hundreds of these types of cases, and I have never had a wife turn out to be wrong about her husband's dalliances. Women have a sixth sense about these things, and men tend to think they're smarter than they are. Like Mr. Webster scheduling a 'work meeting' but booking a cabin under an email that his wife easily snooped on. I mean his password was the pet name he calls his purple-gray Range Rover, Amethyst, and his own birthday. It's like he's asking to get caught.

But Janey's also mentioning something I already noticed. The vibe here is just *off*.

"I think she's an escort. They just haven't 'done the nasty' yet." I use her phrasing automatically, though I couldn't explain why I didn't say 'fuck' the way I normally would.

She hums thoughtfully. "Maybe. But also, there's a small but notable resemblance between them, especially their noses. See the slope? It's cute on her but kinda snouty on him."

"Nose job."

Mr. Webster and the woman sit down on the couch, their knees touching. Now we're getting somewhere. I take a few more pictures of their new position.

"I think they're father-daughter. The vibe is more Dad than Daddy." I don't say anything, and she keeps going, full steam ahead, though I sincerely doubt she has another mental or verbal speed. "I'm good at watching families. I do it all the time at work, and I can tell when people are close and when they're *close*, ya know? My favorite is when 'cousins' come in, but they are not relatives. Or if they are, that's a whole 'nother issue. But their kids don't know that Dad's been dating since Mom died, or that Mom has a secret boyfriend who does more than play bridge with her once a week, so they come up with some story about a long-lost relative who comes to visit when the kids aren't there."

I sense her nodding definitively, like she's certain she's right.

I hate to say it, but she's echoing what I'm seeing in the camera. Mr. Webster and the woman aren't getting any closer, their touches aren't any more intimate, and if anything, they seem to be talking animatedly. If they don't already know each other, their conversation would be more stilted, and if they do know each other, they'd be more comfortable touching. They're somewhere in between close and strangers. I hate the non-definitive 'in between'.

"I'll have to call my office."

Though I'm considering that Mrs. Webster might be my first-ever client to be wrong, or at least wrong about her husband's activities for this particular weekend, I take a few more pictures. Thankfully, Janey doesn't say a word.

What she does is seemingly forget about Mr. Webster and the mystery woman completely because she turns over to her back and stares at the umbrella of trees over us. She's only quiet for a few minutes before she starts talking again. But I suspect her brain has been going lightning fast the whole time because she jumps into a train of thought mid-track. "How many shades of green do you think there are?" she wonders. "There's got to be at least a million hues, some we can't even perceive with our eyes. That's what cones do—see the colors—and the rods see light. Together, that's our vision."

"You sound like a textbook."

"Been accused of worse," she mutters casually. This time, it doesn't seem like she's trying to be quiet because I asked her to, but rather it feels like her entire personality just went small. She even wiggles a bit like the hurt is fresh.

I don't like it. Not one bit. I certainly didn't mean my comment as a dig. "Like what?" I growl as I cut my eyes her way. "By whom?"

She laughs, the sound bright in the woods, and I can't hush her, not when it's such vibrant happiness, but she does it herself, slapping her hand over her mouth and apologizing with her eyes. "Nothing that mattered," she whispers, reassuring me when she's the one who was insulted. "People lash out sometimes, especially when they're hurting, physically or mentally. They shouldn't do it, but when you're in that much pain, spreading it around makes it duller somehow. Sometimes, because it means you're not alone—like misery loves company—or sometimes, because releasing that pain gets it out of your heart. Like popping a pimple—*bloosh*." She flicks her hands like a release of infection, which is a pretty accurate, if not gross, description of stored-up emotional pain.

She's been hurt, that much is obvious. But she's handled it herself and uses it to see the best in others. It's an enviable and inspiring trait. One I don't share. People who hurt me get hurt right back. Exponentially.

"Sounds good for the hurter, but not for the hurt-ee," I reply, lowering the camera and peering at her fully. She's distracting me, which is dangerous, but I'm not sure I care.

She smiles as though that's perfectly acceptable. "I can handle it." But then something draws her attention and her eyes jump to some point above me. "That was an owl! I thought they only flew around at night, but it was right there. Look!"

One look toward the cabin tells me that Mr. Webster and the woman are still sitting on the couch, chatting away. I should pay attention to them. I'm getting paid to do so, after all, but the truth is . . . I can't deny her. I flip over to my back, and she snuggles into my side, getting our faces close together so she can point at an angle I can see. I follow to where her finger is indicating and see a brown-gray owl perched on a branch. But after a quick glance, my eyes are drawn to Janey.

"Beautiful, isn't it?" she says on a wispy breath. She jumps from philosophical enlightenment to childlike excitement over a bird in a whiplash second.

Remembering what she said, I lift the camera to take a few shots of the owl. "Now I've got pictures of birds doing birdy things."

She smiles. I don't see it so much as feel it in the air around us. The stupid picture makes her happy.

I give myself two minutes to enjoy the moment, vowing to get back to surveillance when my internal alarm goes off. But I don't make it thirty seconds until Janey's constant wiggling and squirming is driving me mad.

Is she trying to hump my leg? At that angle?

"What the hell are you doing?"

"My back hurts," she admits as she does the worm dance in the dirt like an actual, literal worm.

I'll admit to irritation. I'm working, she interrupted, and now, she's whining? I also can't let her walk back to the cabin by herself. Not because of bears, which Anderson reassured me haven't roamed these woods in decades but provide an exciting tagline on ads, but because the terrain is rough. I'm surprised —and fine, a little impressed—that she got out here on her own in the first place. But I can't knowingly send her back alone.

I should stay here, watch my target all day if need be, but if I can't, I can still work. I'll get Janey back to the cabin and call the office for more research on Mr. Webster and this not-a-mistress guest he's secretly hosting.

My brain doesn't make the decision to do so, but my body does, and I move to get up, resting on my knees with my butt on my heels, instinctually staying close to the shadows of the tree I'm calling my hunting blind to preserve its integrity as a safe surveillance spot.

I stash my gear once again, knowing I'll have to come back, and offer Janey a hand as I stand. Independent as she is, and probably aware of my annoyance, given the hurt look in her eyes, Janey ignores my offer and moves to stand on her own. Except . . .

"Don't move," I snap sharply, and her eyes dart to me in confusion. "That's poison ivy," I explain, pointing at the three-lobed bush she's reaching for. "Are you allergic?"

"I don't know. I'm not sure I've ever been exposed. In case you hadn't noticed, I'm not exactly the outdoorsy type. Oh, except for that one time I went camping. I couldn't have been more than eight or nine? I was a Girl Scout, troop 481, so I probably learned what poison ivy looks like, but I can't remember. Does it have three leaves? Or four?" She's looking around at the various greenery around her, counting leaves. "I probably didn't get that Scout patch, but I know I got one for pizza making and one for horse care when we went to the stables and I brushed a pony's mane. I think her name was Powder. And also, the pizza making was putting our pepperoni Lunchables in the toaster oven, so I'm not sure that actually counts."

"Three. Four is a lucky clover," I say to answer the most important part of that ramble. "Let me help you." It's not a question this time. The less contact she has with the poison ivy, the better off she'll be. Luckily, I'm one of the fifteen percent of people who aren't allergic, a fact I take advantage of in situations like this.

I help her reverse slowly and invisibly out of my hiding spot, and we make our way carefully back to our cabin, where I guide Janey to the bathroom after a quick stop in the kitchen.

"Strip. You need a cold shower and a wash with dish soap."

She covers her mouth as she laughs. "Nice try, but I'm not getting naked in front of you."

"Don't touch your face," I warn, and her hands fall to her sides. "It's even worse on thin-skinned areas like the lips, eyelids, or nostrils."

Contrary to her words, she looks like she wants to rip her clothes off, not to seduce me, but to scratch the fuck out of herself. All over. Because her wiggle worming has progressed to spastic belly dancing, which I take as a sign that the itch is getting worse.

"Fine." I set the bottle of soap on the edge of the tub and turn to leave. "Cold water. Lots of soap. Don't miss an inch or it'll continue to irritate and then spread."

"Yes, sir," she snaps with an approximation of a salute and a broad smile. For the first time, I notice that one of her teeth has a tiny chip out of it, and I wonder what the story is about that. I'm sure it's interesting. Before I can ask, she pushes me toward the door desperately.

Her hands flat on my chest feel . . . something. I don't know, they just feel. I don't have much contact with people these days, and even the small, teasing gesture is intimate in my book. I don't move an inch. I might even inhale slightly to press my chest into her hands more because her eyes widen. "Calamine lotion's in the first aid kit under the sink," I force out reluctantly, which sounds like I'm snapping at her.

I leave before she can call me on being a roller coaster of a motherfucker, which would be one hundred percent warranted.

That was stupid. I don't do connections, but here I am, wanting to spend time with Janey when I should be working and not stopping her from touching me. I stomp out to the living room and fall to the couch with a heavy exhale to stare at the dark box of the fireplace, trying to discern what the hell is wrong with me.

I don't people. Yeah, it's a verb now. Look it up. Or if it's not, it should be because I'm not good at it. To Janey, I'm probably a grunting caveman-slash-hermit loner who's so out of practice, he can't carry one side of a conversation, so she has to do it all. Maybe that's why she keeps talking so much? And I'm the dumbass listening to her and enjoying the sound of her voice and the way her lips look as they form words.

Fucking idiot.

I need to know if there's a missing family member Mr. Webster might be meeting with, though sending a text to my assistant is more of an intentional distraction than anything.

Target hosted a guest. Doesn't look intimate. Research his family tree —daughter, niece? Blonde, late teens, early- to mid-twenties at most.

I get back a simple check mark in a green box. My assistant Louisa is more of a hermit than I am and abhors conversation. We work remarkably well together.

I hear the shower turn off and the screech of the metal shower curtain rings as it slides open. Behind two inches of wood is a naked, wet Janey, a thought that I should dismiss instantly, but rather, I remember what she looked like running away. The curve of her back, the fullness of her ass, the halo of her hair, the tattoo I want an up-close and personal look at.

I hear her mutter, "Shit." A moment later, she calls out, "Hey, uh, Cole? Can you help me with something?"

Anything.

"What's wrong?" I ask at the door warily, and it opens a crack.

"I can't reach all of my back for the lotion," she explains. "Could you?" Her hand snakes through, holding out the bottle of pink, creamy liquid.

"Yeah," I answer, hearing the huskiness of my own voice. I can't help it, it's an instinctual reaction to her. When she steps away, I push my way into the bathroom, and she yelps in surprise but gives me her back.

Leaning against the counter, her eyes meet mine in the

mirror. Slowly, she inches her tank top up, keeping the front pressed to her breasts and the back lifted almost to her shoulder blades. My eyes rove her skin, seeing bits of pink chalkiness where she's already coated herself, but I also see the area she's talking about where the blotchy, irritated patch is uncovered by the calamine.

I pour a bit of lotion into my hand and gently dab it over the affected area before I blow it dry, a trick I learned a long time ago. Not from poison ivy, but from a particularly bad mosquito infestation around a lake where I was doing surveillance. My client hadn't even needed the pictorial proof that time. The guy had said he was going on a business trip to Sacramento, and after a secret fishing trip with the guys, he came home with tiny, itchy welts all over his body. Mosquito bites were the least worrisome diagnosis his wife suggested upon seeing them. And while I recommended calamine to her, she'd said she preferred to let him suffer the itch he earned from lying, which I found to also be a valid idea.

"Ooh," Janey sighs in relief as I cover more and more spots. But pouting, she adds, "I'm going to be a monster at the wedding, though Paisley will probably prefer that." There's a bitterness to her tone that's unlike her usually sunny outlook. But a moment later, she corrects herself. "Paisley likes to be the center of attention, the prettiest girl in the room, and if there's a day where that should always be the case, it's your wedding day. What I look like won't matter."

I have no idea what Cousin Paisley looks like, but I can't imagine that she's prettier than Janey. Paisley could be a damn runway model and I think Janey would still come out on top of that competition. Janey's . . . interesting. Her looks, her always running mouth, and her mind. She's more than the sum of her parts, even though those parts are pretty damn good all by themselves.

"It'll be fine by then. Don't worry. And you could never be a monster."

She gasps softly, and I jerk my eyes up, looking for what caused her reaction. But then I realize she's simply been watching my every move and expression while I put the calamine on her back. "Thank you," she whispers.

The moment stretches, us staring into each other's eyes in the mirror with my hand frozen on her back. "No problem," I answer, pretending to spread one last dollop of lotion simply because I don't want to stop touching her.

What the fuck is going on with me?

CHAPTER 5
JANEY

IT'S BEEN DAYS. Basically all week, if I'm truthful. I've slept in, watched the trees sway in dawning sunlight, finished a book from my TBR list, and enjoyed my own company all day. It's a luxury I don't think I would've ever gifted myself, so I'm grateful it was essentially forced upon me.

I haven't talked to Henry much, but that's not unusual when he's head-down in a problem, searching out a solution. He gets a little obsessive with a puzzle to solve, and I'm glad he's working so hard to finish in time to still make something out of our vacation.

Henry should be here today. In fact, he should be making the trek from town to the cabin right now, and I've already made the most of my last few hours of solitude by pampering myself with a face mask, a strawberry apricot Red Bull, and another book. It's a good one, too, and I've really chewed through a bunch of it in the peaceful solitude.

You haven't been totally alone.

Granted, Cole is gone for hours at a time, off to spy on Mr. Webster, but when he comes back to the cabin every evening, we have dinner together, then sit and watch the moon rise high into the sky. And we talk.

Well, I talk and he mostly listens. But it's been fun, especially given that for not-speaking, he's more engaged than anyone else.

You mean Henry.

Okay, I'll admit that . . . to myself only. But that's what makes this week all the more interesting. The stark differences I noted that first night have only been amplified with more time. Cole asks about my day, about what I've read, about myself, and he listens to my answers. His attention is singular, focused on what I'm saying even when it's coming out at such a rapid-fire pace that I'm surprised by it.

Not that he shares a lot about himself in return.

Other than the smallest tidbits about his work—like Mr. Webster's name and his own doubts about his potential infidelity—he told me that he's a twin and has a whole gaggle of siblings, which shocked me. For some reason, I pegged him as an only child, but once I pictured him with siblings, all fighting to be heard, I could see him as the lone wolf off to the side, quietly observing and cataloging his brothers and sister.

Nope, this hasn't been the vacation that I imagined, but somehow, it's been exactly what I needed. Best laid plans? Laid to rest. Janey: zero. Universe: score one.

Still thinking about Cole, I flip the chicken breasts I'm studiously watching. I'm not a great chef. Gordon Ramsey is certainly never gonna invite me to prepare dinner for him unless it's to star in *Kitchen Nightmares*. But I've never given anyone food poisoning either, so I'd say I'm right in the middle of semi-decent in the kitchen. Mostly.

I check the clock, both to make sure the chicken has had ample time to reach a safe temperature—gotta protect that no poisoning record!—and because Henry should be here by six o'clock.

After stashing my hopefully-perfectly-cooked chicken in the microwave to stay warm, I glance out the window over the sink. The forest is beginning to darken, and Henry needs to be through the awkward and dangerous drive to the cabin while the sun is still up. Plus, Cole's supposed to come in for a shower and be gone before Henry's arrival. I feel guilty about kicking him to the curb, a.k.a. his truck, for the night, but I don't think Henry will want to share space on what's left of our romantic getaway, and the bedroom loft isn't exactly private.

Stepping out to the back porch, I give the hot tub a long, regretful look. I had such great plans for it but haven't been able to use it with the poison ivy rash, which I'm a bit salty about, but it's my own fault. I prepared for bears but not greenery that could ruin everything.

Or unexpected house guests who would tempt me into the unknown wilds of the forest.

Nope, not thinking about Cole. Or his eyes and fingers roving over my back, drawing heat to places that had nothing to do with an allergic reaction. I'm focusing strictly on the poison ivy rash and that's it. Yep, that's it.

Hopefully, Henry doesn't mind my patchy irritation. The calamine lotion is working, but it's not a quick fix.

I sink onto a porch chair, wrapping a blanket around me and gathering it beneath my chin to call him on speakerphone. It's not that chilly, but worry is pooling in my belly because Henry should be here by now.

"Hello?"

"Hey! Just checking in to see how close you are. The last bit of the drive to the cabin is pretty sketchy, and definitely something that should be done during daylight hours, so hopefully, you're almost—"

He cuts me off abruptly, blurting out, *"I'm not coming."*

"What?" I say in confusion. "Did you work late and decide to come tomorrow instead?" That's so like him. Work, work, work, and lose track of everything other than the issue immediately in front of him. It's sort of cute, if annoying at times. Like these times.

"At all." His tone is flat and cold.

"What do you mean? Is the project not going well?" It's the only thing I can think of. Henry is basically a workaholic, and his work ethic is a good thing. Usually.

"Look, Janey . . . you're uhm . . . great, but I'm super swamped and need to prioritize my own growth trajectory. You understand that. And you're—"

I inhale sharply. "You don't mean the vacation, do you? Are you . . ." Realization hits me like a wrecking ball. "Are you breaking up with me? For work?"

My stomach is somewhere in my ass right now. My nursing professors would say that's not medically possible, but it's exactly what I feel like at this moment.

"*No, no. It's not that. I just . . . you, me, we're not . . .*" He groans and moves around, and I hear the tell-tale squeak of the couch in his apartment. He's not at the office. He's at home, reclining back on the left-end chaise where he always sits, even though he knows I like the spot in the L-shaped corner where I can curl up by the window.

I'm not stupid. And I have experience reading between the lines to hear what he's not saying. He never intended on coming, but he let me believe he was. He let me cook him a romantic– and definitely not poisoned–dinner and worry about his drive while he was chilling at home. He let me tell my whole family that he was coming to the wedding, knowing he wasn't gonna come.

He's stuttering through something about it not being our time yet, but I'm only half listening, too caught up in the swirling tornado in my mind of 'no, no, no' coupled with a high-pitched squealing noise.

"What are you talking about?" I ask when I realize I haven't heard most of what he's said. He laughs, actually snorts like that's funny, and I'm confused for a second until it clicks. He's laughing because that's what he always comments when I go on a rambling tangent and he checks out mentally. Guess the shoe's on the other foot this time. It doesn't feel any better on this side.

I sober with the thought and ask more seriously, "What about the wedding?"

This can't be happening. Not now, not to me. He's making a fool out of me and setting me up for an even worse situation at the wedding. And he knows it.

I can feel tears prick my eyes, and I swallow thickly so Henry won't hear how hurt I am.

No, not hurt. Scared. I'm scared of being with Henry . . . and of *not* being with him. Of the wedding and my family seeing me as a failure all over again. It's all falling apart, but I can fix it. I have to fix it. At least throw some spit and duct tape on it to get through the next few days.

"I told you how important the wedding is for me, and you're bailing on me now?" I don't like the desperation in my voice, but I can't seem to rein it in because I am desperate.

"That's the problem, babe. Meeting your family is a big step, and I don't think we're ready for that," Henry says in a cold but also placating voice. *"Maybe when you get back, we can talk and figure something out. Go back to . . . I don't know, dating?"*

He genuinely sounds as if he thinks I'll agree to that. Of course, I've given him no reason to think I would disagree. Not with anything. That's me, Agreeable, Easygoing, Do Anything for Anyone Janey.

"Dating?" I echo hollowly. "We barely see each other now with all the time you're putting into the McDermott project. And I understand that it's a big opportunity for you, but—" I hear something other than the creaking couch in the background that stops me mid-sentence. I'm making excuses for him, but he's not alone at his apartment. Pieces of a puzzle I didn't even know I was completing fall into place one by one, and I realize the truth. "You're sleeping with someone from the office." The idea comes suddenly, falling off my tongue dully because I can't find any more emotion in my rock-bottom pit. "That's why we haven't had sex in months."

Every single late night, every single 'too tired to come over', every single time he heralded himself as a dedicated, loyal employee, he was with someone else. I can see it all so clearly when only a moment ago, I would've defended him. I want him to tell me I'm wrong so badly, but I already know the truth.

He tries anyway. *"No, I'm not."*

The answer is reflexive, but I can hear the lie plain as day. He might as well have said that he's a green Martian in a skin suit for as believable as that denial was. He's not even trying to convince me, not really, probably assuming that I'll put up with it because . . . well, because I'm Plainy Janey.

Yeah, he knows about my awful family too and the things they said and did to me when I was a kid. He thought some of it was funny and told me I was being too sensitive when I cried fresh tears about something that happened over a decade ago. And now, he's using my own trauma against me. Worse, I'm doing it too.

Yeah, there's a part of me that thinks I should let his infidelity go and be happy with what I have. Maybe that's all I deserve.

"You had me fooled this whole time. I really thought . . ." I stop before I say that I thought this vacation was going to be a new level for our relationship. Not a ring situation, but just more than what we were before. Laughing bitterly, I instead say, "I bet you've been getting a real kick outta what a gullible idiot I am this whole time while I stupidly believed you. Believed *in* you."

"*Janey*."

There's a sixth sense you get as a nurse when a patient isn't doing well. We call it 'circling the drain' because 'imminent death' is too blunt and tends to hurt more. So we couch it in euphemisms and coded language in an attempt to buffer the blunt impact of death. But the reality is there nonetheless, and we all know it.

That's how this feels.

Henry and me, what we were and what I hoped we were becoming, is dying. Right here, right now, in this moment. I can't pretend this didn't happen. I might not deserve more, but I don't deserve this. I'm cut to the core, and the lies unravel whatever stranglehold he had on my heart.

"No." I wish I could say it was a firm, strong answer delivered with fire and brimstone. But that's not who I am. It's soft and quiet, but that doesn't make it any less true. I'm crumbling to pieces, but I have deal breakers. This is one.

"*Don't be like that, babe,*" Henry says, this time sounding legitimately into the conversation for the first time. "*It's nothing, just a way to let off steam when the pressure gets to be too much. It's easy, no strings. Not like what we have.*"

He's admitting it, at least. I won't have to wonder if I overreacted or made it up later. I gather up the few shredded scraps of self-respect I have, knowing that I don't deserve this. Nobody does. "Goodbye, Henry."

I click the red circle, ending the call, and turn my phone off. That'll prevent him from calling me back and from tracking my location. I shake my head in disbelief, remembering how many nights I stared at his dot on that stupid app, waiting to see when he left work. Sometimes, we'd talk while he drove home, or sometimes, he'd come to my place, but I always felt like he was honest because he was where he said he would be.

Never did I think he was getting his rocks off *at* the office.

Guess I'm the sucker. Seriously, how many soap operas have I watched where that's exactly what happens? But I thought we were different. I thought Henry was different.

I pull the blanket tighter around my shoulders, burrowing into it. The night air hasn't gotten any cooler, but my insides feel like ice as the adrenaline dump wears off. I don't know how long I sit like that, replaying our conversations, things Henry's told me, and thoughts I've had about him. About us.

Somehow, it's still only 'getting dark' when Cole climbs the stairs to the back deck. He takes one look at me and my ugly, snotty mess of tears and silently goes inside, leaving me to my pity party. I hear him moving around in the kitchen, pans clanking and the can opener whirring, but I don't know or care what he's doing. Until he slides the door open again.

"Here," he says gruffly.

I pop my head up out of my one-person blanket fort to see what he wants. He's holding out a glass of white wine, poured all the way to the tippy-tippy top, and a deep bowl that has steam rising off it. "What's that?" I ask, not taking it.

I made dinner. Dinner for me and Henry, and he broke up with me by phone instead of telling me before our romantic vacation, so food is the last thing I want.

"Wine. Chicken 'n dumplings. Didn't figure you'd want the chicken you made for the dipshit, but I turned it into comfort food." He says it completely matter-of-factly, with zero emotion, but his calling Henry names tells me that he knows why I'm sitting alone on the back deck.

I've completed the curve around the stages of denial and sadness and am rounding into the anger stage, contemplating ways to bulldoze Henry's existence. Maybe show up to his office and loudly announce his infidelity, asking if sex as a brain break is their norm. Or break into his apartment and erase the characters on his favorite video game. That'd be better than simply destroying the game system. If I did that, he could log into his account on a new one, but deleting the character in-game? Probably the thing that'd hurt him the most, which is ridiculous.

Or maybe move on and be happy. Best revenge is a life well-lived type of deal.

Realistically, I won't do any of those things. They'll stay in my head as ways to torture myself more than Henry, because though I stood up for myself over the phone, I don't have the guts to actually get back at Henry in one of those song-worthy, dramatic maneuvers. I'll simply fade into spinsterhood, living alone forever and adopting a bunch of cats that I name after breakfast dishes like Waffles, Bacon, and Cinnamon Roll.

Sighing heavily, I take the bowl from Cole. "Thanks. How can you be sure he's a dipshit?"

He gives me a dubious look as he sets the wine on the tiny table at my side. "There you go. Let me grab mine and you can tell me all about what a fuckup Henry is."

He disappears, coming back a minute later with a glass of wine and a dinner bowl of his own. He straddles the other lounge chair and flops to its surface. I'm worried for a second that the chair might collapse beneath him, but when it holds steady, I can't help but laugh the tiniest bit. He seems pleased with himself for the small and momentary flicker of improvement in my mood even as I return to my self-pity wallow.

He scoops a spoonful from his bowl, blows on it, and then slurps it down. "This is based on my grandmother's recipe. Had to change it up a little based on what's in the kitchen, but it's not bad," he says conversationally, which is major for him, and any other night, I'd be off and running at the mouth with that small prompt. Tonight, I stare blankly at the bowl in my hands. It does smell good, but I'm not hungry or talkative now. "My grandmother would kick my ass if she knew I used canned biscuits for the dumplings."

It's a non-important fact, but I hear the question there, so I take a small nibble of a dumpling and nod. "S'good." It's all I've got, and I go back to sitting silently and sullenly.

Cole stares off into the dark forest, and at first, I think we're going to have a very quiet dinner with me not providing running commentary on everything from Aardvarks to Zombies. But finally, he offers, "She makes the best chicken pot pie and apple pie on March 14th. Pi day. I look forward to it for 364 days each year and then fight Kyle to selfishly hoard it for myself. It's not his favorite, but he fights me for it anyway because he knows it's mine. He says I'll appreciate it more if I have to fight for it. He's probably not wrong." He falls quiet again but then adds, "She's a great cook and an even better grandma. Been through a lot, and a lesser person would've fallen apart. But not her. Tough times made her strong. I admire that."

I don't think we're talking about his grandmother anymore. Or at least not only about her.

"My sister Kayla, too. She learned from Grandma Betty and my mom. They're all the type of women who've gone most of their lives underestimated." He shrugs like that's to be expected. "Sometimes because of the times they were living in, sometimes because of their looks, sometimes for no damn reason at all. But they come back fighting dirty while staying clean as a whistle." He looks at me, his blue eyes sharp and not missing a thing as he scans my face. "That's when they surprise the fuck out of you."

It feels even more like he's talking about me, but couched in compliments about the women in his life. "How much did you hear?" I ask quietly. "Because I don't feel strong or surprising. I feel . . . stupid."

He chuckles darkly and doesn't answer my question about what he heard. "Janey, you are the biggest fucking surprise I've ever come across."

Why does that sound like such a big compliment? Especially coming from him.

"And I bet Henry is the epitome of a blah, boring, bullshitter," Cole proclaims, his distaste for him obvious. I shrug, not ready to speak ill of him when he was my boyfriend thirty minutes ago. "Let me guess . . . you said he's a software engineer, so he probably thinks he's the smartest man in any room. Definitely thinks he's smarter than you, which he's dead wrong about, and I don't even know him."

I stare at Cole, who's looking off into the forest now. I want him to say more. I'm not fishing for compliments, but my wounded ego could use a little hype party. I was gonna call Mason, but maybe this is better because Mason will remind me that he's been telling me to ditch Henry for months.

"He thinks he's the core of the relationship, but that's his ego talking. The truth is, he's lazy. He never puts forth any real effort and doesn't give a shit about your experience, especially in the sack. You do it all."

Automatically, I try to defend Henry. "He's not that bad."

Cole throws a stormy glare my way and I drop my gaze, feeling chastised though he hasn't responded. After a heavy sigh, he snarls out, "We've been here for days, Janey. He hasn't called or texted you. Not even a 'thinking of you' gif that'd take one second to send. But I see you checking your phone and sending him texts. You even sent him that sunrise selfie you took on the porch yesterday. Did he respond?" He pauses, not to give me time to answer but to stare me down, daring me to lie because he already knows the truth. "He's too lazy to even keep you on the back burner. You put yourself there and stayed long after he turned off the stove."

Ouch! That hurts, a lot. He sounds mad . . . at me. You're not supposed to kick someone when they're down, but he's not holding back. And for someone who doesn't really know me, Cole's got me pinned pretty precisely. Henry too.

Mason's quoted an expression several times that hit a little too close to home, so I've chosen to ignore it, but it whispers in the back of my mind now. *If he wanted to, he would.*

Henry never wanted to . . . anything. If I planned, arranged, put it in his calendar, and reminded him, he'd show up. Sometimes. If he saw value in it. Otherwise, he'd say I never told him about it or claim that work needed him.

Now, I know those were more lies. I can't count how many times he'd tell me that, and I'd question myself or make excuses for him.

God, I'm so stupid. And weak. Cole's right—I've been on the back burner, and not only did I let it happen, but I did it to myself.

Raw, bitter, fresh tears start to burn my eyes. I'm not sad over losing Henry, but it's hitting me that I lost myself. And for what? A whiny, cheating, lying, ferret of a man in clothes he can't afford, with a job he cares about more than anyone else, and who never made me come, even with some directional coaching. Because the entire time I was with Henry, the only way I reached the 'doorway to heaven' was by going up the stairs and twisting the knob myself.

Somehow, Cole knows that too. He knows it all, including how lost I became.

That's not who I am. I know better. I don't put up with that.

But I did. It happened so gradually that I didn't notice, and I gave him way too many chances, thinking things would be better tomorrow, next week, next month. Always better. Because there had to be a silver lining, or what was the point?

The tears fall, running silently down my cheeks. I sniffle quietly so Cole doesn't realize that I'm falling apart, but he keeps his attention on the woods surrounding us and his dinner bowl, giving me a moment of privacy, though he's right by my side.

It's pitch black and completely still around us, and in his stakeout clothes, he blends into the night almost seamlessly until he speaks. "I'm gonna shower before bed." He stands, taking his empty bowl and wine glass with him, but at the back door, he pauses and looks over at me. I can't meet his eyes, too lost in the rambles of my own mind, but I listen when he says firmly, "A man should be willing to work his ass off to be worthy of you. You deserve nothing less, Janey."

He doesn't wait for a response. He simply goes inside, letting that sit on the night air. And my mind.

Alone, I force myself to eat, knowing I need it. I'm not surprised that the chicken 'n dumplings is delicious, even cooled off. I bet Cole cooks all the time, at least for himself. Maybe even for someone special. He's the type who would put in those efforts for his woman.

Not that I need that. Not now. I need to sit with myself and do a bit of healing, not from the breakup, but rather, from the relationship.

I finish the bowl and the whole glass of wine but don't move to go inside. It's nice out here, the sounds of the woods an accompanying song for my melancholy thoughts. The rustle of the leaves in the slight breeze is the melody, and there's a frog somewhere croaking so loudly that it sounds like he's right next to my chair, providing the haunting bass. An owl hoots, and I wonder if it's the same one I saw in the woods by Mr. Webster's cabin.

The door slides open, and Cole reappears, his hair wet and gray shorts slung low over his hips. His chest is bare, and I'm surprised to see just how defined his muscles are. In a purely nursing, medical sort of way, of course. He notices me looking, and one side of his mouth quirks up, like he's not fully committed to smiling.

"I set up a bath for you. Lukewarm water and oatmeal for the itching. Come on inside," he tells me as he takes my bowl from my hands and grabs the empty wine glass too.

Mindlessly, I follow him to the kitchen, where he drops the bowl in the sink and refills my wine glass with another heavy pour. He then guides me to the bathroom, where the tub is filled just like he said, and sets the glass next to a fluffy towel he laid out.

He thought of everything.

Cole turns to go, but I step in front of him to stop him. I drop into his arms, falling into a hug and taking the comfort I need. He freezes in shock for a moment, but then his arms rest heavily on my shoulders, keeping me grounded with their weight as he hugs me back. It's not sexual, just solace, but my cheek pressed to the warm skin of his chest, inhaling the scent of sandalwood soap from his shower and hearing the steady thud of his heart, reminds me that I am a woman.

A sexier, stronger one than I was with Henry. One I will be again, someday, I vow.

"Thank you," I whisper as I release him. When I look up, I half expect to see pity in his blue eyes, but they're blankly shuttered down, giving away none of his thoughts.

"Yeah," he rumbles. Without any more, he turns, and he's gone.

Alone in the bathroom, I stare at myself in the mirror, trying to figure out how in the hell I got here. What I see looking back at me hurts. I'm suddenly Plainy Janey again.

CHAPTER 6
COLE

JANEY IS SNORING UPSTAIRS, but other than that, the cabin is utterly quiet and still. Just me and the glow of my laptop as I work.

I should be researching Mr. Webster, but Louisa is on that, and to be frank, she's better than I am at digitally digging into people's secrets, especially when we're talking a deep dive. Still, I have no doubt she'll find what we need.

The information I'm searching for right now is much easier to track down. It only takes a few quick clicks on social media sites and LinkedIn to get the basics I want to verify and some new insight.

Janey Williams. RN at The Ivy Care Center for the last two years. Graduated with her BSN from the state university before that. Birthdate, July 21st. She's twenty-five years old. Her best friend is a guy named Mason, who also works at The Ivy and is next on my research list. There are a few pictures of Mason, a brunette woman, Janey, and Henry at a baseball game.

I'm glad to put a face with the name, but Henry's pretty much exactly what I expected. Namely, unworthy of her. His smug smile as he looks into the camera makes me want to wipe it off his face . . . with my fist.

Back to Janey. All of what I've discovered so far aligns exactly with what she's told me. She's a what you see is what you get type, a rarity in my line of work and a standard I don't live up to myself.

She follows pages about curly hair, nursing, codependency, and funny cats. Her shared posts are almost exclusively about shelter animals needing a home or reminders to get an annual physical. She's a member of several private book chat groups, which I join under an alias, and they seem to be a way for her to track books she'd like to read. There's an unexpected number of vampire series on that list, which is interesting. Maybe talking isn't the only thing she likes to do with that mouth of hers.

Surprisingly, her online presence is pretty clean. There are no fake profiles I can find, no dating site accounts, and no polarizing posts anywhere.

I think Janey Williams is exactly who she says she is and who I thought she is after only a few days with her. An always-talking, sunshine-spreading, unexpected beauty who believes the best about everything and everyone, except herself.

Which makes what I'm about to do that much easier.

I admittedly have a bit of a savior complex. I've saved more clients than I can count, from their spouses, from work coups, even from themselves. But I keep my professional life and personal life strictly separate. It's a rule I live by, and that has served me well over the years.

Except I'm breaking the rule. For her. Because Janey Williams should have someone put her first for once in her life. And it's going to be me.

Not to be arrogant, but there's no one better suited than me.

I put my laptop away and begin pulling supplies out of the fridge. The last few mornings, she's had yogurt with a sprinkling of Fruity Pebbles for breakfast. Today, that changes.

I don't know if it's the sizzling bacon or steaming hot coffee that does the trick, but a few minutes later, Janey is climbing down the ladder. And watching her come down, her ass swaying side to side as she searches for the next rung, is all sorts of good reasons to make breakfast for her in the morning.

"G'morning," she mumbles, still yawning and stretching.

Her hair is a rat's nest of frizzed curls, there are dark

smudges beneath her eyes and a trace of drool beside her lips, her socks are slouched down to different levels on her shapely calves, and her oversized T-shirt is crooked on her shoulders. She looks like she slept like the dead but didn't get any real rest.

"Breakfast's ready," I tell her in what passes for a chipper, happy tone for me as I set a plate of bacon, eggs, and toast on the island.

"Oh!" She immediately attacks the coffee as she sits. "I need this. Thank you."

I sit next to her with a plate of my own but don't take a bite. Not yet.

After she eats a few mouthfuls and moans her appreciation, I start. "I can't fix what's happened, but I can help with one thing."

Janey pauses with her fork midway to her mouth, and the eggs fall back to the plate. "What?" A weak smile lifts her lips. "Are you gonna spy on Henry?"

She makes it sound like I'm going to hunt him down and rip his dick off. And while the idea was a tempting consideration, I decided not to. That I know all about his work, where he lives, his car make, model, and license plate, his bank accounts, and even what gym he's a member of are just . . . factoids, little pieces of information that might be useful later, but Janey doesn't need to know about. Yet.

"No. As far as I'm concerned, he's in your past and needs to stay there." I frown hard, daring her to disagree, but she stays quiet for a change. "But in your immediate future is your cousin's wedding. I know how upset you are about that, and that is something I can help with."

"How? Are you going to kidnap Paisley? Because I'm not necessarily completely, one hundred percent opposed to that idea. At least in concept." She's joking, I think.

"You do remember that I'm not a spy, hitman, or criminal, right? Despite what my family thinks." I'm joking back, but the serious truth sends her spiraling back down quickly.

"I know," she sighs. "Just wishful thinking. Sorry. You said you can help. How?"

I wish I hadn't squashed her teasing, no matter how slight. She needs to be lifted out of this funk she's in. Hopefully, my next offer will bring the light back to her gray eyes. "I'm going with you to the wedding."

I don't know what I expect. A rush of rambled 'thankyouthankyouthankyou', maybe? But that's not what happens. Instead, she laughs in disbelief. "What?"

"You said going alone to the wedding would be traumatic. Henry's not going, but I can. I'll be your date, stand by your side to have your back against whomever, and make sure you have a great time." Spelled out, it's a simple and easy solution.

Janey shakes her head, making her curls bounce around. "No, I couldn't ask you to do that."

"You didn't," I point out, lifting an eyebrow in an imitation of her own frequent expression. "I'm offering, because you deserve better than Henry, and from what it sounds like, better than your family. You're not in a mental place to walk into that lion's den alone. And I understand what that can be like. So take me. Tell them I'm your boyfriend, and I'll dutifully play the role. I've been undercover enough times that I can make it work. I can make anything work." Okay, so humbleness is not one of my strengths, but I'm not wrong.

Janey blinks at what equates to my rambling the way she does. I'm a man of few words, but I'm suddenly turning into Chatty Chad to talk her into this. Why? I have no idea, but my gut feels like this is the right thing to do.

Maybe it's because she worked with me on the cabin deal? Yeah, that's probably it. It definitely has nothing to do with the damsel in distress deal she's got going on, her beautiful looks, or her sunny personality that I hate to see dimmed by some fuckwit who didn't know what he had.

"That's really nice, but you can't." She shrugs and ducks her head. "Nobody'd believe that, anyway."

I frown and snap, "What do you mean? Why wouldn't they believe it?" I think she's doubting the caliber of my undercover work, which is fucking top-notch. I might not do it often, since I can complete most jobs with surveillance and research, but I can certainly pull off a fake boyfriend appearance.

And if I had any concerns, which I don't, I'd call my brother, Carter. He once had his best friend's sister act like his wife for a business deal. It worked out in the long run, given that she's my sister-in-law now, but it was pretty iffy for a while. But a little poke here and a small prod there, and he'd tell me the whole story of how that went down, which I could use as research for my own role.

Janey lifts her eyes to mine, and I can see the shine of tears there. Shit, she's gonna start crying again and I'm trying to help so she doesn't cry. At least about this. Her crying about dipshit Henry is her own business.

"You're gonna make me say it?" She sounds a little choked, but eventually, she grits her teeth and says, "Look at you, Cole, and look at me. Nobody'd believe you would date me."

"What?!" I'm louder than I intend to be, and Janey recoils as if I slapped her instead of only shouting. I force my voice back down and look at her intently. "The hell are you talking about? You're fucking beautiful."

Her eyes fall again, and quietly, she says, "You don't have to say that."

"I know I don't have to. I want to." I lift her chin with a finger, forcing her eyes to mine. I stare deep into her gray gaze, wanting to make sure she hears me and hears me good. "Because it's the damn honest truth."

I could say more—like that her hair makes my hands itch to grab handfuls, I want to bite her lower lip, and her ass is the stuff of my dreams as of late—but I don't. That'd probably scare the shit out of her, especially when she's so tender after last night's call.

Her lips lift like she's trying to smile but doesn't really feel it. I let my declaration sit with her, giving her time to process and find the silver lining I'm offering in the midst of her rain cloud. It's nearly three silent minutes later, which in Janey time is at least fifteen, maybe twenty, when I feel a shift in her mood.

"It would be nice to not go alone," she murmurs, more to

herself than me. "And having a guy who looks like he walked off a book cover at my side wouldn't hurt." She crunches on a piece of bacon, chewing noisily as she thoughtfully looks me up and down, measuring and appraising my very existence. Straight-faced, she twirls a finger in the air, telling me to spin.

Amused, I stand and turn in a circle with my hands held out to the side.

After what feels like an eternity of her eyes tracing every inch of my body, her lips lift into a pleased smile. A real smile this time. One that I cherish because I'm a greedy bastard who feels like I had something to do with it.

"Will I do?" I taunt. She doesn't have any other options, and let's face it, we both know I look good.

"Are you sure? Like positively, undoubtedly certain?" she asks, her nose crinkled up apprehensively. "You're volunteering to go into a den of wolves while slathered in meat juice. And all of the predators are hidden in cute little doggie costumes that make them seem harmless and fun."

She doesn't want to believe me. Trust must feel like a dangerous option after Henry's betrayal. I get that. I nod, surer than I've ever been. She needs this.

"Just one question, then. Do you have a suit, or do we need to go into town to buy one?"

"That's your only question?" I echo with a chuckle. "Yeah, I've got that covered."

I can see the acceptance dawning on her face as her smile grows by degrees and her eyes brighten. "Oh, my God! Thank you so much," she exclaims in relief as she jumps into my arms for the hug I halfway expected. "I can't believe you're willing to do this for me. You're so sweet, and I really appreciate it. Anything you ever need, I'm your girl. I can be like a helper-spy and go into a women's locker room or spa for you. Something like that, where you can't go." She points at herself like she's the one to call on for that very specific, never-before-happened situation.

I have never been called sweet. Not a single time in my entire life, not even as a kid. But Janey thinks I am, and I've no desire to disavow her of the erroneous judgment, so to keep up appearances, I shift my hips, hoping she won't notice what her innocent touch has done to me.

Pulling back, she drops to her flat feet and confesses, "I have to warn you, though, I wasn't exaggerating. The wedding is going to be awful. I'm a positive Pollyanna type to a fault, but this is so bad that even I can't find a single good thing about it. And I've tried hard. Like so bad that not even good cake will make up for it, and there's a fair to good chance the cake will be gluten-free, organic cardboard too, so there's not even that to look forward to." She sticks her tongue out like she's tasting the gross cake right now. "And, I can't emphasize this enough, Paisley is horrible. I never know what to say to her, and on her wedding day? It's not like I can say anything. So I'm glad you'll be there. Maybe you can do that stone-cold glare you do?" She mimics a narrow-eyed scowl that looks remarkably hilarious on her usually smiling face.

I seamlessly drop into the expression she's talking about, and she plants her hands on my cheeks and stares into my eyes, first right then left. "Yes! Like that! How do you do that? I need you to teach me your ways. That'd come in so handy with patients' families when they get rowdy."

She releases me and falls back to the stool, practicing a few glares. Unsuccessfully, I might add. The closest she comes to a scowl looks more like a pouty kitten.

"I think you have other talents," I say gently as I sit beside her again.

Rolling her eyes, she steals a piece of bacon from my plate, having finished her own. Focusing quickly, she says, "Okay, if you're gonna be my fake boyfriend—that sounds crazy, right?— we need to have our stories straight. Maybe we say you're a doctor and we met at work? Or a fighter pilot? I'm sure they've seen *Top Gun 2.0* and would eat that up. Or go with the obvious and say you're a model."

I choke on my coffee, and she flashes a momentary grin, proud of herself.

"Why don't we stick with the truth? Cleaner that way. I'm a

consultant—that's my usual cover story because it can mean anything—and you're a nurse. We met over dinners that were supposed to be solo, but instead, we got to know each other." I pause to see if she's in agreement, and when she nods, I continue. "What have you told your family or any of the people at the wedding about yourself, your relationship, and dipshit? I don't want to get anything wrong if it can be helped."

She starts to speak but then goes silent. Her brows furrow, and she looks down at her plate. "Uhm, actually . . . not much. Just that I'm dating someone and he works a lot." She lifts her face to meet my gaze. "That's sad, huh? I talk to my parents regularly, but I never shared much about Henry . . . I mean, dipshit. Probably a sign I should've noticed."

Her correction to calling her ex by my nickname for him is progress. Small, but significant.

"It's a good thing now," I reassure her. "What about your family? I researched you, so I've got the basics. But I need to know about them, what you would've shared with a boyfriend."

"Well, you already know Paisley's awful, and . . . wait, what'd you say? You've researched me?" she says, sounding offended.

I shrug noncommittally. "Of course. If it helps, your online presence is remarkably pristine compared to most peoples'. Probably the only ones better are mine and Louisa's."

"Who's Louisa?" she asks. I notice a hint of pink rising in her cheeks.

"Jealous?" I flash a quick, predatory grin. "It's okay if you are. I don't mind if my girlfriends, fake or otherwise, are a little fiery. In fact, maybe I prefer it." I'm hoping to trigger her into it. Not for my sake, but for her own. She's going to need everything she's got to get through this, even with me at her side. She doesn't need to be Kayla-like, able to eviscerate someone in three words or less, but she needs to be her best Janey.

"Humph." She pouts, which for some reason is kinda adorable.

I let her stew in the jealousy for a quick second before explaining her worry away. "Louisa is my assistant, and our relationship is strictly professional. She's also in her fifties, prefers to spend time with her husband and their two Boston Terriers, and is a research machine."

"Good, because I care if my boyfriends, fake or otherwise, are seeing other women." She says it with all the backbone of a strong woman, but I know the cost it's come with. I heard it in her voice last night. That she can fake it a bit bodes well for us.

"Fair is fair. I researched you and should be willing to share myself with you to the same degree. I'm an investigator, own my own bespoke business with top-secret, private clientele. There's no business page listing or 1-800 number to call. I already told you that I have four brothers and a twin sister. Cameron, Carter, Chance, Kayla, and Kyle. What else do you want to know?" I finish.

"Uhm, everything," she answers with her chin in her hands and eager eyes.

"I don't think there's much more to tell. I'm boring and my life is monotonous. Sure, the cases are different, but the job's the same. This stakeout is the most interesting thing I've done in ages, both because of the location outside the city and my cabinmate." I give her a sly grin that she ducks away from, but I see the soft smile she's trying to hide. Confident I've made my case about what she's bringing to the table, I offer, "Fire away. Hit me with whatever questions you want. I'm an open book."

I've never uttered those words in my life, but I find that for Janey, they're true.

I want her to know me. And I want to know her too.

But only so we can pull off this fake boyfriend thing, of course.

CHAPTER 7
JANEY

WITH PERMISSION TO ask anything I want, my brain short-circuits and I ask everything at once, the words tumbling over one another in a rush for freedom.

"How did you become an investigator? What's been your wildest case and why? Do you and your twin have that twin-telepathy thing? If so, is it weird because like, how do you turn it off when you're doing private stuff? Or oh, God, what if you couldn't? That'd be awful. If you could be any animal, what would it be? That one's not as strange as it sounds. It's a proven psychology trick that speaks to what you value most. Have you ever had a nickname, and if so, how'd you get it? Do you have pet peeves or things that make you angry? I promise if you'll tell me what, I won't do it. That way, you won't get mad when you're helping me. Have you ever been in love?" My eyes go wide and my mouth drops open into an O of horror. "Oh, my God, do you have a girlfriend? Or a wife? Or a husband? Basically, is there anyone who's going to feel some sort of way about this little adventure you've agreed to go on with me?"

It's an entire unwieldy, immense blob of verbiage, but I can't seem to stop it from pouring forth until the idea of Cole having someone in his life hits me. He told me Louisa is his assistant. He hasn't told me anything about anyone past, but recently, I've come to find out that's not exactly enough information to rule out the existence of a significant other. On the other hand, I don't actually know whether Henry told his co-worker about me . . . and us. Knowing him, he probably didn't.

Cole is blank-faced staring at me.

I think I've scared him already. It wouldn't be the first time my exuberance put someone off. I've been on several first dates that ended before the entrees arrived, but my perspective is that those guys weren't meant for me if a little nervous chatterboxing was too hard to handle. That's dating—seeing if your weirdness fits with another person's weirdness in a complementary way.

But Cole chuckles deep in his chest, and my nervousness untwists itself in my chest like a shoestring knot that someone just tugged the string on. The sound is foreign coming from him, and it makes his whole face soften in a way I couldn't have imagined. It makes him look relaxed and not at all scared. Or scary.

Ticking off answers on his fingers, he replies, "Long story. This one. No, thank God, and fuck off for the awful imagery of Kayla that way. Human, top of the hierarchy. Cole Slaw, because my grandma made it for a picnic once and I ate it until I got sick. Name didn't stick very long because I can't even think about it anymore without gagging." He shakes his head like he's ridding himself of the thought. "Uhm . . . I cataloged every question you asked, but I'm forgetting some in the middle. I remember the important one, though." He looks directly into my eyes, silently demanding that I listen, understand, and believe this truth. "No girlfriend, wife, or anything like that. Cheating pisses me off, and it's not something I could ever do, not for a case. And not for a friend."

I smile at the rough raspiness that's entered his voice, showing the depth of his feelings about cheating. It makes sense that'd be his position when he sees case after case of how devastating it can be. I like that. It's definitely something we have in common.

And he called me a friend!

I like having friends, especially hot guy types who are willing to help me and don't freak out when I rapid-fire questions.

Which I actually don't remember. Embarrassed, I say, "Could

you remind me what questions you answered? I kinda forgot what I asked."

He doesn't bat an eye, just obliges easily. "You asked how I became an investigator and my wildest case. Mr. and Mrs. Webster are by far my wildest, most interesting, and favorite case. Not because of them but because of you."

I swear I swoon, literally spinning in a circle on my stool, at his sweet words. I'm not used to kindness, but this is more than that. Cole's repairing damage in my soul that I buried long ago and like to pretend doesn't exist.

He doesn't ignore me when I ramble. He doesn't tell me to shut up. He doesn't think I'm stupid or boring or forgettable.

He listens. He pays attention. He cares.

It sounds like so little, but the truth is, in my experience, it's a lot. And it's a rare person who behaves the way Cole does. Too many people have gone the opposite way with me.

"Really?" I ask, hoping it's not too pathetic. He lifts one wry brow, and it's all the reassurance I need. "Thank you. You don't understand how much that means to me."

"It's true," he says once more. "As for becoming an investigator, it was mostly by accident. I went to school for a bit, but it wasn't for me. My older brothers rocked that shit, business school all the way, though Chance struggled a bit. But not like me. I would go to classes, and boredom would set in, which led to anger, and basically, I said 'fuck it' to everything and dropped out of college. I was hanging out at my local bar when a guy came in, asking about one of the bartenders." He gets a faraway look in his eyes like he's remembering. "I figured out that he was looking for a deadbeat dad, asked a few questions to confirm the bartender was the right guy, and told the PI where he could find him because fuck that guy. He was letting his kid go hungry while buying college co-eds drinks every night." His lips are curled in distaste as he tells that part of the story, but then he shrugs and the anger melts away like it never existed.

I wonder if it really disappeared, though, or if Cole pushed it down deep like I do. I cover any hurt with smiles and rainbows and the belief that everything'll be okay. I think he covers it with grumpiness and scowls that probably are intended to be scary, but they make me fluttery inside.

"To thank me, the PI offered me a couple of bucks," he continues, "but I turned it down. I was living off my college fund then, doing fine on my own and too proud to actually work. But a few days later, he asked if I would sit on a subject for him. It was a pretty basic assignment, but I felt a thrill, a satisfaction with it that I never felt with academic work. And that was it. I never stopped."

He sips his coffee like we're casually talking about the weather and not sharing his entire life story in basically one breath.

"Wow," I respond. "That sounds meant to be. You were in the right place at the right time to meet your mentor. Hey, what about the bartender? Did the PI find him? Did he get the child support for the kid? He's not still struggling, is he? Because I know some state resources and charitable non-profits that could help."

Cole's eyes narrow as he looks at me in confusion. And then he smiles. Again! I'm keeping track at this point.

"You would help, wouldn't you?" he asks wonderingly.

"Of course." I reach for my phone, already thinking of the social workers I deal with at the care center. Usually, they specialize in adult care, but there are several who do both child and adult resource assistance.

Cole places his hand over mine, stopping me. His skin is warm, and his touch sends shocks of awareness through my entire body even as my focus zeroes in on the connection. I look at his hand to see if he's got one of those handshake zapper things clowns used to use on unsuspecting marks because his touch feels that electrified. But it's just him . . . touching me.

I look up and meet his eyes, which have gone soft. "The kid's fine. Mom too. The PI had a few words with the bartender, who tried the ole 'I'm barely scraping by' act. The PI planned to serve him papers, but the kid needed money faster."

"Did you give them money?" I ask hopefully. He said he was living on his college fund at the time. I don't know what kind of money he's talking about, but I'd be digging in couch cushions if a kid needed food. Surely, Cole's the same. Everybody'd do that.

"No, I didn't give them money." He smiles again, but this time's different. It's only with one side of his lips and it looks . . . cold and dangerous. A shiver runs down my spine, but it's not in fear. No sirree, I kinda want him to look at me like that, which is stupid, but it reminds me of the sexy vampires in my books.

"I was an asshole back then. In a different way than I am now. In my mind, I didn't have anything to lose, so I waited for the bartender—his name was Gary—to come in one night. Ordered my usual whiskey, but instead of on the rocks, I took a straight shot for courage and told Gary that we were taking a walk because I had something to talk to him about." He pauses and gives me an appraising glance, as if checking to see if I'm on board with whatever he's about to tell me.

Oh, my God, did he kill Gary? He said he's not a killer or criminal, but it's not like people go around announcing that. Did I miss that?

But I don't make a move to get away. I sit right where I am, willing to listen because if Cole did something bad, there had to be a reason, right? Maybe Gary attacked him first?

"You should see your face right now," he murmurs, his voice low as he cups my cheek and peers into my eyes. A muscle twitches in his jaw. "Whatever you're thinking, it's not that bad, Janey. I swear."

Oh.

"Oh!" I sag into my chair and try to figure out what I'm thinking. Is that disappointment I'm feeling? Was I proud that Cole was willing to defend a child I didn't know existed five minutes ago to the death?

Cole stares ahead stoically, his gaze fixed out the kitchen window, and quietly confesses, "I marched him to the nearest ATM, had him clean out his savings account of every penny he had, and told him that if he said a word about it, I'd tell every sorority sister and college girl in the state that he was intentionally infecting them with STDs and tell every bar owner in town that he stole from the till and sold alcohol out the back door. He'd be unhireable and unfuckable in under an hour." He drops his chin, a cloud of shame overtaking him. "I would handle things differently now, but I thought I was untouchable back then."

"What'd you do with the money?" I ask.

He turns his head a few degrees, looking up at me in surprise. "What do you think? Gave it to the kid's mom. Told her it was back pay and probably all she'd ever see, but if she needed anything, to give me a call."

Oh. Well, that's not all that bad. It's even kinda admirable in a way. "And Gary?"

"Left town shortly after. Took me all of two days to find him. He still doesn't send child support, but the kid's better off without him. I just keep an eye on them." He sighs as a shudder runs through his muscles. "I've never told anyone that story. You and Gary are the only ones who know about that night."

I feel honored that he would trust me with something so secret and can't fight the urge to hug him. Well, it's a side hug because I mostly press my chest to his bicep and cheek to his shoulder, but that still counts in my book.

After a moment, he shifts to curl his arms around me and it's a for-real hug. Pressed against him, I vow, "I know I'm a blabber-mouth about basically everything, but I will never tell a soul an actual secret. I'm proud of you for doing such a big thing for that kid."

He pulls back, putting a few inches between us, but it's only to look into my eyes. Bewildered, he asks, "You're proud that I basically robbed a guy and threatened to fuck his life completely up?"

I roll my eyes. "Well, don't say it like that. You saved a kid from starving, like Robin Hood, taking the money from a guy who should've given it willingly to give to the child who should've received it in the first place."

"You're . . . something else," he grumbles, but there's a hint of one of his happy smiles beneath the grumping.

I don't mean to. I don't plan it. And I certainly don't think about it. But I place a gentle kiss to the side of his mouth, catching the edge of that tiny smile with my lips. It's over too fast for him to pucker and kiss me back—not that he'd want to! —but I get the quick sense of rough stubble and soft lips before I pull back and smile.

His eyes have gone dark and hard. "Don't mess with monsters, Janey. You never know what'll happen."

He's doing the cold, hard, asshole thing again in an instant, trying to put up a big old brick wall between us, but I've already seen behind the curtain, Mr. Oz. Grinning, I reply, "You're not a monster. You're a grumpy Muppet at best. Like Oscar, the grouchy one in the trashcan, who always tries to scare everyone away but secretly likes people." I place another quick peck to the end of his nose and grin wide, proud of myself for being right about Cole from the get-go.

He does a good job at creating a forcefield around himself, and most people don't make the effort to pass it. But if you do, he's an entirely different person deep, deep, deep down inside.

"I'm gonna shower, but thank you for breakfast. And thank you for going to the wedding with me. It means more than you could possibly know," I tell him. I get up, reaching to take my coffee with me, but Cole moves faster.

I don't know how I get there, but I'm suddenly backed against the cabinets and Cole is pressed against me, a hand gripping the counter on either side of my hips to lock me in the cage of his arms. I gasp, my hands finding their way to his chest.

"I'm not who you think I am," he growls. And then his lips are on mine.

There's no gentle touching, no tasting, and definitely no get-to-know-ya testing. Cole takes my mouth and my breath, roughly kissing me like I've never been kissed before. Actually, I don't know that what I've done before qualifies as kissing now that I'm experiencing this all-consuming devouring. He tilts his head to the other side like he wants to have me every way he can, and I fight to keep up, wanting him as much as he apparently wants me.

He wants me?

I don't know what flippy-floppy world I've entered, but I like it here and want to stay because believable or not, the proof is pressed between us. He can't fake the thick, hard evidence that Cole Harrington wants me, Plainy Janey Williams.

But too soon, Cole groans and presses his forehead to mine, stopping the kiss. I can feel the heat of his breath on my lips, which seem puffier than they were a minute ago.

"Don't see things that aren't there in me, Janey."

I think it's supposed to be a warning, one of his shields going up between us, but I see him, the real him, and it's not so scary. "Don't be afraid to let me see everything," I challenge.

Before he can protest, I duck out of his arms, heading down the hall to the bathroom.

I'm not sure if he'll follow me to argue that I'm imagining his good-guy, ooey-gooey center. Or follow me to fuck me on the bathroom vanity. Or run from my unflinching view that everyone, including him, is good deep down. I'm kinda excited to see, though.

I hear the front door open and then close and have my answer.

CHAPTER 8
COLE

"BREATHE. In through your nose, two, three, four. Out through your mouth, two, three, four." Janey stops talking to herself for a moment to actually do the breathing exercise, but after only one round, she goes back to her pep talk. "It's gonna be fine. Lovely, even. We'll walk in, say hello, and hug Mom, Dad, and Jessica. We'll sit down and enjoy dinner."

We're driving into Bridgeport for Paisley's rehearsal dinner, and Janey's been freaking out all day. She took two showers, saying she needed to rewash her hair because 'it wasn't acting right', but it looked beautiful to me both times. She has on makeup tonight, making her lashes dark and long, her cheeks extra pink, and her lips shiny. And her dress? Fuck me, her dress.

She walked out of the bathroom in bare feet and a dress that had all my blood running south in a heartbeat. I'm a complete sucker for one thing and one thing only . . . sundresses, and though it's a fancy version, that's what Janey chose to wear tonight.

It's peach with tiny flowers all over and floppy ties at the shoulders that make me want to undo them and test gravity, and the hem falls to below her knees. She'd done a twirl and it'd flared out, tempting me with a peek of her knees. Her knees, for fuck's sake. Knees I've seen all week in her shorts but that suddenly seemed newly interesting when she hid them away like there was a fresh mystery to find.

Oh, there's a mystery under that dress I want to explore, but it's not Janey's knees. It's higher, much higher.

Fuck, I sound like Kyle.

Get it together, Harrington!

Janey's still itemizing things out like bullet points on a to-do list. She's up to dessert and clapping politely through the toasts now. I do the same thing sometimes because it helps me feel in control when there's a chance everything might go haywire, and I wonder if she's doing it for similar reasons.

"Tell me about your parents and sister," I demand as a way to distract her, another effective coping mechanism.

"Huh?" she utters, opening her eyes where I suspect she was visualizing tonight's dinner as she talked it through. "Oh, yeah. The more info you have, the better this'll go."

Mom, Dad, and Jessica. That's the sum total of Janey's immediate family, and I want to know everything. Not because I need it to play the boyfriend role but because I want to know everything about Janey. And morbidly, the people who've hurt her. For no reason in particular . . . none at all.

"They're the Three Musketeers, which left me on the outside, mostly. I completely understand why, though." She sounds resigned to that reality, something I can't agree with in the slightest. I harrumph in response, and she tries to convince me.

"My parents adopted my sister when she was barely two, basically saving her from the rough start at life she'd been born into. I was fourteen and through the worst of it with my family. I'd figured out that staying 'out of sight, out of mind' was my best bet, and I was already looking for the silver lining in literally everything by then. So when they brought home an adorable almost-toddler, I had this dream that we'd be sisters and Jessica would be my friend. I mean, I had friends at school and stuff—I wasn't a total outcast, thank God—but not in my family, you know?"

She goes quiet, and I reach over to take her hand in mine, running my thumb along the soft skin between her thumb and index finger. She sighs like she's got the weight of the world on her shoulders, and capable as they may be, she was only a child. It shouldn't have been her that had to carry pain from what should've been a happy time.

"Instead, she became the instant center of attention, coddled and spoiled in nearly every way to make up for her early years' mistreatment, and through no fault of her own," she says emphatically, making excuses for her family, "she made me even more of an outsider. Only this time, it wasn't in my extended family. It was in my own home. Mom joked that Jessica was their 'Do-Over Child' and that they wouldn't make the same mistakes with her that they made with me."

"That's bullshit," I snap.

I don't know if she believes me because she adds, "Fourteen-year-old me had a teeny-tiny moment of hope that they finally saw how awful they'd been to me and wanted to be better. But no. Now? Twenty-five-year-old me hopes that someday, Jessica will mature beyond the thirteen-year-old princess my parents have created and we'll eventually become the friends I wished for."

In my opinion, she's moved beyond 'looking for the silver lining' there and is spit-polishing a nickel, hoping it'll shine up like silver.

"And your parents?" I ask tightly. This is a bad line of questioning before we walk into the rehearsal dinner. Not for Janey, but for me. I'm supposed to play the charming, loving boyfriend, but mostly, I want to rip Janey's family a new one for not recognizing what an amazing human she is.

"If you ask them, they were good parents and the proof of that is that I'm an upstanding, independent adult with a job. That's their stamp of achievement as far as they're concerned."

She shrugs it off casually, though her lips have tilted fully upside down. I've never seen her frown. Even when dipshit was breaking up with her, her lips were only pressed into a straight, flat line. I hate that her family is what prompts the expression now. It shouldn't be like that.

I've got my own troubles with my family—an emotionally distant dad, a mom who makes up for it by loving too hard, brothers who fought for ranking in a fake hierarchy and one who opted out of that nonsense, and a sister who's weary from years of second-mothering us all. And a partridge in a pear tree or some shit.

But Janey's different. She's too good to have to suffer through hell at a place and time that should be your safe spot. Home. Family. Childhood.

Her family should've been the ones to love and appreciate her, but instead they used their position of power to squash her, making her doubt her own worth. The consequences for that are still echoing in her heart and mind. Hell, even in her relationships, like with dipshit.

I grit my teeth so I don't tell her what I think about her shitty parents and bitchy sister, mostly because I want to go into the rehearsal dinner and help her, and if she thinks I might go Asshole Mode on them, she'll bail on this whole thing.

Which I don't want because she needs this on multiple levels, and I don't want to take it from her.

"They never noticed the difficulties I had growing up," Janey continues about her parents, not noticing my thinly held grip on my anger, "and to be honest, I never told them. It wouldn't do any good to bring it up now. Better to let that hurt live under the rug where I've already tap-danced it down until it's flat enough to not trip me up anymore."

She forces a smile to her face, but it looks brittle and artificial. "Tonight's about Paisley and Max. That's it. Get in and get out unscathed."

We're quiet for the rest of the drive. I think Janey's gone back to listing out the activities of tonight's festivities. I'm figuring out whether there's a way to get her dad out back for a little chat.

I pull into the parking lot of a steak restaurant that's known for two things: a pricey menu and an air of snobbery that's rarer than the steaks they serve. I don't know Janey's family's financial situation, but I'm a bit surprised, I have to admit.

My family wouldn't give a place like this a second thought, but I'm well aware that we're in a different tax bracket than most. Well, my parents are.

"Why're you going to the rehearsal dinner if you're not in the wedding?" I ask, realizing that though I haven't been to many weddings, that's unusual.

"Paisley wanted a big woo-di-hoo with her family and Max's family breaking bread together. And yes, I know what you're thinking—isn't that what the reception is for? And you'd be right, yes, it is. But what Paisley wants, Paisley gets, so a family affair rehearsal dinner it is. The bridal party did the practice run earlier today, but dinner is an all-hands-on-deck situation."

With what Janey's told me about Paisley, I'm not surprised. One more opportunity to be the center of attention sounds right up her alley.

There's a valet in front of the restaurant, but I think Janey could use one last moment to collect herself before this shitshow begins, so I drive past him to park on my own. "Stay there," I tell her before I get out and walk around the truck to her door. I open it and take her hand to help her down, making sure she's steady since she's no longer barefoot in that damn sundress but is wearing nude strappy heels. This close, I can see the line of her cleavage and am tempted to trace it with a finger and then my tongue, teasing her breasts until she forgets about her family's drama.

Completely unaware of the filthy thoughts running through my mind and still surprised at the mildest chivalrous gesture, she quietly says, "Thank you."

I've got no issue with women who want to open their own doors and don't need their chair pulled out, but Janey likes those things. I suspect she's never been treated that way, and I plan to show her how a man should cherish her in all the everyday, small ways.

"You ready?" I ask, keeping her in the open doorway with

one hand on the truck and one on the door. There's no one around to hear us, but this is a private conversation. Only she and I know what's about to happen, and it needs to stay that way. If she says no, I'll help her climb back in the truck and have her roaring down the highway, heading back to the cabin, in under sixty seconds.

"Yep! Let's go introduce everyone to my awesome, hot, smart, rich boyfriend!" she says, sounding like she's channeling a cheerleader on pep rally day. Rah, rah, sis, boom, bah!

It's fake. Obviously so, and I sense she needs a little encouragement to do this. She needs to at least partially feel like it's real.

I lean into her, murmuring so close that my lips brush hers. "Call me your boyfriend again, beautiful."

I feel her breath whoosh out and grin victoriously. She's not thinking about Paisley or her parents or her sister now. She's thinking about me and only me. And not that I'm some fake stand-in that she's lying about.

For a moment, it feels *real*.

"You're not a boy . . . or a friend . . . or a boyfriend. You're something else entirely," she whispers, and now her smile looks real.

"Tonight, I'm yours and you're mine," I prompt with a meaningful look, "and don't forget it."

I take her hand in mine, press a kiss to her wrist, and lead her toward the restaurant. It's showtime.

I'm nervous. Not that I'd show that to Janey or anyone else. But this undercover gig feels bigger and more important than any job I've had before. Janey needs this to go perfectly, and I'll do anything to make sure that happens.

We follow the hostess's directions to the private back room and I open the door, then press a hand to the small of Janey's back to guide her in. The space is filled with dark walnut paneling, rich carpeting, and staid oil paintings of cattle and ranchers. The long, white tablecloth-covered table in the center of the room is covered with brightly polished silver, sparkling stemware, and a gathering of greenery and white flowers that meanders down the middle.

Though the room is full of people, no one so much as glances our way to notice Janey's arrival. Even so, she takes my hand again and squeezes . . . hard. I can feel her nerves ratcheting up like she's entering the Thunderdome and will have to fight to the death instead of having dinner with her family.

"We're fine. You're fine," I whisper in her ear, keeping an eye on the room though I glance down at her chest, which is rising and falling too quickly. "Slow down your breathing. I've got you."

"There's Mom and Dad," she says.

I follow her gaze, clocking the two people I need to impress the most.

Janey's mom, Eileen, is short and thin, has a brunette bob that brushes around her jaw, and is wearing a blue dress with large red flowers along the hem, which is touching the tops of her knees. Her shoes are sensible block heels and her jewelry is minimal, only a tennis bracelet that I bet she pulls out of her jewelry box for special occasions.

Janey's dad, Leo, is tall and has a round belly I suspect is from a more-than-occasional beer. His head is freshly shaved, and his smile looks easy as he listens to whatever Eileen is saying. Leo's wearing boots, khaki slacks, and a green polo shirt with a pair of reading glasses tucked into the button placket.

They seem slightly underdressed for the occasion, but all in all, they look remarkably . . . normal. Which is surprisingly not uncommon when you're talking about people who are shitty parents. They're rarely the scary monsters we expect them to be. More often, the worst of the worst look like your neighbors, which is the scariest part of all.

"Let's go introduce me," I say, pulling Janey toward them. I have a few choice words for these two.

And the rest of the family too.

———

Janey

I can't do this. I should've told Cole no. I should've laughed at how ridiculous the very idea of his playing my boyfriend is. But I wanted it to work and had myself believing it would right up until we walked into this room.

Now, sticking my head in the sand ostrich-style is sounding like a better plan. I want to run back to the cabin and hide. Skip the rehearsal dinner, skip the wedding, and go back to work next week like nothing happened.

But Cole is having none of Plan B, Janey the Ostrich Queen.

He marches straight up to my parents and interrupts whatever conversation they were having by extending his hand toward my dad. "Mr. Williams? I'm Cole, Janey's boyfriend. Been looking forward to meeting you."

Dad recoils in surprise, from the interruption and Cole's very direct—and charming?—introduction. "Oh, uh . . . nice to meet you, Cole. Call me Leo," Dad answers as he shakes Cole's hand.

Cole shakes Mom's hand, charming her too. "Your daughter has told me so much about you two. I've been looking forward to this," he repeats.

Mom and Dad smile wanly, not hearing the thinly veiled threat in his words, but I hear it loud and clear. I've spent enough time with Cole over the past week to be able to get that much of a read on him.

Warily, I plaster myself to Cole's side like I could hold him back if he decided to defend my honor or something insane. "So, yeah . . . this is Cole. Yep, my boyfriend, Cole. That's him." He glances at me and lifts a brow, the tiniest hint of a smile on the left side of his mouth. I should add that to the count, but I've completely forgotten what number I'm on, so I just enjoy it. "Oh! And Cole, this is my mom, Eileen, and dad, Leo."

Mom and Dad exchange a look. I know that look—it's the same one they made when I excitedly told them I'd won the fourth-grade spelling bee. They want to believe me, but they don't. Not really. And okay, I'd admittedly been a little confused about the spelling bee. I won for my class, not the whole grade, but I didn't realize there was a difference. And I definitely didn't know I'd have to go onstage in front of the whole school to compete against the other classes' winners. I mumbled my answer into the microphone and Mrs. Beckman declared it incorrect, even though I spelled hippopotamus right. I wouldn't spell it h-i-p-p-A-p-o-t-a-m-u-s because then it would be a hippa, not a hippo.

So I do what I do best and launch into a monologue. "Yeah, we've been looking forward to this. Cole's been super busy at work, but I told him we couldn't miss Paisley's wedding, and here we are. Me and my boyfriend, Cole. Are they gonna get started soon? I'm starving. I don't think I had lunch today. Did we have lunch today?" I ask Cole.

"You made charcuterie boards," he reminds me, "and we ate cheese cubes, lunch meat, and crackers all day."

"Oh, yeah!" I say too brightly.

Dad leans over with a grin to tell Cole, "Probably a good thing she didn't cook for you. She's better at burning than baking, right, honey?" Dad jokes. "Remember the bacon?"

The last time I cooked anything at home was when I was eighteen, and yeah, I might've set the smoke alarm off that time, but for all Dad knows, I'm a chef now. I'm not, of course, but he doesn't know that. He doesn't care. In his mind, the joke's set in stone, forever and ever, amen.

"Really? She's great in the kitchen now," Cole says thoughtfully. "Keeps me well-fed for sure." He pats his flat stomach, drawing attention to how fit he is.

He's seen me make sandwiches, soup, pizza rolls, and the chicken that was supposed to be for Henry, but if you heard him complimenting me, you'd think I serve up Michelin-rated dinners on the regular. It's definitely a little bit of false bragging, but I'm happy for it.

"Well, I taught her everything she knows," Mom adds. That's true, actually. Mom taught me how to make chicken that won't poison anyone and ground beef with a sprinkle of packaged seasonings. Other than that, she shooed me out of the kitchen because I was in her way.

"How's the garden?" I ask Dad, choosing a topic that I know will last.

His face lights up the way it always does when he talks about his babies, the flowers, bushes, and plants he cares for. Within seconds, he's off, telling us all about the new fiddle leaf fig he 'rescued' from the plant store while Mom looks at him like he's the most interesting man on the planet, though I'm sure she's heard this story ten times already.

And I'm happily listening, glad the attention is off Cole and me, until a voice says, "Hey, Sideshow!"

It's Jessica. She was allowed to watch *The Simpsons* from a young age, something I couldn't do until I was a teen, and bestowed me with the clown nickname because of my wild red curls. The name's nothing new, but it's annoying all the same. In the hopes of shutting it down for the eight hundred thousand, fifty-eighth time, I ask, "Aren't you tired of that yet?"

She laughs like that's ridiculous. Like Dad, Jessica prefers her humor dipped in plaster and written in stone, to forever be humorous. To her, at least.

Cole does something I've never been able to do—shut Jessica up. He wraps one of my ringlets around his finger, tugging gently. "I love Janey's hair. It's different and beautiful, not boring, plain brown." He sounds wistful about my hair, all the while, insulting Jessica's brown tresses.

Ooh, he's a slick one. Shutting down Dad about my cooking and Jessica with her annoying nickname.

I'm secretly thrilled and have to shift from one foot to the other to keep from doing a happy dance.

"Who're you?" Jessica asks with narrowed eyes.

"Cole, Janey's boyfriend," he answers proudly, forcibly dragging his attention away from me to glance at her. He doesn't bother asking who she is, and I can see that it irks Jessica.

I'm going to hell for it, but I'm glad Cole's here, playing the part of my boyfriend. Just seeing the looks on all their faces makes whatever eternal damnation I'll suffer worth it.

"Oh, there's Paisley," Mom says in a hushed voice like we're not all here to see her. And she's off on the topic of the day. Not meeting my boyfriend for the first time, of course. That's small potatoes.

The wedding, though? *That's* important.

"I haven't seen her dress yet, but you know it's going to be gorgeous. Paisley wouldn't have it any other way." Mom nods, certain of that. "They went into town and tried on dozens of them before she picked one, but it's been all hush-hush, top secret."

She looks left and right like someone might overhear her gossiping. "I hope she picked a white one, at least. Wedding dresses should be white . . . and lacy . . . and elegant." She's obviously given this a lot of thought. "You know, kids these days are getting married in pink dresses? And black ones? I saw it on a TV show and thought 'that's not a wedding dress', but I guess if that's what she wants . . ." She trails off, shrugging like it's none of her business seconds after judging an entire industry. Mom's a traditionalist, to say the least.

"Well, Paisley'll look beautiful, I'm sure," Dad comments, on Mom's side no matter what. She could say that the moon's made of dried Oreo filling and he'd nod agreeably.

"They're having the ceremony at that event center," Mom says as she starts rehashing everything she knows about the impending nuptials.

"I'm a *junior* bridesmaid. Can you believe that shit?" Jessica sneers when Mom pauses to take a breath. She somehow manages to make it sound like a brag that she's more than me, but at the same time, completely beneath her to be a 'junior' anything.

"Jessica, please watch your language. Young ladies don't speak like that," Mom corrects her gently.

If I'd cursed when I was thirteen, especially in a fancy restaurant, I would've been grounded for life. Not that I would've dared to say that . . . well, not where Mom could hear. But Jessica? She curses loud, proud, and with no care and is barely reprimanded. Somehow, that's supposed to be one of those 'mistakes' they're correcting with her.

Jessica rolls her eyes at the admonishment. "Whatever. It's stupid that I'm not a regular bridesmaid. It's not like I'm a child."

"Beg to differ," I mutter under my breath, thinking no one will hear me. Or listen.

But Mom does.

"Janey!" she hisses. "Be nice to your sister. Her feelings are a little hurt is all. She's sensitive, you know."

She's sensitive. Jessica? The Menace is sensitive?

Meanwhile, Jessica's grinning like the Cheshire Cat at having gotten away with her rudeness.

"Everyone, please sit down. Dinner is served," Uncle Teddy announces formally. He's wearing a button-up shirt and bolo tie, black slacks, and boat shoes. An odd combination of not-formal attire, but for him, it's pretty razzle-dazzle. Uncle Teddy's probably one of my favorite people in my family, mostly because he used to give us as many Otter Pops as we wanted and made sure I got my favorite purple ones every time. That was partially because Paisley wanted the red ones so she could pretend they were lipstick, but still, at least I got my favorite too.

What can I say, my standards for favorite are pretty low in my family. All it takes is a popsicle and you're it.

Next to him stands Aunt Glenda. She's wearing a gold gown that looks more wedding-like than dinner-like, but she looks really pretty in it.

And then there's Paisley and Max.

Paisley is wearing a white satin nightgown-type dress with a draped neckline that shows her thin frame. Her hair is curled and pulled up around her face with rhinestone clips, and she looks deliriously happy. Her fiancé, Max, is wearing a black suit, a white dress shirt, and a blue tie.

Max's outfit is basically the same as Cole's, but there's a noticeable difference in fit and quality between the two.

Earlier today, Cole had come back with a black garment bag, confusing the hell out of me since I thought he was on a stakeout in the middle of the forest. But he'd explained that Mr. Webster was gone and he'd made the trip to get clothes for tonight's dinner and tomorrow's wedding. I'd told him the jacket wasn't necessary, but he'd insisted, saying he'd have it in case I got cold.

That alone had warmed me enough for the entire evening.

Well, that and the fact that Cole looks good in a suit. His shoulders seem extra broad, his tie matches his eyes perfectly, and as comfortable as he seems in tactical stake-out gear, he seems surprisingly right at home in fancy clothes too.

We sit and dinner is actually . . . okay.

There are toasts, but everyone's fixated on the bride and groom, and I can comfortably disappear into the group of guests, which is good because I can only focus on Cole. He's completely at ease, smiling and laughing along with everyone at the right times, clapping politely, and eating with all three forks like he knows what he's doing.

Meanwhile, I'm struggling to cut my overdone steak and trying to decide whether I should pick up the potato wedges and eat them like fries or dice them up. I glance to Cole for guidance, and he stabs a small piece with his fork and offers me a bite.

"These are really good. We'll have to make them at home," he murmurs. It's between us, but the table is full of people so others can't help but hear.

"What? Uh, yeah, we should," I answer clumsily after swallowing the bit he fed me. It is a good potato, but what follows is the real spice that leaves me wanting more.

He places a chaste kiss on my lips, quick as a blink, like he's comfortable doing that anytime he wants, and then goes back to listening to one of the groomsmen wax poetic about Max's college days.

He's playing the doting boyfriend so perfectly that if he's not careful, I'm going to forget that he's acting.

After dinner, everyone mingles around the room again, chatting about tomorrow's ceremony.

I excuse myself to the restroom, but as I'm touching up my makeup, I freeze, caught in the lounge area by Paisley and another cousin, Nikki. They're coming in the door and haven't seen me yet, but Paisley's laughing and says incredulously, "He's real? I mean, she RSVPed for two, but I totally thought this was one of those 'he goes to another school' type of things."

Nikki laughs and agrees, "Me too!"

Paisley's not done and suggests, "Maybe he's a fake boyfriend? I've read about those in books. Or" —she giggles— "I could see her paying him."

"Totally," Nikki answers. "I mean, talk about an odd couple. Look at him and look at her," she scoffs.

I drop my lip gloss to the counter with a clatter and Paisley gasps, sounding about as fake as a three-dollar bill. "Oh, Janey! We didn't know you were in here."

They knew. I can see it on their faces—the fake shock, the evil glint in their eyes, the triumphant smiles they can't quite control. They intentionally walked in here, knowing I'd be alone and defenseless, to taunt and tease me.

And I let them.

Most days, I'd have something to say. I'm not the mousey little girl they remember from when we were kids. I'm stronger now, but I'm also too freshly hurt to find anything in my mind. For once, it's completely silent and blank.

"Excuse me," I say, trying to brush past them to escape.

But rather than getting out, Cole pushes his way in . . . to the women's restroom. Well, it's the lounge part, not where people are peeing, but still. He shouldn't be in here.

His eyes are stony and cold, and the charming gentleman from all evening is gone, replaced with the hard man he can be. Is it strange that I'm glad to see this version of Cole? I think it's closer to the real him, not the fake chuckle-chuckle guy he's been for some of tonight's conversations.

"This door is so thin that I could hear every word you two said and it's fucking disgusting. That sort of disrespect might be accepted by everyone else, but it's not acceptable to me. And not to Janey. You think we're an odd couple? Not sure you're one to judge since your husband has been eyeing every woman here all night—the waitress, the hostess, the blonde bridesmaid," he sneers at Nikki.

"He has not," she insists, but there's doubt in her eyes.

I don't know whether that's true or not, but if Nikki's hubby was eyeing someone else, Cole would definitely be the one to notice. And that particular bridesmaid is Nikki's sister, who has a sordid history of her own and has actually slept with a couple of Nikki's boyfriends over the years.

"And you? Ringleader of the Bitches? What proof do you want?" he demands of Paisley. "Want to know Janey's favorite drink? Red Bull—strawberry apricot flavor. Toothbrush? Purple. Sleeps? Middle of the bed. Tattoo? Right here on her hip. It's my good luck charm, and every time I think of her, I like to grab ahold of it." He echoes his words with action, firmly gripping my hip right over my flower tattoo as he yanks me to his side. "Position? Knees thrown over my shoulders as I worship her," he finishes with a crude lick of his lips. "Want to see it right here or are you satisfied?"

My cousins are red faced and horrified. I'm about to attack him and demand what he just described because it sounds amazing, and like his kiss, something I've never experienced. And I have no doubt that Cole can deliver.

There's a knock on the door. "Uhm, ladies?" Uncle Teddy asks from the other side. Judging by his tone, the door is thin enough that everyone's heard this part of our conversation too.

"We have to go," I ramble. "Right now. Right now," I repeat as I grab Cole's hand and drag him out of the restroom, through the room of people, who are definitely looking at me now, and out of the restaurant.

"Janey Susannah Williams," Dad shouts, but I keep hustling without so much as a glance his way.

"Oh, my God, oh, my God, oh, my God," I mutter over and over as Cole walks me to his truck. "What the hell just happened?"

"I shut your bitchy cousin up and made sure that, on the eve of her wedding, all she'll be thinking about is you getting fucked like you should be. And like she never will be, judging by Max."

"What?" I screech.

Am I mad? Am I impressed? Have I gone crazy and imagined that horror show?

Maybe all three. Probably all of those and more.

Except Cole's smiling like he's proud of himself as he starts the truck and waves to the crowd of people—my family!—who followed us out of the restaurant. The last thing I see is Mom's frown. She doesn't look disappointed, though. No, she looks like she expected as much from me.

CHAPTER 9
COLE

JANEY'S quiet the whole way back. I'm pretty sure this is her version of furious. She doesn't turn her anger outward, shouting it from the rooftops and raging against others. No, her anger burns deep and hot, hurting her more than anyone else.

When we get back, I park behind her little yellow SUV that hasn't moved all week. I don't want her to bolt in the middle of the night. She probably wouldn't, but I'm taking no chances. It'd be too dangerous, and I'm not done with this job. Or her. And I'm not sure what to expect from Pissed Off Janey, but running away isn't going to happen, even if it takes blocking in her car and propping up against the front door to catch a few Zs. Holding her hostage? Not an issue for me.

I go around to open her door, but she's done it herself, hopping out of the truck to the dirt, purposefully not letting me help her as an act of rebellion. She wobbles slightly in her heels, and I reach out to catch her, but she jerks her arm away and marches past me, into the cabin.

Shit.

Inside, Janey's opening and closing the handful of cabinet doors like she's looking for something, but I suspect it's more about the slamming doors than a kitchen scavenger hunt. Her heels click-clack across the floor, and she occasionally huffs in annoyance when a cabinet doesn't have the thing she's looking for, whatever that is. Probably my head on a silver platter.

She wouldn't be the first or the last to hope for that particular menu item.

"That could've gone better," I start.

Janey turns gray eyes on me that are surprisingly fire-filled. There's a spitfire inside her after all, and I'm glad to finally meet her.

Where was she when Henry was being an asshole? Why didn't she come out and tell her cousins to fuck off tonight?

This Janey could've done both of those things easily. But she's beginning with me. I can take it. If Janey needs to rage at someone, let it be me. I'm virtually a stranger and will be out of her life after the wedding, so I'm safe. I'll gladly let her use me for target practice.

I lean against the counter, crossing my arms over my chest as I watch her flit about the kitchen. I risk asking, "What're you looking for?"

"The corkscrew. After all that" —she waves her hand around wildly in the vague direction of the restaurant— "I need a glass of wine," she answers shortly, still opening and closing things— drawers now.

I open the fridge, take out the wine we started last night, and pop the cork out with my teeth before setting it on the counter closest to her. Janey takes one look at it and lunges for it, upending it in two hands to take a solid swallow. When she's had enough, she drops it to the counter with a *thunk* and swipes her lips with the back of her hand. Her gloss is long gone, leaving her lips bare and pouty.

"Better?"

"No," she snaps as she bends over to undo her heels. She kicks them off carelessly, standing barefoot, but when she looks at me again a moment later, her eyes are the tiniest bit softer thanks to the alcohol. "What the hell was that? We talked it through—go in, be charming and cute, a couple they'd all believe. You were supposed to bolster me up and help keep my family at arm's length, like my own personal bodyguard or something. Lay low, draw no attention, be completely forgettable to them like I usually am." She takes another drink.

"I mean, yeah, later, I'd have to face facts and tell 'em we broke up or something, but that's a problem for Future-Janey. This Week-Janey" —she points at her chest— "wanted to make it through the rehearsal dinner and the Wedding from Hell with zero drama. That's it. But *pfft!*, there went that plan." She's pacing, randomly turning this way and that in the tiny space.

"That was never going to happen and you know it," I argue, keeping my voice steady even though I want to shake some sense into her. Her family is a nightmare and she damn well knows it. I'd even venture to say that as bad as she made them sound, in person, they're worse. "Paisley wasn't going to let you waltz in, with or without a boyfriend, and leave you alone. You're her favorite punching bag and she's not done playing with you. The question is, are you done letting her?"

"Ugh!" The noise is a combination of shock, hurt, and betrayal. She wants to be insulted by my blunt words, but I'm right and she knows it. She just doesn't want it to be that way. She paints over her family's shortcomings with excuses that her childhood wasn't that bad, but it was fucking bad enough, and it's continuing now.

She deserves so much better.

She deserves the best. Her heart is too tender, her soul too good for the shit those people shovel onto her. And this is my weakness—I want to save her, help her, make her see that she could never be forgettable because she wiggles into your psyche with sunshine and smiles, happy dances, and excitement over the simplest things, somehow making everything more interesting.

I rip the Band-Aid off slowly, knowing that I'm going to cause more damage as I tell her, "Janey, I was in the hallway. They fucking passed me to get to you, thinking they were safe because I wouldn't follow them into the ladies' room. You know that, right? They walked in there, talking shit and wanting you to hear. They meant to hurt you." I implore her to hear me, to understand that what I'm telling her is the God's honest, ugly truth about her cousins.

"They said they didn't know I was in there," she says quietly, wanting to sweep it away like she's done so many times before, but she knows. Something she saw in their faces tonight . . . she knows they did it on purpose. So though she's making excuses for them, they're only lip service.

"I waited . . . waited for you to tell them to fuck off, but you didn't. So I did what you asked me to do—protect you from them. Maybe it wasn't the way you wanted, but I can guarantee you that none of them see you as weak tonight. They probably think your boyfriend is a psycho," I admit, "but not that you're weak. Not that you froze. Not that you are anything other than a loved, cherished, beautiful woman with a man who cares deeply for you and will defend you, no matter what it takes." My voice is steel as I say, "That's what they'll remember."

"Oh," she says, almost inaudibly with her eyes staring holes in the floor.

I threw a lot at her, and not a single thing was a soft ball. I basically told her that her family is full of manipulative shrews—hey, nice to meet ya!—and I'm sure she's reeling, probably trying to figure out a way to spin it the way she always does. I'm a grumpy, loner asshole, so I'm starting at a deficit, but I can't think of a single way she can silver-lining her way out of this one and that's got to hurt.

So I give her a moment to process.

I fill two mugs with hot water and pull a box of cheap hot cocoa mix from a cabinet. Silently, I stir the powder into the water, letting the marshmallows rise to the top. "Sit on the porch with me?" I ask stoically, but there's something akin to hope in my gut.

Janey lifts her chin, looking at me with clear eyes. She's still working it through, but she's getting there, little by little.

"Okay," she answers, sounding defeated.

On the porch, I set the mugs on the little table and wait for her to sit first, but she doesn't move. Taking the cue, I sit on the lounge chair that's become 'mine' over the last week, expecting her to sit in 'hers'.

Instead, she stands beside me with a look I can't decipher. "Janey?"

In answer, she sits down with me, arranging herself between my outstretched legs and leaning back against my chest. I'm shocked, but there's no way I'm going to ask her to move. I grab the blanket from behind me and throw it over her to keep her warm, though I'm burning up like a furnace at her being this close.

My cock's already growing in my slacks, and there's no way she can't feel the effect she has on me, so I don't bother trying to hide it.

"I'm really sorry your family sucks," I say as I press a kiss to the top of her head. Her curls are soft and spring up around my face, tickling me and making me smile instinctually. Janey's got a lot of ways to do that, though, even if she doesn't see them all.

"God, they really do, don't they?" she answers sadly with a humorless laugh. But her voice is lighter than I would've expected. It's a small difference, but I notice it anyway.

I should've known—she's been through hell tonight, but she bounces back, finding a happy place even if she has to create it herself. That's what she does best—create happiness.

"Can we talk about something else? Tell me how awful your family is to make me feel better." She wiggles, snuggling in deeper to the blanket and rubbing over my hardness. I swallow thickly, doing my best to ignore it and focus on what she needs, not what my dick wants.

"Yeah, uh . . ." I stare into the forest, trying to think of a story that'll help, not just be comparatively worse. And then I've got it. "My brother, Chance, he's a real goody two-shoes. Never met a rule he didn't follow, a goal he didn't smash—"

"So, the opposite of you?" she teases, and I can hear the small smile in her voice. I wish I could see it, but the night surrounding us is too dark, broken only by the light of the moon. I can imagine it, though, her lips lifted wide to show the little chipped tooth that makes her smile that much more intriguing.

I chuckle. "I'm not that bad. That'd be my brother, Kyle. He's the real heavy-duty rebel of the family and won't follow even a good rule just to be contrary. I'm somewhere in between. I'll follow rules if I agree with them. But I've got a healthy dose of 'ends justify the means' when the situation warrants." She nods in agreement, and I go on. "Karma, being the bitch she is, brought Samantha into Chance's life. She says what's on her mind with zero fucks or platitudes and basically drove him crazy from minute one when she spilled a bag of dicks at his feet."

Janey gasps in shock and I explain, "She's a relationship therapist and sells sex toys to supplement her practice. Anyway, Chance brought Samantha home to meet the family, kinda how you did with me tonight. Except Grandpa Chuck's old-school. He asked, flat-out at the dinner table, if she was a gold-digger."

"He did not," Janey whispers, horrified.

"Yep. And Samantha told everyone—Grandpa Chuck, Grandma Beth, Mom, Dad, all of the siblings, plus Aunt Vivian, my cousin, and his fiancée—that she was only in it for the dick, so he didn't need to worry about the pre-nup he informed her she'd have to sign. I thought Grandpa was going to have a heart attack right then and there. It was awesome."

I think back to that dinner fondly. Chance has always been uptight, and Samantha is good for him. And despite her arguing to the contrary, they are engaged now, though I don't know what they decided to do about the pre-nup. It's not my business unless Chance makes it so.

Besides, I already ran a background check on my sister-in-law to be and her best friend, Luna, who is married to my other brother, Carter. They're clean, criminally speaking.

"She sounds kinda awesome," Janey says. "Maybe she could teach me her ways?"

"No. You don't need to be like Samantha any more than I need to be like Chance. I mean, he's my brother, but the man probably irons his socks and reads tax code for fun on Friday nights. You need to be the best Janey, and that's enough. It's always been enough and always will be."

I feel her sink into me, relaxing more and more, and feel relieved that she's not angry anymore and seems to be listening.

"You think so?"

I nod, though she can't see me. "I know so. You're special, Janey. Your family . . . some of them are too stupid to see it. And the ones who do? They try to snuff it out so you don't realize the truth."

"What's that?"

"That you're amazing," I rasp, my voice deep and intense. This isn't a pep talk anymore, or building up her confidence. This is me selfishly confessing what I think about her, what I feel about her.

She wiggles, turning in my lap to look up at me. There's just enough moonlight that I can see her eyes jump from mine to my lips. So soft that I almost think I imagine it, she says, "Thank you. For tonight, for doing what I couldn't do, and even for calling me out. For . . . everything. You're amazing too, Cole."

She's too close. The smell of whatever perfume she put on earlier is invading my nose, and the feel of her pressed against me is too much. I should stop, but I'm not a good man. I'm only pretending to be because I can help her.

I cup her jaw in my hand and take her lips in a searing kiss, pouring everything I feel into her. I don't have words. I'm shit at them anyway, but I want her to understand.

All the times I've glimpsed her smiling at the morning sun and wanted to feel her smile against my lips. All the days I've spent lying in the forest, watching Mr. Webster, but actually wondering what she was doing at the cabin. All the showers I've listened to her take, going insane that she was naked only feet from me but off-limits. All the beauty I see not only in her pretty face and sexy body, but in her heart, mind, and soul. And all the times I've wanted to follow her up that ladder to her bed and fuck her hard and deep and long, something I suspect she hasn't had in a while.

Fuck, I want her.

But she's at a crossroads, with Henry, with her family, and

most importantly, with herself. I won't take advantage. I want to help her, not be someone else who hurts her.

So as much as it literally pains me to stop, I do. "Janey," I say, her mouth still moving with mine as she tries to kiss me back. "Stop."

She freezes instantly, and though she doesn't move from the lounge chair, there's a gaping distance between us. "Sorry, sorry . . . I got carried away with the whole fake boyfriend thing," she apologizes, her voice artificially high, taking the blame though I'm the one who overstepped.

She wiggles like she's going to get up, and I grab her, keeping her right where she is so she feels how hard she's made me. Hell, she can probably feel the precum leaking from my cock at this point because I'm that on edge from kissing her. "I'm not rejecting you. I want you. Fuck, do I want you," I grit out. "But you're not ready—not after everything that's happened. You don't owe me anything."

"Yeah, I understand. Thanks. I just . . . I'm . . ." She fakes a huge yawn, stretching an arm overhead. "I'm really tired after tonight. I think I'll turn in and see if I can get some sleep, 'kay?"

She's rambling again, each word tumbling on top of the last, and this time, when she moves to get up, I let her. She needs to run right now, but I know she's not going far.

I stay on the porch as she goes inside, taking her barely sipped hot cocoa to the kitchen. I force myself not to follow her as she goes into the bathroom and changes into her pajamas. I don't let myself watch as she climbs the ladder, knowing her ass is swaying side to side with each step. Only after a few minutes, when I'm sure she's settled, do I get up and go inside.

I drop my mug in the sink too and make my way to the bathroom. I turn the shower on, letting it get steamy while I stare at myself in the mirror. I'm a fucking idiot. I've done everything I could this week to be a non-threatening, non-asshole, helpful cabinmate, and then I go and fuck it up by not doing the one thing I want to do most—fuck Janey. How does that make any sense?

That's not the only thing you want to do.

You want to help her too.

That's true. This whole fake boyfriend thing was my idea because I heard the desperation in her voice when she pleaded with the dipshit to go to the wedding, and it broke something inside me. But even playing savior, I'm not used to caring more about someone else's heart than I am my own dick. It's weird and uncomfortable. I don't like it.

I realize I forgot my bag in the front closet and quietly open the bathroom door in case Janey's already fallen asleep.

But two steps into the hallway, I realize that Janey's not sleeping at all. Those quiet, muffled sounds aren't snores. They're . . .

Motherfucker.

Janey's touching herself. She thinks I'm in the shower and won't hear her, but I can hear every slick move of her hand and hitched breath.

I don't think. At least not consciously, though there must be some degree of thought in my brain because I don't charge up the ladder to take over pleasuring her myself.

But I do slowly, silently unzip my slacks and slip my hand into my boxers, wrapping it around my cock.

I have to be agonizingly careful so she doesn't hear me and completely quiet so I can hear her, but I stroke up and down my length, using the precum that's pouring forth to ease the motion. I imagine it's Janey's juices running down my cock, her tight walls gripping me, and her neck I'm stifling my groans into and not my arm.

It's delicious torture, listening to her pants get faster and faster, and when her breathing stops, I know she's on the edge, the same as I am. "Cole . . . *yes* . . ." she whispers as she shatters.

She said my name.

I erupt over my hand, spasms racking through my body as I come for her, even though she hasn't touched me. We joked about it earlier—that for tonight, she's mine and I'm hers—but this is for her, the same way that cum on her fingers is mine.

CHAPTER 10
JANEY

I CONSIDER SNEAKING out of the cabin dark and early in the morning to avoid Cole after that embarrassing rejection last night. I got carried away and mistook his kindness for something else. And no, it wasn't a good 'heart' pressed into my back like a thick iron rod when we lay there, but Cole's physical reaction to my squirming around didn't mean he actually wanted me and it was silly of me to think otherwise.

He's playing a part, Janey. Undercover, fake boyfriend, that's it. And you need him to do that for a few more hours, so suck it up, buttercup, and don't make things weird.

Because though I've also considered not going to Paisley's wedding after the catastrophe of the rehearsal dinner, nothing's really changed. In fact, it's almost worse. If I don't go, my whole family will think I'm embarrassed by last night, which I was. Embarrassed, mad, horrified, angry, and more, but I'd need an emotion wheel to decipher and label everything.

But now that I've had some time to think about it, I'm also grateful that Cole said and did what he did.

Was it mortifying? Yes, absolutely. Was it warranted? Probably.

Has anyone ever had my back and stood up for me that way? Never.

And it's sexy as hell.

Maybe that's why I basically threw myself at him?

What's even sexier is that he didn't do it for himself. He did it for me because he thinks I deserve better than the way my family treats me. And I do. I just forgot for a little bit.

I've done a lot of work since leaving home—reading books, joining online groups, and some intense self-therapy. I set out to become better, stronger, and happier. And most of the time, I am. But old, bad habits are comfortable, albeit sneaky tricksters, and I've fallen back into them more readily than I would've thought.

"The cost of someone else's happiness shouldn't be my own. I'm worthy of self-preservation and celebration and shouldn't be made to feel guilty for doing so," I tell myself, reciting a quote that's helped me over the years.

Because that's exactly what my family has done my whole life —made me the butt of the joke, ignored my hurt, valued others over me. And for what? They're not any happier than I am, not really.

So with a clear head, I'm choosing to not do that anymore. I'm not participating in their stupid games and I'm not winning any more stupid prizes.

Nope.

What I'm going to do is go to Paisley's wedding with my head held high, my back straight, my curls wild, and Cole on my arm. Just in case I freak out again, which definitely won't happen. Probably.

Going will prove to them and to myself that their opinion means nothing. And then after tonight, I can go back to living my happy, healthy life without them. Without Henry too.

Because yeah, I see how he's basically the 2.0 of my family and I reacted the same way, allowing myself to be undervalued like Cole said. It hurt—a lot—but he's right. And I'm not that girl anymore. I refuse to be.

I give myself a good stare down in the bathroom mirror. "Janey Williams, you can do this. Be yourself, go in there, and show them all that you're a badass."

Okay, 'Janey' and 'badass' probably don't belong in the same sentence, but I'm sticking with it.

"I'm a badass," I tell my reflection one more time for good luck and then walk out into the living room.

Cole rises from the couch like he's been listening for my footsteps. Which means he could probably hear my pep talk.

"Were you eavesdropping?" I ask with narrowed eyes.

He stares back blankly for two blinks before saying, "Nope. Didn't hear a thing." Then, being the charming distracter that he is, he says, "You look beautiful."

"Thank you. It has pockets," I inform him, doing the cursory showcase of the silky, silvery gray wrap dress's pockets by slipping my hands into them and holding the skirt out wide. The slit up the front pulls apart, flashing my thighs, and Cole's eyes go dark as he zeroes in on my skin.

"Whoops! Guess I shouldn't do that tonight," I say brightly, but I'm not ashamed at all. Seeing his eyes like that is better than any amount of self-pep talk in a mirror.

He mumbles something under his breath, but he's too far away for me to hear it clearly. It kinda sounds like, "Unless you want to kill me, get someone else killed, or get fucked in the bathroom."

"What?" I ask, sure I'm wrong.

"Nothing," he answers. "You look beautiful. The color matches your eyes."

Nodding, I tell him, "That's why I got it. Unexpected bonus points that it hides what's left of my rash."

My poison ivy is clearing up nicely thanks to Cole's home remedies. It still itches some, but it doesn't look too bad at least, and my dress covers up all of my afflicted areas. I think I look sexy in it too, as it features a dramatic low V-neck but covers everything else with long, puffy sleeves, darts along the bodice and full back, and a hemline that swings shy of my ankles.

"You look nice too. I like your suit, and we sorta match." I hold my sleeve up to the gray pinstripe on his black suit.

Cole's ignoring last night too, falling right back into his role with ease, taking my hand, wrapping my arm over his like he's escorting me somewhere fancy, and walking me to the front door. "Ready?"

I take a deep breath. "Yeah, I am. Let's do this."

"That's my badass," he quips. Shocked, my eyes jump to his, and I find that he's sporting one of those tiny half-smiles of his. He totally heard my pep talk.

————

The wedding is stunning, of course.

Max shuffles around nervously but stands at the front of the room and recites his vows to Paisley without a stutter. Paisley's dress is indeed white and fits her like a lacy second skin from the sweetheart neckline to her knees before fluffing out in tiny, pleated ruffles. Her rhinestone belt matches the clip in her hair, and her veil doesn't even get stuck on her bouquet. It's like Lady Luck—that bitch!—is on her side.

I secretly wish Paisley tripped down the aisle, or Max objected to his own wedding, or they lost the rings. Something. Anything that would maybe be a funny story ten years down the line but today would leave Paisley mortified.

None of those things happen. Neither does anything else exciting. It's a boring, picture-perfect ceremony, straight out of a bridal magazine. Martha Stewart herself would approve.

"The things at the bottom of her dress look like the lacy circles Grandma Beth had on the living room tables when I was a kid," Cole whispers at one point.

I press my lips together, trying not to laugh. "Doilies?" I clarify, and he nods with a self-satisfied smirk. I glance at Paisley's dress again, squinting slightly. I can see it. But it's probably difficult to make white lace not look doily-ish, I think. Then again, I've never looked at wedding dresses, so what do I know?

The reception looks like a magazine shoot too, with crystal vases filled with pale blue flowers in the middle of each table, a shiny, white-lacquered dance floor with Paisley and Max's monogram, and lights that are changing with the music the DJ is pumping into the space. Right now, it's classics, giving the room a formal ambiance, but given his setup, I bet we can expect some dance hits later.

As we enter, Mom is the first to beeline straight toward us. "Janey, do not embarrass me tonight." It's an order and an admonishment for last night all rolled up in one, and though it's vaguely threatening, she says it with a smile like she's lovingly greeting me. That part's just for show.

Before I can respond, she hustles away to talk to other, more important, people.

I don't react. I purposefully let her worries wash off my back. She doesn't control me. Her control over me stopped when I turned eighteen and left home. Anything past that is me giving her power she doesn't deserve, I remind myself.

Cole leans in, his breath hot over my ear as he whispers, "I don't like your mom. Or any of these people."

I smile, thankful that someone other than me sees through their bullshit. But there's one issue there. "You've already told me you don't like people anyway, so of course, you don't like them."

"You're wrong on one point," Cole murmurs, his voice deep and thrilling. "I like you."

I swear my heart skips a beat, like full-on, EKG-worthy arrhythmia, especially when our eyes lock. Cole is serious, his jaw set and gaze boring deep into mine. I want to believe him, but his mixed signals are nearly the size of banner flags. Does he mean that or is it part of the adoring boyfriend role? I'm not sure.

"Well, look what the cat dragged in," a voice says, drawing both our attention. Nikki is wearing her baby blue bridesmaid dress and an evil grin. "I didn't figure you'd show your face after that appalling business last night. It was all anyone could talk about after you ran out like a dog with its tail between its legs."

She's picking and poking, trying to find the angle that'll hurt the most and garner the biggest reaction. We've played this game before and she's always won.

No more. Never again, I vow. And though I've told myself

that before, this time is different. This time, I mean it with my whole heart.

I'm not going to sink to their level and be bitchy back, even though there's a part of me that'd like to. I'm going to be my best Janey, focus on the good, and get out of here without expending any more energy than I already have toward people who don't deserve it. That's my version of badass. Not fighting fire with fire, but rather, not fighting at all, not because I can't, but because I don't want to.

Instead of shrinking the way I've done in the past, I stand taller, lean forward a little into her hate-filled gaze, and stare back stone-faced, not giving any quarter.

It works. After a moment, Nikki *harrumphs*, not satisfied with my lack of reaction. "Guess you've got your guard dog tonight too, huh? Ruff, ruff!" She barks—literally makes actual barking noises—at Cole, suggesting that's he's some lapdog protector.

And now she's done it.

He's letting me do this on my own . . . when it's about me. But when Nikki takes him on, he's ready and way better prepared than she could ever be.

"You must've been embarrassed that everyone heard you and Paisley being bitches. Janey's told me how hard you two always worked to keep it on the down low," he says, his voice flat and hard. He could make a scene again. Nikki definitely deserves it. But he's restraining himself. "Especially since from what I can tell, the two of you never left that high school, mean girl mentality behind. Even now, we've barely walked in the door and you're running over here, tripping over your cheap, synthetic extensions to steal her moment of happiness. It's pathetic," he spits out.

Nikki's jaw drops open, making her look like shocked Pikachu. I'm ninety-nine percent sure she's never been talked to this way. And I should probably squeeze Cole's hand to call him off or something since I'm trying to be the bigger person here, but he's saying all the things I've thought over the years and I can't stop him. A deep, evil part of me is enjoying it too much.

Is it still bad if I let someone else do the dirty work?

Maybe. But letting Cole be his true self doesn't make me any less of a badass. He's just one too, in a deliciously different way.

"By the way, where's that high school boyfriend you locked down by 'forgetting' your birth control pills?" Cole finishes with a downright deadly look on his face.

What? I didn't know that. How does Cole know that? Or is he making an educated guess?

Either way, Nikki's head swivels around wildly. Is she checking to see if anyone overheard that? Or looking for her husband? Either way, when she sees him, her eyes go wide before narrowing sharply. He's standing with her sister. There are a couple of other people talking to them too, but her husband and sister simply standing next to each other is enough to have her stomping away from us and across the room.

I lean into Cole's side and he wraps his arm around my waist. "Too much?" he asks.

"No, it was perfect," I admit.

We stand around quietly for a while, watching the festivities. A few people stop by to chat and meet Cole, and Nikki was right about one thing—everyone heard what Cole said last night. But he's not embarrassed by it in the slightest. In fact, he tells Uncle Teddy that he's proud to love a good woman the best he can.

I think he means love, like with his heart, but given the sly glance Uncle Teddy throws him, he thinks he means with his dick.

At some point, Cole whispers, "Stop wiggling. It makes you look nervous."

"My dress is irritating the rash on my hip," I confess, well aware that I've been mindlessly scratching.

"When it itches, tell me and I'll take care of it."

Confused, I look at him with furrowed brows.

"Tell me," he repeats, a sense of command in his voice.

So I do. I give him a pitiful look, knowing the desire to scratch the hell out of my hip is in my eyes, and he grips it hard right over the rash, squeezing my flesh. It's painful, it's heaven, it soothes the itch better than my nails have all week.

He uses his hold on me to guide me to the dance floor, and I try to argue. "I can't dance."

"I can," he replies simply. It's all that's needed, too, as with his hand on my hip, occasionally kneading the flesh there, I let him lead me around the floor. Oddly enough, when I'm not thinking about dancing, I'm not too bad. Of course, that's mostly because I'm following Cole's hand, wanting his touch for several reasons right now.

"How'd you learn to do this?" I ask as he spins me in a circle.

"No choice. Mom decreed that we'd learn, so we did," he says easily. "Even Kyle knows how. Had to put it to practice at Dad's office parties, especially at Christmas."

I try to imagine Cole as a boy, learning a traditional foxtrot or waltz and performing at a cotillion. I can't quite picture it. "What else did you have to learn?"

He's quiet for a while, swaying with me but lost in his thoughts.

"That being alone is for the best sometimes," he admits finally. "But it's good to have people you can count on when shit gets fucked up." His voice has gone roughly contemplative, and he doesn't offer any more so I'm not sure exactly what he's talking about, but I can surmise that I'm not the only one whose family puts the 'fun' in dysfunctional.

We make it through dinner, cake, and about five too many boring toasts about Paisley and Max, without any drama. I'm this close to being home free.

But then the DJ plays Queen Beyonce. "Can I get all my single ladies to the dance floor, please?"

I don't move, but Aunt Glenda scoots past the table and basically shoves me out of my chair onto the dance floor. "Go on, Janey Sue." I hate it when she calls me that. My middle name is Susannah, which I already don't like, but when she shortens it, I sound like I have a pet pig that I dress up with in matching seasonal costumes for the county fair parade.

To be clear, I've never so much as touched a live pig, much less owned one, though I did have several different collars for my calico cat when I was a kid and would change those out. But Mr. Pennyfoot liked that.

I look back, and Cole sends me a wink. *You've got this*, that wink says. And he's right.

I stand in the gathering of single ladies on the floor, Jessica elbowing to get in front of me despite being a literal child. And though my family's bad, they're not going to marry her off child-bride style, so she shouldn't even be out here.

"That bouquet is mine. Touch it and I'll cry," she hisses at me. She doesn't mean a cute, little, boo-hoo, sad cry. Jessica will throw a literal tear-soaked tantrum to get her way.

Of course, that only makes me want that stupid bouquet more than my next breath.

I'm standing up to Nikki, not letting Paisley intimidate me, not letting Mom get into my head, and Jessica can sit all the way down. At the kids' table where she belongs!

I've had enough. That ribbon-wrapped bundle of blue roses and baby's breath has an entirely new meaning, like it's a trophy for me telling my family to fuck off, something I've never had the guts to do.

Paisley scans the group, likely looking for a preferred brides-maid to catch her precious flowers, but little does she know, they're mine. All mine.

With a smile, she turns around. The photographer has her do a couple of practice tosses with overly exaggerated, fake looks of excitement while she clicks away, and then the count starts . . .

"One . . . two . . . three!"

Paisley tosses the bouquet over her shoulder, and everyone scrambles. Dozens of arms reach high, fighting to catch it, and I'm pretty sure I accidentally drop-elbow Jessica in the head, but somehow, the flowers land roses-down right into my hand and I grip them tightly.

Someone tries to wrestle it away from me, but I jerk it into my body like a wayward football and rush out of the group. Once I'm clear, I hold it up victoriously, rose petals falling loose from the rough handling, and shout, "I got it!"

There's a round of polite applause and Paisley whirls around angrily. "No, it wasn't supposed to be you! That's Hannah's! Give it to her!"

The photographer is clicking away, taking shots of me with the now wilted bouquet but then turning to take a burst of shots of Paisley, who's definitely not looking her best. If looks could kill, I'd be a puddle of Janey Juice at her feet.

Doubt that's going to be in the wedding album!

"Nope, rules are rules. I caught it, it's mine," I shoot back, suddenly ready to throw down over this bouquet. If Paisley's expecting me to give in and hand it over to Hannah, she's dead wrong. Not this time.

Something's changed from last night till tonight.

It's me.

Even with the distance we've had, I think I was holding on to a thread of hope that my family would eventually be decent, and that's why those habits were so easy to fall back into. But I'm finally fully realizing that my family won't ever change, so I need to quit giving in to them, worrying about their reactions, and caring what they think.

There's a clarity in my mind and heart that I've never felt before, and the weight of all of their drama is simply gone. At least for the moment.

I just need to be Janey. The best Janey Williams I can be, I remember Cole saying.

And they can take it or leave it, and honestly, there are several who don't get the choice. I'm choosing to leave them . . . starting with my biggest childhood bully, Paisley Roberts. Oops, I mean Paisley McMahan since she's taking Max's last name.

People say standing up to a bully will make them leave you alone, and maybe that works if the bully is coming from a place of insecurity, but Paisley's sitting on a throne of entitlement, so challenging her, particularly in a time that's already emotionally charged, isn't gonna be that easy. She's not backing down.

No, she lets loose with a harpy shriek, running toward me with outstretched hands, her long, French-manicured nails looking like claws. She grabs at the bouquet but also gets a handful of my hair, which she yanks hard.

"Give. It. To. Hannah!" she orders.

Verbal warfare? Not my forte. Physical? Even less so, despite my telling Cole that I know karate. But I flail about, doing my best to get Paisley off me. It looks and feels more like bad grappling, and we fall to the floor, brawling around like drunk girls at a mud-wrestling competition. Only there's no mud, just a supposed-to-be-classy, monogrammed dance floor.

I kick out a leg, which Paisley counters by wrapping her own giraffe length leg around it. I manage to get an arm out—not the one holding the bouquet which I'm still holding tightly—and push at Paisley's chest, getting a little space between us. But it's not enough. She must be part honey badger or something because where she was mean before, she's now essentially feral.

"Let go!" I scream. "Help!"

The next thing I know, Paisley is being physically lifted off me. Cole has had quite enough of my family's shenanigans and has literally lifted the bride with one hand by the back of her dress, prying her fingers from the mess of my curls with his other. It doesn't escape my notice that not a single one of my family tried to stop Paisley. Max's family I can probably excuse because they're in shock, but my family has seen this before.

"Ow! You're hurting me!" Paisley whines loudly. "Daddy, he's breaking my nails!"

"Then let go," Cole roars. He sounds pissed. I feel Paisley's hand finally relax as she releases my curls from her fist, and she's lifted fully clear of me.

Instead of throwing her across the floor, Cole sets Paisley down with a modicum of restraint. She in return stomps her foot in full on tantrum mode. "You ruined my wedding! You ruin everything!" she screeches at me like I'm the one who attacked her.

"What did I do?" I ask as Cole helps pull me to my feet. "Catch the bouquet you threw?"

I scan the room, thinking surely, everyone sees how crazy Paisley is now.

But they're not looking at Paisley. They're looking at me and Cole, who's kneeling to help smooth my dress into place. I glance down at him, kinda wondering what's taking so long. Did I rip my skirt in the melee? Flash everyone my panties? Worse?

He's on one knee, his blue eyes looking extra intense like he's trying to tell me something I can't decipher as he takes my hands in his own, holding the bouquet with me. And then I see the tiny lift of his lips, just on one side. That's his amused smile.

"Janey Susannah Williams, you are the best and brightest thing in my life. You see good in the world where I see none. You feel compassion for those who deserve none. You love with abandon and without any self-preservation, inspiring me to finally believe that love exists."

"Oh, my God, what are you doing?" I ask quietly, grabbing under his elbow and pulling in an attempt to make him stand up.

It sounds like he's proposing, which is ridiculous, of course. We barely know each other. And at my cousin's wedding certainly isn't the place. Even if I don't care about the Miss Manners rulebook at this point.

Cole doesn't move or let me move him. He stares into my eyes, and then I see it—the twinkle there.

He's proposing. At my bitchy cousin's wedding. In front of my whole dysfunctional family.

The same way he said he barged into the bathroom last night so that no one would be talking about me and Paisley, but rather about me and Cole, that's what he's doing again. He's helping make this whole moment about something bigger, better, and brighter than whatever that bouquet beatdown was.

No one will talk about Paisley's cake—which was in fact as bland as I expected—or her basic vows, cookie cutter reception, or even her doily dress. They'll talk about my engagement in the middle of the dance floor to a man who loves me, Janey Williams, with all his heart.

I should probably feel bad about stealing Paisley's spotlight. But I don't. This is the culmination of years and years and years of mistreatment at her hand. And I didn't want any of this. Again, my plan was to show up, be invisible, and go home. Paisley is the one who started it with her catty comments last night, and she's the one who attacked me tonight. This is payback for her own actions.

I tear up. Not about Paisley and this whole sordid mess, but because the man at my feet, who's a self-proclaimed grump, is willing to go so far as my fake boyfriend that he's proposing. That's so sweet.

I squeeze his hands and nod to let him know I understand.

His smile grows. "Will you do me the honor of letting me be your husband so I can love, cherish, and worship you all the days of our lives?"

Wow.

I know he's faking, but that's a damn good way to ask someone to marry you. It seems everyone else agrees too because there are sniffles and *awws* coming from all around us. Granted, that's probably Max's family, not mine, but still . . . Cole's awesome and we all know it.

"Yes!" I shout. And then I say it again in case he didn't hear me, or you know, the valet outside wasn't listening. "*YES!*"

"*No!*" Paisley screams, but no one's listening to her.

Cole stands and sweeps me into his arms, spinning us around in a fairy-tale moment that feels utterly magical. This is the kind of love I deserve, and I won't settle for less ever again.

I mean, this is fake. I know that. But the real thing should be like this, with googly eyes, pounding hearts, and butterfly-filled stomachs.

Then, to top it all off, he kisses me.

And fake proposal or not, the kiss is very real. His lips are soft, though they press against mine firmly. His arms tighten around my waist, and I feel his fingertips press into my left hip, right over my tattoo, and remember what he said about it being a good luck charm. I thought he was making that up, but it feels true right now too. He nips my lip, one tiny bit of sharpness to keep me from floating away, and lowers my feet to the ground.

Cole's smile is bright and wide, like he's truly happy as he accepts congratulations from everyone. They talk to him more than me, but I don't care. They're my family, but their hold on me is gone.

CHAPTER 11
COLE

"OH, my God! We did it! We did it!" Janey shouts as she dances and jumps around the living room of the cabin. She lost her heels in the truck and is currently barefooted with her gray dress swishing around her legs as she moves. "Did you see their faces? That was epic!"

She throws a few air punches and then a really bad kick, scaring me that she's gonna fall but also giving me a shot of her black panties. "I was like *bam, bam,* and *hi-yah* when I was fighting Paisley."

She wasn't. Not at all. The girl can't fight, which makes it that much more endearing that she thinks she can.

I chuckle as I sit down on the couch to kick my shoes off.

She freezes. "I feel . . ."

She presses her hands to her stomach, and for a second, I think she's gonna say she feels sick because the look on her face is weird. But then she lets out a long breath, and though it makes no logical sense, she even *looks* a few inches taller.

"I feel free," she finishes.

She's been chattering away since we left the wedding, thanking me profusely and then asking if I saw the scratch on her face from Paisley's nails, which I definitely did. When I jerked Paisley from Janey and saw the red streak down her cheek, it was all I could do to not destroy Paisley in front of everyone for daring to mar Janey that way. Not physically—I wouldn't attack a woman. But with everything I know about Miss Paisley Roberts, now Mrs. Paisley McMahan, I could destroy her marriage and the rest of her life without ever leaving the dance floor.

I approached being Janey's fake boyfriend the same way I would any undercover assignment and researched everyone who might play a part in the ruse—the bride, the groom, her parents and sister, the bridal party, and even aunts and uncles. That's how I knew about Nikki's birth control mishap—for the love of fuck, do not post things on social media, people!—but that's nothing compared to the skeletons in Paisley's closet.

I thought about spilling all the tea to Janey, thinking maybe it'd help her see that Paisley wasn't so scary, but I'm glad I didn't. If I'd made Paisley less, Janey wouldn't feel so triumphant about tackling her bully now. As it stands, Janey confronted, stood up to, and defeated the biggest monster of her life on her own.

Well, I helped a little.

But that freedom she's feeling, it's hers and hers alone. She earned it.

"I'm glad," I tell her as I relax, letting my legs spread out and laying an arm along the back of the couch to enjoy her celebration.

But she's done dancing. She launches herself at me, straddling my lap with a knee on either side of my hips and her core hovering just over my dick, which is standing up at attention now. Janey places a hand on each of my shoulders and smiles as she looks me in the eye. "Thank you so much, Cole. I can't explain how much that meant to me."

I can see it in her eyes, can read it in her mind, and I try to stop her. "Janey, what I said last night . . . it's still true. You don't owe me anything. I'm glad to help."

It's true. Helping is what I do. But I never get this involved, go off-plan the way I did, or give a shit about the end result. Janey's different. I'm breaking all my own rules for her, and that wide, perfectly imperfect smile is all the payback I need or want.

She places a finger over my lips and shushes me. "Shut up, I have something to say." Her eyes go wide at her own words. "Sorry, I'm still a little riled up, I think."

But I want to hear it, whatever's on her mind. I move my hands to her hips, giving the left one a squeeze, and her eyes flutter shut for a moment. When they reopen, she looks determined to say what she wants to say.

Her voice is quiet but strong as she tells me, "Last night, you said you wanted me but didn't want me to feel like I owed you anything. But I do."

I growl angrily, not liking where this is headed. She gives me a pretty decent glare, or at least one that's better than her previous attempts, so I let her have her moment.

"You helped me find me again," she continues. "And I'm not having sex with you because of that."

"We're not having sex at all," I snap, the reminder more for me than her. "But I need you to get up or I'm gonna forget that I'm being a gentleman with you," I warn her because she's relaxing too, her core getting closer and closer to resting fully over mine. And I'm this close to shoving her panties aside, unzipping my slacks, and jerking her down to sit on my cock, rather than my lap.

She doesn't move.

"Yes," she purrs, "We are. I want to have sex with you because I owe me, Cole."

"What? No."

She continues talking like I didn't say a word, running right over me, "I haven't had sex in months, never had an orgasm with Henry—"

I rumble, "Don't say his name when you're sitting on my cock, Janey."

Pink rises in her cheeks at my gruff tone and crude language. But rather than putting her off, I swear she's trying to get herself roughly fucked because she moves her hips back and forth, barely brushing over the ridge in my pants. "Or what?" she says softly. "You'll fuck his name right out of my mouth?"

I pull her down hard, moving her hips myself, not for her

pleasure, but to rub myself with her heat. I expect her to be appalled or jerk away and skitter from the big, scary asshole guy, but she . . .

Fuck me, she moans.

Her head falls back, exposing the length of her neck, and her hands move to my chest for leverage as she bucks, using me.

"I need this. I deserve this. I owe myself an experience with a sexy man." She's talking to herself, but then she lifts her head to look at me again. "I think you can make my body do things I've only read about. I want you, Cole."

Every word is coupled with a stroke of her pussy against my cock, and though I'm fighting to keep control, I'm losing the battle. "Janey."

She's begging for it. I'm pleading for her to stop. Only one of us is going to get our way. And the way things are going, I'm going to lose this battle.

"Last night, I wanted you to help me forget." She shakes her head, her curls dancing wildly and her eyes slipping shut again. "But that's not . . . help me remember . . . me," she pants out.

Fuck. That's my damn kryptonite. She wants me to help her.

I can sure as shit do that.

I take her jaw in one hand, holding it firmly to force her hazy eyes to mine. I need her thinking clearly, especially after the excitement of tonight. "You're sure?"

She dips her chin once, pushing into my hand. "I'm sure. I want this. I want you."

I'm going to hell for all the things I've already done in my life. But this? This is going to be the pinnacle of my worsts and my undoing. Janey is going to be the example of when I should've done better, been better, and instead chose my own selfishness.

The least I can do is make it good for her. I don't want to only make her remember herself. I want to show her all the things she never imagined were possible.

I can give her that, I vow. It's a slight salve to my already guilty conscience, but it's enough to break the restraint I'm desperately holding on to.

I take her mouth with a vengeance. All the hunger I've pushed down for the last week bubbles to the surface as I kiss her, and to my surprise, she kisses me back with more sexy confidence than I would've thought she possessed.

Fuck Henry for not taking full advantage of all Janey is capable of. I won't make the same mistake.

I trace my hands down her neck, across her collarbones, and lower to cup her breasts. Janey sighs, lifting into my touch, and I rub my thumbs over her hardening nipples. A quick release of the tie at her waist, and I jerk the neck of her dress open, exposing her to my hungry eyes. Her bra is black, matching the panties she's already flashed tonight, and I slide the straps from her shoulders, letting the cups fall loosely.

Dragging a finger over the tender flesh, I delight at the softness of her skin and her responsiveness as she arches to meet my touch. Both of us needing more, I lean into her, covering her nipple with kisses and licks before sucking it into my hot mouth.

Janey wraps her arms around my head, holding me to her as I punish her with pleasure.

Know your worth.

Demand to be treated like the amazing woman you are.

No excuses for assholes—not your family, not friends, not even me.

I groan at that thought and bite her sharply for lowering herself to be with me.

She deserves more than a fuck on the couch, but I'm too impatient to haul her up the ladder to a bed, so this'll have to do. I lift her off my lap, tossing her to the couch, where she bounces and lets out a squeak of surprise. And then I'm over her, kneeling between her spread thighs.

Pushing her dress the rest of the way off, it puddles beneath her body in a satiny sea of gray, but it's still not enough. I need to touch her. I yank my shirt off, only half the buttons undone, and Janey tries to follow my lead, reaching behind her back to undo her bra, but I stop her. "Let me."

Uncertainly, she pulls her hands back, and I slip mine beneath her to undo the hooks. I pull the bra from her and let it fall to the floor, doing the same with her panties. Nude before me, she squirms nervously, suddenly looking shy as my eyes rove over her body.

I see it all. Her full breasts that she's trying to push together with her arms, the sweep of her hip covered with the floral tattoo, the softness of her belly she's tensing, and the shiny wetness in the short curls over her pussy. Every freckle, scar, line, and curve . . .

"Beautiful," I say huskily. "Fucking gorgeous."

She absolutely is—inside and out.

Her smile is soft and filled with relief, like she doesn't understand that I'm the lucky one here. But I'll show her.

I lean down, spreading her legs with my shoulders, and kiss the sensitive spots along the insides of her thighs, purposefully moving higher and higher in the tiniest of increments. I dance my fingertips over the outer lips of her pussy, feeling the slickness of her arousal and spreading it around as I pull her open. Her hips buck up, looking for more, and I feel the evil grin stretch my mouth. Fuck, she's going to be heaven.

I drag one finger through her juices, testing and teasing at her opening, before slowly pushing into her. Her groan of pleasure is music to my ears, and she takes my finger so easily, I immediately add another one. I fuck her with two thick fingers, curling them up to stroke along her front wall.

"*Oh*," she sighs as she suddenly grabs ahold of my hair with one hand and the couch with the other. "There."

I chuckle darkly. I know where she needs to be touched, but I need to discover how she likes it. Slow, soft, and gentle? Rough, fast, and hard? Somewhere in between? Both?

Fuck.

I shift uncomfortably, my slacks squeezing my cock to the point of near pain. But I stay focused on Janey. This is for her.

Petting that spot inside, I kiss everywhere but exactly where she wants me. I want her on my hand first so I can watch her take me, my fingers disappearing inside her warmth and reappearing glistening with her arousal. I drive into her slow and deep, grinding her clit with my palm every few strokes, and it's not long before she's soaking my hand and her cries are getting louder and higher pitched. I press down on her belly, right over her curls, and plunge my fingers into her again and again, pushing her to the point of no return.

With a soft, breathless cry, she shatters. Spasms rack through her body, and she bucks wildly as she chases her pleasure, and I stay with her the whole time, drawing it out as long as possible until her movements become jerky like she's trying to get away.

I growl. "Good girl. That's one."

She laughs like I'm joking, but I'm dead serious. Especially when I slip my fingers into my mouth, sucking her orgasm from them and savoring every bit, which makes her eyes pop open wide in surprise.

Has no one ever appreciated her this way? Their fucking loss because she's sweet as nectar, and I can't wait for more.

Holding her arms out to welcome me into her embrace, she says, "I can't do more. Just come here."

I let her pull me on top of her and pin her with my weight to kiss her deeply, wanting her to taste how delicious she is. When her tongue touches mine, she quivers, and I let her memorize her specialness before starting all over again . . . laying kisses along her jaw, down her neck, to her breasts. I kiss over her belly, trace part of her tattoo with my tongue, and worship her entire body before finally settling back between her thighs.

"Cole?" she whispers.

"Mmhmm?" I answer, already looking at her pretty, puffy lips and anticipating how good she's going to taste. And more importantly, how good I'm going to make her feel.

"You don't have to—" she starts.

I cut her off, growling, "I *get* to, Janey. I haven't done a damn thing I haven't wanted to in years. This?" I lick a long line from her entrance to her clit and groan at her sweetness as she shudders. "I get to do, and it's a fucking honor."

"Oh," she murmurs, still not sure. A second later, she repeats the sound, only it's a whole lot more pleasure-filled because I'm devouring her like a starving man. The slight taste from my fingers is nothing like drinking directly from her. I was gentle before, but I'm impatient for more now and I'm working her hard and deep.

My fingers find that spot inside again, and I pump into her quickly as I batter her clit with my tongue. She's going crazy beneath me, somehow fighting me off and holding me to her all at the same time. "I–I . . . oh, my God!" she shouts, coming again.

I don't go easy on her. She's proving she can handle it, so I take the flat of my fingers and swipe them across her entire pussy so fast that my hand's a blur. She comes again, or maybe she's still coming? I'm not sure, but her face is contorted in pleasure, her mouth open and eyes squinched shut, and her short nails are digging into my shoulders like she's afraid I'll leave her a mess like this.

I'm not going anywhere.

Except I've got to get out of these fucking pants.

When she's recovering, I stand up and shove my slacks and underwear off as fast as I can. My cock virtually sighs in relief at the freedom until I take myself in hand, squeezing tightly at my base to stave off the orgasm that's already too close. She said it'd been a long time for her. Well, it's been a while for me too, and I'm afraid I'm going to come too quickly and not get to enjoy being inside Janey for as long as I'd like.

Slight pain doing its job, I kneel on the couch between Janey's legs once more, lining up with her entrance. I drag my head through her folds, groaning at the luxury of being the lucky asshole to touch her this way and reminding myself of the mission . . . help her remember who she is so she feels like herself again after this is over.

Don't be a selfish prick, Harrington.

This is all about her. "Janey, Janey, Janey . . ." I mumble.

"What?" she asks, worry wrinkling her brows.

I didn't realize I was talking, saying her name aloud. Instead of explaining that she's in my head, I push forward slowly, feeling her stretch around my cock as I fill her inch by inch.

"Mmm, Cole," she moans. "*Yes . . .*"

She feels even better than I imagined, wrapped around my

cock like a hot, slick vise. I give her a few thrusts, letting her adjust to the invasion, and when her eyes meet mine, clear and bright, I can't hold back anymore.

I fall forward, propping up with one hand beside her head on the couch pillow and one hand gripping her leg, which is lifted in the air. Her hands grasp my hips then move up to grab my waist instead. "Fuck," I grunt.

Deeply and powerfully, I begin to I fuck her. I swear, I mean to be sweet and gentle, but I'm too far gone, and her jagged breathing says she doesn't mind my rough abuse of her pretty pussy.

I keep my eyes locked on hers as I slam into her again and again, and the harder and deeper I go, the more blissed out she looks. Her gray eyes even roll back, her lashes fluttering closed when I speed up, pistoning into her and bottoming out with every stroke.

I could do this forever, fuck Janey all day, every day. Make up for her mistreatment by soothing it over with orgasms until her sunny outlook makes sense because all she knows is pleasure.

With a roar, I pull out of her, coming in hot, pulsing jets onto her. My cum covers her pussy, messily dripping over her lips, and shooting up onto her belly, coating her in white. But she's close again too, so I shove my still-hard cock back into her, using my cum to rub her clit while I fuck her with every last bit I have to give.

"One more. You deserve it," I promise her.

And like she finally believes that, she pulses around my cock, milking any cum I had left with her orgasm.

It's the most beautiful thing I've ever seen in my entire life.

CHAPTER 12
JANEY

WHEN I FIRST ARRIVED AT the cabin, I imagined snuggling up in the treehouse-like loft with a cup of coffee and a book for hours.

Waking up in the cozy bed wrapped in Cole's arms is even better.

I stay still, watching him. His brows are furrowed and his lips are pressed together, like whatever he's dreaming about is pissing him off. Carefully, I soothe him by tracing a single finger through the coarse hair on his chest, drawing shapes I don't recognize because I can't not touch him.

Last night was more than I could've imagined. And I've imagined a lot over the last week. But even with all my book-spiration, I didn't think guys like Cole actually existed—ones who care, who want your happiness, and who derive pleasure from seeing you boneless from orgasm after orgasm. I think Cole decided to make up for my lack of man-made orgasms over the last year in one night.

And whoo, he succeeded.

"G'morning, beautiful," he grumbles. I dart my eyes up, guilty for having woken him, but he's got a sleepy smile beneath half-open eyes. That smile alone is worth the guilt.

"Sorry, I didn't mean to wake you," I tell him quietly, not wanting to break the spell between us. He chuckles, pulling me in tighter against him. He might be asleep, but there are certain parts that are not. Hello, morning wood!

"I've been awake for almost an hour. Didn't want to disturb you," he replies as he buries his nose into my neck and places a soft kiss there, right over my pulse.

"Liar," I accuse with a smile as I tilt my head for more kisses. "You were all frowny, probably fighting bad guys in your dreams. I was soothing you."

"Soothing? By torturing me? By dragging the slowest finger ever, closer and closer to my cock? By taking so long, it said 'fuck it' and decided to meet you halfway." Every accusation is partnered with a rough kiss or suck or nip along my neck, jaw, and shoulder.

He's right. I was mindlessly getting lower and lower, from his chest to his abs and over his hip, studiously avoiding his thick hardness because it felt intrusive and selfish to interrupt his sleep with my desire.

But oh, boy, is he awake now!

I let my whole hand run over his abs, feeling the bump of each one below the sprinkling of hair, and then follow the trail lower to where it becomes his base. He groans deep in his chest as his hips buck. I can see the tightness in his belly where he's holding himself back.

I feel drunk with power. This monster of a man letting me control him, control this . . . control us.

"Can I touch you?" I whisper.

"Fuck." He shudders. "Anything you want, Janey."

I have a filthy thought, something I haven't done too many times before but want to try now. Henry always said I wasn't good at it, so why bother? But I don't think Cole will mind if I'm bad at it.

Maybe he'll think you're good. And I bet he'll be happy to tell you what to do otherwise.

I throw the blankets off and move lower on the bed to kneel between Cole's spread legs. He lifts his head from the pillow we shared to peer at me curiously. Keeping our eyes locked, I lean forward and place a kiss to his head. It's a chaste, grandma-cheek-worthy kiss, but he groans like it's delicious agony as his head falls back to the pillow and his eyes slam shut.

Emboldened, I lick a circle around the crown, then take him into my mouth. I suck and lick, lick and suck, exploring him and his reactions. I feel invincible when Cole's hands fist the sheet beneath him as his breath goes jagged. "Goddammit," he grits out.

I smile to myself and swallow him deeper into my mouth, teasing along the entrance to my throat to see how much of him I can take. When he spills a bit of pre-cum, I want more, so I find a rhythm, bobbing up and down the length of him.

Cole threads a hand into my hair, gripping tightly at the base of my head, and I tense, expecting him to take control. *You're not doing it good enough.* But he just scratches along my scalp, almost playing with my hair, releasing and grabbing it over and over while I work him.

"Janey, baby . . . you gotta stop or I'm gonna—" he warns, his meaning clear.

I want him to come. I want to make him explode in my mouth. I want to taste him, swallow him, and know that I, Janey Williams, did that all on my own. Because I'm a Blow Job Queen and I want a sash, crown, and scepter. Okay, maybe not, but whatever I'm doing is working for Cole and that's what counts.

I pant, "Do it," and swallow him again, bobbing my head, my cheeks hollowed out against his shaft.

Permission given, Cole stops holding himself back, and I feel his entire body go taut as I take him to the edge. His balls tighten against my hand, and then he jerks, curling in on himself and around me as he roars. "Fuck, yes . . ." He grunts as jet after jet of salty heat fills my mouth. I gulp it down hungrily, like it's my reward for a job well done.

It's not a crown, but I'm definitely happy with the prize.

I expect Cole to flop to the bed in spent exhaustion when he's done. That's what Henry would've done once his needs were met. But again, Cole is nothing like Henry.

He grabs under my arms, hauling me up his body until I'm

straddling his face. "Whoo!" I holler in surprise at the change in position.

Cole wraps his arms over my thighs and pulls my lips apart, teasing over my clit with his thumb. "My turn." Before I can say anything, his tongue is on me, licking and sucking my clit and dipping down to tease along my entrance.

It feels strange to sit over him this way, but when I look down, he seems more than happy with the arrangement, so I relax, letting myself drop lower. I can see the hint of a smile at my surrender, and it reassures me.

My hands press against the cool glass of the window above the bed, and when I look outside at the trees, I feel exposed in a way that should scare me. But with Cole here, I know I'm safe. It's just me, him, and maybe that wayward daytime owl to see us.

It doesn't take long for Cole to expertly get me to the point of no return, and he growls against my flesh when I spasm over him. I'm still trembling when he moves me again, pushing me back down his body and centering my core over his hard-again dick.

I wiggle to help us align and then feel him fill me, inch by thick inch, until I've taken all of him and I'm seated completely on him. I roll my hips around, enjoying the stretch of fullness. Cole touches places inside me that have never been touched, in more ways than one.

We find a pace together, not him fucking me or me riding him but us working together to give each other pleasure. His hands slip along my sides, up to my breasts to tease over the stiff nipples, and I swear an electric current shoots from them straight to my clit. I fall forward, meeting Cole in a sloppy kiss. He tastes like me, and I know I taste like him, but that only adds to my arousal.

Sex with Cole is all-encompassing like there's no wrong, only right, only pleasure.

And when he grips my hips, squeezing the left one sharply, I shatter again. He holds me tightly, keeping me together as my body tries to launch into the atmosphere, and I feel the hot pulses of his orgasm filling me too.

I'm still panting and recovering when Cole murmurs, "I meant great morning, beautiful."

I don't get it at first. My brain is still a mushy mess of bliss, and my body is ready for a nap even though I haven't gotten out of bed yet. But then . . . he said 'good morning, beautiful' earlier.

I lift up from my collapsed flop and peer at him with the one eye I can get open. The other is refusing on principle alone. "Was that a joke?" He shrugs but is grinning widely. "Oh, no, I think I broke you," I say, feigning distress. "Your grumpy, asshole persona just needed a morning blow job, a couple of orgasms—two, mind you." I hold up two fingers to illustrate the number. "And now you're all Jokey McJokester."

He chuckles, deep and rough, as he gathers me into his arms. He's slipped out of me, and I can feel the rush of our juices leaking out to coat us, but Cole doesn't seem to care at all, so I try not to worry about it either as we snuggle in a comfortable, complacent quiet.

Is this what it's supposed to feel like all the time? It's amazing.

Henry didn't want sweat, cum, or spit on him before, during, or after sex. It was nothing like this, with touching and caressing, appreciating each other's bodies, and wanting the other person's pleasure. This is infinitely better.

Sex shouldn't be sterile and mechanically cold. It should be messy, fun, and full of surprises, I decide.

"Hey, where'd you go?" Cole asks quietly, and when I focus on the here and now again, he's looking at me with concern in his blue eyes.

I don't want to tell him that I was thinking about Henry. Or well, not about him, exactly, but about how much I've missed out on . . . about how much I gave up. And for what?

Last night, I felt like I'd found myself again. Today, I'm sad that I lost her at all, but I'm going to learn from the hard-won lesson. So, I say the next thing on my perpetually-busy mind. "I was thinking about breakfast. More specifically, about what you're going to make for breakfast."

He doesn't believe me, but he lets me lie and keep my thoughts to myself this time. "On it. Biscuits and sausage gravy?" Cole answers, waiting for my approval. When I nod, he helps me from the bed.

He goes down the ladder first, and unlike his gentlemanly behavior earlier this week, this time, he stares up at me the whole way down, even tilting his head to get a better view of me from below when I wiggle flirtatiously. We make our way to the kitchen, where Cole pulls an apron on over his bare body—gotta protect the goods!—and I wrap up in a blanket from the couch.

"I like naked breakfast," I tell him dreamily, and he turns to give me a shot of his butt with a cocky smirk thrown over his shoulder. "It feels naughty." I start the coffee maker, then sit at the island to watch him work. Talk about a morning show.

Cole is a good cook—or better than me, at least—and he expertly peels apart biscuits from a popping can, adds milk to a dry package of cream gravy, and browns sausage on the stovetop, which he adds to the gravy. Once he layers it all onto plates, he sets them on the island. After grabbing a blanket of his own, which he wraps around his waist towel-style, he sits beside me and we eat.

This is it.

My reservation is up today, and Mr. Webster left two days ago, which means Cole should already be home, working in his office or doing whatever he planned to do before meeting me. He stayed longer to help me, and now, that's done too.

"I like it here. It feels like a little pocket of paradise where we're the only two people alive and nothing else matters. I'm dreading going back to . . ." I think about what exactly I'd like to hide away from and settle on, "Life. I mean, I love my job and miss the people there, but I could also stay here, holed up away from the world with you. We could get groceries delivered to the main road, take walks in the forest, watch the sunrise and sunset every day, hang out in the hot tub, and start every day with orgasms and end with more orgasms. We could just stay . . . here."

It's a ridiculous dream and I know it, but I want it all the same.

I love my life, my job, my friends. But there's something magical about this cabin away from everything, where responsibilities don't exist, rules are ignored, and all that matters is today because tomorrow is an eternity away.

Cole frowns and wipes his mouth with a napkin. Because yes, after cooking us naked breakfast, he sets the table, pours us coffee, adding sugar to mine the way I like, and uses utensils properly. It's the little things, but it makes me feel like even a lazy Sunday breakfast is a valuable experience. He makes it feel like I'm worth making it important.

"That sounds good. Mostly the no annoying people part."

I grin, teasing with wide, fake-innocent eyes, "Aww, are you calling me not-annoying?"

His lip lifts in a small smile at the barely-a-compliment I'm giving myself. "What's next for you?"

I catch the little add-on there where he's specifically asking about me, like we aren't a thing anymore. Not that we ever were, but part of why I wish we could stay here is because of Cole. All week has been fun, and last night-slash-this morning was amazing.

Maybe I need a sex-cation with Cole?

But I don't suggest that. Instead, I answer his question. "I'm driving home this morning, then I have laundry to do and groceries to buy because tomorrow is a regular Monday for me. I'll be taking reports by seven a.m. and handing out meds by eight."

The weight of reality crashes down on me. Imagining a typical workday, I say, "I'll take care of my patients all day, and Mason'll force me to go out for dinner, even after I tell him I bought food, by reminding me that I can't cook. And we'll talk about my vacation and the wedding. He doesn't know about you yet, and I can't wait to tell him about the sexy stranger I almost killed with bear spray and my ninja skills but ended up seducing into helping me escape my family's death grip." I curl my hands like claws and wrinkle my nose like my family is full of literal monsters.

"Sounds like a hell of a Monday," Cole says in a monotone, disinterested voice that sounds too familiar. He might as well have said 'mmhmm, yeah, sure' for all the inflection in his words. Is he really that suddenly uninterested? Or is there something more to it?

"You?" I prompt, trying to reengage the way we've been all week.

He shrugs. "Home. Work. Repeat."

"Won't any of your friends or family check on you? You've been gone longer than expected. Are they worried?" I ask in concern. "Oh, you probably texted them already, right?"

He looks at me with his brows low over his blue eyes. "Nobody knows I'm gone. They don't know when I'm there either. I show up for dinners when I can, or if they're mandatory, because that usually means shit's hitting the fan, which is good entertainment more often than not. But, no . . ." He finishes with a shrug like it's completely normal that no one knows when he leaves home for an entire week.

It's shocking. I told Mason my plans, including giving him the link to the cabin's ad, the emails from Anderson, and my expected route to and from the cabin. I also have a neighbor getting my mail and watching my place for any suspicious activity. If I didn't show up today, there'd be at least two people who'd call the police and report me missing, and I'd probably be on the news by Tuesday, Wednesday at the latest, because Mason wouldn't leave the networks alone until they were running ticker tapes at the bottom . . . *Have you seen this woman? She needs to show up to work because we're out of ratio! And oh, yeah, she's my bestie.*

But really, I have people who would care and that's important.

"You can text me when you get home," I offer. It's a bigger deal than it sounds like and I know it. I'm asking if he wants to continue us outside the fantasy world of the cabin and the fake boyfriend deal.

I hold my breath, waiting.

"Janey," he says gently.

Nope, nope, not doing that 'let her down easy' tone. Not today, not any day.

I rush to smooth over the awkwardness I've created. "I mean, someone should know you're okay and didn't drive into a ditch along the way home. It doesn't have to be me." I laugh, but it's high and forced and sounds fake even to my ears.

I should've taken the win of an amazing week with an even more amazing stranger and been grateful. And I am. So grateful for everything Cole's done for me. But I pushed too far.

"You finished?" Cole says flatly, pointing to my plate with a jerk of his chin. He's nearly hugging his empty plate, slouched forward with a hand pressed to the island on either side of it. I glance from his plate to mine, which has a few bites left, but the tasty breakfast is sitting like a rock in my stomach now and I couldn't eat another bite if I tried.

"Oh! Yes, but I'll do the dishes." I'm up, tucking my blanket around me tighter because I suddenly feel nakedly vulnerable. The face-sitting, ride 'em cowgirl, Blow Job Queen that I was an hour ago is gone.

But I won't forget that she exists. I worked too hard to find her.

With my head held high, I grab our plates and head to the sink to escape Cole's non-answer answer. He doesn't want to talk or text me later, not telling me he's home safe or anything else, and that's okay. That was our deal and that's fine. Totally fine. "Dishes are on my check-out checklist from Anderson," I inform him. "I wouldn't want to get hit with a fee for not doing everything. I need to clean the kitchen, load the sheets into the washer, and grab the towels from the bathroom."

"Okay," Cole answers. "Mind if I shower first?"

"No, no, of course not," I say brightly, waving him off with bubble-coated hands because despite my plans to put the plates in the washer, I poured dish soap all over them and am scrubbing them with a sponge.

Once the bathroom door closes, I sag. "Way to go, Janey. Things were going great and then you turn Stage-Five Clinger on the poor man who just did you a huge favor by playing the part of your doting boyfriend. Well, fiancé. But still? It's nothing more, nothing less. Just a fake deal to help and some life-altering, no-strings-attached sex. That's it." I scrub the plate with a vengeance, like it's the one that messed up. Mocking myself, I say again, "Text me when you get home! Good God, could you sound any more desperate?"

I rush through a wipe down of the kitchen, climb upstairs, and strip the bed. When I throw the sex-scented sheets over the railing, they hit the floor downstairs with a satisfying *schlump*. After a quick tidy in the bedroom, I climb back down the ladder and load the sheets in the washing machine. I fluff the pillows on the couch, giving them a karate chop, check the back porch for any stray blankets, and basically, make the cabin look as unlived-in as possible.

Like this week never happened.

That sort of hurts, right in that spot where memories reside in your heart. That spot that makes you want to carve initials in tree trunks, take a picture, get a tattoo, or something. I want more, like some type of souvenir to commemorate the good times we had here. Because this past week should be more than just memories . . . shouldn't it?

When I hear the bathroom door open, I pounce, passing Cole in the doorway. "My turn," I chirp. Once behind the door, I let the fake smile fall, along with my blanket.

I pull my hair into a puff of frizzy curls, knowing I'm doing that both to hurry and because the frizz is from Cole's hands and I stupidly don't want to let that go yet. I take a speed shower, get dressed, and shove my toiletries into my suitcase. One last glance around the bathroom and it, too, looks empty and uninhabited. I pile up the towels in front of the still-running washer and grab my bag.

In the living room, I find Cole sitting on the couch, his elbows resting on his spread knees and his eyes unfocused as he stares into the cold, black fireplace.

"I'm ready. Out by ten a.m. like Anderson said," I announce cheerfully as I drag my suitcase to the front door.

"Here. Let me," Cole says as he reaches for my bag.

I keep pulling it along. "No worries. I've got it. Been hauling this thing around myself for ages. One time, I had to roll it through the airport, bumping around this way and that, trying not to take out any kids, only to find out that it was overweight at the boarding gate. They said it was too heavy and made me check it. I mean, the weight is on the plane either way, whether it's below in the cargo area or in the overhead bins, so I don't know why it mattered, but rules are rules, ya know? And it would've fit in the overhead! It's a small bag. I think it was heavy because I was bringing back rocks from the beach. But it's lighter now, no rocks at all this time. Though I did take a leaf from the tree by the back porch as a keepsake. It's pressed into one of my books. I want to save it to remember this trip—I mean, the pretty forest."

I stop rambling, mostly because I've said too much about what this trip meant to me, but also because I've bump-bumped my suitcase to the back of my car. "Sioux-B, you ready to make that scary drive back through the woods again?" I ask her as I lift the bag into the SUV. It was nice to have Cole help with things this week, but I'm used to taking care of things myself and being self-sufficient, and it's time to get back to that.

Which is totally fine. I'm good at it.

I slam the hatchback and turn to Cole. "Thank you. What you did for me this week means more than you'll ever under-stand, and I really appreciate it," I say with a true smile. "Thanks for not letting a teensy-weensy, unimportant thing like a bear spray attack-slash-introduction get in the way of our being friends."

I lift up to my toes, throwing my arms over his broad shoul-ders for a hug. I feel his palm cup my hip and wait for the squeeze, but it doesn't come. Not this time. He hugs me back politely, like a gentleman and nothing more. Like this morning didn't happen.

"Wait."

Hope springs in my heart. Is he going to say something

meaningful? Or do something sweet? Maybe he changed his mind and wants to stay in this fantasy world too?

He hustles toward his truck and digs around in the back seat for something. He comes back with a little white card which he holds out to me. "Here."

I take the card and look at it uncertainly.

Cole Harrington
555-349-8731

It's his business card. He's giving me his business card.

I swallow thickly and force a smile to my lips. "Thanks. Yeah, I uh . . . thanks, Cole." I put the card in my back pocket and try to figure out what to do now. I've already said thank you and hugged him goodbye. The only thing left to do is . . . leave.

"Well, uh . . . 'bye, I guess."

He opens my door for me, waits for me to get in, and then closes the door too. All perfectly kind, and I'm doing okay until he taps Sioux-B's roof. "Drive safe," he says.

I look up one more time into his blue eyes, which are emotionless and empty. His jaw is set, and his lips are pressed together. He looks . . . cold. Like a stranger. Nothing like the man who grinned up at me from between my legs hours ago.

Grimly, I drive away, slowly and carefully adding distance between us as I make my way through the forest and back to the main road.

"Let's go home, Sioux-B," I tell my car.

Hopefully, I can get to the main road before the tears start. That'd be helpful, at least. No way can I get safely down this trail otherwise.

I almost make it too.

CHAPTER 13
COLE

"DRIVE. SAFE. FUCKING DRIVE SAFE?" I say out loud, watching the taillights disappear into the trees. "What the fuck was that?" I'm apparently taking a play from Janey's book and talking to myself now.

I don't know what happened between sitting down to breakfast and Janey turning into a cleaning Tasmanian devil, but I'm sure I fucked up somewhere. She asked about me texting her, and I wanted to say yes. Fuck knows, I want to text her. I want to follow her home, see where she lives, make her come in her own bed. Hell, I want to do laundry and go to the grocery store with her.

But I shouldn't, and I know that.

She needs time.

This week has been a whirlwind of changing directions for her, and in this pocket of non-reality, she's been okay. But she's going to get home, see Henry's socks on her bedroom floor, or her Mom is going to call, or any one of a dozen other things, and she's going to have to face it on her own. She'll have to decide for herself how she wants to react, and as frustrating as it is, I need to let her do that.

Is there a chance she'll go back to Henry? I hate to say it, but I've seen it happen before, women who deserve so much better but have settled for so long that they don't know any other way, so they keep reconciling, hoping for a different outcome that never happens.

Is there a possibility that her mom is going to say Janey embarrassed her family by refusing to give in to Paisley? Also, yes. And Janey might actually apologize for what we did.

She's spent her whole life making sure everyone else is happy, and I think she forgets that she deserves to be happy too. Truly happy, not just a forced focus on the good without ever acknowledging the bad.

I want her to find that—in herself, for herself.

When that happens . . . I'll find her again. Because I might've let her leave, but I didn't let her go.

———

"I understand, Mrs. Webster. I can send you the photos if you'd like, but there's nothing in them," I tell my client over coffee a few days later.

"He was with her for days! And you got nothing?" she screeches so loudly that people three tables away look at us with interest. I thought she'd be glad to find out that I saw no evidence of her husband cheating, but that doesn't seem to be the case.

Gritting my teeth to remain professional, I repeat, "I completed surveillance for four days. During that time, they sat in the living room and kitchen together. Any time he went to the cabin's bedroom or bathroom, she remained visible in the public spaces." I check my notes even though I don't need to, having already told her this information. "She left every evening by six p.m., not spending the night a single time. They never touched intimately. No contact beyond a hug. This should be good news," I remind her.

She huffs out a disappointed sigh. "Yeah, thanks for nothing."

"I'm still looking into the woman. I'll be in contact when I have a name." I don't tell Mrs. Webster that I have suspicions about the identity of the not-a-mistress. I don't think it'd do any good right now when I don't have the complete facts, but Louisa's making progress.

"Whatever," she snaps. She stands, grabbing her to-go cup of mocha-chai-berry-blast-frappe, or whatever the hell that monstrosity of syrups and whipped cream is, and stomps to the door, her heels sharp on the tile floor the whole way.

Eyes in the coffee shop follow her and then flick back to me expectantly, eager to see me make the next move.

This is why I hate people.

I sip my own black coffee, staring back at the gawkers one by one until they drop their gazes and go back to their own phones, laptops, and business.

It's been ten minutes and the baristas are churning out orders hand over fist when the door opens. I glance that way naturally, cataloging the newcomer, only to find it's Kayla.

Fuck.

I'm not in the mood for anyone in my family right now. I'm grumpy from dealing with Mrs. Webster and frustrated because I haven't seen Janey in days. Is she at work? Home? With Dipshit?

That thought brings a deep scowl to my face.

"Hey!" she says with a surprised smile. "What're you doing on my side of town? And who pissed in your coffee?"

She sits down uninvited, but I'm smart enough to not tell Kayla to get lost. Besides, I can feel fresh interest around me from the few remaining people who saw Mrs. Webster stomp out and now a new woman's sitting with me. It's another suspicious-appearing situation that's completely innocent. Not that any of them think so. They probably think I have dates meeting me, one right after the other, serial player style. I want to yell at them all, 'One was a client, one's my sister, and neither are any of your fucking business.'

"Work," I answer both of Kayla's questions without explaining anything. At least she didn't mean to run into me. That gets her a bit of patience.

She nods, not pressuring for information she knows I won't give. I don't know when or why my job became such a secret, but it's been this way for years now and I have zero intention of changing it. I'm not a suit and tie guy like my siblings, minus Kyle, of course. I would go insane trapped in an office, playing nice with arrogant assholes like they do, but they wouldn't understand that. And Dad would be disappointed, not that I care what he thinks, and Mom would worry every time I went out on a gig, and I wouldn't put her through that.

"Me too," she groans in agreement. "I have a meeting this afternoon but needed a caffeine infusion first. Hang on, let me order."

She goes up to the register and returns moments later with an Americano in hand. I swear in that time, she made friends with the order taker, the coffee maker, and the lady sitting closest to the bar. Kayla's good at things like that. I think she got all the charm allotment for the two of us.

"What's your meeting about?" I ask when she sits back down.

She takes a sip before diving in to tell me, "Cameron's got us on the hook for a former amusement park that's fallen into disrepair. Feral teenagers have taken it over, so now it has a bit of a sordid reputation as an illegal rave spot. Definitely going to need some major reframing if we're going to turn a profit with it, but I think we've got a good shot. What do you think of Unicorn Universe?"

I picture my niece, Grace, at an amusement park full of unicorn themed rides, sweets, and souvenirs. Gracie isn't your typical nine-year-old who'd be running through a park shouting 'best day ever!' with giddy happiness at a mere unicorn carousel. She's more the type that'll tell you the animation is lame and the unicorn-horn hot dogs are filled with nitrites. But she's the outlier and I think most kids would be the former rather than Gracie's latter.

"Sounds like a goldmine," I declare, though I have no idea because again, I'm not a business brain like Kayla. But I do have one idea. "You should sell those headbands with unicorn horns on them and have a coliseum filled with balloons where the kids can ram their heads into them. Pop, pop, pop!"

Kayla laughs and acts like she's writing that idea down.

"Increase liability insurance," she notes. "What about you? I haven't seen or heard from you in a while."

Kayla would make a top-notch interrogator. She was trained by the best—Mom. Who was trained by the original—Grandma Beth. Technically, Grandma Beth is Dad's mom, but she and Mom have been like two peas in a pod since all us kids were twinkles in the sky.

They're three generations with interrogation skills that would make the CIA jealous. They don't need truth serums, or bright lights, or waterboarding either. Their weapons of choice are a few select words, a smile, and blue eyes that see to your soul, revealing every secret you ever thought to keep.

Having learned from Mom, Kayla doesn't pry or go straight for the jugular, but she's paying attention to every nuance of my expression, voice, and movements. I adjust accordingly, keeping my face straight, my voice level, and my body completely still. If eighty percent of communication is non-verbal, I'm not saying shit.

I'm about to answer with something flippant like 'been here and there' or 'just busy'. But then I remember Janey's expression when I said no one knows when I'm out of town. I brushed it off at the time because Louisa knows. She knows everything. But if something went wrong, my family wouldn't even know to contact Louisa. They don't know she exists. They barely know I exist, which is mostly by design.

"I need to give you someone's phone number," I tell Kayla begrudgingly. "For emergencies. Like if anything happened with Gracie or the family and you couldn't get ahold of me, you could call her."

I said the magic word.

"Her?" Kayla echoes, her ears virtually perked up in interest like one of those poufy, purse-type, yippy dogs.

"Calm down. Louisa is my assistant. She knows where I am at all times," I explain as I send the contact to Kayla's phone. Even as I downplay it, I'm smiling a little despite myself. "I'm trusting you—only for emergencies," I remind her.

She narrows her eyes, giving me a calculating glare. Considering Kayla and I are fraternal twins, we look remarkably similar. When we were babies and both bald, we even looked identical, which is why Mom always dressed us in pink and blue. As adults, though our looks have changed and we both have hair, our expressions are sometimes scarily alike. Like now. I might as well be looking in a mirror.

"What happened?" Kayla demands. "Why now?"

Okay, change of plans. She's definitely going for the jugular now.

"Nothing. I was reminded that someone should know where I am, and Louisa does. If something happens to me, she has orders to contact Mom. But if something happened at home, you wouldn't know how to find me. Now you do."

I shrug like it's no big deal, even though it's a big fucking deal. This is the closest I've let anyone get to my work, and though Kayla's not asking outright, I know she's curious as hell.

"You were reminded? By whom?"

The woman who's invaded my every waking thought and sleeping dream. The woman who I'm doing my best to not stalk so she can have time to heal. The woman I want to call right now so I can listen to her ramble on about absolutely anything because I never realized how quiet my house, office, car, and life are until her.

I don't say any of that. I don't have to. Despite not having twin telepathy, Kayla is grinning like I just told her all my deepest, darkest secrets. "Whoever she is, I like her already. Do you know that you've said approximately twenty times more words since I sat down than you usually would? You're making small talk, for God's sake. Asking about my work, offering information, and looking like you're going to murder whoever stole your favorite puppy."

"I always ask about stuff," I argue, not touching the other things because she's one hundred percent right about those.

She lifts a wry brow, shutting me down. "No, you don't. And that's okay. Anything you do say is important, which means this conversation" —she points from herself to me— "is important."

I take a sip of my now-cold coffee, the bitterness feeling like home. But it doesn't have to be like this. Janey showed me that.

Her family is awful, and while I've never been particularly fond of mine, they're nothing like hers, and I don't give them enough credit for that. Maybe I can start with Kayla?

Slowly, carefully, I confess, "I met someone."

Fuck, that's a huge admission right there. And rather than a weight lifting off my shoulders, it settles there heavily, making it that much more real.

Kayla looks ready to explode with questions, but she's doing a fairly decent job of holding herself back, so I try again.

"She's a talker, and at first, that meant I didn't have to talk. Like, at all, which was pretty great," I say sarcastically. "But then, it became easier and we . . . talked." I don't think I've used the word 'talk' that many times in my entire life combined.

"I think I love her. Listen to you waxing poetic about all the ways she's changed you for the better."

"I didn't say that."

Undeterred, Kayla asks, "When do we meet her?"

I shake my head. "It's not like that. That wasn't the deal."

"Deal? What deal?" Kayla's on full alert now. "I don't like the sound of that."

"Her boyfriend broke up with her right before an important family event, so I offered to take her to a wedding. She needed a friend. That's it." That's not close to 'it' but I've already said too much.

"Tell me you didn't pull some stupid Carter-esque stunt." She presses fingers to her forehead right above her brows, talking to the ceiling with closed eyes. I'm pretty sure I've seen Mom react the same way to various things us boys have done. "You're too smart for that. Tell me, Cole."

She's talking about my second-oldest brother, Carter, who decided to take his best friend's little sister to a client meeting as his 'wife'. It worked out in the long run, but it was messy, for Carter, his now-actual wife, Luna, the company, and even the client. And that's almost exactly what I did. I even considered calling Carter for advice. But I don't tell Kayla any of that.

"Her family is bad, Kayla," I answer without answering. "Not like ours. Bad like . . . mean and hurtful. And she's this bright sunshine that sees beauty in the ugliest of people. She called me 'sweet', for fuck's sake." I'm not explaining it right, not really, but I don't know how to express how good Janey is and how shitty her family is without getting angry all over again.

"You can be sweet," Kayla repeats, but she sounds pissed about it. "So what did you do?"

I don't reply, and Kayla leans across the table, her voice low and hard-edged and her eyes icy. "I can call Kyle right now. Have him stop by and fuck your shit up." The threat is real and meant whole-heartedly.

It's a legitimate threat, too. I could take Kyle . . . once upon a time. He's my little brother, after all. But these days, he's more jacked than all of us brothers put together and has zero sense of self-preservation. He'd probably enjoy beating the information out of me. Or just beating me up for the hell of it, no reason needed.

I growl but admit, "Told them I was her boyfriend." Kayla lifts a brow, knowing there's more and not accepting anything less than all of it. Right now. I roll my eyes and sigh. "And fake proposed to her in the middle of the dance floor so everyone would remember that and not the wedding."

I expect shock. Horror, maybe. But Kayla laughs loudly. She covers her mouth, trying to contain it, but it escapes, becoming even more boisterous.

People are looking at us again.

"You did not!"

"Shut up," I snap. "It's not funny. Janey caught the bouquet, and the bride literally attacked her."

Still laughing, she says, "It's hilarious! You . . . proposed . . . during someone else's wedding? That's awful . . . so wrong." She's shaking her head and waving a hand like she wants me to stop talking so she can get control of her giggles and catch her breath.

When I glare, she only laughs harder. And people definitely heard her say I proposed to someone because she said it at one hundred decibels and this damn coffee shop echoes like crazy. They've probably decided I've got another woman sitting at home now because there are several women giving me stink eyes who were looking at me with interest when I came in earlier.

Not that I care about any of them.

Eventually, she finally sobers enough to speak, but she's still laughing as she asks, "She okay . . . from the . . . whoo . . . pull it together . . . attack?"

"Physically? Yeah. Emotionally? Probably not," I growl, anger rising as I remember the scratch Paisley left on Janey's cheek and the look of terror in her eyes when I yanked Paisley off her. "Which is why you're not meeting her."

"You mean why you're sitting here moping and not at her place right now," she corrects.

I amp it up and give her my top-notch, go-to-hell scowl. She grins, unfazed, as she wipes the tears from her eyes.

"This is why I don't tell you shit. I'm sharing important information here, for the first time in the history of fuck-all, and you're laughing about it." Okay, so I'm a little grumpy that Kayla isn't treating this like the groundbreaking deal that it is. I'm growing over here, trying new things and whatnot, and she's giving me a hard time in return.

"What would you do without me? All of you are stupid as can be," she says, and I'm pretty sure she's talking about me and my brothers. Or maybe all men? "Call her."

She moves to grab my phone, and I snatch it out of her reach. "She needs time. I'm giving her time." It's basically my mantra at this point. I've said it to myself so many times this week.

Kayla pins me with a pretty decent version of my own fuck-you look, all humor gone now, and I get a glimpse of why she's a scary force to be reckoned with at work. Carter told me that once, and I'd thought it was amusing, but I see it now. "Never thought I'd say this to you of all people, Cole, but . . ." She lets it drag out for maximum impact. "You are a coward." She says it matter-of-factly, which makes it cut that much deeper. "You run away from the family, and now you're running away from this woman. Janey, you said her name is? You're right. Don't call her. If she's as great as you say she is, she deserves a man who will be there for her, not cut and run when she needs you most."

Fuck. That hurts.

"That's not what I'm doing," I declare. But it sounds a little lame in my ears even as I say it. "I'm trying to do the right thing here, for Janey's sake."

"No, you're keeping her at arm's length like you do everyone because she's in a messy situation and she makes you feel something, which you don't like. And no one calls you on it because what would be the use? You'd grouse at them and ignore it, probably disappear for a while. But this one conversation with you has been more real than we've had in years. And I liked it."

She doesn't sound like she's liked it or likes me very much at this moment.

"And now I have to go be happy-happy-joy-joy and sell Unicorn Universe to some asshat who'll probably look at my boobs the whole time," she finishes, standing up to leave.

"Wait. What?" She said a lot and I'm mad as fuck, but she's still my sister and I'll destroy anyone who disrespects her that way.

Kayla waves her hand dismissively. "Not. The. Important. Part. Cole." She bends down, getting in my face. "Call her."

And with that order, she takes her coffee, purse, and my certainty that I'm doing the right thing by staying away from Janey with her out the door.

CHAPTER 14
JANEY

"GOOD MORNING, MRS. MICHAELSON!" I sing as I enter her room. "How're you today?"

Of course, she doesn't say anything, but that's expected. I open the blinds to let some sunshine in, check the machines at her bedside, and then focus on the woman herself. "You look good. Like you slept well." I pause as though she responds. "Me? Pretty well too. I was up reading—I got the new Vampire King book I've been waiting on—but I forced myself to stop at chapter five. Dragul had just spotted his latest victim-slash-soulmate, so it was nearly impossible, but I made myself promise when I started it that I would only read for a bit, not all night."

Truthfully, I'd been distracted while I was reading, which is not a problem I usually have. I fall into books and imaginary worlds like they're building around me, brick by brick and word by word. But since I got back from the cabin, my thoughts have been preoccupied with one thing . . .

Cole.

I've wondered what he's doing. If he's on a case or even in town. Shoot, I've wondered if he's dead in a ditch along the winding road home because no one would know to look for him.

But I've also remembered . . . his touch, his array of smiles, his kindness, and his grumpy charm.

I miss him. Despite the painfully weird goodbye, I miss him.

I've done a good job of staying busy, though. I've worked, catching up with my patients and the other staff because life went on without me here. Ariella, one of the aides, is pregnant with her third, and we're excitedly planning a baby shower, even though she's barely twelve weeks. Dr. Vincetti announced his upcoming retirement and subsequent plans to travel with his husband. Mr. Culderon's son, who we don't like, came in flashing a ten-dollar fake Rolex, thinking it would impress the staff and we'd treat his father differently, which of course, we don't. We continue our top-notch care, regardless. Mrs. Michaelson has a sore on her hip, a common concern for bedbound patients, and I've made it my personal mission to heal it with love, positivity, and a healthy dose of prescription ointment. And best of all . . .

"I did it," Mason says from the doorway. "You were right, and I finally listened. I did it."

I look up from the spread of wound care items in front of me. "Of course, I was right," I answer automatically. "What was I right about this time?"

Mason comes in, taking position on the other side of the bed to assist . . . and gossip. "About me and Greta," he answers with an eye roll. "As the announcers would say, it's *ovah!*"

"What? Oh, no, Mase! I'm so sorry!" I truly am. Though I worried they weren't a good fit because she didn't appreciate Mason's awesomeness, I hate that he's hurting, which I know he is beneath his macho man guise.

"I'm not. Unfortunately, she made it easy. She told me that my bare chin looked *so good*," he mocks, "and was rubbing all over my face like a cat in heat. Then, like she was testing a stolen credit card and got approved for the candy bar at the gas station, she went straight for the 70-inch TV and said I should shave the 'stache too and maybe get an undercut and a hard part. And then we could go shopping." He throws his voice falsely high and whiny. "Won't that be fun?"

"Ooh, that's not good." I wince.

"Right? I'm not some dude bro who needs a makeover to

pass as human. And want to know the worst part?" he asks, sounding like this is going to be a head-run off a cliff.

I cringe, preparing for something like she wanted to shop for engagement rings or wanted Mason to get her name tattooed on his chest in three-inch tall Gothic letters.

"It's gonna take months to grow my beard back out," he finishes, sounding exasperated. He sighs heavily and holds gauze out for me. "I'm not one of those guys who sprouts facial hair like a werewolf. It's gonna take time, but it's happening, Mrs. Michaelson. You just wait. Mason's getting his groove back." He dances, wiggling his hips and kicking out a leg, but conversationally including our patient like she's been involved the whole time, something he learned from me.

I laugh in surprise at his good-natured, Golden Retriever-esque response to a breakup. Considering mine was more tears and pathetically begging for Henry to at least go to the wedding, I'm impressed by Mason.

Not that I'm still in that headspace. I'm more in the Henry Who? mindset now.

"Congratulations, then?" I say carefully.

Mason dips his chin, agreeing that congrats are in order. "You know what this means, right?" he says. "You and me, both single and ready to mingle. We should get drinks tonight and see who's out there."

There's never been anything between Mason and me, so I know he's not asking me 'out', but even the idea of sitting in some club, sipping an overpriced, watered-down drink and making myself available for any Tom, Dick, or Henry to choose me sounds dreadful. Especially when I already know who I want. He just didn't want me.

Not that I'm bitter! I'm fully in my Janey-Self-Love era, taking care of me, myself, and I and remembering why I left my family in the first place, and analyzing why the hell I got caught up with Henry, who treated me like a second thought, so I don't do either of those things again.

As I've recently been reminded, I'm a strong, beautiful woman worthy of more, and any man who doesn't appreciate that can go. As Ariana Grande famously said . . . thank you, next!

Somehow, it doesn't sound so badass when I tell Mason, "Can't, I have a date with a bottle of wine, takeout pasta, a hair treatment, a collagen face mask, and Dragul tonight. I'm gonna be naughty and go all . . . the . . . way . . . to chapter fifteen." I shimmy my shoulders in giddy excitement as I make my reading sound dirtier than spreading book pages. "Already promised Mrs. Michaelson that I'll tell her how Tiffany gets snared in Dragul's seductive web of nips and nibbles." Finished with my patient's wound treatment, I throw away the trash, yank my gloves off with a snap, and then load up on waterless soap from the dispenser on the wall.

"Your vampire guy, who's like a thousand years old and has lived through war, the rise and fall of civilizations, and the advent of sour gummies as an entire genre of candy, is in love with someone named Tiffany?" Mason echoes, his face screwed up in distaste. "Let me guess, she's twenty-one, has zero life experience, but they're somehow inter-cosmically connected?" Mason laces his foamy soap covered fingers together to illustrate.

"*Maybe*," I concede. He's pretty spot-on, but he doesn't have to ick my yum like that. And in my defense, Tiffany is the reincarnation of Dragul's first love from when he was human, so . . . there's that.

We walk down the hall together toward the nurse's station, greeting other patients as we do a cursory scan to make sure they're okay. Some are sitting up in their rooms, doing puzzles or listening to the radio. Others prefer to socialize by sitting in the hallway or the den area, which is better known as Gossip Garden—and if you think a care center full of old folks doesn't have more gossip swirling than the *Big Brother* house, you'd be mistaken.

I sit down at a computer to document Mrs. Michaelson's care, and Mason leans against the counter.

"Hey, Pam, help me out," he says to the lady writing on the big whiteboard behind the desk. At first glance, with her short, white hair, big round glasses, and baggy scrubs that hang from her spindly frame, you might think Pam's a patient, but she's one of the longest tenured and hardest working aides here. She never flinches from a mess, is the first to jump in and do whatever's needed, and honestly, should've retired at least five years ago but says she'd rather get paid for taking care of old folks than take care of her old husband for free.

She gives Mason a wary look, which is valid considering he could be asking for help with what to order for lunch or with cleaning up feces.

"I'm trying to get Janey to go out tonight, but she's ditching me for a book boyfriend with fangs and a hard-on for a bitch named—" Mason stops abruptly, changing gears. "How does a vampire get an erection? They have no blood. That's the point of all the bitey-biting, right? But they've got enough to go all . . ." He throws his forearm out, hand fisted at the end, like that's supposed to be Dragul's erection.

Although with the way he's written, Mason's not that far off if I'm being a hundred percent honest.

"Baby, do that again and you'll be the one giving blood. Look at those veins!" Pam quips as she grabs Mason's arm and traces the thick vein in his forearm. If she had a needle in her pocket and the law on her side to allow her to actually draw blood, I think she'd already be wrapping a tourniquet around Mason's bicep.

"It's definitely giving . . . nurse porn!" Gabriella, our charge nurse, agrees. She's been here for years and is actually the one who hired me to work on the ward. My interview with her consisted of her trying to talk me out of working here and suggesting that I do travel nursing instead to 'pad my bank account while I'm young'. But I'd been sure then and I'm still sure now. I love it here, and Gabriella is a big part of that. She's the boss, but she's a good one, with a bit of motherly love—of both the tough variety and the kind variety—for everyone, staff and patients.

Mason laughs at her assessment and does a few biceps curls

to pump his arm up even more. "Ya think that's hot? Check this out," he tells Gabriella as he flexes hard.

"Aww, so cute. You think women like that?" she teases back in a pitying voice. "Nah, show me a man with a belly. If he eats, I know I'll eat and my kids'll eat. Plus, a man with some cake will appreciate my snacks." She pats her own curvy butt enthusiastically, which is extended beyond both sides of the chair she's sitting in.

Mason's ready, though, and throws back, "If he's not hitting the gym, how's he gonna hold you up, flip you over, and uh-uh?" He mimes spanking all that ass, and Pam and Gabriella burst out laughing.

"My knees and back don't want or need all that anymore. Hell, I need three pillows to get me in the right position and give me Posturepedic support so I can walk after," Pam says, divulging entirely too much information.

"Ooh, yes. Getchu one of the wedge pillows," Gabriella agrees. "Puts everything at just the right height so nobody's gotta work too hard."

Mason looks stunned. And confused. I'm mostly enjoying the show of them teasing each other.

"I can't with you two," Mason finally decides with a laugh, waving his hands in front of his face like he's wiping away that imagery. "But I need one of you to tell this one" —he points at me— "to stop pining after Forest Frank n' Beans and go out for drinks with me tonight."

"Who?" Gabriella asks.

I give her a bare bones rendition, explaining, "I met a guy, and he did me a favor and took me to my cousin's wedding. We had an amazing time—"

"She means there was no pillow needed, other than the one she was screaming 'yes, yes, yes' into," Mason interjects. I swat his stupidly-big shoulder as Gabriella and Pam grin. I maybe shouldn't have told Mason as many details as I did.

"As I was saying, we had an amazing time, and then he gave me a business card as a goodbye." Gabriella recoils, disgust wrinkling her face, and I rush to add, "But it's fine. I'm thankful he helped me with the wedding and reminded me that I deserve better than my ex or my family." I smile, topping off the story with a happy ending.

Not that kind, but a mental one at least.

Mason and Gabriella lock eyes, having a conversation between the two of them. I know Mason well enough to read what he's saying—'You see what I'm dealing with here? Help me.'

Seemingly forgetting that the mission was to talk me into going out, Gabriella spins in her chair, fingertips going to her keyboard and her back straight like things are dead-serious now. "Name? Any identifying information?" she demands, sounding more boss-like than usual.

"What?" I ask, looking from her to Mason.

"Cole," Mason answers for me. Yeah, I definitely told him too damn much. "She's got a picture too."

"Perfect."

"What're you doing?" I look over Gabriella's shoulder as she clicks away on the computer. She's already done a search for 'Cole + Bridgeport' which gives hundreds of returns. I blanch. "No, you don't have to do all that. It's fine."

"Janey, I'm a single mother in her forties who's been back in the dating cesspool for years. I have a PhD in tracking down men, their wives, their kids, their mugshots and records, and various other things. You have to be a detective these days to keep yourself safe because these men are all out here being so creative with the truth, and I'm looking for a forever, not a for-never. And so are you."

Well, she's right about that. If my options are cat-motherhood or a relationship, I want the relationship to be long-term and worth it.

"He's an investigator," I add. "I don't think you'll find anything, though, because he said he researched me and complimented me on my online presence. Said it was locked down and clean and that the only ones better were his and his assistant's."

That was definitely the wrong thing to say.

· · ·

Gabriella's brows climb her forehead, and her eyes go wide in displeasure. "That means he's married," she tells me gently. But then her temper flares up in my defense. "Probably has four kids with three different baby mommas, a job that he 'travels' for, and is likely a felon. That's basically like a guy telling you he's an FBI agent, and 'he could tell you things, but then he'd have to kill you'." Fired up, she turns to Mason and accuses, "Why do guys think that's funny? We're out in these streets, fighting for our literal lives, and they joke like that? No sir, no thank you. Automatic block and report."

And I'm reminded all over again about why I'm not going for drinks with Mason. The dating scene is awful and I want no part of it.

I'm going home, reading a book, and maybe looking up shelter cats to happily start my spinster collection. Because I'm enough—me, myself, and I.

CHAPTER 15
JANEY

AND THAT'S what my life becomes. Day after day, go to work, smile, gab with everyone, go home, and bury myself in my books.

At least, until the day Gabriella tells me she found something. Which is how I find myself pacing back and forth in front of a nondescript building on the edge of downtown Bridgeport. I watch my reflection in the mirrored windows.

"Go in. What's the worst that could happen?" I tell my reflection. Of course, I've got a reply. I've always got a reply. "He's married like Gabriella warned and his gorgeous wife is inside with their adorable mini-Coles crawling around on the floor. My ovaries explode, my heart breaks, and I say something stupid like 'I can't stop thinking about your stupid half-smile because you made me come more times in twelve hours than I have in the entirety of the last year.'"

A man who is walking by overhears me and says, "Well, hi there."

Embarrassed, I wave but keep my pacing loop of indecision, and he drifts off, leaving the crazy lady, even if she is spouting out sexual nonsense on a busy sidewalk in the middle of the afternoon.

He's not married. Gabriella is pretty sure of that. In fact, she eventually agreed that Cole's online presence looks as clean as he said it did but warned that I should still be cautious.

"Maybe he'll be glad to see me?" I suggest to myself.

Still, I should've called. That would be the reasonable thing to do considering he gave me his phone number. But I'm not doing reasonable anymore. Part of the New Janey regime is that I'm making big moves. If it'll make me happy, I do it.

Which is why I'm here.

Cole made me happy. In the ugliest of moments, when the worst thing I could've imagined happened, he supported me and made me smile. And I want to tell him so.

I approach the door, noting the engraving on the frosted glass, *BS Consulting*. I giggle a little, wondering if it actually means bullshit. That's the kind of thing Cole would do, especially when he's handing clients' bullshit all day, every day.

Inside, I enter a large room that's almost empty. Immediately in front of me is a white modular desk, where a pretty blonde woman sits with a welcoming smile. To the right is a grouping of four chairs and a coffee table. It's sparse, modern, and vaguely expensive-looking for being nearly bare. Like an art gallery.

"I wondered what you were going to decide," the blonde says, sounding amused but polite.

When I don't answer and look at her in confusion, she points to the windows with a bemused expression. Yep, they're completely transparent on this side. "You could see me pacing back and forth?" I question stupidly.

Her smile grows, but it seems friendly. "Sure could. Can I help you?"

"I'm looking for Cole Harrington," I blurt out. "My friend—well, she's my boss—helped me track him down. He's a hard-to-find man, like nearly impossible, but Gabriella—that's my friend-slash-boss—is good. Like Cole-should-offer-her-a-job level good," I recommend with a nod. "Once she had his name, she looked up property records for the county. There's a bunch, especially under C. Harrington, but a lot of those seemed like they might be Cole's brothers' properties. This one seemed different, so I thought maybe it was his. Is it?"

Her eyes get wider and wider as I spill out Gabriella's entire research process in a single breath.

"Sorry, I shouldn't have come. I'll just go."

I turn to make a run for it, but a door I didn't see opens across the room. And *he* comes in. Big as life, twice as sexy, and crossing the open room like he's about to conquer the world . . . or tackle me. I don't know which, but just seeing him again stops my heart for a moment. He's in a light blue dress shirt today, one of those types with a white collar and cuffs, to go with his black pants, no tie, but shined dress shoes that click on the tile of the foyer.

And I want him. God help me, I want him.

"Janey?" Cole growls, snapping me back to reality. "What's wrong?"

"Uhm, what?" I squeak. "Nothing, nothing's wrong. I was just in the neighborhood and thought I'd stop by." Instead of explaining how I tracked him down again, I say, "Did you know there's an Italian place around the corner that's been there since 1924? It was a speak-easy during Prohibition years, or at least that's what the sign out front says. I passed it a few times as I was walking the block, trying to talk myself into coming in."

"She doesn't have an appointment," the receptionist offers.

Not listening to either of us, Cole is suddenly in front of me, his blue eyes scanning me head to toe like I might be broken, physically or mentally. Little does he know, despite my current attack of nerves, I'm the best I've been in years.

I see worry and confusion and something else that I could almost mistake for lust before his gaze shutters down, going blank.

Frowny face aside, he looks good. His shirt looks perfectly fitted to his superhero upper body, and his dress pants are just *slightly* tight in all the right places to remind me of what he's got. His jaw is covered with a couple of days' worth of scruff that I want to scratch my fingers through, and his lips look kissable.

"Amanda, close up for the day and go home. Thank you," Cole says as I watch his lips move. I presume he's talking to the receptionist because I don't know how to do those things. And of course, my name's not Amanda.

Cole takes my hand and yanks me across the room past the grouping of chairs. I glance back to find Amada watching in shock. He does the magic trick with the invisible door again, and in an instant, I'm in an echoing stairwell.

"Are you sleeping with her?" I ask. I have so many questions, but that's the one that pops out of my mouth first.

"Who?" Cole replies, climbing stairs and pulling me with him. I swear I see a tiny hint of a smile, but I probably imagined it because a nanosecond later, he's frowning again. "Amanda? No. She answers the phone and greets clients. She doesn't even know what I do."

"Oh." I think about what an odd job that must be, but I can understand doing just about anything that'll pay the bills these days. "Is Louisa here?"

He shakes his head. "Works from home."

"Oh, yeah, I remember."

We approach another door, and Cole types a code into a keypad. I hear the click of the lock and then he pushes the door open, revealing a private apartment.

"Is this where you live?" I ask, looking around curiously.

It's a lot like downstairs—austere, empty, modern, but with a sense of luxury. It doesn't feel particularly homey, like the leather couch doesn't seem like a place where you flop to binge watch TV and I wouldn't dream of putting my feet on the glass coffee table. Overall, it feels anonymous.

Which makes me sad for Cole. He should have a place to relax and be at home. Especially after spending days lying on the forest floor to surveil someone, which reminds me . . .

"Did you find out about Mr. Webster's guest yet?"

He's guided me to the couch and nearly shoved me down onto it—I was right, it's not comfortable at all—and is looming over me, looking furious. Done with my questions, he demands, "What the fuck are you doing here?"

Once upon a time, I would've flinched. I would've shrunk down and probably even apologized for disturbing him. And I'm sad to say, that time wasn't all too long ago. But I've remembered who I am, who I've worked to become.

That week in the woods might've started my spiritual rehabilitation, and Cole's reminder that I deserve better helped more than he'll ever know, but I'm the one fixing my insides and doing a really good job at it, if I do say so myself.

Cole, on the other hand, seems to have returned to his former grumpy self.

"Excuse me?" I reply. "I went through all this trouble of finding you—no easy task, mind you—because I wanted to tell you something." He blinks, blank-faced, but I'm pretty sure he's gritting his teeth. I forge ahead, doing this for me more than him. "Thank you. That's it. You helped me with the wedding, and I said thanks for that. But you did so much more, and I'm doing really well now. I'm not perfectly fine, but I'm not broken either. I'm healing, seeing the good in situations that have them, and not making excuses for those that don't. For the first time, I'm not worried about what everyone else is feeling or thinking. I'm making myself happy. Yeah, I'm happy. So, thank you."

He huffs a laugh. "You tracked me down to tell me *that?*"

I stand up, facing him as close to eye-to-eye as I can get. But it's not enough, so I step up onto the fancy-schmancy couch that definitely shouldn't have shoes on it so I'm even with him. "No, and also, screw you. It hurt my feelings when you gave me your business card and dismissed me like I was a pity fuck. I didn't deserve that."

I did not mean to say that. I didn't practice that speech a single time before coming. But now that it's out in the open, I realize how true it is and I'm glad I said it. New Janey isn't pulling any punches. Truth jabs here, come 'n get 'em!

But Cole leans in, our noses touching and his eyes probing into mine. What I said hit him beyond whatever shields he's putting up. "You were never a pity fuck. I wanted you so badly, I almost climbed that fucking ladder a million times, and I jacked off listening to you touch yourself."

I gasp as heat floods my cheeks. "What!"

"And I've done it nearly daily since getting back, wishing it was you each and every time," he adds, his voice low and intense. "But I've forced myself to stay away as much as I could, knowing you need time to heal and that you don't need me fucking up your process. But it's been hard." His hands are curling and uncurling at his sides like he's fighting himself, holding back from touching me. "I've wanted to bang on your door, take you into my arms, wipe away your tears, and fix things for you. That's what I do—save people, help them, fix shit. But you don't need me to do that for you. You'll do it on your own eventually, and then I'll be standing on your sidewalk, proud as hell and ready to fuck you like you deserve."

Okay, none of that was on my Bingo card for today.

Cole makes it sound like he wants me but has been staying away because . . . I don't even know why?

"I don't get what you're saying. What are you talking about? You've been to my house?" I ask in confused shock as I step down from the couch. There are probably shoeprints on the nice leather, but I can't care right now.

"I left you alone. I swear, I did. But then Kayla called me a coward, and I couldn't anymore." He runs his fingers through his hair, scrubbing over his scalp punishingly. "There's a short-term rental across the street, four houses down. So, I watched and waited. But you were—"

Wait. WHAT?

I cut him off. "Did you say that you're staying by my house? Watching me? Like a stakeout, like you were doing with Mr. Webster?"

He shrugs casually, like a little mild stalking is a totally normal activity. "It's what I do," he explains.

A million thoughts are running through my head at once. I mean, that's not unusual for him, professionally speaking, but it's really weird for me. If this were one of my books, it might be darkly romantic. But it's not. This is real, and after a lifetime of trying to be as invisible as possible, I feel seen in a way that's startlingly uncomfortable.

Has he watched me crying? Dancing around my living room,

having Angry Girl Music solo raves? Has he watched me touch myself? And so much more.

I feel exposed and vulnerable and really stupid for not noticing him right across the street. Heat fills my cheeks, panic blooms in my gut, and I need . . . to escape.

"I need to go." I virtually bolt for the door, only to find it locked. "Let me out," I say, my eyes fixated on the white surface.

Cole walks up behind me, his chest so close to my back that I can feel the heavy weight of his presence. Even now, there's a small piece of me that wants to lean back and fall into him. But I don't.

I can't.

CHAPTER 16
COLE

I'M AN ASSHOLE. I warned her that I was, but she didn't believe me. Hell, she had me not believing it for a while.

I let Janey out of my apartment, feeling the panic roll off her in waves. I should've stopped right then and there. But did I?

Fuck no.

I had to make sure she got home okay, so I followed her instead.

I watched and waited, waited and watched for two whole days. That's forty-eight hours, 2880 minutes, or 172,800 seconds. That's got to be a record or something, right? Not for me, I've done longer stake-outs, but for a man to stay away from the woman he's obsessed with? Call up the *Guinness Book of World Records* because I'm pretty sure I'm destined for page twenty-two for this feat of restraint.

And what did Janey do for those two days? Nothing.

Locked inside her house for the weekend, she didn't even order food, which made me worry whether she was eating enough because I know she can't cook. She didn't have any visitors, and a quick check of her friend's social media showed that Mason was on the lake with a bunch of guys, which made me realize she didn't tell him about my watching her. Everything she's shared about him makes me think he's a great friend and good guy. If he knew, he'd be busting down the door to confront me himself. But he didn't.

She's hiding away, alone, with the blinds closed, probably starving to death, and it's my fault.

I need to explain to her that I wasn't being creepy. I was . . . okay, am . . . checking on her to make sure she's healing okay. That's all.

So, this morning, when her front door opens bright and early, I'm ready and waiting and step outside as she's walking to her bright yellow car.

My plan is to meet her in her driveway and tell her all the things I should've said but didn't because I was so surprised to find her standing in my office—the one no one knows about but she somehow found. The things I didn't say because it was all I could do to not gather her in my arms, kiss the shit out of her, and bury myself inside her right there on my couch.

She's ready too, looking across the street like she expects me to be there. "I'm going to work," she shouts across the street. "But you already knew that, didn't you?"

There's a hint of an edge in her tone, but mostly, she sounds resigned, like she's already made excuses for me in her mind, and that pisses me off. She shouldn't be forgiving me for this, or at least not this easily. She should be stringing me up by my balls and making me grovel for it.

Before I can begin to apologize, she gets in her car and drives off while I'm still dumbstruck and standing on the front steps, watching her go.

One of our neighbors—Jim Zadowski, according to online info—walks past, looking extremely curious. He waves and shouts, "Morning!" He's short and heavyset, on a mission to lower his blood pressure, according to his My Fitness Pal posts, and walks with a teeny-tiny Yorkie named Captain.

"Morning," I grumble back as I shut the door.

I sit down in the living room chair that's become my second home over the last days because it has the perfect view of Janey's house and an electrical outlet where I can plug in my laptop so I can watch Janey and work at the same time. I've got a new case that's mostly drudging through this guy's social media content, and if I have to watch another diesel engine overhaul or live streaming discussion about horsepower versus torque to see if he's drinking while the kids are at school, I will yank my own eyeballs out.

I haven't quite reached the point of talking to myself aloud like Janey does, but I'm definitely calling myself some choice names because if she won't do it, I'll do it myself. Fuck, I wish I had at least some basic communication skills so I could explain all this to Janey.

But I can wait until this afternoon when she gets home and talk to her then. That's only another eight and a half hours from now. Pfft, I can do that long standing like a statue, and nearly did one time.

This'll be easy. I can even work to stay distracted. I'll just wait for her to get home.

An hour later . . .

If I were a smart man, I'd run this idea by Kayla first, especially since she's the one who got me into this mess by calling me a coward. But I don't want her to tell me I'm an idiot. I already know that. So, I don't call her, or anyone else, to discuss my new plan.

I pull into The Ivy Care Center parking lot. From the outside, it looks well-maintained and welcoming, with flowers blooming in pots on either side of the front door and a fresh coat of paint on the bricks. It's a pleasant façade for a place that's really not much more than a comfortable place to die.

I grab the gas station bag from the seat beside me and then the box of treats I picked up too. I might not know how to 'people' as myself, but I've got practice faking the charm that comes naturally to most others. And using food as a way in has always served me well.

I press the doorbell by the front door. *"Hello. Welcome to The Ivy. Can I help you?"* a disembodied voice says.

Leaning toward the camera, I slap a charismatic smile on my face and say, "I'm here to see Janey Williams. And I brought treats for her friends."

"Is she expecting you?"

Huh, better security than some Forbes 100 corporations. I'm impressed.

I let my smile fall, looking conspiratorial at the inhuman camera like it's an old friend. Quietly, I confide, "It's a surprise. I'm hoping to sweep her away for lunch, but just in case she's too busy, I brought her favorite strawberry apricot Red Bull, some trail mix, with the requisite extra bag of M&Ms to make it actually worth it."

The laughter on the other side tells me everything I need to know. I'm in.

The door buzzes. "Come on in."

Inside, a smiling woman sits behind a large desk that's covered with stacks and stacks of paper—my worst nightmare, non-digital records. "You know the way to our Janey's heart, don't you?" she says by way of greeting.

"I'd like to think so," I reply as I glance down at her name tag. "Hopefully, yours too, Jackie. I brought these for everyone else." I hold out the box filled with bagels, donuts, and mini muffins.

"Ooh! Gimme that!" She squeals happily as she takes it from my hand. "I'll put it in the break room and tell Janey she's got a visitor, but I won't tell her who . . .?" She trails off, expectantly prompting me for my name.

"Cole Harrington. Janey and I are friends," I say with a half-smile, making it clear that we're considerably more.

"Well, you can be my friend too, Cole, if you keep bringing treats like this. Hang tight, it might be a while," Jackie says, pointing to a chair. Getting up, she disappears down a hallway, presumably to put the snacks in the break room for everyone.

It's been about thirty minutes, during which time five different staff members have done drive-bys to scope me out or tell me thank you for the bagels. But the man approaching now doesn't seem like he works here.

"I hear you'd like to see our Janey," he says, sounding fatherly. He's tall, thin, with a full head of thick, white hair. His navy sweater hangs off his shoulders, his khaki slacks are baggy and piled up at the ankle, and he's shuffling around in suede house shoes.

But I know that this man's opinion carries weight where it matters. I stand, holding out a hand respectfully. "Yes sir. Cole Harrington."

He shakes my hand more firmly than I would've expected. "Ace Culderon. Or at least that's what they called me back in the service."

"It's a good name, Mr. Culderon." I can play the charming date to a pseudo-father figure if it's necessary to get to Janey. I've done worse for less, and at this point, I'd do just about anything to get in front of her and explain myself.

"Call me Ace," he offers. "You play?" He points a gnarled finger at a side table with a marble chess board.

"A bit," I answer with a shrug. I learned as a kid from Grandpa Chuck and have played a bit over the years, but not enough to be good.

"Me too. Sit down," Ace instructs. I make sure he moves to the chair and sits down okay and then settle myself across from him. "You start."

He's given me the advantage of playing white, which already tells me that he expects to win easily against me. Otherwise, he would've taken the advantage for himself. We play quietly for a few turns, feeling each other out.

"What're your intentions?" Ace asks after taking one of my pawns with his knight. Though his eyes never leave the board, I sense he's sizing me up and doesn't mean my plans with the game.

"To take Janey to lunch. We have some things to talk about."

"Mm-hmm," he hums. "You the one who broke her heart? Coming to make amends and beg her to take you back?" he asks blandly, but his nonchalance is as big a façade as my charm is.

"Not exactly." I'm not sure how much he knows about Janey's personal life, but given the stink eye he's shooting at me with his yellow-tinged eye, I'd say it's enough to be pissed. And protective of Janey. "We met recently. Her other guy broke up with her, and I stepped in as a date for a wedding."

"You are him, then. She talked about that other fella a bit, but she came back from her vacation and all the nurses up there been a'tittering about the new man she met. Peep, peep, peep like hens, all of 'em." He scans the board, already knowing his play but making me wait so I'm forced to hear him out. "Heard a few of 'em tell her 'good luck' on Friday, so I figured she was gonna have herself a good weekend too. But this morning? Well, something's dulled that girl's shine and I don't like it a bit." Ace moves his queen and sits back, letting me chew on that.

Janey might not have confided in Ace, but he knows a lot and I can appreciate his observant nature. "That does sound like me," I agree. "But I'm here to fix it."

He eyes the gas station bag beside me. "Gonna take more than some fizzy water and candy. Where're the flowers, the sharp suit, the clean-shaven face?" he demands as he scans me head-to-toe with a raised brow, obviously finding my jeans, T-shirt, and scruff lacking.

"I thought of that, but I figured she's around flowers all day." Focusing on the one thing I can address, I gesture to the three fresh arrangements in the lobby, presuming there are more scattered throughout the facility. "I wanted to get her something . . . specific that'd brighten her day. And I'm hoping to take her to lunch, not a five-star restaurant." I look down the hallway, wishing she were walking this way to get me out of this conversation.

Almost like she heard my prayer, I see Janey coming. Her scrubs are purple today, her hair pulled into a puff of curls on her crown, and her sensible rubber shoes squeak slightly on the linoleum floor. She looks gorgeous, especially when I see her back ramrod straight, her chin jutted out, and her eyes narrowed in on me.

"Mr. Culderon, is this man bothering you?" she asks,

ignoring me to gift the old man with a warm smile I'd kill to have aimed in my direction.

"Nah, we were playing a friendly game of chess, weren't we, Cole? By the way, checkmate." He moves his queen again, and with a scan of the board, I can see that he's got me. I've got no counters, and he's good enough that I didn't even see it coming.

"Good game, Ace," I reply, laying my king down on the board. "Thank you."

He stands and holds out his hand. When I take it, I'm surprised at his firm grip again. "Don't hurt this nice lady's heart or I'll tear you up. Ya hear me?" he warns.

"Heard, sir." I'm not afraid of Ace, but that doesn't mean I can't be respectful. His heart's in the right place, and for all I know, he's the mafia kingpin of the care center.

Ace shuffles off, leaving Janey and me alone though Jackie is back at her desk, typing something into the computer from a stack of paper. I'm pretty sure that if I could see her screen, she's typing nothing but gibberish as her ears are tuned in on Janey and me.

"What are you doing here?" Janey hisses, trying to keep her voice down.

It's ironically the same thing I asked her when she showed up to my workplace, but I don't point out that particular similarity. Jackie is watching us like a hungry hawk wanting some gossip, so I match Janey's volume, keeping my voice low as I say, "Hoping to take you to lunch and apologize. I shouldn't have invaded like that. Your home is a sanctuary and I fucked that up. I'm sorry."

Apologies are not my strong suit. I can't actually remember the last time I apologized for anything. Maybe a throw-away 'I'm sorry' when I tell a client bad news, but to actually mean it? Not in ages.

"Psst! Show her what's in the bag!" Jackie advises excitedly from across the room.

Janey looks over her shoulder to her co-worker, then back to me, so I grab the bag and hold it out to her. As she looks inside,

I explain, "Those are your favorites, so I figured they'd be welcome, even if I wasn't."

She's holding them to her chest like precious treasure. "You got the peanut butter M&Ms too?"

"Yeah, because you pour those in the trail mix, mix them up, and then there are two kinds of candy in every handful. And no raisins either because they're gross—squishy and chewy like gum, but you're supposed to swallow them." I'm quoting the rant about the 'perfect trail mix' Janey made one afternoon when I came back from a stakeout to find her pouring a share-size bag of M&Ms into her trail mix and shaking it up. I'd been distracted by the bouncing of her breasts, but I'd heard what she was saying too.

She looks at the can of Red Bull and mumbles, "It's the strawberry apricot one too."

"Yeah."

Of course it is. That's the only one she drinks.

Staring at the can, she says, "A couple of summers ago, we had a patient who refused to eat anything but French fries and slushies. It didn't meet her nutritional needs at all, but she told us that she was old and could eat what she wanted. So, her daughter brought her a strawberry apricot slushie with her fries one day, not realizing it had an energy drink in it." Janey smiles at the memory, then laughs, "She was like the Energizer Bunny, talking and laughing and sitting up in the den. Then she started demanding one every day, so we made her a deal. For every swallow of protein drink she took, she'd get a drink of the slushie. Maybe it was wrong, and it shouldn't have worked, but it did."

She goes quiet, lost in the past, and Jackie adds, "Oh, I loved Mrs. James, and that daughter of hers was as caring as could be."

Hearing the past tense, I ask, "What happened?"

Janey meets my eyes, and I can read the answer there before she says it. "She passed away. But her last days were better for it. Her daughter came every day to bring her that slushie, and she had enough energy to make those visits matter. And now, I'm addicted to these silly things, which are so bad for me, but they remind me that days are what you make of them."

I can honestly say that I've never given more than two shits about what I'm drinking. Is it cold or hot when it should be? Alcoholic or not? Taste good? But not Janey. A simple drink is an experience to be appreciated, and she can find a way to smile about a beloved patient's life while mourning their death.

"I'm sorry. It sounds like you did everything you could for her." I don't know what to say. Death isn't part of my daily life the way it is for Janey, but I want her to know that I'm sorry she has to carry that grief.

She nods with a sad smile, then sighs, and the happy mask reappears as she pushes those feelings down.

"Lunch?" I prompt hopefully.

"No," she answers firmly.

My heart sinks. I really fucked up this time. I fucked up so badly that the kindest woman in the world, the one who makes excuses for the worst of the worst, won't forgive me. It hurts, but it's warranted.

"Bring pizza at six thirty. Don't be late." She smiles, her eyes dancing with laughter, and I realize that she just got me. She read me, and she knew exactly what she was doing. She lifts to her toes, presses a quick peck of a kiss to my cheek, and spins to swish away down the hall.

I can feel the grin stretching my lips. She's giving me a chance, and I'm going to make damn sure I'm worth it.

I'm halfway to the door when I hear a whoop of excitement from where Janey disappeared. Okay, she's happy too. She's mad, she's justifiably unsure of what I did, but I'll explain that. And then hopefully, we can start fresh.

CHAPTER 17
JANEY

TODAY HAS BEEN INTERESTING. I spent all weekend huddled up in my house, alternating between thinking about Cole—and I admit, peering through the blinds to stare at the house across the street—and reading my book. As expected, Tiffany fell for Dragul, but it's not an easy situation. I mean, she doesn't know vampires exist and Dragul needs to literally suck her blood to bind them as soul mates. Definitely some challenges to overcome there.

A lot like Cole and me.

Have I forgiven him for stalking me? No. I'm too nice, not stupid. And what he did is beyond any boundary I can imagine having. But when he showed up at work today, there was something in his eyes that called to me. He's sorry. He said it, but that's easily faked. His eyes, though . . . there was truth in them, so I'm willing to hear him out.

And he did bring my favorite snacks. A small but significant gesture. Could he have learned about those from spying on me? Yes. But he also quoted nearly word-for-word what I'd said about my trail mix concoction. It was a silly, throwaway ramble that most people would've ignored, but Cole listened and remembered. That makes me feel seen in an entirely different way than I did on Friday when I freaked out about his being across the street.

His listening that closely makes me feel important, like I'm worth his time and attention. "Which I totally am!" I remind myself as I spritz water over my head and scrunch my curls to freshen them up.

I listened to him too, though. And though I might've panicked at his place, I also heard his explosion of emotion before I found out about the stalking. I heard him say that he was trying to give me space to heal and not interfere because he knew I could do it on my own, and that he was proud of how strong and capable I am. Those are words that have never been directed at me before, not by my own talkative mind nor anyone around me. But Cole sees that in me and he's right.

"I'm a total badass." One last look in the mirror and I'm ready—cleaned up after work, dressed in jeans and a striped T-shirt that hangs off one shoulder, and mentally prepared to listen.

And excited to see Cole.

Yeah, that part's probably stupid, but I can't help it. I missed him after leaving the cabin, and there's a piece of me, not that far deep down, that's giddily jumping up and down at the idea of the hot guy coming to see me.

Maybe he can give you more orgasms?

No, that's not what tonight's about. Tonight's a reset, a new beginning in the real world, not the fake one we started at the cabin.

———

"Come in," I say as I open the door at exactly six thirty.

"Thanks." Cole's wearing the same jeans and T-shirt from this morning, but I can smell a fresh dose of cologne as he passes by. Oh, wait . . . that's the pizza he's carrying.

"This is my favorite pizza place!" I exclaim as I take the box and set it on the coffee table. I grab plates and napkins from the kitchen and gesture for him to sit on the couch. "What kind did you get? I didn't think to tell you my favorite, but I'm not too picky. Unless you got pineapple or anchovies. Neither belong on pizza as far as I'm concerned, but I can pick them off if I need to."

When I sit beside him, Cole looks tense. His hands are clasped between his spread thighs and his eyes are flitting from the pizza to me. Finally, he sighs. "Gonna be honest. Went to two different places and asked if they'd ever delivered to this address, then got a repeat of your previous order. It's meat lovers with jalapeños."

He investigated me and my pizza habits. I blink, not sure what to think about that. It's definitely going above and beyond, but also . . . who does that?

Like he can sense me waffling, Cole opens the box and serves me the biggest of the eight slices. I'm not too proud to say that food is the way to my heart after a long day at work, so I take a big bite. I swear, the smallest surrender drops his shoulders two inches, and Cole seems much more relaxed as he takes a slice for himself.

I let him take a bite, then ask, "Stalking, huh?"

He chokes, his eyes going wide as he shakes his head. "No . . . well . . . maybe a little. But for good reason," he forces out as he swallows.

I hold my hand out, giving him the floor to explain himself, and take another bite of pizza. Cole sets his plate on the table and wipes his hands on his jeans, not like they're greasy but like he's nervous. But Cole doesn't get nervous. Or at least not that I've ever seen.

"That morning," he starts, not needing to say which one he's talking about, "I wanted to say yes, that we could talk . . . after. But you'd had all these big life things thrown at you like wrecking balls and I didn't want to be a distraction." He's talking slowly, carefully choosing each word. "I wanted to wait" —he pauses, searching for the right words— "for you to find you again."

I swallow my bite of pizza and give him a tiny hint of a glare. "I found myself in that cabin, partially thanks to you. And then you made me feel disposable. At least with my family, I was expecting it."

Okay, that last bit might be a bit mean, but it's the truth. Cole's rejection hit me out of left field after the amazing morning we'd had, and though I played it off, it hurt . . . a lot.

"Fuck," he hisses, sounding angry with himself. "I'm sorry."

"Get to the stalking. Explain that," I prompt. "How'd you end up across the street from me and I didn't even realize it?"

"That's my job." He shrugs. "I'm good at it." But then he adds, "I saw Kayla and took your advice. Gave her Louisa's name and number so someone would know if I was dead in a ditch. And Kayla said I was different, so I told her . . ." He licks his lips and looks me dead in my eyes. "About you. She said I was a coward for not calling."

I laugh. "She's right."

"She usually is," he admits with a smile that says he's not mad about that. "But I didn't want to interfere . . . no, that's not true." He sighs and scrubs his hands over his face, searching the ceiling like the answers are written there. "I wanted you to do it on your own, wanted you to know you could handle anything because apparently, I'm shitty at making connections and tend to run away from scary things like emotions. Or so I've been told by someone who'd know."

He rolls his eyes, but I can see that whoever said that hurt him. I'm guessing Kayla since it sounds like she's the one who called him out on everything.

It's a lot to think about, so I grab a second slice of pizza and chew thoughtfully as I work my way through everything he's said and done.

"You were really sweet at the cabin and definitely didn't have to step up for the whole wedding thing, especially to the extent you did, so those are points in your favor," I mutter. Cole tries to say something, and I hold a hand up. "Not talking to you. Let me think."

He clacks his mouth shut but then smiles at my not-at-all-silent methods.

"You definitely have the 'if he wanted to, he would' camp in your favor. I don't think you have a back burner," I say, remembering what everyone said about Henry that I finally realized was absolutely true. "You're like a grill, all flames, all the time, with a side of 'get it your way' because you pay attention to stuff like that and go above and beyond." I point to the pizza box as proof. "I thought you'd dumped me, but you didn't. You didn't leave when times got tough. You were supporting at a distance, which is different. But good-different, I think."

"What do you think?" he asks, reaching his limit for patience.

I smile and teasingly ask, "You promise not to stalk me again? Maybe just ask what I'm thinking or feeling instead?" It seems like a reasonable suggestion, but Cole shakes his head.

"How about both? A little stalking—for good reasons only—and I'll do my best to communicate like a human instead of a grunting Neanderthal."

I consider his counter and nod. "Deal. Have you figured out my favorite ice cream place yet?"

"Trick question," Cole responds with a smirk. "You like sangria popsicles from the cart at the park."

He's right, those are the best. "They're so good! Like grown-up Otter Pops," I tell him.

———

Cole

We finish the pizza, and I would take her for popsicles, but the park closes at sunset and the cart guy is long-gone home. But I'm happy—hell, fucking overjoyed—to sit on the couch with Janey and listen to her tell me everything.

She starts with how everyone at work breathed a sigh of relief when she told them about her and Henry, rallying around her to proclaim his assholery. They practically swooned for her when she told them about her wedding date, even teasing her about her fake fiancé after she told them about the Bouquet Battle and ensuing mid-reception proposal. Without even pausing, Janey tells me how her boss, Gabriella, tracked me down.

That segues into how Amanda saw her pacing back and forth outside my building, and she was mortified. Dropping that line, Janey moves on to how worried she is for poor Mrs. Michaelson, who's definitely not long for this world. Then I hear all about the book she's reading and about how the vampiric hero is somewhat like me at times. But before explaining that, she's off and gushing about the adorable kitten she saw on a shelter page.

I listen, cataloging it all. I've missed listening to her talk, her enthusiasm for everything working its way into my blood, making me appreciate all the little things she notices in every day.

"It's getting late," she says hours later. I know she has to be up early. Her alarm goes off at five thirty every morning so she can make it to her seven a.m. shift, so I don't push it. I don't want her driving and working tired. Her safety and her patients' safety are too important.

"I have a question," I blurt out as she walks me to the door.

I should probably think this through, but I don't want or need to. I'm following my gut—or is my heart? I'm not good at differentiating, apparently.

Janey looks at me with bright, trusting eyes, completely unworried about whatever I'm going to say, which is a relief after everything it's taken to get here. Tonight's deep dive into my emotions and thoughts was difficult and unnerving, but I did it. For her.

"Will you go to dinner with me . . . at my parents' house?" I lift my brows doubtfully, knowing it's a big ask. "They're not as bad as yours, no offense, but it's fair to say it won't be a good time. Other than the fact that you'll be with me, of course," I tease, but I'm serious about the warning. "There's one of those mandatory deals happening and I thought—"

"Yes!" she squeals. "Of course! Will I get to meet Kayla? And Samantha? And your mom! I feel like I already know them, like we're besties. Or gonna be, at least. Oh, maybe I'll get to pet Nutbuster, too!"

I chuckle at her enthusiasm. When I got the text that I'm expected at dinner to discuss Chance's upcoming wedding, enthusiasm wasn't my reaction. Annoyance was more like it. But I find myself smiling now. They're going to love Janey, and she'll love them, of course, even the ones who don't deserve it.

"Thank you," I say as I back her into the door until her shoulders are touching it. I trace her jaw with a fingertip, inhaling sharply at the slightest contact. "Fuck, I've missed you."

"Me?" she echoes with a sultry smile.

"You, Janey Williams. I need to taste you, see if you're as sweet as I remember." I take her jaw in both hands, holding her still with every intention of sipping at her gently, teasing us both.

"Oh," she sighs, but my lips are already on hers, so I swallow the breath and lose all control.

I was right, but also wrong. She's sweet, maybe even more so than I thought, but she's also spicy from the jalapeños and her own comfort in her skin. She meets me hungrily, giving as good as she takes, wrapping her arms around my waist and leaning into me.

Fuck her right here against the door, my cock suggests, and on some level, I agree. I want to be buried inside her again, feel the pulsing of her orgasm as she's impaled on my cock, and hear her crying out my name.

But not yet.

We're starting over in a lot of ways. With some history, yes, but still . . . this is different, and better.

This is real in a way I've never been before with anyone.

So I kiss her with everything I have, trying to say all the things I didn't tonight—that she's amazing, that I'm obsessed with her, that nothing scares me but she's fucking terrifying, that I want to listen to her ramble all day, every day because it's so damn quiet and lonely without her.

I hope she hears it all, straight from my lips to hers.

CHAPTER 18
JANEY

I'VE NEVER BEEN to a meet-the-family dinner, especially not when the family is as large as Cole's, so I'm not sure what to expect. But I've seen enough movies to know one thing . . .

"Will your mom show me your baby pictures? Like tiny, naked Cole in the bathtub?" I wonder hopefully. "I bet you were so cute and squishable. Probably with big, chubby cheeks and a twinkle in your little eye. Or were you already grumpy and glaring at everyone?"

I clap my hands happily, imagining a baby Cole with his arms crossed over his chest, an old-soul frown on his face, and a judge-y side eye for anyone who dared get close enough to do something annoying like shake a rattle at him.

His grip on the steering wheel tightens, the leather creaking ominously. "No, I burned them all," he replies brusquely, but I'm at least eighty percent sure he's kidding. Probably.

He has a sense of humor, it's just drier than Death Valley in August. But I'm not going to give up. Not when he's opening up for me and really trying to be more human.

"I bet she'll tell me some stories, though. Maybe the time you scored the winning goal or were named Prom King? That seems like you." I grin, now imagining Cole as a teenager. "You were probably the type that all the girls chased after you. Star athlete, Mr. Popularity, straight-As, and a partridge in a pear tree, right?" I guess.

He chuckles hollowly at my description of him. "You couldn't be more wrong. You know how you wanted your parents to see you, maybe pay some fucking attention for once?" He cuts his eyes to me in the passenger seat of his truck as we speed down the highway.

"Yeah?" That's sadly true. Seeking attention was a delicate balance because I didn't want to be a target, but I did want to be considered, loved, and understood. I just wasn't.

"Well, my goal was to be invisible. Nothing good came out of getting attention in my house. My older brothers—you'll meet them tonight—clamored for Dad's approval, even if they had to stand on each other's necks to get it. Kayla escaped the worst of the mindfuckery and got noticed because she was unique in our dick fest. But me? If Dad forgot I existed, that was for the best. Then, he wouldn't pressure me to be like him because that was the last thing I wanted. Same held true at school. Didn't want teachers calling home, for anything good or bad. So, I shot for high Bs and usually got them. I mostly tried to coast, completely unnoticed, through the middle of everything, everywhere I was."

"Oh." That's awful and it makes me angry for him. "I'm sorry. What about your mom?"

He shrugs, focusing on the road again. "She's great, but she was so busy back then. There's a lot of unwritten rules in a family like ours, social events you're expected to attend and roles you have to uphold. And Mom did it all. She ran from fire to fire, keeping all of us in line, Dad included, while simultaneously fundraising for this and coordinating for that. I didn't want to be a burden, so I stayed out of trouble as far as she knew, and out of the way."

"They don't know you at all, do they?" I realize. "Don't know what a sweet, caring, slightly crazy guy you are?" I sound wistful, but he really is a great man and it's sad he doesn't show them that side of himself.

He shakes his head, but there's a hint of a smile on his lips at the way I'm describing him now. "No, only you know that."

"Lucky me." I sigh dreamily, meaning to keep that reaction inside for a change, but my mouth lets it fly free anyway. Cole grins fully then and reaches over to take my hand, places a gentle kiss to the back of it, and rests them on the console between us.

I do feel genuinely fortunate to know the real Cole and can't imagine how his family has been able to ignore him all these years. I can feel his presence almost before he enters a room, like he's thinking about me so hard that my Spidey senses know it. His intensity, his focus, his care for what he holds dear is a powerful draw, but according to him, his family somehow doesn't even notice it. How can that be?

Minutes later, we're driving down a long street with a tall, wrought iron fence on the right. I'm thinking it's a nature preserve or something with all the trees until Cole turns into a small drive with a gate. There's nobody here, but with a push of a button on his steering wheel, the gate starts opening to admit us.

"That's your house?" I blurt out. That's rude enough, but of course, I keep going with zero filter. "I have no idea what I was expecting, but it sure wasn't *that*. I mean, you mentioned your family has money, but *this*? This isn't wealthy, it's *Richie Rich riiiich*."

As we drive through the gate, I'm looking left and right, craning my neck to see everything. The house is huge, white, with wide stairs going up to the double front door. In the middle of the parking lot out front—yes, I'm calling it a *lot* in my head because once you get past being able to park six or seven cars, calling it a driveway really sounds stupid—is a fountain with a naked guy surrounded by arcing sprays of water.

"It's home," Cole says simply. Now I can see how easily he could be invisible here. He could go off to another wing of the house, and nobody would give it—or him—a second thought.

Money doesn't make the man, of that, I'm sure. But I could compile every penny my whole family's made in the entirety of their life, and we could maybe pay the electric bill one time for a place like this, so though it's 'home' to Cole, it's hard for me to not be intimidated by this much flash.

"Are you sure I'm dressed okay?" I question, smoothing a palm over my skirt. Cole said the dress code is casual, so I chose a silk camisole tank in emerald that goes great with my hair and a long, flowy skirt that makes me feel feminine and not at all schlumpy like my usual scrubs. My outfit isn't the issue, but I might be. Because what I'm really asking is 'am I okay to be here?'

Cole glances my way, reading my reaction in a fraction of a second. Not that I'm hiding it. I know my eyes are wide, my jaw is dropped open, and . . . oops, I'm pointing at the fountain like a tourist in Rome!

"You look gorgeous," Cole assures me, then adds, "also, if shit goes sideways, I fully expect you to have my back like I had yours with Paisley's deal."

I gawk at him in shock, replaying all the ways he superheroed for me, up to and including a fake proposal, and contemplating ways to do that myself. "You want me to propose?" I murmur in confusion.

"I mean you'll have to tell them that I'm an asshole who blackmailed you into coming," he corrects with a sly grin. "I've got a reputation to uphold."

And I'm reminded again that he doesn't let anyone in. Not really.

But he's learning to with me.

"Your secret's safe," I offer, locking my lips and throwing away an imaginary key.

Cole parks, opens my door, and walks me up the front steps. He knocks but then wraps his arm around my waist, squeezing my hip. I look at him quickly, but his face is completely blank—as if he didn't just do that, as if he doesn't know it makes me want him, as if we're not walking into a foreign world I can't imagine. He told Paisley it grounded him. Well, I think he's grounding me right now too because though my heart is racing, I do manage to take a breath.

An older man opens the door, holding it wide for us to enter. He's probably in his sixties, with salt and pepper hair, a friendly smile, and wrinkles that let me know he's spent a fair portion of his life in the sun.

"Hey, Ira. How're you?" Cole asks the man.

They shake hands like old friends, but Cole didn't mention anyone named Ira, so I'm not sure who this man is to him until Cole gestures to me. "Janey, this is Ira. Technically, he's the house manager. Mostly, he kept Mom from calling the police on the daily by helping me sneak in and out safely. Ira, this is Janey. She's the main reason I get into trouble these days." He laughs heartily, and Ira does too, their camaraderie obvious.

"I don't get you into trouble," I start to argue, then concede, "Well, there was that time . . ."

Cole lifts a wry brow my way, and I shut up because he's actually not wrong.

"Nice to meet you, Ira," I tell the smiling man who's looking from Cole to me with glee in his dark eyes.

"You too, Janey." To Cole, he says, "Everyone's in the living room. Need me to unlock the side door just in case?"

Cole huffs a laugh. "Not necessary anymore. But thanks."

Hand in hand, we walk through the marble-tiled foyer and into a living room. I'm holding my breath, expecting Cole's arrival to be some grand entrance. But I'm actually struck by how familiar this feels because we enter the room, and no one reacts in the slightest—until Cole clears his throat.

"Cole! You came," a woman says in surprise. She rushes him, looking delighted as she reaches her arms out to hug him. I'm guessing she's Cole's mother because he hugs her back easily. "And you brought . . . a friend?" she adds a beat later. She obviously didn't expect me, but she didn't expect Cole either, even though he described this as a mandatory family dinner.

"This is Janey. Janey, this is my mom, Miranda."

I hold out a hand, but Miranda apparently hugs everyone because she wraps her arms around my shoulders too, patting me on the back gently. "It's so nice to meet you, Janey," she gushes with a bright smile. She reminds me of a television mom from the '80s—perfectly coiffed blonde hair, smart slacks and summer-weight sweater, designer flats, and a welcoming aura.

"You too," I reply as she releases me.

Next, of course, I meet Kayla. It's obvious who she is because she's nearly identical to Cole, like they're the same person in different fonts—one male, one female. Her hair is long, down her back in loose, beachy waves, her blue eyes are dancing with excitement, and her dress is definitely not casual. She looks like she came straight from the boardroom to dinner in a slim, gray shift dress and patent black stilettos.

"I'm Kayla, and believe it or not, I've heard so much about you," she informs me, though the sly look she's throwing at Cole says differently. I'm guessing their definitions of 'so much' are probably a bit different. "Guess you took my advice and called her?" she boasts.

Cole answers cryptically, "You couldn't be more wrong if you tried."

The stalking situation doesn't seem like polite conversation, nor something Cole would want to share, given his evasive verbal maneuvers, so I jump in with a bright smile and offer, "We reconnected. That's all that matters."

Kayla nods, mostly satisfied. "I'll take it."

Cole points around the room, introducing me to everyone else. "Cameron and his daughter, Gracie. Carter and Luna. Chance and Samantha. And my dad, Charles." I wave to everyone, maybe a little more enthusiastically to Samantha after Cole's story about what she said at her first family dinner. I hope mine's not quite so dramatic, but also, I'd like to be her friend.

"Hi, everyone. Nice to meet you," I say as I look around the room.

Though Miranda is blonde and blue-eyed too, Cole's brothers seem to be carbon copies of their father, with something in their curious and calculating gazes that echoes Charles's perfectly. Gracie is cute from what I can tell, but I can only see the top of her head because she's deeply involved in a video game on an iPad, making sound effects as she destroys something onscreen with what I can guess is some type of blaster. There's Luna and Samantha, side-by-side like besties. The gang's all here, except for . . . Kyle. But Cole said that as much as he usually dips out early, Kyle goes for the late arrival, usually showing up for dessert and a little hellraising.

"Have a seat, dear. Tell us all about you. Maybe there'll be something my daughter doesn't already know," Miranda says kindly, teasing Kayla. The look that passes from one woman to the other is full of love and humor, something I can honestly say I've never experienced with my own mom. A teeny-tiny knife of jealousy stabs my heart.

"No interrogation," Cole grunts, though he does lead us over to a couch where he sits directly beside me, our knees touching and his arm thrown over the back to encase me protectively.

I swear everyone's looking at us like we're exhibits in a zoo, and unconsciously, I sink into Cole's side a bit, which makes him pull me in even more. By the time he's got us situated, we're pressed together, hip to hip, thigh to thigh, knee to knee, and my shoulder is in front of his chest. I'm one half-scoot away from literally being in his lap, which only makes his family gawk more.

But respecting her son's grumpy decree, Miranda redirects the conversation. "Fine, well, we were talking about the wedding. Chance and Samantha are days away from saying 'I do'," she informs me, politely looping me into the family conversation.

I nod and smile at Samantha. "Congratulations."

At the same time, Cole informs her, "Got a plus-one now."

He pats my hip, and I swear I melt quicker than ice on a summer day. But . . .

"Oh, that's okay," I argue. "I'm sure you've already done the seating arrangements and caterer numbers. I wouldn't want to impose or anything, especially with a last-minute addition. I can't imagine how stressed you must be. *Not* that you look stressed," I correct quickly, horrified at my runaway mouth. "You look beautiful. But weddings are . . . a lot."

Cole leans over, and though he's close to my ear, he doesn't whisper. Just loud enough for everyone to hear, he says, "I went with you to your family shindig, which was damn near hell, so you can come to mine and save me from them. Fair's fair." I jerk my eyes to his, glaring at his rudeness, but stop when I see the spark lighting his blue eyes. I even see the tiny lift of the barest smile. He's kidding, both about his family and any wedding tit-for-tat situation between us.

But they don't see that. They see the grumpy asshole and nothing more.

Not catching Cole's humor in the slightest and most definitely misinterpreting his smile, Samantha interjects, "Damn, Cole! Don't snarl at her. You're hard enough to like as it is. Don't make it harder." Then, to me, she adds, "Janey, of course you're welcome. The Vanisher always had a plus-one. We just didn't think he'd use it. We figured we'd be lucky if *he* showed up." She throws shade more skillfully than an umbrella, and with a deadly, fake-innocence smile too.

I like it, but considering her target, I don't like it too. This is going to be complicated.

"I said I'd be there," Cole grumbles.

Given the disbelieving look Chance is shooting him, I suspect Cole says that about a lot of things and then bails at the last second. Likely for work, but I bet it's more often that he wants to avoid peopling and they take that as some type of flakiness or commentary on where they rate with him.

He's as misunderstood here as I am in my own family, but his family is different from mine, and I need to remember that. Mine doesn't want me other than for a convenient target. Cole's family loves him. That much is obvious.

They just don't understand him.

But his mom was visibly thrilled to see him tonight. Kayla encouraged him to call me because she knew it would make him happy, and she wants that for him. Even the brothers whom Cole holds himself apart from are watching me, analyzing whether I'm a good risk or a bad risk for their brother because they care about him. I can't speak about Charles, since he hasn't said a word since we walked in, but one asshole out of a family of seven is a pretty good statistic.

They're not perfect, but no family is. They're made of flawed people who love each other imperfectly. But sometimes, they're worth it, like in Cole's case.

I bet if I can get Cole to the wedding, I can help them all see how amazing he is. Because despite his teasing about wanting to be saved from them, it's obvious how much he cares for his family too. Every story he's told about them has made that abundantly clear. He's proud of them, loves them, and even protects them whether they realize it or not.

"Thank you. I'd love to come," I tell Samantha, putting my plan Cole: Recognize the Awesomeness into play.

That settled, everyone jumps headfirst into discussing the wedding—what they're wearing, where they're supposed to be and at what time, what's expected of everyone, and more. I sit back and watch, channeling Cole's surveillance tips to listen and learn. Surprisingly, they're so interesting, I don't think I ramble aloud a single time.

"Can I see you in my office before dinner, gentlemen?" Charles says mid-wedding conversation.

Cameron hops up like he was expecting the question. Carter and Chance are slower to rise, both giving kisses to their respective brides—Carter on Luna's forehead, and Chance to Samantha's lips, which he then rubs a thumb over with a raised brow. The look that passes between them is hotter than a volcano.

Cole sighs heavily as he squeezes my hand. He doesn't want to leave me, but I'll be fine. It's not like his family is going to behave worse than mine. I'm in no danger of attack, verbal or physical. Or at least I don't think I am, so I smile up at him encouragingly as he stands. Besides, this'll give me a chance to move deeper into phase one of my plan.

"Got your bear spray in your purse?" he teases straight-faced.

"Yep. My aim's dead-on too," I reply with a smile because we both know that's not true in the slightest.

When the guys leave, Miranda stands too. "Gracie-girl, let's go check on dinner. I want to make sure we've got your dinosaur nuggets in the oven."

The child doesn't look up from the iPad, but she must've heard because she robotically stands and somehow follows

Miranda from the room without bumping into a single piece of furniture or wall.

Which leaves me with Luna, Samantha, and Kayla. And given the way they're looking at me, I'm woefully unprepared for this conversation. Maybe I really should've brought my bear spray? If not for protection, I could hand them out like party favors and maybe then they'd like me?

"It's okay, we don't bite," Luna reassures me with a smile that reaches her eyes, which are behind thick, black frames that give her a slightly nerdy vibe.

Samantha scoffs. "Speak for yourself, girl. Chance has teeth marks on his ass as we speak." My eyes shoot open wide in shock, and she adds, "But I only bite him. For the most part. He likes it that way."

Luna swats her arm and scolds, "Don't scare her."

Samantha shrugs, unbothered by the reproach. "Just being honest. Sometimes, you gotta be quiet and the only thing to muffle a cry is your own arm. And a little bitey-bite is perfectly normal and natural behavior that calls back to our primal natures."

"Ladies," Kayla snaps, "we've got limited time before they all get back."

Luna and Samantha understand Kayla perfectly, and all three turn back on me with single-minded focus. They've seemed nice all evening, but Cole's request for no-interrogation went null and void as soon as Miranda left in a quest for the perfect dino nuggie, and we all know it.

"What do you want to know?" I ask, figuring I might as well face this head-on. Cole said his family doesn't really know him, and this is my chance to help with that and show them that he's really a great guy. Mostly.

"Everything," Luna admits on a long exhale. "Start with how you met."

Samantha nods, pointing at Luna like 'yeah, what she said', so I explain the bear spray joke Cole made. "I thought he was a bear at first, so I had protection. But finding a strange man in your cabin in the middle of nowhere was even worse than a grizzly, so I sprayed him. Well, I tried to, but it kinda went *pffft*." I show the arc the spray took, falling to the floor unsuccessfully. "He chased me, my towel fell off so I was butt-ass naked—I know that's not the expression, but that's how I said it as a kid and it stuck, so I always say it like that. Anyway, I ran into the bathroom and locked myself in. He was yelling at me, banging on the door like he was gonna rip it off the hinges because he thought I broke in. Turns out, we were both wrong and there was a mix-up in the bookings. He offered to pay for my vacation if I would let him use the shower every night, which I thought was super generous, so I said we could share the cabin." I tell the whole saga in one breath, the women all hanging on my every word, and finish with a shrug like that's a perfectly normal meet-cute story.

"Did you get all that?" Luna asks out of the side of her mouth, her eyes never leaving me. Kayla nods in answer, and Luna adds, "I feel like I should've recorded all that so I could play it back in slow motion or something."

"You get used to it," I assure her. "Cole likes when I ramble."

Luna fights a smile as she whispers, "I bet. Someone's got to carry the conversational load."

"Huh, you said *load*," Samantha laughs, but almost instantly, she groans, "Oh, God, I'm spending way too much time with twenty-year-old boys, aren't I? That was awful."

"So you're in the cabin together?" Kayla prompts, sticking with her more serious approach of information gathering.

"Yeah, and at no point in there did you think . . . this is a bad idea? Sleeping in a cabin in the 'middle of nowhere', as you said, with a grunting Neanderthal a foot taller and wider than you who'd already shown anger management issues?" Samantha asks, now sounding like she thinks I might be too stupid to live. I suddenly remember that she's a psychologist and is probably analyzing my (lack of) self-preservation skills.

"Of course, I did, but I trusted my gut. I could tell that Cole was sweet and kind, caring, and considerate. I mean, maybe not at first, but there were circumstances there. After that, he slept on the couch, made me coffee, and . . . Oh! You should've seen how gentle he was putting lotion on my back when I got poison ivy." I'm throwing out his good points like I'm narrating his highlight reel, but they don't look like they believe me.

"It rubs the lotion on its skin," Luna says vacantly, and I think it's a quote from an old movie because it doesn't sound like her voice.

"Did he push you into the poison ivy in the first place?" Samantha suggests, and I laugh at the idea of Cole pushing me anywhere.

Maybe to the bed?

Well, yeah . . . that'd be fine. But that's not the kind of shove Samantha means.

"What? Of course not. I was lying in it when we were—" Oops! I stop abruptly. Selling them on Cole's awesomeness doesn't include telling them what he does. He's intentionally kept that secret, and it's his truth to share. So, I can't say we were spying on Mr. Webster. Instead, I continue, "Uhm, watching an owl that flew overhead. I didn't recognize that it was poison ivy when I laid down. I probably still wouldn't, even though Cole told me how many leaves it has. But just between us, if someone held up two pictures of plants and asked me to identify the one that turned my back and hip into scaly patches of hellacious itchiness, I wouldn't have any idea."

"Lying in the forest, watching an owl?" Kayla repeats doubtfully.

"Yep, that's what we were doing," I confirm. It sounds like a lie even to my ears, but given the sparkle in the three women's gazes, they don't suspect we were doing something with Cole's job. They think we were engaging in some 'nature nookie' when I was exposed to the poison ivy. Not wanting to discuss that any more than his work, I rush to add "But Cole helped me up, put calamine lotion on all the areas I couldn't reach, and took great care of me. He even ran an oatmeal bath for me one night."

I look at them expectantly, hoping they can see it now. A jerk wouldn't do that. It's irrefutable proof that Cole's awesome.

"Okay, I'll accept that he was decent in the woods," Kayla offers, with Luna and Samantha nodding along like they concur.

"What happened when you got back? I saw him at the coffee shop and he was in bad shape, giving me his assistant's number in case of emergency and talking non-stop about the someone he met."

"He did?" I can feel the happy hearts bursting out of my eyes at that good news. Cole said as much already, but his version sounded less romantic than the way she's telling it.

"He also told me about your shitty family attacking you over a bouquet. Sorry about that," she says.

"What the fuck?" Samantha mouths, probably trying to imagine something like that at her own wedding and failing because it was seriously crazy.

"Yeah, they're not great," I admit. "But I'm okay. Or I'm getting to be. They're not bad people, but that doesn't mean they're good for me."

"Somebody's been doing their therapy work," Samantha praises with a light golf-style clap. "I don't know your family, but hearing that, can I add . . . it's completely acceptable to cut people out of your life for your own sanity. Fuck knows, I have. Toxic is toxic, and you don't have to keep exposing yourself to radioactive waste because you share a bloodline with it."

She's definitely in psychologist mode, but it sounds pretty personal too. "Thanks. I'm doing better every day. Of course, it helps that no one's called me since the wedding. They're probably waiting on me to apologize, which isn't happening."

It's a reminder to myself, one that I haven't needed as much anymore. I honestly haven't even thought of my family in days, and considering they're probably still gossiping about my audacity at keeping the bouquet, that says something—about us both.

"Yes! Good girl!" Samantha cheers. "Peace doesn't come easy or cheap, but once you let go of the war, knowing it's for the last time, you feel so damn good." She pats her chest with a serene smile I suspect is hard-won given her comment about cutting toxicity out of her life even if it's a blood relative.

Oh, yeah, I'm pretty sure we just became friends. Or maybe she's my new therapist? Either way, or both, I'll take it!

I realize I'm doing a little happy dance, tapping my feet on the floor, when Kayla catches my eye, lifting a perfectly arched brow. I remember she asked a question. "Oh, yeah, when we got back. Well, we didn't leave on the best of terms. He gave me his card with his phone number," I reveal carefully, keeping his business privacy in mind.

As expected, they gasp. "He did not," Luna says.

Samantha and Kayla speak over each other, but it's some version of 'what an idiot', only significantly less polite.

I feel like I'm gossiping with the girls . . . in a good way, like when the nurses all get together at the desk to bitch about admin. I think we're building friendships with every word and I'm so glad.

"I know, right?" I agree, rolling my eyes. "It was boneheaded, but it was for a good reason. Anyway, I've got a friend who's part of the FBI—the female bureau of investigation. She helped me track him down, and I showed up unannounced. He was surprised, to say the least." I laugh, remembering the look on his face, which was more a combination of pissed off and terrified.

"Did he sweep you into his arms and tell you how much he'd missed you?" Luna asks dreamily, picturing a very different type of reunion than what's in the books I read. Or what actually happened.

"Not exactly," I answer, drawling it out dramatically. "We were a mess there for a bit. He freaked, then I freaked. Then he showed up at my house even though I hadn't told him where I lived." I shrug at the absurdity of it all.

Kayla's perfect brows jump up her forehead—both of them this time, Luna's jaw drops open, and Samantha says, "Oh, hell no."

"It was fine. We both kinda went a little overboard. But that's how we are, I guess," I explain. They don't look like they understand at all, so I try again. "You know the saying 'if he wanted to, he would'?" They nod, not sure where I'm going with this and still worried about Cole showing up at my house, which I'll admit would be valid . . . if it wasn't Cole. "Let's just say, Cole *wants* to. After a lifetime of people not wanting me, or only wanting me when it's convenient for them, he's attentive in ways I never even dreamed of and certainly didn't think any man would be. He's . . . sweet, intensely so, and quiet, but he's watchful, taking it all in and seeing things others don't. He sees . . . me." The confession is more meaningful than I expected, but it's undeniably true.

"We've both had some missteps," I admit, "but I have no doubt that his heart's in the right place, and he's always . . . trying to show me he cares. Deeply."

That's not nearly enough to describe how this man who is grumpy, short, and borders on complete assholery to everyone else is beyond kind with me. For me. To me. But I hope it's a start for them to see that maybe what they've always thought isn't actually true. Or at least, it's not anymore.

Cole might've been the kid who snuck out to avoid them all, but I think deep down, he wants to be a part of what his family has become. He's just not sure how to get there now that he's on the outside.

Footsteps in the hallway draw our attention, and we all turn to look, finding the guys returning from their private conversation. Chance looks furious. Actually, they all look angry, so I don't think their talk went well.

Cole comes to my side, moving me so that he's between me and the other women. "Good?" he asks quietly, clearly concerned about me despite whatever just happened with his father.

I smile and nod reassuringly. "Yeah, I was telling them how awesome you are."

He chuckles, deep and low in his belly. "Yeah, right. Waste of breath."

But given the way Kayla's looking at him, like she's seeing him for the first time, I don't think it was.

"Dinner's ready," Charles says.

We move into a formal dining room, which looks far less comfortable than the living room, taking seats around a large rectangular table set with a lineup of silverware on either side of each plate. Now I know why Cole was so comfortable with the place setting at Paisley's wedding. Her fancy-fancy is probably his family's picnic setting.

As talk about the wedding continues, Samantha reminds Grace about how important the role of flower girl is, and I can't help but compare the little girl's happy smile to my sister's brattiness about being a junior bridesmaid. Now that she's put her iPad away, Grace's energetic and cuter than a basketful of kittens. I think I'm gonna like her a lot.

"Don't worry, girl. I got this," Grace tells Samantha, sounding more like fifteen than the nine-ish I think she actually is. "I'll scatter them, not chunk them at people, same as last time." She tilts her head thoughtfully, wrinkling her nose, "Unless someone does something stupid like petting me on the head like a dog or pinching my cheeks and calling me adorable." She makes it sound like that's the worst insult someone could possibly say to her. "In that case, they're definitely gonna catch these hands. And probably a few rose petals up the nose."

"Deal," Samantha approves, laughing good-naturedly. "If someone did that to me, I'd probably kick 'em in the nuts."

"What?" Cameron sputters, checking in for the first time during the whole conversation. "Don't tell her that."

"Self-defense is a necessary skillset for every woman, at every age," she advises him. To Grace, she says, "Protect yourself from anyone who makes you uncomfortable. I don't care who they are. If you don't like it, don't want it, and aren't an emphatic 'yes', they're the ones who're wrong. Not you."

"She's a kid, not dating frat bros on Tinder," Cameron argues.

"Right," Samantha agrees, "and this is when kids learn, so that by the time they get on Tinder, their boundaries are solidified and they know what's acceptable. And what's not."

Grace's not the only one ping-ponging their eyes from Samantha to Cameron as they debate. We're all watching.

"Well, when the school calls because she beat up some boy who was flirting on the playground, I'll tell them you're coming to pick her up." He says it like a threat, or at the least, an annoyance.

Samantha takes it as a golden opportunity. "Please do. I'd be happy to coach them on appropriate interventions, none of which include 'boys will be boys' or excusing bad behavior. And then Gracie and I will get ice cream and discuss outdated expectations and how she can ignore them before I take her to the club and introduce her to our new martial arts teacher for a lesson. Actually, that might be our next girl date. Whatcha say, Gracie?"

I thought I wanted to be Samantha's friend. I think I want to be *her*. She's a beast.

Grace looks excited but cuts her eyes uncertainly to her dad, not sure if she can show her true feelings. Cameron sighs then tells his daughter, "Don't throw the petals. Do the 'drop them down the aisle' thing like you're supposed to." To Samantha, he adds, "Unless that's an outdated expectation you'd like her to ignore?" He goes quiet again. His lips are pressed into a thin line, his back straight and shoulders wide, and his blue eyes are stone cold.

I try to think about what Cole's said about Cameron but can't think of anything other than he's the oldest and the second coming of his dad, which isn't a compliment in Cole's eyes. I can see why he'd say that, though, because Charles is silently lording over the table with the same stern expression.

"Dad, I've done this before. I know how," Grace reassures him, suddenly sounding mature in an entirely different way. I wonder how often she goes back and forth from sassy pre-teen to taking care of her dad's feelings.

"Of course," Cameron agrees, smiling at her warmly, "it'll be perfect."

Slowly, conversation starts up again.

"Bread," Cole says at one point, putting another slice on my plate right as I slip the last bite of the previous one into my mouth. While I'm observing his family, he's watching me, taking in my every expression and move.

"Thanks. This is delicious. Do you know how to make it?" I ask quietly as I chew the sourdough heaven, meaning for it be between us. Cole dips his chin once, saying yes and probably putting it on his to-do list for our next dinner in.

"Cole cooks?" Kayla asks, overhearing me.

I swallow, feeling eyes on me again. The girls especially are watching with interest, but everyone heard Kayla, so I answer aloud. "Yeah, he's great in the kitchen. Thank goodness because my special talent is burning water," I joke truthfully.

"Huh," she says with a slightly puzzled frown. I can almost see her putting new information into an existing puzzle, replacing pieces that have been there for years.

My plan is absolutely, one hundred percent, for sure working! Probably.

CHAPTER 19
COLE

"WHY DO we have to do this again?" Carter complains. He's standing on a pedestal with a woman kneeling at his feet, so you'd think he'd be hunky dory with the situation. He's definitely always been the type to appreciate a bit of hero worship.

Unfortunately, the woman isn't Luna. It's the tailor.

"Be still, please," she mumbles around the pins in her mouth.

Chance sighs and snaps, "Do you have a burgundy suit? Didn't think so. So let the woman do her job and quit being a diva."

Damn. Wedding stress must be getting to Chance because he's the usually the most polite and well-spoken of us all. I can't remember the last time he was this snippy.

Even chastised, Carter still wants to get the last word in. "I'm just saying, we all have black suits. Or gray suits. And they're perfectly fine for a wedding, so I was wondering why we can't wear those?"

"Samantha wants burgundy pants and vests, ivory shirts, and floral ties," Chance says, sounding like he's quoting his bride-to-be.

"And what Samantha wants, Samantha gets," Cameron interjects sardonically.

He's pissy from getting put in his place at dinner a few days ago, but Samantha was right and we all knew it. Fuck, even he knew it! He wouldn't want Gracie getting disrespected and thinking she had to take it, though maybe there should be a step between head-pats and ball-busting? Like a 'don't touch me' scream?

But then I imagine some kid at school pinching Gracie's cheeks—either ones, face or butt—and decide Samantha was right. If that were to happen, they'd be damn lucky for her to show up and not me. Gracie's my ride-or-die. She's all of our ride-or-dies. As in, anyone who hurts her dies.

Cameron's a good father, or he wants to be and tries his best to be. But he's broken inside from the loss of his wife, Gracie's mother, and that alone makes it difficult for him to function, much less function at the level he should. It doesn't help that Gracie is the spitting image of her mom, and though she was small when her mother died, she somehow acts like her too. We all step in to help as much as possible, covering for Cameron when needed and making sure Gracie has all the love we can give her, but it doesn't make up for the loss, and we all know that.

Cameron especially knows that, which I know makes him feel guilty. That of course feeds into his inner demons because he too feels that loss in his own heart, and the whole fucking cycle perpetuates itself. At this point, it might take an angel to shake him free. Or remove the stick from his ass.

"About this? Absolutely," Chance answers Cameron. He points an accusatory finger at Carter. "How many weddings did you even have? How many times did you have us all playing along with your mess? All I'm asking is for you to quit bitching and *put. On. The. Damn. Burgundy. Shit.*"

Well, fuck. I'm impressed. Chance is the best of us, truly. He's self-aware, helps others, makes a difference in the world, and all that jazz. He also rarely curses, so for him to square up to Carter that way and start throwing three-dollar words around, he's furious.

In solidarity, I decide to wear the outfit Samantha wants without comment, floral tie and all. I shoot Kyle a look and find him grinning about the whole situation. He must think all this is fucking hilarious because he doesn't do fancy clothes, serious events, and empty traditions.

He missed that mandatory dinner completely because he likes to do things that'll piss Dad off, and no-showing a family meal basically puts him at number one on Dad's shit list. But since Dad's not coming to the fitting appointments, Kyle was right on time, arriving on his loud motorcycle, wearing dirty jeans and a tank top, with mud on his boots and days' worth of scruff on his face. He said he spent the morning 'working' and when we asked 'on what?', he'd smirked and answered 'Maggie's house.'

My brothers had rolled their eyes and grumbled about him having a latest and greatest woman who'll probably only last the week, and Kyle hadn't denied it. But I secretly keep up with my family, and I know Maggie's House is the dog rescue Kyle volunteers at, usually taking shelter dogs on socialization playdates with his dog, Peanut Butter, but occasionally doing work on their kennel area. Which makes me hope that's actually mud on his boots and not dog shit.

I sniff, not smelling anything foul, so odds are fair to good that it's dirt. This time.

"My turn?" Kyle offers as the tailor finishes measuring Carter. She blushes when Kyle toes off his boots and steps onto her pedestal in his socked feet. "Do your worst . . . or best. Your call," he tells her with a wink, and I swear she blushes even more. Most of the time, Kyle's ninety percent charming bullshit and ten percent serious guy. Every once in a while, that'll switch, but it takes a lot for him to be sincere about anything, and wedding attire isn't enough to warrant it.

While Kyle gets measured, he meets my eyes in the mirror. "A birdie told me you've got a new lady love."

That bird's name is Kayla. She probably filled him in on everything he missed at dinner. I hate that she does that because she's not his fucking secretary and it only enables him to continue to flake on us.

"Yeah." If he wanted more info, he should've been at dinner. I know I'm one to talk—well, okay, not talk, but judge—but I show up at least. I might stay on the outskirts, not share anything, and dip early, but I come for the important shit. Unlike Kyle.

"Luna said Janey's got you wrapped her around her little finger," Carter offers, wiggling his pinkie in the air. "Drawing her baths, cooking her dinner, and playing hero with grand gestures in front of her family." I can almost hear Luna's description in his words, but where Carter makes it sound like I'm a pussy, I'd bet my left nut that Luna made it sound romantic. She's an author, and while she specializes in action graphic novels, she's a lover at heart. And Carter has less than zero room to give me shit because I know Luna has him doing Disney sing-alongs on the regular. Wrapped? Yeah, he is.

Chance chuckles. "To hear Samantha tell it, you're an obsessive asshole who fucked her, bailed, and then stalked her to get her back. She seemed to think a police report and possible restraining order were good ideas."

Kyle's hanging on every word, and I wonder what Kayla's version was, but he doesn't offer any details, only asking, "Which is it?"

With a nonchalant shrug, I admit, "Both."

Laughing, Kyle says, "Sounds about right." But he must move with the laughter because he hisses an instant later and the tailor, who's at his back, winces.

"Sowwy," she says, her mouth full of pins again. I wonder if she's ever swallowed one? It seems like a dangerous way to go about her work, but what do I know? "Almosth done."

"Catch me up. What's she like?" Kyle asks.

"Most importantly, mine," I snap. Kyle can't help it, women flock to him. They always have. Over the years, especially when we were younger, more than a couple of ex-girlfriends asked if I'd hook them up with him after our breakup, which I always declined. As far as I know, when a girl I've dated approached him directly, Kyle told them to fuck off too. But Janey's different and I don't want any misunderstanding.

Kyle holds both hands up, causing the tailor to inhale sharply.

I think she pokes him on purpose this time, but he brushes it off with a glance her way. "No worries, bro. I meant like . . . how'd she get you all . . . *like that?*" He waves his hands in my general direction, indicating my current mood, which isn't all too different from my usual mood.

That's not true.

Normally, I would've wanted to go first for the fittings, get the hell outta dodge, and not fuck with all this brotherly love shit. But here I am, willingly going last and hanging out with my brothers for the better part of the day. The entire day. I can't remember the last time I did that. If I ever did.

I'm quiet for too long, but my brothers are patient fuckers and wait me out until I finally admit, "She's different. She sees good in everything, even me, and it's kinda nice to not think the world is a shithole for a change."

Nobody says anything. Even the tailor freezes. And all eyes are on me.

Fucking annoying people. I should've stuck with my usual—make it short and get gone.

The room bursts into rowdy teasing with everyone talking over each other.

"Hell, that was nearly poetic, man!" Cameron quips.

"She sees good in *you?*" Carter says, making it sound like that's impossible.

"Ah ma gawd," the tailor mutters.

"Wow." Short and simple, to the point . . . that's Chance.

But it's Kyle who responds with the most sincerity, not sounding like he means it any other way than with kindness. "Can't wait to meet her."

I acknowledge Kyle with a grateful nod, ignoring my other brothers' shit-stirring.

After a moment, Chance clears his throat. "Much as I hate to interrupt this love fest, Marvin and Noah are going to be here soon. Can we please not act like *us* in front of them?"

Marvin is Samantha's stepdad, and Noah is her stepbrother. The step-titles are new. Samantha's mom, Susan, and Marvin did a courthouse ceremony about four months ago, and from what I've seen in my research, they're absolutely disgustingly in love. I'm happy for them, especially since it's a second marriage for them both—Susan's first marriage ended in an unexpected and ugly divorce, and Marvin's first wife sadly passed away. They're making the best of a new opportunity at happiness, though, blending their lives and kids—Noah, Samantha, and her younger sister, Olivia—together as delicately as possible.

Nobody argues, so Chance takes that as begrudging agreement on everyone's part. And none too soon because the front door opens, and Marvin and Noah come in just minutes later.

"Hey, everybody! How's it going?" Marvin hollers. He's a big personality, always has a smile on his face, and I don't think he's ever met a stranger. People he doesn't know are merely friends waiting to be made.

Or people waiting to fuck you over, I tell myself automatically. But Marvin doesn't feel that way, and so far in his life, I guess it's worked out for him.

"Marvin!" Chance answers, approaching the man with open arms. They embrace, then Chance hugs Noah too, who's a near clone of his dad minus a few years and plus a few inches of height. "Thanks for coming. Kyle's finishing, then it's Cole's turn, and then you're up."

Noah is part of the wedding party too, which is gonna be huge. Chance is a traditionalist and wants all of his brothers by his side, plus Noah. Samantha's having a matching large group on her side of the aisle—Luna and Kayla, of course, and Olivia, plus her friends, Jaxx and Sara.

"Sounds good," Noah replies, taking a chair to wait his turn.

"While we wait, there's something I want to talk to you about," Marvin tells Chance. But then he looks around the room. "With all of you." He's stone-faced, with a line of worry between his brows.

"What's wrong?" Chance says, instantly on high alert at the unusual expression on Marvin's face.

He doesn't ask about Samantha directly, probably because he saw her this morning, which was only a few hours ago, and he's been texting her all day. But the only people who'll get Marvin to be this serious are his girls—Susan, Samantha, and Olivia.

Marvin's jovial tone has vanished, replaced with a somberness that seems foreign on the man. "We got a call this morning . . . from Glenn."

The only people to react are Chance, because I'm sure Samantha has talked about her father, and me, because of course, I researched Samantha's whole family when she and Chance got engaged. I grit my teeth to hide the gut punch. Chance doesn't bother.

"What the hell does he want?" he demands. Again, for a man who doesn't usually curse, this is a trigger button that could start World War III. Chance will do anything for Samantha, including and not limited to annihilating her dad for her.

"To come walk his baby girl down the aisle." Marvin is doing his level best to keep a stiff upper lip while talking about his wife's ex-husband, but on the inside, I bet there's lava on the verge of eruption.

Glenn and Susan were married for years, but like in too many cases, she carried the weight of their entire world on her shoulders. Glenn took that for granted and started cheating, ultimately leaving his family for his mistress without a glance back. Until now, apparently.

"No." Chance's response leaves no room for interpretation, but he still adds, "Absolutely not. He wasn't invited for a reason, and he's not walking Samantha anywhere."

"I know," Marvin agrees, "but I wanted you to know because Susan's in a tizzy, worrying that he's going to show up." To all of us, he says, "That's where you come in. Historically, one of the roles groomsmen played was that of protector. If Glenn comes, we all need to be ready. I don't want anything to ruin Samantha's day."

For having such a shit father, Samantha lucked out in the stepfather department.

"Of course," Chance vows, then looks around the room, making sure we're on board with the plan.

"Want me to go preemptive? Find him, kill him, keep him

away from Samantha forever? Glenn Redding, right?" I question like I don't already have a file on the man.

I know where he lives and works, where he banks, his secret Tinder profile account, his new wife's name and what days she fucks around with her trainer, and more. I could blow his life up in under a minute from where I'm sitting and be out clean. Or if I needed to, I could find him tonight for a more hands-on approach. It's just a matter of travel time.

Realizing my brothers are looking at me strangely, I laugh like I'm kidding even though I'm dead serious. Chance is my brother, and though we might not have the best relationship, I'll go to the mat for him, and by default, Samantha. But they already half-wonder whether I'm a hitman, so they're probably taking my offer as genuine.

Which, this time, it is.

"I don't think that's necessary," Marvin answers me, though Chance looks like he may be considering it. "Susan's talking to Samantha today, letting her know gently, but I want everyone on the same page."

"Page one through epilogue, keep Samantha out of prison," Chance says.

Honestly, he's probably right. If Glenn shows up, it won't be us protecting Samantha from him. It'll be the other way around. Samantha can probably hurt her dad in much more creative ways than I could. Most of them might even be legal.

We finish our fittings, and as planned, I stand still and don't say a word, not even about the floral socks that go with the tie. As we're heading out the door, I corner Chance.

"Let me know if you need anything. Just between us." I give him a pointed look, and though his jaw is set tight with frustration, he nods.

"Thanks." He holds his hand out, and I shake it firmly, a vow agreed upon between us with no words needed.

We might not be close, but when push comes to shove, I've got his back, whatever that entails.

CHAPTER 20
JANEY

"YOU'RE GOOD TO DRIVE YOURSELF?" Cole confirms, though I've said as much the three previous times he's asked.

It's cute. He came over this morning with coffee, muffins, and reassurances that Chance's wedding will be nothing like Paisley's. I have no doubt that's true, but Cole seems concerned I'm going to bail on him like Paisley's drama has contaminated weddings forever for me. Little does he know, I'm excited about today. Another wedding with him, with his family? I can't wait.

He's leaned back on my kitchen counter, one ankle crossed over the other, arms crossed over his chest, and a worried frown on his lips.

I step in front of him, pressing my body against his and placing a kiss to his lips, hoping to turn that frown upside down. "I'm a big girl. I can go to a wedding by myself. You have things to do with Chance before the ceremony, and that's totally fine. I'll meet you at the reception."

In answer, he wraps his arms around me, hauling me up to my tippy toes to claim my mouth in a kiss full of promises. We haven't had sex again since reconnecting, and I'm tempted to leap onto him like a spider monkey, wrap my legs around him, and impale myself with the hardness I can feel behind his zipper. I'm ready, so ready, even thinking he was going to strip me down by my front door after our pizza date when we talked things through. But he didn't then, and he doesn't now, making no move to take us any further than where we are and what we're doing, which is admittedly great.

He kisses the stuffing out of me as his hands trace over my curves, cupping and squeezing and branding me with his touch to the point it feels like he's exploring my soul.

I'm hopeful, moaning at the feel of him sandwiched between us, and though I've had a grip on his shirt, I release it to slide my hands under the fabric. When I touch his skin, rediscovering his tight abs, Cole groans. So, I touch him more, running my short nails up to his chest and down to the trail of hair that disappears into his jeans.

He shudders beneath my touch. I, Janey Williams, make this man, Cole Harrington, quiver with only my hands. I feel powerful, I feel sexy, I feel . . . horny! I start to undo the button at his waist, ready to take what I want.

"Fuck," he groans. "Wait . . . stop . . . stop."

I freeze in shock. "What?" I whisper, hoping I heard him wrong. Maybe he's talking to himself? Telling his dick to wait and trying to stop himself from coming too soon? I certainly can't judge a man for talking to himself, given my personal verbal habits.

He wraps his hand over mine, not removing it but holding me still with my palm pressed over the thick ridge in his jeans. "Not yet. I want to take my time with you, not fuck you and then rush out."

That's sweet and all, but . . .

"Quickie?" I ask hopefully and feel him jump behind my hand. At least one part of Cole is very on board with the idea.

"I'm not a quickie guy," he says, tilting my chin up with a finger. "Not with you, Janey."

I want to pout, but that he feels like there's something special between us makes my heart sing too.

"Tonight? Can you wait?" he murmurs against my ear, nuzzling the sensitive flesh there with his nose and then nipping my earlobe with his teeth. "If you can't, I'll take care of you and leave with your taste on my tongue and fingers. Do you need that?"

I hear what he's promising. It's not sex. He'll give me pleasure, probably leaving me sticky and blissfully exhausted from orgasms, but not let himself come. He doesn't have time, not if he wants to get to his brother when he's supposed to, and he needs to do that. It's important for them to see the efforts he makes for them.

I want to say yes. Touching myself to thoughts of Cole over the last few days is nothing compared to the way Cole works my body. But selfishness isn't who I am.

"If you can wait, I can wait," I answer, trying to convince myself to believe my own words. But I can hear the quaver in my voice as I do so.

Cole smiles, his thumb tracing my puffy lower lip. "Now who's grumpy?" he teases, but he sounds as disappointed by waiting as I am. He kisses me again, but this time it's gentle and soft, not to build the heat we're both trying to tamp down. It's an apology and a promise. A to-be-continued.

His phone dings with an alarm, interrupting even our small kisses, and I know I made the right decision. He has to go, but he takes the time to press his forehead to mine. "Text me when you get there?"

I smile. "I'll be fine. I can handle . . ." I stop when he gives me a pointed look and joke, "Or you could put an AirTag on me if you'd rather?"

"Don't tempt me, woman."

Okay, so that should probably be worrisome. Samantha the Therapist would counsel me to run for the hills from the stalkery guy. So why does Cole's obsessive nature feel romantic to me? I'm probably unwell, and it's likely from my childhood trauma, but whatever it is, I don't care when he looks at me like I'm his whole world.

And it's not like I haven't already considered that he's going to leave for a job and I won't know where he is and had my own freak-out about it.

"I'll text you," I vow.

———

Cole

Leaving Janey this morning without sinking into her is the hardest thing I've ever had to do. I couldn't even adjust myself in my jeans without fear of shooting off like a firework. But I have to meet my brothers.

Today is one of the most important days of Chance's life, and I'm going to stand by his side in solidarity. Though I would never tell her as much—because *words* and *people*—Samantha is too good for my brother. Not because he's a bad guy. He's great, actually, but Samantha's in a league of her own and Chance couldn't have found a better partner to create a little chaos in his rigid, planned to the nth degree, scheduled life.

As evidenced by where Samantha chose to have the wedding.

Years ago, Chance started a club of sorts. It's part mentorship, part gym, part self-improvement, and all his pride and joy. Called the Gentlemen's Club, it was an entire dick fest until Samantha came along and started teaching classes about dating, relationships, sex, and more to the members. Now, the two of them spend nearly every waking moment inside the club's walls, so you'd think they'd want somewhere else—*anywhere else*—for their wedding.

Hell, with Chance bankrolling it or Mom and Dad pitching in, the wedding could be at the Ritz-Carlton if Samantha requested it. But no. She wants to say their vows in the place that's most important to them—the club. Chance did hire both a wedding coordinator and a designer to turn the indoor gym into a reception space and the outdoor ball court into a ceremony space, but it's never going to be as fancy as a regular wedding venue. But that's not what matters to Chance and Samantha, and I'm glad. To me, it shows that though they're so diametrically different on the surface, underneath all the trappings, they value the same things.

I park in the empty lot next door—a purchase Chance recently invested in for possible future expansion of the club— noting the cars and trucks already here. Looks like I'm the last Harrington to arrive, so it's a good thing I didn't stay at Janey's. Even if I really would've liked to.

I walk through the big double doors, glancing up at the fancy, gold, lion's head sculpture above them. Chance might be practical and a bit stuffy, but he knows how to represent, and the lion is the club's mascot of sorts.

"Hello?" I bellow. "Where are you all?"

"Cole? Back here," Chance shouts. I follow his voice, passing by a team of people who are in the finishing stages of decorating. It looks good to me, with flowers, lights, and dozens of round tables already set for dinner.

Down the hall, I find the guys in what I'm guessing is a classroom, given the stacks of chairs on one wall. It appears they're getting ready . . . with glasses of amber liquid in their hands. Chance passes me one as a greeting and then lifts his in the air.

"Guys, I want to tell you how much your being here means to me," he starts, already sounding emotional for this early in the day's activities. "I wasn't sure we'd get to this point. You know how Samantha is."

We chuckle good-naturedly, remembering the time we all got together like this to discuss their relationship and Chance had confessed to being desperately in love with Samantha but unable to tell her because she's a track star-certified runner from anything resembling love, relationships, and commitment. Well, she was. I think now, instead of running away, she'd run straight to Chance in any situation. Even if he fucked up, she would chase him to kick his ass, not kick him to the curb.

"But here we are, and I'm thankful for each and every one of you." Chance clinks his glass to mine and then works his way around the room until he's saluted us all.

"To Chance and Samantha," Dad says, and we echo the toast before all swallowing our shot in one go. Chance must've sprung for the good stuff because the whiskey is smooth as silk and warms my belly.

Time flies as we get ready, and before I know it, it's almost go time and my phone is dinging in my back pocket. When I check it, I find a text from Janey. She's here. I smile, pleased she actually texted me and didn't blow it off like I'm overbearing.

"Hey, Chance, I'm gonna grab Janey. Be right back." He nods, in the midst of posing for some staged photos of his socks and cufflinks.

Is that a thing? Pictures of wedding day socks? Who'd want that and why? I'm not sure, but at least it gives me the moment to sneak away.

I exit a side door, walking around the building so I don't have to fight my way through the arriving guests, and into the lot. Janey's bright yellow car is easy to spot, her red hair even more so.

I creep up behind her and wrap my arms around her waist. She squeals and wiggles wildly before realizing its me. "Hey," I growl in her ear as I let her feet back to the ground, making sure she's steady in her heels before releasing her.

She whirls, fire in her eyes and a smile on her face. "What are you doing out here? You scared me!"

"I have that effect," I agree solemnly, and she laughs. "I wanted to escort you in and make sure you're settled."

She beams like the simple gesture means so much. To her, it does. To me, it's the least I can do since I invited her as my plus-one but will be standing up for the ceremony.

"You look beautiful."

She's wearing the same gray satin wrap dress that she wore to Paisley's wedding, which was gorgeous on her then, but now that I know how easy it is to undo one little tie and gain access to her whole body . . . it's fucking stunning.

"You too," she says, looking me up and down.

"It's pink. And floral," I complain. But I don't really mean it. I don't give a rat's ass about what I wear as long as it's functional. And today, the function is 'don't piss off Samantha' and so far, this is working.

"You make it look manly and sexy," Janey growls, mimicking me except for the excessively pouty face. "But I do think I prefer you in jeans and bare feet . . . or nothing at all." Her gray eyes sparkle as she bats her lashes at me.

I groan, counting down the hours until we can get the hell out of here and go back to Janey's. Or my place. Or the closest hotel. Or anywhere we don't have to leave for the next three to four business days.

She laughs and pats my chest. "Come on. The sooner this starts, the sooner it'll be over."

I swear she's reading my mind.

We weave through the lot toward the door, but I stop when I see a man and a woman getting out of a car off to the left. "Shit."

"What's wrong?" Janey asks, automatically freezing at my side.

I step in front of her, explaining quickly. "That's Glenn, Samantha's dad, and Ashley, his mistress-turned-wife. They can't be here."

Her eyes narrow, immediately with me. "What do you want me to do?"

I'm sure that if I asked, Janey would jump on someone's back like an overhyped labradoodle and use her non-karate moves in an attempt to fight them. But I need more substantial backup to prevent a bigger problem. I consider sending Janey, but I know where the guys are. She might get lost in the maze of hallways or throngs of people. "Stall them. Be right back."

I give her a pointed look, and she nods, so I bolt for the side door I came through moments ago. Inside, I poke my head into the ready room, keeping my voice low so I don't get everyone's attention. I only need one person. "Kyle."

He looks up and must see something in my face because he immediately sets his drink down, already heading my way. Once clear of other ears, he asks, "What's up?"

"Glenn."

It's all I have to say for Kyle to be ready. There's a reason I grabbed him and not one of my other brothers, who are more the polished, use your words types. Kyle? If he can't charm you into doing what he wants, he has no qualms about punching you until you make the right decision. I hope it doesn't come to that, but if it does? He's who I want at my side.

We speed walk outside, breaking into a jog around the building as soon as we're clear. "There," I tell him, jerking my chin toward Glenn.

Janey is kneeling down, her purse contents scattered everywhere, and Ashley's attempting to help stuff it all back into Janey's tiny clutch. But Janey's delaying her with every item she picks up.

"Sorry! I'm such a klutz! I've got it all, except for what I need. Band-Aid? Got it. Tampon? Yep. Breath mint? Two flavors. These peppermint ones are the best because they double as a fix for an upset tummy," she rambles, putting her skills to good use as she holds up a red Altoids tin. "I'm always prepared. For anything. Like a Girl Scout. Or is that the Boy Scout motto? I can't remember. But if you slice your finger open, I'm your girl. Cool, calm, collected, and could probably whip up some butterfly stitches in a pinch if necessary. But a safety pin to keep from flashing the whole wedding party? Nope. Apparently not."

She meets Ashley's eyes with a self-deprecating smile, and I wonder what in the world she said to get them to stop. Then I realize she's holding her skirt together. She didn't use a pin for the dress last time and doesn't need one today, either, but it's a great cover, keeping them out here long enough for me to get back with Kyle.

We step up, and Janey switches gears, quickly and easily shoving everything into her purse now that she doesn't need to stall them any longer. She flashes me a smile, proud of herself. I give her a tiny nod of appreciation, keeping my mean face on as she steps out of the way.

I square up to Glenn, giving him a withering glare. "Leave now," I order. "You're not welcome here."

This isn't a negotiation or conversation. It's a declaration, of peace if he chooses wisely, or war if he chooses unwisely.

He blusters, used to being the one to give commands, not

take them. "I don't know who you think you are, but I'm the father of the bride. Now, if you'll excuse me."

He tries to push past me, bumping my shoulder like he's the threat here, but I don't move an inch. Kyle steps up to my side, creating a united front.

"I know who you are. You're a sperm donor who bailed on your family for new pussy, and Samantha doesn't want you here," I tell him, low and harsh. "That's why you weren't invited."

I'm not holding back.

I've worked cases with some real assholes—guys who've taken out loans in their wife's name, hid money, hid children, cleaned out retirement funds so they couldn't be split in the divorce, and more. But Glenn is worse than most. Because he hurt my family. Samantha's been part of my family for months now, ever since Chance fell in love with her. Today only makes it official.

And this man left Samantha penniless, full of distrust, and traumatized while Susan was working her ass off to pay bills and fighting to keep her family together, and Olivia was hurt and angrily lashing out.

Yeah, I know exactly who he is.

"I'm going in there and walking my daughter down the aisle. I raised her, so I earned that right."

"You didn't earn shit," I spit. "You're not a father."

He rears back, blatantly telegraphing that he's going to throw a punch, and I don't do a thing to stop it. I want him to hit me. Once.

The impact is pretty solid for a man his age and condition, but it glances off my cheekbone, right below my eye. There's a roar in my ears, but distantly, I hear Janey gasp, and I glance over to make sure she's not close to the action.

Then Kyle does what Kyle does best.

He throws a solid uppercut to Glenn's gut, folding him in half. I expect him to stay down, but Glenn comes back with another punch of his own. He's giving it his all, but he's fighting in slow motion, trying to take on two guys half his age. Not that we're pummeling him. We want him gone, not *gone*.

So we stop when he holds up a hand in surrender, bent over with the other hand propping him up on his knee. "Tell her I'm here. She'll want me here."

He's delusional, utterly delusional if he thinks telling Samantha that he's here will be good for him. Has he met his daughter? She'll march out here in her wedding dress, beat the hell out of him herself, and spit out some things that'll have him rocking like a baby in therapy for the rest of his life.

And I'd happily stand back and watch her do it, except today's her wedding day, and this shit stain isn't going to mess that up for her.

"She doesn't want you. Doesn't think of you. Doesn't care enough about you to hate you," Kyle snarls, doing a good job on his own of giving the man a dose of Samantha-truths.

"But—" he stammers, catching his breath enough to stand straight again.

"Fine. You don't like his way?" I ask, jerking my chin toward Kyle. "Let's try my way, Mike *Glenndale*," I say grimly, using his fake name from Tinder. He flinches instantly, and I know I've found a weak point. "Address? 360 Boxwood Lane. Bank account? 25674320." I spare a glance at Ashley, seeing the unease in her eyes. Glenn sees it too.

"Who the fuck are you?" he sputters.

"Samantha's family. Now leave. Or would you like to discuss your recent '*business trip*' to Ohio?"

"What's he talking about, Glenn?" Ashley demands, her voice shrill and accusing, especially for a woman who slept with someone else's husband and then married him. If there's one thing I've learned in my business, it's *if they'll do it with you, they'll do it to you*, and Ashley'd be wise to listen to that particular advice.

But either Glenn's had enough or he really doesn't want to discuss Ohio. "Fine. Just tell her—"

Kyle interrupts him. "Nothing. We're not telling her a damn thing. You fucked around on your family, sounds like you're fucking around on this one too, and if you don't want to enter the find-out phase, you should go." He curls his hands into fists, the knuckles cracking with the movement.

Glenn takes one last stab at dominance, pointing a finger at Kyle. "I'm calling the police on you for assault."

Kyle laughs in his face as he knocks his hand away. "You think this place doesn't have cameras? Video and audio that'll show you trespassing on private property, punching my brother first, and then getting your ass whooped to keep you from crashing a wedding you weren't invited to? Yeah, see how that works out. Maybe we'll press charges too. You want a restraining order filed against you by your own daughter?"

I don't know if Samantha would actually do that, but it seems to be threat enough to finally get Glenn to see reality. This isn't happening. He's not getting in. He's not getting near Samantha, Susan, or Olivia ever again. Not on my watch. Not on my family's watch.

Knowing he's beat, Glenn grabs Ashley's hand and nearly drags her back across the lot toward their car. As they go, I can hear her asking, "What happened in Ohio?"

Serves him right.

My first priority is Janey, and I turn to her, doing a quick scan. She looks okay, uninjured and not mad at least, but there's an odd look in her eyes. "That was sexy," she whispers. "I did my best stalling them, but that was . . . wow." She sighs dreamily, and I wish I could speed the clock up and make it tonight already because I want her making that sound while full of my cock.

"You must be Janey?" Kyle says from behind me.

Janey leans to the side to peek around me. "Yep, and you must be Kyle. Nice to finally meet you. I hoped to meet everyone at dinner the other day, but you weren't there. Cole said you might not be since you like pissing your dad off. But I knew who you were like that," she says, snapping her fingers, "even though you're not a copy/paste like the other guys, because Cole wouldn't have just anybody at his side for something like that."

She points in the direction where Glenn disappeared. "It'd have to be someone he trusts. So . . . yeah, nice to meet you."

Kyle chuckles. "I get it already. I see why this works. You, zero words. Her, all the words. Am I right?"

I glare at him, not answering, but I guess that's answer in and of itself. Still, to be sure, I add, "Fuck off."

"Hey, let me check your face," Janey tells me. She lifts up on her toes, pressing gentle fingertips to my eye socket and peering into my eye as she tells me to look left, right, up, and down. "It's gonna be tender and it's gonna bruise because it's already a bit red, but it's not broken or anything."

I take her hand, placing a kiss to the middle of her palm. "I'm fine. And thanks for not stepping in like I did with Paisley's fight."

Her eyes widen. "You're right! Weddings are supposed to be all lovey-dovey and romantic, so why do we keep getting into fights at them? Is it us? Are we the problem?" She's joking, but I tilt my head like I'm considering it.

"Have you considered that it's just *him*?" Kyle suggests, gesturing at me. I throw him a dirty look, and he shrugs, unconcerned. "We need to get back."

"Yeah, let me walk Janey in and I'll meet you."

But Janey shakes her head. "I'm fine. Go, be with your brothers."

She's amazing. After all she witnessed, she's smiling and taking it all in stride, ready to celebrate Chance and Samantha. I press a quick kiss to her cheek and then turn to Kyle. We take off at a jog, heading to the side door. Kyle talks out of the side of his mouth as we go. "We gonna talk about that?"

Telling Glenn's secrets also highlighted some of mine. Most people don't know shit like that about others, so I know Kyle's questioning how accurate their guesses about my job might be.

"No."

He laughs. "Didn't think so."

Inside, the wedding coordinator seems flustered. Spying us, she whisper-yells, "There you are! Get in line!"

"Yes, ma'am," Kyle answers with a grin, and instantly, she responds with a smile of her own.

I don't know how he does it. I could fucking recite poetry and women would run for the hills. But Kyle flashes one smile and has them melting at his feet.

Janey doesn't seem to mind your lack of a way with words.

Thank fuck.

CHAPTER 21
JANEY

I WALK through double doors of some sort of club-slash-gym only to find that it's been turned into a fairytale inside. The first thing I see is a reception desk that has gorgeous photos of Chance and Samantha in every size. I pause to look at them, oohing and ahhing probably way too much over the cuter ones, then hurry inside as a woman dressed in all black invites us to find our seats.

I follow the other straggling guests down a hallway and out another door, finding myself in a courtyard of sorts. Literally, I guess, because there are basketball hoops on either end, but they've been reimagined as part of the décor with chandeliers replacing the nets and white tulle draped from one to the other, creating a canopy over the rows of gold chairs. The court itself has been covered with glossy white tiles, and one sideline has an archway for the couple to stand beneath for the ceremony.

It's creative, it's beautiful, and apparently, it's go-time because the woman in black is looking over the audience expectantly.

"Is this seat taken?" I ask a woman seated on the groom's side. When she smiles and says 'it is now', I feel welcome and know I made the right choice to come with Cole. Not that there was ever any doubt. I wouldn't want to be anywhere else today, especially not after seeing Cole in action with Samantha's dad.

I'm not a person who appreciates violence. I don't want to watch UFC fights with guys beating each other bloody, and I don't like posturing guys who throw punches over presumed slights like cutting you off in traffic. But I don't blame Kyle for defending his family.

And I certainly appreciate the smart, slick way Cole did it without lifting a fist. He would've, and I know that. But he didn't have to.

I wish Cole's family knew the lengths he would go to for them, the things he'd do for them. Maybe then they'd see who he is. Kyle got a peek tonight, so that's something. I hope he compares notes with Kayla because she seemed to see Cole differently at dinner.

The soft music changes, garnering everyone's attention.

An older man in a black suit escorts a woman in a mauve dress down the aisle. They sit up front on Chance's side, so they must be Cole's grandparents. Then Charles and Miranda walk in, arm in arm, to sit.

I notice that the front row on Samantha's side where family would usually sit is nearly empty, only occupied by one man, and that breaks my heart for her, especially after what I saw in the parking lot. But despite her lack of family, she's surrounded by people who love her.

That resonates with me, given my own family. I still haven't spoken to them, and maybe that should make me feel abandoned and alone. In the past, it would've. But honestly, I've felt lonely with them for a long time, and being without their constant nitpicking, gaslighting, and insults has felt . . . good. I'm happier without them, which is sad, but the truth. And like Samantha, maybe I can find a circle of people who love me too. A family of a different sort. Starting with Cole.

An officiant walks in, taking his place beneath the archway. He's followed by the groomsmen, who're led by a tall, skinny younger man who looks nothing like the Harringtons, and then all the brothers—Cole, Kyle, Cameron, and Carter, who seems to be the best man.

Cole looks handsome, despite his mild complaints about the

burgundy—not pink!—suit and floral tie. It's expertly tailored, the pants showing off his butt as he walks past. When he gets to his place beneath the large arch, his eyes sweep over the crowd.

At first, I think he's making sure Glenn didn't sneak in after all, but then he finds me and he smiles, and a happy little tingle starts in my tummy as I wiggle in my seat.

He was looking for me!

I love that he does things like that, and coming out to escort me in, and so much more. He makes me feel important and cherished, something I've never felt in a relationship. Or in life, honestly.

The bridesmaids are next—a brunette, a woman with pitch black hair and severe eyeliner, a teenager, and then Kayla and Luna. Last but certainly not least, Grace slow steps down the aisle, dropping petals precisely. As she passes, I can hear her talking to herself, "Drop, don't throw. Drop, don't throw."

I laugh to myself, sensing a kindred spirit.

The music changes again, and at the officiant's gesture, we stand.

The doors at the back of the club open again, and we get our first look at the bride. She's walking with her mother, who looks like she's been crying. But Samantha looks clear-eyed and excited as she walks down the aisle in her white gown, which is architectural and modern, with a folded portrait collar that wraps around her arms, leaving her shoulders bare, and a long, column skirt. As she walks, I think I see blue Converse sneakers peeking out from underneath.

Her mom pecks her cheek, then sits with the man in the front row as Samantha takes Chance's hand. They look into each other's eyes like they're the only two people in the room, and Chance mouths something. Though I can't read his lips from here, Samantha smiles softly, so I feel like it was something romantic.

"Please be seated," the officiant says. "For those of you who don't know me, I'm Evan White, Chance's best friend and business partner. And no one was more surprised than I was when he asked me to officiate his wedding. Usually, he's stealing the mic from me at every opportunity." He pauses for the answering chuckle. He's clearly a slick public speaker. "But I promised to stick to Chance's script, so he's trusting me." Evan lifts his brows, silently joking that it was a stupid choice on Chance's part.

But contrary to the taunt, Evan does a great job. The ceremony is personal, with what seem to be private jokes between the bride and groom, along with some highlights of their love story. At one point, Evan steps off to the side, turning his microphone off, and Samantha and Chance say their vows quietly, to each other alone, which feels meaningful and intimate.

I may not know them well, but even I can tell the ceremony is uniquely theirs, with the romance and love shining brightly between Chance and Samantha for all to see. I tear up a little, and the woman next to me hands me a tissue. "Thanks," I whisper.

Though he's doing his job as groomsman, Cole's attention has drifted to me time after time. I feel his eyes now and see that he's frowning, watching me closely and concerned about my crying. I smile back to reassure him that I'm fine, just a happily blubbering mess over the sparkle of someone else's love.

Evan pronounces them husband and wife, but before he can invite them to celebrate with a kiss, Chance is already sweeping Samantha into his arms and kissing her. It's no chaste, polite, public kiss either, but rather a bold declaration of their passion and love, and I smile and dab at my eyes again.

They finish off by walking down the aisle hand in hand, with matching brilliant smiles on their faces. The wedding party is next, Cole escorting the bridesmaid with pitch black hair and eyeliner. He's completely polite, but there's a tiny part of me who doesn't like her hand on Cole, even if it's simply resting on his forearm, both of them making the minimum necessary contact for the role.

I'm such a weirdo! I'm not a jealous woman, especially when there's zero reason to be, but I also want to shout 'mine!' like a toddler. Which is silly.

As he passes by my aisle, he looks my way and I force a smile to my lips.

Don't be weird, Janey! Don't go stage-five clinger over something that's perfectly innocent.

The rest of recessional walks down the aisle and through the doors into the building. As Grace goes in, we hear her loud sigh and exasperation as she says, "See, Dad? I told you I could do it! I ate that! Like no crumbs, dead-ass."

Giggles and chuckles erupt at her prideful adorableness, even with the language, and then slowly, we rise to go inside too, following the wedding coordinator's invitation to proceed to the reception area.

I don't make it that far because halfway down the hall, a door opens and Cole snatches my hand, pulling me into an empty room. "Whoa!" I squeal in surprise as he shuts the door behind me.

Pinned against the door with Cole caging me in, a hand on either side of my head, I look up at him. His eyes are dark, his jaw tense, and his nostrils flaring slightly with his jagged breathing. "You okay?" he demands, his voice husky.

"Yeah," I answer in confusion, not sure what's brought on this level of intensity.

He runs a thumb over my cheek and places a gentle kiss there, just below my eye. Then he does the same to the other side. "You were crying."

"Happy tears," I explain. "You can tell how much Chance and Samantha love each other."

His brow furrows. "You looked mad when we were walking out."

"No, I smiled at you. You look handsome," I argue. Both are true statements, but he's not wrong. I was . . . mad-ish. Angry-adjacent. Irritated by proxy.

"You smiled with your mouth, but not your eyes," he counters. "Don't hide from me. What's wrong?"

That's a harder confession to make because it's a lot more dangerous. "I didn't like . . . I mean, not that I have any right . . .

but—" I stammer, not sure how to explain that I had a momentary fit of jealousy for no good reason.

"Tell me. Whatever it is, I'll fix it."

He would. I could probably say anything, and Cole would do his best to repair or change whatever's upset me without making me feel stupid.

Or needy, my heart shouts.

"She was touching you," I confess quietly, embarrassed at my own overreaction.

I watch a smile bloom across his lips in slow motion, reaching his blue eyes and making them sparkle. "You're jealous?"

He sounds incredulous. Like he has no idea how sexy he is, how amazing he is, and how much I want him. He's teaching me what a relationship should be like, and like a greedy girl, I want more of it. I've never had anything that was mine. My whole life, I've had to share, had to make do with less, and was given scraps —of time, attention, and love.

But not with Cole. I want him, all of him, all the time, all mine.

Okay, my weirdo flag is starting to rise higher on the flagpole. But I can't help it. Cole's different from anyone I've ever known.

My face falls as his smile grows. He's laughing at me, and I feel stupid after all.

"Janey," he murmurs, forcing my chin up until I meet his eyes. And I see something other than pity or humor there. I see heat and hunger. I see fire and passion. I see . . . something I'm too scared to label because it's only been a few weeks, but I feel it too. "If you knew the things I'd do to keep you, you wouldn't worry about anyone else. You'd worry about *me*."

Okay, that should probably be worrisome. But it's not. At all.

He likes that I didn't want that woman touching him. He likes that I'm a jealous, greedy girl for him. Are we both weirdos? For each other?

Probably. Because when he kisses me, sipping at my lips like he's claiming them all over again, I feel like no one else exists. There's no need to worry or feel jealous because there's only us.

"Let's go home," Cole rumbles against my mouth. "I want to show you that you're the only one who matters."

I can feel what he's talking about—in the heat from this morning that's sprung back to life between us with only a kiss, in the thick, hard ridge pressed against my stomach, and in the achiness deep in my own core that only he can fix.

But I'm not the only person who matters. He has a whole family on the other side of this door that wants and needs him. They want him to be a part of this special event, and though he'd probably deny it, he wants that too.

It's hard, but I shake my head, knowing it's the right thing to do. "Tonight," I remind us both. "First, let's celebrate Chance and Samantha."

He groans like he knows I'm right but is no more eager than I am to admit it. "Hate that fucker."

But there's no hatred in the statement. In fact, he sounds pretty fond of his brother.

Cole adjusts himself in his slacks while I straighten my dress, and hand-in-hand, we rejoin the party.

———

The reception is gorgeous!

The round tables are set with gold chargers, gold-rimmed plates, and gold silverware, all centered around a grouping of flowers, greenery, and brass candlesticks holding burgundy candles. There's a wall of greenery with a neon light that says *Harrington* and a dance floor with black and white checkerboard flooring. The lighting is soft and romantic, especially with the lit candles on every table.

Cole leads me through the tables until we find one with some of the other wedding party members. He pulls a chair out for me next to Kayla, and after I sit, he pushes me in before sitting down on my other side. Around the table are Carter, Luna, Kyle, Kayla, and Cameron. It looks like Grace has claimed the last chair, but she's nowhere in sight right now.

"Thought you left already," Carter says, a brow raised like he's truly surprised to see Cole.

"Thought about it, but Janey likes you fuckers, so . . ." He trails off, making it sound like I'm the only reason he's still here.

Carter nods, not looking like he believes that for a second. "What happened to your face?" He touches his cheek, right below his eye. "It's red after one of your usual disappearing acts, but it wasn't this morning."

Cole squeezes my hand beneath the table, and I press my lips together so I don't ramble out the whole parking lot story in one breath. "Must be the lighting," Cole says dismissively as he turns his head to the dance floor, purposefully giving Carter the good side without a bruise.

"We already saw the video, asshole." Carter rolls his eyes when Cole's head whips back around. "You think Kyle didn't tell us at the first possible opportunity?"

Cole doesn't say anything. Nobody says anything for a long minute.

Finally, gritting his teeth, Cole asks, "Chance? Samantha?"

Kyle shakes his head, pointing across the room to the smiling bride and groom who are in the middle of the dance floor. "Chance, yeah. That's how we saw the video. But he's not telling Samantha today. He said thanks and that he'd take care of it from here."

"Then why the fuck are we talking about it?" Cole bites out.

Kyle chuckles, completely unbothered by Cole's gruff response. "Because you went all Liam Neeson with a special set of skills on his ass and it was cool as fuck. Do me next. What do you know?" He makes it sound like Cole did a psychic medium reading trick on Glenn and seems genuinely excited to hear what secrets Cole knows about him.

"Nothing."

Cole's trying to shut down the conversation, but Cameron's not having any of that. "Do we need to be worried about you? I know we joke around, but is what you do legal? I don't care about the family name or any shit like that, but you know Mom would bankrupt herself to save you. Don't make that necessary."

He sounds like a true older brother—bossy, worried, loyal, caring, arrogant.

Cole turns a full-force glare on Cameron. "No need to worry about me, man. You never have in the past, so why start now?"

"What's that supposed to mean?" Cameron demands, his eyes narrowed.

"It means you don't know me at all. You never have." Cole says it to Cameron, but I can feel all his brothers and Kayla recoil at the accusation.

Kayla's the first to recover, replying, "And whose fault is that?" When Cole turns angry eyes on her, she doesn't flinch in the slightest. In fact, she leans into it, her blue eyes shooting daggers too. They really are two sides of the same coin. "We don't actually think you're some assassin criminal, Cole. But a complete and total asshole? Yeah, you're definitely that. You don't share the most basic of information, you disappear for days at a time without telling anyone, missing dinners and events, which makes us all worry where the hell you are and what the fuck you're doing. And now you're sitting here, acting like we're supposed to be chasing you down, begging for your attention and any morsel of information you deem us worthy of. I fucking cried when you told me your assistant's name and number!" she reveals, bitter anger woven through every word. "Do you know how ridiculous that is?"

She doesn't wait for him to answer, barreling on, "Newsflash, we've all got our own shit to deal with, so if you want to be a hermit and distance yourself, we're gonna respect that. Not because we don't care but because we *do*. So if that's what you want, we give it to you because for some asinine reason, we love you. And it's not only because I shared a womb with you."

With that, she pushes back from the table and stomps away.

The brothers turn angry glares to Cole. Luna and I meet wide-eyed gazes, her eyes behind black-framed glasses that amplify them, and I can read that she feels like an intruder into this family situation the same way I do. I should've given Cole some privacy, but he wrapped his arm around my back several minutes ago and has been squeezing my hip like he wanted me to stay.

"Oh, you dun *fucked* up now," Kyle drawls out, sounding slightly amused at the drama. "I hope you know her Amazon password because you're gonna need to buy her entire wish list to apologize for *that*." He waves his hands around, indicating the entirety that is Cole.

Cole sighs, watching Kayla make her way through the room and out into the hallway.

He leans over and whispers into my ear. "Wait right here. I'll be back, okay?"

I nod, and he presses a quick kiss to my temple before following after Kayla. I'm glad he's going to make amends with her, except when he leaves, I'm stuck with four Harrington brothers who're staring me down like I'm the enemy.

"What do you know?" Carter demands. His blue eyes are nothing like Cole's, which telegraph his every thought and emotion, at least to me. Carter's gaze is cold, calculating, and vaguely threatening.

I bite my cheeks, literally suck them in fishie-style and bite down on them to keep from speaking. My default mode is full-ramble, and that's *not* what I should do right now. I can nudge, I can encourage, I can highlight Cole's awesomeness, but anything Cole tells or doesn't tell his family is his choice to make, not mine.

So I shake my head, begging them with my eyes not to ask again.

Surprisingly, it's Luna who backs me up. "Leave her alone. Her loyalty's to Cole, not you, and rightfully so. If you want to fix things with your brother, that's your responsibility, and Janey's not a shortcut to figuring him out."

"Fix things with him? You mean he needs to fix things with us," Cameron counters.

Luna shrugs as she sadly declares, "Sounds like nothing's getting fixed, then."

I think my plan *Cole: Recognize the Awesomeness* just took a sharp nosedive into the failure zone.

CHAPTER 22
COLE

"KAYLA!" I shout down the hall, but she doesn't turn around. In fact, I think she walks faster, trying to get away from me.

Going so far as to enter an office, she tries to shut the door in my face, but I push back, forcing my way in. "What the fuck?" I mutter as she finally gives in.

She whirls away so I can't see her face, and though her back is ramrod straight, I have the sense that she's hiding tears from me. "Kayla?" I say, quietly this time.

"Just leave me be, Cole. It's fine. Give me a few minutes. I'll be back." Her speech is stilted and nasally. Clearly, she's crying or on the verge of tears.

"I didn't know," I confess. It's only a few words, and to some, it might seem like the barest of revelations, but to me? It's significant.

Kayla spins around, her eyes bloodshot and glittery but filled with fire. "You didn't know what? That we all talk about you, comparing notes on who talked to you last or saw you last because we're worried about you? That every time there's a plane crash, shooting, natural disaster, or anything tragic in the whole world, we're terrified that you're there because we have no idea where you are or what you're doing . . . ever?" She's pacing back and forth across the room, her voice getting louder and more hostile with every lap.

"Or how many times Mom has called 'mandatory dinners' over stupid shit so we can lay eyes on you as proof of life? That Cameron doesn't tell Gracie you'll be at her school events because he doesn't trust you'll actually come and the last thing that little girl needs is another adult in her life who doesn't show the fuck up when they're supposed to?"

She pivots, making another trip back across the room. "Or that we hate that you keep yourself apart from the rest of us like we're not worth your oh-so-valuable time? That we tell each other all kinds of stuff, but you don't trust us with anything? I don't even know where you live, for fuck's sake. Janey FBI-ed that info, and I wanted to scratch her eyes out for it because you let her in, but not any of us."

I try to speak, but she cuts me off. "I'm not mad at her for it. I'm glad, actually! Because I want you to have someone who makes you happy, even if it's not us. But selfishly, I want my brother. I want *us*." She waves a hand around wildly, indicating me and her, and all the rest of my siblings back in the reception. "We all do. Except you."

Her every word is a stab to my heart. I didn't know . . . *any of that*. I thought they didn't care whether I was there or not, if they talked to me or not, even if I existed or not. I had no idea they were watching the news and comparing notes, tracking me down, and protecting my beloved niece from me.

I shake my head, trying to make sense of everything I've always thought with what Kayla's saying now.

Kayla gives me point-two seconds to process, and when I don't spill my guts, she strides toward the door, shoulder bumping past me. "Fucking asshole."

"Wait."

To my surprise, she does.

Maybe I shouldn't be surprised, though. That's the problem. Kayla's always been there for me. I just thought it was begrudgingly so. Maybe that's not the case and I only felt that way because of my own misguided perceptions.

"I didn't know any of that," I start. It's harder than I imagined to say actual words to explain the chaos I'm feeling.

She huffs and mutters, "Idiot."

"I know. I'm figuring that out. Right now, so give me a minute to catch up," I beg. She narrows her eyes, and I add, "Please."

That seems to set her back a few notches, which is ridiculous. A simple nicety shouldn't be so foreign that my sister is shocked by my usage of it. Right? Am I that much of an asshole?

Yes.

The truth is . . . I am. Or I always have been. But I can change that. I hope.

"We grew up in different families," I say, trying to explain a lifetime. "I mean, they were the same, but they were different to us." I look up, focusing on Kayla. I see her strength and determination, but also her kindness and second mothering. "You got the best of Mom and Dad, and I mean that in the most complimentary way possible. I got . . . nothing. Or at least I felt like I did. I didn't matter. Cameron and Carter were fighting for top dog, Chance dipped out to do his own thing that he loved, Kyle was being a dick at every opportunity. And I skated by on the outskirts, watching. I've always done that, so I didn't know any of what you said—that you worried, that you cared, that you gave a shit at all."

I close my eyes, remembering my teen years in a new light. "I thought I was waiting to be invited in, which never happened, and that only confirmed that I didn't matter. But maybe I didn't make it seem like . . . I wanted that?" Kayla said they were trying to respect my wishes to be left alone, so maybe that's what was happening back then too?

"Did you want us to send you a gold-embossed, wax-sealed invitation with your name calligraphed on the envelope?" Kayla scoffs, swiping at her eyes. But her tone is lighter now, like her anger is dissolving as I share my thoughts and feelings. She's figuring stuff out too, like we're both finally seeing a full picture at the same time.

I huff out a chuckle. "Maybe? Though I probably would've ripped it up and thrown it in the trash," I confess with a bit of embarrassment.

"You would've pissed on it and set it on the dining room table for us to find," she suggests.

I shake my head. "Nah, that's Kyle. I wouldn't have wanted a scene. I spent most of that time wanting to disappear."

She laughs through her drying tears and nods, agreeing with me. "Are we that annoying?" she asks, the honesty in the question a wake-up call I didn't know I needed.

I tilt my head, acting like I'm thinking about her question, but the truth is harder to accept. "No, I think *I* am. How've you put up with me all these years?"

I don't think we need to go through every day of our childhood, memory by memory, or even our adulthood, to analyze what we thought happened versus what actually happened, but I definitely have a lot of personal reflection to do. And I have to reexamine how I'm going to behave with my family moving forward.

"It's been tough," she confesses with a heavy sigh, "but I feel like *this* is better. You?" She points from herself to me. "I didn't realize how much *I* had to say on the matter."

"Me neither. I'm glad you went first, though, because otherwise, I think this would've been 'fuck this, fuck you, and fuck off.'" I mimic my own grumpy, grunty, gruff way of talking.

I know that's true. If Kayla hadn't raked me over the coals, I don't think I would've ever seen things from her point of view. And if I hadn't seen how Janey's family treated her, I don't think I would've seen the good in my own family, either.

And something else Kayla said comes back.

"Don't be mad at Janey, 'kay? She's dealing with a lot." I place a hand on my own chest so she knows exactly what I mean. "And as much of a shitshow as we are, her family's worse. I'd really like for you and her to be friends." It's as much of a plea as I can make, and it's still not for me to be part of the inner circle of my family, but for Janey to be.

Kayla laughs. "Are you kidding? We love her! She's all sweet and nice, you're this asshole extraordinaire, but she has you tamed. Pulling out chairs, running out to greet her, and feeding her? It's adorable. She's like a lion tamer-slash-magician or something," she teases, which from Kayla is a major compliment. More seriously, she says, "We like her, and more importantly, we like her for you. She's good for you."

I can feel heat on my cheeks. Not that I'm blushing. I don't fucking blush. It's just warm in here or something. "Thanks. I think so too."

"Plus, it sounds like you're both a bit . . . strange," Kayla teases, spinning a finger by her temple. "She tracked you down, you showed up at her house?"

I guess Janey told them that. "Did she tell you I showed up at her job with her favorite snacks too?" I brag.

Kayla's brow lifts into a sharp arch. "Did she *tell* you where she worked?"

"Gonna have to plead the fifth," I answer with a grimace because Janey said 'long term care facility', but I definitely found the name when I did research on her.

"That's a lot," Kayla decrees, looking dubious about my overly zealous pursuit of Janey.

"It works." I shrug, but I'm fighting to hide my grin because yeah, we definitely work.

"Come on, then. Your lion tamer is probably worried about you. And hopefully, our brothers haven't scared her off."

Fuck. I've been gone too long. "If they've done anything to Janey, I'm going to kill them." When Kayla glares at me, I amend, "Not literally. But figuratively? Hell, yeah."

Thankfully, Janey's sitting at the table where I left her. She and Luna are talking easily and both smiling. I slip back into my chair, placing my arm around Janey's back and cupping her hip. She immediately beams at me. "Okay?" she asks, chancing a glance at Kayla before her eyes return to mine. "You were gone for a good bit."

"Yeah, he admitted to his asshole ways, begged for forgiveness, and agreed to come to dinner at Mom and Dad's for the next three months without complaint," Kayla answers for me.

"The hell I did—" I interject.

"That's amazing!" Janey squeals, punching the air with her little fists. "I knew my plan would work and they'd see how awesome you are! I mean, how could they not? You're all growly and grouchy, but inside, you're such a sweetie. I'm so happy!" Janey leans over, pressing her lips to my cheek, but even with the kiss, I can feel her smile.

I look over to Kayla, finding her blinking innocently with a smile of her own. She played me. Like a damn pro. She's good.

"You too, of course," she tells Janey. "You're always welcome."

Janey gasps. "Really? Oh, my God. Thank you. I'd absolutely love to come. What should I bring? I'm not a good cook, but I can buy the best pie you've ever had. Wait . . . no, you said Grandma Beth makes homemade apple pie which is your favorite, so I'll pick up a cake or something. Or wine! Should I get red or white? I like white, usually, but if we're having beef, then I should get red instead."

Kayla's eyes sparkle when Janey mentions Grandma Beth's apple pie. I've obviously shared that with Janey, and like Kayla said, she wants me to talk to her and my brothers, but she's happy I'm sharing with anyone. "Bring that asshole and we'll call it good," she reassures Janey while pointing at me. "Really, Mom likes to cook or she'll have someone cater if she's not feeling it."

"Deal!" Janey shouts, agreeing easily.

Later, when Kayla and Luna leave us, saying they're going to mingle, I turn to Janey. "Thank you," I tell her, my voice a bit choked.

She smiles, but there's worry in her gray eyes as she instantly knows what I'm talking about. "Did it go okay? You and Kayla seemed much better, but I know that couldn't have been an easy conversation. I'm sorry for being the trigger that caused it."

"What?" I ask with a frown. "You didn't trigger anything."

She swallows thickly. "If you hadn't had to come out for me, you wouldn't have had to fight Glenn, and then your family wouldn't have seen what you did. Well, what you said, I guess."

I can hear what she's doing. Her whole life, anything that went wrong was blamed on her. Paisley overreacting to a bouquet toss? Janey's fault. Jessica not getting her way? Somehow, Janey's fault. Her bully not getting to continue tormenting her? Still, Janey's fault. She's so used to being blamed that she's blaming herself, only now, it's for my mistakes.

I put a finger over her lips, shushing her. "If I hadn't gone out there for you, Glenn would've made his way inside and that mess would've happened in the lobby where everyone would've heard and seen. That would've been infinitely worse. Besides, none of this" —I gesture to the table like my siblings are still there— "is your fault. It's my fault for being a shitty brother."

She doesn't look sure but asks hopefully, "But it's better now?"

I nod. "Yeah, thanks to you. It's better. Not fixed, but maybe one day . . ." I drift off, wondering how in the hell I'm going to repair an entire lifetime of mistakes I've made with my siblings, who aren't perfect either.

And that's before I even consider Mom and Dad.

―――――

The rest of the reception is smooth sailing. Chance and Samantha dance the night away, seemingly oblivious to any earlier drama, a delicious dinner is served, toasts are made, and Dad gives a speech about how he always knew Chance was special, earning an eye roll from me that I at least attempt to hide, and how he's glad he's found a woman equally as special. Considering their first meeting, that's major progress, especially for Dad.

As great as it is, I nearly fling my half-burned sparkler in the metal trash can after the send-off because I'm way past ready to go home. I take Janey's hand and nearly haul her to the parking lot.

"I'll follow you?" she asks, looking up at me through half-open lashes while we're standing at the door to her yellow car.

She means back to my place or her place. But I want her to have the chance to lead with everything. She's more than capable and deserves the right to be in control . . . for now.

"Where? To do what?" I ask, letting all the hunger I feel for her weave through the words as I twirl one of her red curls around my finger. "Your choice."

"Is your bed as uncomfortable as your couch?" she asks with a shy smile. Her fingers are tiptoeing up my abdomen to my chest, where she drags a fingertip over the skin of my neck just above my collar. I've never thought myself particularly sensitive there, but right now, it might be enough to make me come. Flirty Janey, when she feels that she's got me in the palm of her hand, is a beautiful sight.

"I have no idea. It's a bed. It's a couch." I never thought about it honestly, and I don't have the blood flow to think about it now.

"Let's find out," she purrs.

I nearly shove her into her car, making sure she doesn't flash any of the other wedding guests who are also all over the parking lot. I can't risk a kiss, so I close her door, tap the top of her car, and growl, "Follow me, and keep up."

She laughs, not offended at my caveman orders. In fact, when I back my truck out, she's parked right behind me, already having trailed after me in her car. She's as ready as I am. We've waited long enough.

I beat my own personal record on how fast I can drive between Chance's club and my place, and that's saying something because the former record was set when Samantha was missing and we were rallying around Chance, fearing the worst.

But we make it, parking in the private garage, and in moments we're in the elevator. Janey's wiggling around like an excited kid about to get ice cream, and I'm at my limit, wanting her to wiggle like that on me.

I step in front of her and pick her up by her hips. She wraps her legs around me easily, her dress falling open from the waist down. The moment I feel the heat of her pussy over my hard cock, I groan and use my grip on her to pull her against me harder. "Fuck."

She shudders, and though our mouths meet, our breaths mingling, neither of us can concentrate enough to kiss. All our attention is focused on the area where we're almost connected in the way we want. So close, but too far.

Luckily, it's only two stories from the garage to my place, and thirty-seven steps from my front door to my bedside. Not that I'm counting now, but I already know, having counted it out in case I ever needed to make an exit in the dark.

I toss Janey back to the fluffy surface, and she bounces. "Whoo! Definitely softer," she squeals, answering her own earlier question.

Her eager hands go to the tie at her waist, and I stop her, undoing it myself. I yank the dress open with a snap and see that she's in a matching black bra and panty set. But this one's different from before. It's delicate and sheer, letting her nipples and pretty pussy peek through. She wore this for me, knowing that we promised tonight was the night. And though it's been hell to wait, I'm glad we did. For this moment right here, when I know this means as much to her as it does to me.

"So beautiful," I praise, running my hands up her legs, over her hips, and across her belly. I cup her breasts, lifting them into my palms and then teasing at the already hard nipples before falling over her, resting on one elbow so I can take the hard nub into my mouth through the fabric. I feel Janey's hands weave into my hair, clutching me to her as she arches her back.

"Oh!" she cries, her fingers digging into my scalp as she begs for more.

I suck and lick her through the fabric as I undo the clasp between her breasts, and her bra opens for me like her dress did. Flesh bared, I finally taste her, licking circles around one nipple, then the other. While I work her, I use one hand to jerk my tie off and start unbuttoning my vest.

"Take 'em off," Janey murmurs. Lost in bliss, she wants more of me too, so I pause to stand at the bedside and rip my shirt off. I toe my shoes off while I'm undoing my pants and let them drop along with my underwear. Nude in front of her, I take my cock in hand, squeezing the base tightly to balance out the pleasure of being with Janey. Again. Finally.

She sits up, leaving her dress and bra behind on the bed, and smiles sweetly before folding forward to place a gentle kiss to my crown. I'm watching closely and see the string of precum follow her lips as she glances up, and when she licks her lips, happily tasting me, a rough groan rumbles through my chest. The groan turns into a grunt an instant later when she takes me into her warm mouth, swallowing me deeply in one stroke.

Fuck. I can't do this for long.

But it feels so good.

Greedily, I look down, watching her take me. I even gather her curls into my fist so I can see better. She always looks beautiful, but with a mouthful of my cock? Stunning.

I need to touch her, though. More than my own release, I need to pleasure her.

I reach my other hand beneath her to pinch her nipple, rolling it in my fingers. Her answering gasp lets me slip into her throat, and she gags a little. I pull back, apologizing even though it felt amazing. "Sorry."

"Do it again," she says. I can see tears in the corners of her eyes from the gag, but she's smiling as she looks at my cock in wonder. But I don't think she's impressed with me. No, she's impressed with herself.

And that's sexy as hell.

I let her bob up and down, fucking me with her mouth and tongue, and every few strokes, I pinch her nipple and thrust in, making her take me deeper. She's surprised every time but seems to enjoy it. So do I, and it doesn't take long before I'm on edge. "Janey—" I warn.

"Mm-hmm," she moans around me, nodding her head. She hears my warning and wants me to come in her mouth.

I can't help it. I've lost all control. She's stolen it and holds all the power.

I buck into her mouth wildly, slipping into her throat over and over again as she gags. But she comes back for more every time, fighting to keep suction around me, forcing me to stay deep.

She swallows as I roar, pumping jet after jet of hot cum into her throat. The explosion, as amazing as it is, does nothing to ease my hunger for her, and as soon as it's done, I push Janey back onto the bed. She looks pleased with herself, maybe even proud for making me come with her mouth.

I slide her panties down her legs carelessly, delighting at the arousal that coats them. She's fucking soaked . . . for me. And I want to drink it all, savor every drop until she gives me more. I push her legs open, creating space for myself, and dive in for her center.

She's shaved smooth this time, no short red curls, and I realize again that she wants this as much as I do. She got ready tonight thinking about us, and though I don't have any signs like fancy lingerie or extra prep time, I want to show her how much I thought about it too.

So I do the one thing I can.

Gripping her thighs tightly, I hold her open, letting my eyes trace every inch of her, following my eyes with my tongue and fingers. I lick, suck, and caress her pussy, giving her everything I have to bring her pleasure, all the while, keeping my eye on her, watching for what makes her writhe, spasm, and moan.

I cataloged every reaction she made last time, but each time is different, and I want to do what's best for Janey now. Today, in this minute, whatever will make her crazed with ecstasy.

Sliding two fingers inside her, I pet that spot she loves and batter my tongue over her clit, helping her build toward a powerful release. She needs it, has earned it after waiting so long for it. Soon, I'm pressed as deep as I can go and rubbing her inner wall ferociously while sucking hard on her clit. It's all she can withstand, and she moans out my name as she shatters apart, her whole body spasming.

I want to prolong it, but I need to be inside her . . . now. I stand, hauling her to the edge of the bed and throwing her legs into the air. She catches herself, choosing to support her own legs instead of resting them on my shoulders, while I line up with her entrance and slam into her. I grip her hips, pulling her onto me over and over again, still feeling the flutters of her inner walls.

She's slick, hot, and squeezing me like a vise. She's fucking heaven.

I thrust into her, the slapping sounds of our bodies the harmony to our grunts and moans. But she's too far away. I need to touch more of her . . . all of her. Testing, I lean forward, seeing when her flexibility gives way. To my delight, she folds nearly in half, her knees almost to her shoulders, and I find her hands, interweaving our fingers. Holding our conjoined hands to the bed, I stare deeply into Janey's eyes.

"Come for me." It's about as much dirty talk as I've ever done. Hell, it's more words than I used in a whole day before Janey. But she's making it easier to say what I feel. And right now, I want to feel her sweet pussy quivering all around me while staring deep into her eyes, knowing I'm the one she wants.

That she wants *me*.

That she's *mine*.

I've never felt less worthy, but fuck, am I glad that Janey sees something in me that others don't, because I'm too selfish to give her up now. I want her. All of her, every day, forever.

"Cole!" she shouts. Her eyes roll and her lashes flutter, but she fights to keep them open, letting me see all of her as she comes. Her nose crinkles, her brow furrows, her mouth falls open. It's glorious, and I've never felt more fortunate to witness something. I could see one of the wonders of the world, and it would pale in comparison to the sight of Janey orgasming on my cock.

It's too much for me to take, and I again spill into her. My cock jerks with every pulse, but what's really exploding is my heart. I don't have words for it, don't have words for much of anything, but there's something in my chest that feels strange.

I yank out of her, knowing my cum will leak out too and wanting to use it. I swipe my hand through the mess at her opening and smear it over her sensitive clit, marking her with our combined cream.

"Oh! I can't!" she squeals as she squirms to get away.

I pin her thighs back with one arm, keeping her bent in half and her pussy exposed for me. "You deserve it. You deserve everything," I vow as I speed up, my movements swiping over her whole pussy as my hand becomes a blur.

Her cries get higher pitched, to the point where she's almost screaming, but she's not fighting me anymore. She's on the cusp of something big, and we can both feel it. My cock is leaking after my orgasm, but it's nothing compared to the juices pouring forth from Janey. Her whole body goes tight, her mouth opens in a silent scream, her eyes slam shut, and her fingers turn into claws against the bedding.

I guide her through it, letting her drift away this time, knowing she'll come back . . . to me. Because I think I know what this feeling is. I've just never felt it before.

CHAPTER 23
JANEY

"YOU SEEM DIFFERENT," Mason tells me at work the next week.

He's right. I am different. And that's thanks to Cole.

And myself.

I can admit now that I was angry and hurt by Cole's dismissal after our week at the cabin. But I can also see that he was right to let me have time alone to heal and find my balance again. Because he's definitely thrown me for a whirlwind of a loop-di-doo.

I never knew a relationship of any sort could be this . . . all-encompassing. No, that's not it. Cole hasn't taken over my life. I still go to work, enjoy my patients and friends, and have read ten more chapters of Dragul and Tiffany—which isn't as much as usual and I still have forty-eight to go.

But the intensity with him is unlike anything I've known. It feels like he's aware of me on a primal, cellular level. He knows when I get to a good part in my book by my breathing and wants me to share the excitement. He listens to not only what I say about my day but hears how I feel about it and responds to that, and when he looks at me with those blue eyes of his, I feel as though he sees my soul and likes every bit of it, even the dark parts I've worked so hard to pretend don't exist.

And the sex?

Holy hell. I'm not sure what Cole and I do even qualifies as sex. It's like soul-gasms each and every time. He has kissed every inch of my body, from the spine of my back to the sensitive spot beneath my ear, my pinkie toes to the crooks of my elbows. There's no dive and done, or worse, leaving me to handle things myself. He takes his time every time, building a connection between us that makes me feel claimed, body and soul. He pours himself into me, physically but also emotionally, unflinchingly meeting my eyes with every orgasm like he's wowed by what happens between us and it wouldn't, couldn't, be possible with anyone else.

I'm glad he gave me time to be ready for him, for this, for us. I'm not sure I would've been able to handle it otherwise. But now? I appreciate Cole for what and who he is, the same way he does with me.

"I'm happy," I answer Mason. I still ramble too much. It's a habit I'll never break, but I also find that I can say what I'm thinking or feeling without all the distractions in my head. I'm not as worried about what people will say back or think, so I don't have to couch my answers in loads of extra information to keep any negative reactions at bay.

"Regular servings of deep dicking will do that," he teases with a grin. He hasn't dated since breaking up with Greta, but his beard is on its way to regrowing, and he's seemed happier without Greta's constant 'fixing' of things that weren't wrong in the first place. "How're things with Prince Charming?"

I laugh. Everyone here thinks they met Cole when he came up to bring me snacks, and no matter how many times I tell them that he's usually a Grumpy Gus who doesn't like people, only me, they won't believe me. His charming mask was too good.

"So great!" I gush. I want to say more, but I also get that Cole and I are different, individually and together, and like Luna, Samantha, and Kayla, not everyone will understand the way we are with each other. At least not at first. When Mason waves a hand, signaling 'gimme more', I stick to the basics. "We went to his brother's wedding and it was stunning. All gold and white, with flowers and tulle everywhere. I met his whole family again, all the brothers and his sister. Plus, his mom and dad, and even his grandparents. That was just a drive-by on the dance floor, but his grandma is the cutest and told me she loved my hair." I grin widely, remembering the older couple swaying to a Sinatra song. "And all week, we've been taking turns staying at each other's places. It feels cozy, like I know he'll be sitting on the couch, waiting for me when I get home. We'll curl up, talk, and *stuff*, and then fall asleep in each other's arms. It's really . . . *adjectives, adjectives, adjectives*," I finish, waving my hands around as I run out of descriptors for how happy I am.

Mason smiles back. "I'm happy for you. Make sure you tell Gabriella that too. She could use a happily ever after ending, even if it's someone else's, to help her keep the faith that there are good ones out there."

Frowning, I ask, "Did something happen?"

Mason looks over his shoulder, making sure no one else is at the nurse's station to overhear, but still whispers, "Yeah, it didn't get too far, thankfully. Let's just say there's a reason she does full recon on guys before meeting them in person. The dating pool is a dark, ugly place with sharks hiding in plain sight."

"Oh! I hate that. Maybe her Prince Charming is still out there, and she'll find him soon. Or maybe he'll stumble into her remote cabin in the woods, and she'll attack him with bear spray?" I suggest hopefully, knowing that sounds like a worst-case scenario, not a best, but it worked for me.

"Yeah," Mason says with a shrug. "She's okay. Could probably use a pick-me-up, though." Quieter, he adds, "Or a hook-up without a record or an STI."

I cringe. That makes me sad for Gabriella who is gorgeous, brilliant, and so big-hearted. But one day, she'll find The One. I have to believe that. And then all the hardships will be a part of her story on how she found happiness. In the meantime, the struggle is real.

"Other than *stuff*, what's on the agenda for tonight?" Mason asks, using my euphemism for sex. I'm not a prude, but I also don't go around spilling private details, despite the fact that I basically share everything else, intentionally or not.

"Oh, my God! I haven't told you?" I say, then slap my hand over my mouth because that was definitely too loud. Too late, though, because one of the lights on the screen comes on. I hold a finger up to Mason and answer, "Yes, Mrs. Donald?"

"Somebody's screaming in pain down the hall. I know you hear it too, but you're sitting on your lazy rump roasts, letting her cry out like a wounded seagull. *Raaaawrch*," she screeches, not sounding anything like I did.

"I'm sorry, ma'am. I'll check up and down the hall," I reassure her, knowing full-well that what she heard was me, but I'm not going to admit that.

For every kind, nice patient we have, there are always a few who're unhappy in their old age, somehow thinking they'd escape the passage of time and feeling betrayed that their golden years aren't as imagined. Mrs. Donald is one of those and always mad at someone for something, even when it's been a perfectly lovely day. I once heard her complaining that she didn't finish a puzzle fast enough. Not that a piece was missing, or it didn't look like the picture on the box, but that she had arbitrarily decided that it would take her no more than an hour, and it took her all afternoon. We'd tried praising her speed, which was remarkably good for a woman of her age and eyesight. Even going so far as comparing her to competitive puzzlers, which is surprisingly actually a thing. She wasn't having it and pouted for days, refusing her pudding at dinner and any other attempts at puzzles.

I hang up to find Mason touching his nose. "Not it."

I roll my eyes. I'm the one who disturbed Mrs. Donald, so it's only fair that I be the one to go tell her that everything's fine on the hall. But first . . .

"We're having a family dinner at Cole's tonight. All the siblings and spouses are coming over!" I'm being quiet, but my excitement is palpable. My plan to bring Cole and his siblings together wasn't a failure after all, and in fact, it was his idea to invite them over for dinner.

If there were a gold medal in successful plans, well . . . I wouldn't get it because it was super-rough there for a minute, but I'd totally get a participation ribbon.

"Sounds like one big, happy family," Mason muses.

He's wrong. The Harringtons haven't been happy for a long time. There are feelings of hurt and betrayal, of being judged and dismissed, and a ridiculous amount of male posturing in their past. But even in their mess, they'd do anything for each other. That's what makes them family. Not the blood they share, not the history they wrote together from vastly different perspectives.

They love each other in spite of being family, not because they are.

Seeing that shines a new light on my family too. They think sharing blood trumps everything. My parents, sister, cousins, and even beyond think they can do anything and not suffer any consequences because blood is thicker than water.

But it's not. Family can be those you choose. If you're lucky, you can choose the people you're born into. If not, you can choose others to be your family.

I'm choosing Cole.

And if possible, I'd like to choose the Harringtons too.

"Hopefully, they will be if I have anything to do with it," I tell Mason. "I'll go tell Mrs. Donald that everything's fine if you go check on Mrs. Michaelson. She's due for a new bag."

Mason holds up a bag of saline that's prepped and ready. "On it. Good luck."

He means with Mrs. Donald, but I mentally store the well-wish away for tonight's dinner, which is important to Cole and his siblings in a way I'm not sure I can even fathom.

———

Cole and I are standing in the private garage below his office, waiting for his siblings to arrive. He told them the address and that there was parking, but not much else. I think he wants to surprise them more than he wants to keep secrets. Or maybe it's just a habit that needs to be worked on.

Either way, with only that small bit of information, they all readily agreed to come, which I think bodes well for this big reveal. Well, what I assume is a big reveal because I think he's going to tell them everything tonight. It won't undo years of hurt in one night, but I'd be lying if I said I wasn't hoping it heals some of the damage that's weighed Cole down for so long.

He told me what Kayla and he talked about and how confused it made him, but he's been mostly silently working it out in his mind ever since. That's been hard for me because I'm a talk-talk-talker, but I've tried to respect his mental space and process.

But the fact that he initiated this dinner speaks volumes. Loud, clear, resounding volumes.

I hear the gate rolling up and hold my breath.

Like they planned it, everyone arrives at pretty much the same time. Carter and Luna carpooled with Chance and Samantha, who surprisingly don't look tan from their island honeymoon. Cameron comes in a luxury sedan, and Kyle roars in on a motorcycle.

Once we're all gathered together, Cameron begins the inter-rogation. "Where are we? Thought we were having dinner? If I got a babysitter for you to get us tangled up in something—"

Cole's jaw is tight, his shoulders down and back like he's expecting trouble when he interrupts to answer, "We are. At my place. Here."

I plaster myself to Cole's side supportively, knowing that those few words equate to a neon welcome sign into his entire life, and he wraps his arm around me, grateful for the support to get to this point. It takes a single heartbeat for what he's said to sink in, and then they look around with renewed interest.

"You live above the offices?" Cameron surmises, sounding much less cranky now.

"Yeah, my office. My home. My building," Cole says without an ounce of pride, simply stating facts.

Kyle's response is first and loudest, his shock echoing against the surrounding concrete. "You own the whole fucking building?"

Cameron's eyes narrow, scanning Cole's face for any sign of a lie. Carter looks around, and I can almost see him doing math in his head like that meme with the lady superimposed by geometric shapes and formulas. Luna said Carter sometimes does property investments with her brother, so he'd know what a building this size, in this location, would cost. Chance smiles easily, though I'm not sure if that has anything to do with Cole or his newlywed bliss. Kayla . . . doesn't seem surprised.

"About damn time," she rumbles with an eye roll.

"What?" Cole looks at her in shock.

"Janey's friend isn't the only one with a certification in FBI-ing," she explains with a heavy amount of 'duh' on the words. "I figured if she could find you, I could find you." She turns to me, her blue eyes dancing with curiosity, and inquires, "How long did it take your friend?" But she immediately holds up a hand, stopping me from answering. "Actually, better yet, don't tell me. I don't want to be pissed if it took me longer. I'm a little competitive after living with these guys my whole life." She jerks her head toward her brothers, who seem well aware of her cutthroat streak.

I laugh and say, "C. Harrington, seriously? Not like he was hiding it well, but there were a lot of listings to go through." Kayla looks at me like 'don't I know it?' and we share a smile.

Cole gawks at me, suddenly realizing that we never discussed the details of how I found him. He looks proud and . . . turned on by the lengths I went to in tracking him down.

"I'll be fixing that LLC name, apparently," Cole says flatly, but his lip quirks. He's not mad at all, not even that I found a loophole in his top-secret operation.

"I've got a guy who can help with that if you want," Chance offers. "He's a club alumnus who specializes in corporate law now. He's done podcasts with Evan and me, talks to the guys about setting goals, and gives me a friends and family discount." Rather than a brag of 'knowing someone' to make himself sound important, Chance sounds like a proud parent who witnessed their kid go from Troublemaker to Rockstar Adult.

Cole nods in appreciation. "You wanna see around or what?"

Of course, everyone does.

Cole walks us to a door, puts in a code, and ushers us into the stairwell. We follow him up one flight, waiting as he does another code to enter the office level.

"You've got this place locked up tighter than my ass the last time I went to jail," Kyle jokes.

Chance chokes down a laugh, and I think I hear him murmur to Samantha, "Don't knock it till you try it."

At the same time, Cameron rolls his eyes. "You haven't been to jail." He sounds certain of that.

Ignoring them all, Cole says, "Paranoia partnered with a need for discretion." He doesn't explain further until we enter his office area. Seeing it again, through everyone else's eyes this time, I look around, noting the sterile, modern, anonymous feeling. "This is the home base of BS Consulting. That's me. I do private investigations for a select clientele."

"You *are* a hitman, fuck yeah!" Kyle announces loudly. And with shockingly little alarm. "Anybody we'd know? And what's the going rate? I've got a bit saved up and a few folks I wouldn't mind 86ing from the face of the Earth." He draws a line across his neck with his thumb and then lets his head fall to the side, his eyes closed and tongue sticking out.

Of all the brothers, I'm figuring him out the most easily. He uses humor and sharp sarcasm to lighten things up anytime something important is going on, never letting anyone or anything get too heavy. I wonder if he's ever serious, though.

Cole glares at him with raised brows. "Haven't been one before. Thinking of branching out now, though. Wanna be my practice dummy?"

Kyle busts out into laughter, not expecting Cole's answering wry joke. Because he is kidding. Mostly.

"What do you investigate?" Cameron questions. He looks thoughtful, like he's considering this new information logically and rationally, turning it over in his mind to see how it affects them all.

"Whatever I choose to. Clients come to me, tell me what they want, and I decide if it's worth my time and interest." Cole's process is considerably more in-depth than what he's making it sound like. I've seen him researching for hours while we sit on the couch in the evenings, and he's gone on stakeouts twice in the last week. Locally, thankfully, and he did tell me where he was going and when he'd be back. I still worried, of course, and nearly attacked him when he walked through the door, both with kisses and a full, rambling report of how much I missed him.

"What's worth your time and interest?" Cameron asks, digging for more. I thought he was being a bossy older brother before, but I can hear the undercurrent of worry in his voice. Not for himself or the family but for Cole. He wants to make sure his brother is safe.

"Corporate espionage, high-profit divorce, child custody, stuff like that. I'm not loaning my talents out to enemy countries or anything." Cole's answer is glib, but he nods at Cameron, saying without saying that he hears him and he's careful.

Cole leads us back into the stairwell and up to his living space. "Home, sweet home," he says without a smile. This is hard for him. I know it is. He's spent his whole life thinking his family didn't care about him, so finding out that they care a lot has set his world view on tilt, reframing a lifetime of feeling left-out and forgotten into something more like self-isolation.

He's still regaining his balance.

And going so far as to welcome them into his private sanctuary is a vulnerability I don't think he could've exposed a few weeks ago.

But now? Here he is, showing them his soul. And I'm standing at his side like the sunshiniest, loudest cheerleader to have ever existed.

"Dude, your decorator phoned it in. Looks like a page out of Architectural Digest," Kyle declares as he launches himself at the couch and puts his boots up on the coffee table. "You're boring as hell, but you've got more pizzazz than this. You need a pillow or something. Forget doing a hit and hit a TJ Maxx, for fuck's sake."

Somehow, that's enough to break the ice and we all sit down in the living room. I think everyone realizes that Cole's shared a lot tonight, and though they have a million questions, they don't have to be asked all at once. So, though they're still looking around and taking it all in, conversation slowly turns to things other than Cole's secret life.

Like Chance and Samantha's honeymoon, which was beachy, sandy, and reportedly did not include visiting a single tourist hot spot. I'm pretty sure they went from the airport to the hotel suite and back, only surfacing from each other for food.

And Cameron's need for a new nanny because Grace ran off another one, which is apparently not all that uncommon. Kyle suggests getting a puppy, not as a reward, but as a way to teach her calmness and responsibility, but Cameron's not hearing that at all no matter how many times Kyle declares that Gracie is great with his dog, Peanut Butter, and is a virtual angel when she's at his place.

When we move to the dining table, Cole mentions it's never been used, and instead of its being an awkward reminder of how alone he's been, Kyle makes a joke about popping his dinner cherry and everyone laughs. With a growl of fake annoyance, and secret appreciation for Kyle's irreverence, Cole serves up the meal he and I made together.

Well, he made it, and I grabbed ingredients, set timers, and stirred a few things after he showed me how to because apparently, whipping, folding, and stirring are all different things.

It's a family dinner unlike any I've ever had. Nobody cries, nobody gets their feelings hurt, everyone talks kindly unless teasing each other, and then it's with good intentions. It's everything I wished, hoped, and pretended my family dinners were for my whole life.

The Harrington siblings have it. Or more accurately, they're creating it right before my eyes.

"How do you like being a nurse at The Ivy, Janey?" Kayla asks, turning the conversation to me.

Hearing her mention my work makes me think of something. But first, I answer her question, recognizing that she's trying to include me, and I want to be a part of what this family has going on because it's truly special. "I love it. I always wanted to be a nurse and kinda fell into long-term care work, but I'm so glad I did. It's hard, especially when we lose patients who've been with us for a while, but I like helping make their days, however many they have left, the best they can be, especially when their families can't always be there for whatever reason." Before she can ask a follow-up, I switch directions on her, wondering if she and Mason might be a good match. "Kayla, random question . . . how do you feel about facial hair?"

"On me? Veto and scheduling an urgent waxing appointment. On other women? You do you, boo. On a guy? It depends. Are we talking neat and cared for, or full-on, scraggly bird's nest with lunch left buried in it?"

"The first, of course!" I answer with a laugh.

"Then no." She grins, having gotten me good. "To be fair, it was a no either way. Why?"

"Oh," I say sadly. "I have a friend who's recently single and thought—"

She interrupts me, holding a palm up. "And veto that too. The last thing I need is to be set up on a blind date. Not only no, but *Hell. No.*"

It sounds like there might be bad history there, but either way, hearing her solid disinterest, I don't press. Instead, I nod. "I get it. No worries."

Chance sees the opening, though, and jokes, "I don't know, Kayla. A blind date where they don't know what they're getting into might be the only way. Because a guy would have to have big, clanging, brass ones to approach you. You're kinda intimidating, in case you didn't know."

Kayla blinks twice, feigning vacancy before delivering a death blow. "You are intimidate-*ed*. Men are intimidate-*ed*. That doesn't mean I am intimidate-*ing*. It's a failure on their part, not a weakness in mine."

Samantha reaches across the table and high-fives Kayla. "Damn straight."

Chance chuckles. "So big, brass ones is what you're looking for, then? Noted."

Kayla shrugs carelessly, laughing back. "If that's what it takes."

I think diamond-hard, boulder-sized balls of pure courage is more like it, but I keep that to myself, too impressed by—and maybe a bit scared of—Kayla to tease her. Instead, I give her an out of the conversation I unintentionally started. "Anybody want apple pie? It's not Grandma Beth's, but it's her recipe," I brag, placing my hand on Cole's shoulder.

"You made apple pie? Grandma's apple pie?" Kyle echoes incredulously. "Fuck yeah, I want some of that. Bring it on!" He picks up his fork and holds it at the ready, grinning at Cole with childlike excitement.

"You get the last piece," Cole declares. "Otherwise, no one else'll get any."

"Fair enough," Kyle agrees with no shame.

CHAPTER 24
COLE

I DON'T ANSWER my phone for many people. Not many people have this number because it's not the one on my card, but rather my personal one. So when it rings, I know it's actually worth my time.

"Hello."

"I have an update for you on the Webster case," Louisa clips out, her fingers clicking on a keyboard in the background. She's always like this—no greeting, no niceties, straight to the point, which I appreciate.

"Go ahead."

"I've got the unknown woman's current name and details, but no connection between her and Webster yet. Her social media doesn't mention him by name or anything that suspiciously points to him. No overlap in friends, family, history, etc. But her history is sketchy at best."

She pauses for a breath, and I ask, "Criminal?"

"No." Her fingers fly over the keyboard and she reads, "Mother, deceased. Father, unlisted. Ward of the foster care system, starting at age five. There's a list of homes before she was adopted at . . ." *Click, click, click*. "Fifteen."

"That's unusual," I murmur. A cute five-year-old didn't get adopted, but a fifteen-year-old with a hard life did? That's not the norm, nor would it typically bode well for a teen in today's system.

"Yeah. Ran away by sixteen, started using her mother's last name again a couple of years ago, but legally, it's still her adoptive parents', which is why it took me so long. I'll send her contact info to you now." There's a *whoosh* sound as the email leaves Louisa's computer, and a moment later, my computer makes its little *ding-ding* of delivery.

"Thanks." I go to hang up, but Louisa clears her throat.

"There's more," she says, and I can tell *this* is actually why she called. I'm quiet, waiting for her to share what she's found. "Mr. Webster had a heart attack last week, died at St. Joseph's. No signs of foul play, being treated as natural causes."

"But . . ." I prompt. Suspicious timing, but if there's no police investigation, it shouldn't warrant that particular tone in Louisa's voice.

"The wife, Mrs. Webster, is doing a quick run to settle the will. Considering there are significant assets, it seemed . . . interesting."

I agree, it does. I told Mrs. Webster that I didn't think the woman her husband met with was a marital threat, but maybe she knows something we don't. It wouldn't be the first time a client has done some digging of their own after I handed them a shovel and a prime dig spot.

"Thanks. I'll follow up."

We hang up, and I make a couple more phone calls. Tonight, Janey and I won't be curled up on the couch for a cozy night and then move to her bed, which is admittedly more comfortable than mine.

———

"Thank you for meeting me," I tell Riley Stefano. The woman from the cabin, whose hair is now striped in black and pink, is wearing wide-legged jeans, clunky tennis shoes, a cropped band T-shirt, and a half-pound of chunky jewelry as she sits across the table from me and Janey at a diner of her choosing.

"You said it was important," she explains. She's bouncing her leg, which might make her seem nervous, but it feels more like she's staying at-the-ready for anything, especially given the way her eyes jump around the room, watching for danger from every angle. I don't think she trusts easily or even at all, which makes sense with the history Louisa described. "So, what's up?"

I take a sip of my coffee and lean back, wanting to seem as non-threatening as possible when I say this part because I can only guess how bad it's going to sound to a woman like Riley. "I'm a private investigator. During one of my cases, you became a person of interest."

"Me?" she snaps. In an instant, she's standing, ready to bolt. "Tell Austin that I'm gone, or you couldn't find me, or whatever."

"Wait!" Janey pleads. "We don't know anything about Austin. That's not what this is about."

This is why I asked her to come with me. A woman like Riley wouldn't consider sitting down with me, even in a public place. But Janey has an aura of kindness, which I thought might help. Turns out, I was right, because though she looks suspicious, Riley sits down again.

I want to ask who Austin is and maybe see if Riley could use a bit of help dealing with that situation. But first, I've got to find out who the fuck she is to Mr. Webster. I pull out my phone, showing her the picture I took of her and Webster in the cabin.

As expected, she turns narrowed, eagle-sharp eyes on me. "What the fuck? That was private."

"Hence, my being a private investigator," I answer. "Who is Webster to you?"

"Why do you want to know?" she counters, not giving up anything.

Janey leans forward, her eyes soft and her words gentle as she says, "Riley, Mr. Webster had a heart attack last week. He passed away. I'm so sorry."

I'd bet she's had this exact conversation dozens of times before, but I can see that it weighs on her each and every time. She doesn't know Riley, didn't know Mr. Webster, but is now an inextricable part of this moment for the woman across the table. But Janey willingly carries that responsibility with grace, kindness, and care.

"What?" Riley whispers, her face looking like she just got slapped. Her tough façade slips as she sags in her chair. She picks up my phone, looking at the picture of her and Webster with glittery eyes, even touching his face on the screen.

"Who was he to you?" I ask, trying my best to mimic Janey's tone.

Riley frowns and dashes away a stray tear with the back of her hand. "My birth father. This was the first time we met. He didn't even know I existed." She smiles sadly. "Probably a good thing, or he would've died sooner. Everyone does. I'm like a curse."

"No such thing," I say, disagreeing on principle. "People live. People die. It's the circle of life, and too often, that's some hard to swallow shit. Doesn't have anything to do with you." Okay, that's the truth, but it might've been too blunt because Janey gives me a pretty solid side-eye glare, and when Riley looks up from my phone, she's gone frosty again.

"Said like someone who's never lost someone," she replies bitterly. "At least I found him before."

"You found him?" Janey echoes, prompting her to say more.

Riley nods and then sighs heavily. Ignoring me completely, which is probably for the better, she tells Janey her story.

"My mom and him knew each other in college. She didn't even know his last name. It was a hook-up, a one-time thing. She didn't realize she was pregnant with me until almost seven months later, and by then, Will was gone. She tried asking around to find out who he was."

She shrugs like that was unsuccessful. "But he was just *poof*! Mom had me, and we were okay for a while. Until she got cancer."

Riley goes quiet, lost in memories for a long minute. When she restarts her story, she's skipped what must've been the hardest part. "I got shipped off to foster care. I was a terror. Mad, sad, wanted to die to be with my mom, and took it out on everyone, especially the people who were trying to give me a home."

Janey reaches across the table and takes Riley's hand, comforting her. "I'm sorry about your mom. You must've been so scared."

Riley doesn't flinch away from the contact or the kind words. In fact, I think it gives her the strength to continue a story I'm not sure she's ever told. "One of the kids at the first foster home ODed, which meant all the kids had to go somewhere else, and that started the roller coaster. There were some good ones, with nice people who gave a shit, but I lost count at some point." She drops her eyes to the table, staring unblinkingly at the white laminate surface. "Eventually, one of the foster families adopted me. Not because they loved me but because if I was 'theirs', the state didn't do checks on me as often, and I could take care of the younger ones and keep the house while they cashed the checks. They promised that when I was eighteen, they'd add me to the 'payroll', as they called it, basically meaning that as another adult in the house, they could foster more kids and make more money. Of course, I'd have to pay for room and board, though." She huffs out a bitter, mirthless laugh.

"I left. Worked, slept on couches, and eventually got myself pulled together. I'm doing good now. Ironically, after all that, I'm a nanny, so I still take care of kids, but it's on my own terms." She seems more present now, like she's here with Janey and me and has finally found a seed of happiness. "The family I work for, they're really great, and last Christmas, they got me one of those DNA kit things. They knew I always wondered . . . couldn't help it, you know?" She frowns, seeming almost embarrassed by her reasonable desire to know who she is and where she came from.

"The results came back with a match. William Webster. My biological father. I reached out to him, and he wanted to meet me."

Riley glances down at the phone again, but the screen has gone dark. I reach over and wake it back up so she can see the picture of her and her father again. She touches his face, and an errant tear runs down her cheek.

"I'm glad you told me," she whispers. "Otherwise, I would've thought he didn't want—" She cuts off what she was going to say with a choked sob.

"I'm sorry you didn't get to spend more time with him," Janey replies.

"Riley," I say carefully, not wanting to spook her after everything she shared, "Will's wife is doing all the paperwork after his death. As his daughter, there are assets you're likely entitled to. If you need help with a lawyer, I can connect you with one. Pro bono." I don't add that I'll be covering that cost because there's no way Riley has the funds to bankroll something like that.

She's shaking her head, refusing me before I finish offering. "No, no, no. I don't want his money or anything. I want . . ." she pauses, correcting herself, "*wanted* to get to know him. And I did."

I'm not sure she understands what she's potentially giving up. The Websters aren't top one-percenters or anything, but they have enough that Riley could probably set herself up for life if she handled an inheritance properly. "He doesn't have other children, nobody other than his wife. She knows about you." I wouldn't usually divulge that, even under threat of prison or death, but this situation feels different from most. Riley feels different from most clients I work with. And she's not even my client.

"She knows about me?" Riley repeats, a thread of hope woven in the question, and I realize that the way I phrased it makes it sound like Will told his wife about his long-lost daughter.

"That Will was meeting with you, not who you were to him," I correct. "She thought he was sneaking away for other reasons." I leave that open to interpretation, having probably shared too much already.

Riley's shoulders droop and her face falls. She studiously picks at her fingers for a long minute while she thinks and then sighs as she meets my eyes again. "Thank you for telling me what happened. And for the offer to help. I really appreciate it. But I got what I needed in that cabin in the woods. I wanted a family, a history, a place where I belonged. That's all I ever wanted, and for a minute, I had it. That's more than some people get, so I guess in some ways, I'm lucky. I had a great mom who loved me so hard, she fought to stay with me long after she was ready to let go. And a dad who was excited to meet me, said he loved me, and wanted to get to know me. I wish I'd known them longer, but I'm really blessed to have known them at all." She places her hand on her chest, tears falling openly now.

Janey's crying too, dabbing her eyes with a napkin, and I clear my throat while discretely swiping at my own eyes.

This woman, who's been through so much, is sitting here with more love and hope in her shattered and stomped-on heart than I could possibly imagine. It makes me disappointed in myself for not appreciating my own family, who're not perfect but are at least here and willing to repair some of the shit we've gone through.

"I'm gonna go, but thanks," Riley says once more.

She stands, but I stop her. "Wait. Here, take this." I hold out a business card. "Call me anytime, for anything. If I can help in any way, call."

Riley takes the card, slipping it into her pocket without looking at it. I don't think I'll ever hear from her again.

Janey's more hands-on, standing and holding her arms out. Riley and Janey embrace for a long time, having found a connection in a moment of pain. "You're okay. Always have been, always will be," Janey tells her. I sense that she's said those words to herself more than a few times when things were rough.

"You know it," Riley replies. In some ways, they're kindred spirits, and both are stronger for this moment of shared kinship.

As Riley walks out of the coffee shop, Janey sits down and falls into my arms. I run a soothing hand up and down her back, comforting her until she's cried out.

"That was awful, but I'm glad she got to meet her dad after all these years," Janey says when she's calmed down enough to speak. She's turned, tucked into my side so that her head's resting on my shoulder.

"I'm more shocked she didn't want to go after the cash." It's crude, but unfortunately true. Not many could see a pile of money that they have legal claim to and walk away from it because it wasn't what mattered to them. The person was.

"You know how she said she found her family in that cabin in the woods?" Janey whispers.

"Yeah?"

She lifts her head, looking me in the eyes. Her gray ones are bloodshot, pink, and puffy, but she looks gorgeous to me. Her big heart, even when it's hurting, is beautiful. "I did too."

She doesn't mean her family of assholes. She means me. I'm her family.

And truthfully, she's mine.

But it's more than that. Meeting Janey in that cabin not only gave me her, but she's managed to somehow give me all my siblings, bringing us together in a way we've never been before. Janey did that, with her smiles and sunshine, hopes and silver linings.

But it's all her. My Janey.

"Me too," I answer, placing a gentle kiss to her lips. "You ready to go home?"

Her smile is all the answer I need, so I wave at the waitress. She holds a hand up, letting me know she'll be right with me.

"I'm gonna freshen up really quick," Janey tells me, pointing at her eyes and then the restroom across the diner.

"Alright, I'll be right here," I say. I watch her walk across the room, and once she's safely in the restroom, I pull out my phone to text Louisa.

Person of Interest = daughter from college hookup. No interest in pursuing inheritance. No need to notify client. Webster case, closed.

It seems harsh to summarize the last forty-five minutes into four emotionless sentences, but it's all the record needs to reflect. The tears, the story, the heartfelt connection, those aren't for an impersonal record. They're for me, Janey, and Riley, who I truly hope will continue to do well.

CHAPTER 25
JANEY

IN THE RESTROOM, I blow my nose and wash my hands, splash the cool water on my face and tap my fingers under my eyes, hoping to dissipate the puffiness a bit. I can't wash away the evidence of all the crying, but that's okay. It was worth every tear to see Riley walk out with her head held high and her back straight, knowing that she has a place in the world—one she was created from, and one she carved out herself with hard work.

"As good as it's gonna get," I tell my reflection in the mirror over the sink. Still, I tap at my cheeks a little, giving them a bit of rosy color before I open the door and walk back into the restaurant.

I'm barely out of the restroom when I hear my name. "Janey?"

I glance to my left and see Henry, sitting alone at a table with a cup of coffee. He looks the same as he always did. His hair's freshly trimmed, his face clean-shaven even though it's late in the day, his tie is precisely centered on his throat, and his sleeves are folded back carefully to showcase his expensive watch.

"I thought that was you. Hey!" he says with a friendly smile. Like we're old buddies running into each other and he's not an ex who cheated on me, abandoned me, and made me feel like I was worth less than gum on his shoe.

Actually, that part was probably *partially* my fault. He didn't do the things he should've, and that blame rests solely on his shoulders, but I didn't demand more or expect better. And I accepted his bare minimum time and time again while making excuses for him. That's on me.

I know better now. I would never stoop that low.

This time, it's Henry who's rambling, not me. "You look great. How're you doing? Have a seat and we can catch up." He points at the chair across from him, welcoming me to sit with him and assuming I'll be glad to do so.

"Are you serious?" I snap, indignant that he would think I'd fall right back into his arms that easily.

"What?" he shrugs like my reaction is completely irrational. When he sees the anger on my face, he actually chuckles. "Don't be like that. Look, I'm sorry, okay?"

He makes it sound like his apologizing is doing me a favor. That what he did was no more than being late for a cup of coffee or something.

"I was just so loaded with deadlines, projects, and upgrades. And you were all 'meet the family!'" He mimics the happy excitement I had about that with disdain. "I figured some time would do us both good, ya know? And I didn't want to take all the stress out on you. I needed a release valve from the pressure cooker at work. That's all it was. You know how it is." He smiles like that's enough because that's *it*, that's all he's got. That's his apology, explanation, and justification. The sum total is worth less than the air he wasted to say them.

"You don't have to apologize for what your so-called 'stress' did to you. But what you did to me? That was wrong. That's what you should apologize for," I tell him, calmly but firmly.

I'm not the same Janey he knew before.

I'm not the same person I was then.

I've grown stronger, changed for the better, and learned what it really means to have a partner stand at your side and at your back, even when things go to hell in a fiery handbasket.

He doesn't say a word, only stammers senselessly, which definitely doesn't resemble a true apology, so I keep going. "I'll own that I let it go on too long, but you did too. You were more than happy to be hurtful, dismissive, and cruel to me. I learned from it. Have you? Or are you still the jerk you always were, out for yourself, no matter the cost to anyone else?"

"Wait a minute, it wasn't all bad. We had some good times. If you've forgotten, I could remind you," he says with a sleepy-eyed smile, dragging a fingertip around the rim of his coffee mug like that's supposed to be sexy, even though I know he couldn't find a clit with an anatomy drawing, a headlamp, and a tour guide.

"No. Hell. No." I hold up both hands, giving him my palms in the universal 'stop' sign. I think I'm channeling Kayla as I do it, but it works now the way it worked for her.

Henry's smile falters, and I think for the first time, he's realizing that I'm not the forgiving, weak, scrap-accepting woman I used to be. I'm strong, powerful, and know my worth. And my new and improved expectations are astronomical and still being surpassed each and every day by one man.

Cole.

"Whatever. You look like shit. Your eyes are all bloodshot, your hair's frizzy, and you smell like old people," Henry accuses, despite his earlier claims to the contrary.

Truthfully, I saw myself in the bathroom mirror and I do look awful. Not that it matters because that has nothing to do with Henry's bluster now. He's lashing out, trying to hurt me again, and using the easiest weapon he can—my appearance—to put me down and make himself feel superior.

"That's enough," a gruff voice says behind me.

I smile, not needing to turn around. I knew Cole was listening from afar, letting me have my moment to shine and trusting that I could handle myself while keeping watch over me. I sink back into him, letting my back rest against his solid chest, and he places possessive hands on my shoulders.

"Who's this?" Henry demands, sounding angry at the idea that I might have found someone else despite having been screwing around on me while we were actually together.

"My boyfriend," I answer with a smirk. It's never seemed sillier to describe Cole as a 'boy', but the look on Henry's face at that reply is worth it. I laugh. "Did you think I was sitting around pining for *you*?"

I give him a look up and down, knowing that he's already comparing himself to Cole and finding himself lacking. Not in the ways that truly matter, like heart and soul, but in the things Henry values—money, attractiveness, and dominance.

Yeah, Henry knows my trigger spots. But I know his too. I avoided them at all costs while we were together, no matter how many times he trampled over mine. But now? I feel free to say what I've thought so many times before. Ironically, for all the rambling I did, I somehow kept the truth tucked deep inside, filtering that from Henry.

"You made me weak because you liked feeling superior to me," I say, and Henry starts to argue. I keep talking, taking some of the blame, "And I let you. But I'm better now. Not because Cole made me strong but because *I* did." I pat myself on the chest proudly and then smile. "Bonus, he likes that because he can handle my best me. I'm happy now, for the first time ever."

"You forgot to tell him how I worship your sexy body until you've come so many times, you pass out in my arms," Cole stage-whispers in my ear, loud enough for Henry, and those close, to hear.

I have to laugh. He's letting me have my 'I am woman, hear me roar' moment, but he's still possessive and wants to shamelessly claim me.

The ladies at the next table, who've apparently been eavesdropping, cheer. "Ooh, girl, did you hear that?"

"Yeah, and what he said," I add, feeling a blush creep up my neck.

"Whatever," Henry snaps, still eyeing Cole like he's considering possible angles where he might come out on top but finding none.

The truth is Cole is ten times the man Henry will ever be. Not because he's stronger, richer, or more attractive. Or because he's perfect, because he's definitely not. It's because I don't have to wonder where I stand with him. He's upfront and honest to a fault. I don't have to search for silver linings in Cole. He's all gray, all the time, but that's somehow exactly what I need. I don't have to hide any part of myself, not even the weird ones, with Cole. He accepts me as I am and celebrates everything about me.

I'm done here. I'm glad to have had this opportunity to tell Henry what I think, but it won't change anything for him. He'll brush me off easily, the way he always did. But it did change something for me. I have a sharper clarity now on my relationship with Cole and what it means.

"Let's go home," I tell Cole.

He doesn't answer, just guides me away from Henry. I don't look back, not even once. I don't need to. That part of my life is over. That version of myself is gone.

I'm sure Cole looks back, though, because he chuckles at my side as we exit the diner.

Outside, he stops us, creating a safe space for me with my back against the wall and his hands on my hips. "You okay?" he asks, lifting my chin with a finger. When I meet his eyes, he's gazing at me in wonder.

"Yeah," I answer, then reconsider. "Actually, better than okay. It felt so good to finally say all that," I confess.

Cole grins, looking proud of me. "It was sexy as hell."

The recognition is hard-won, but I fought for it, earning it myself . . . but with Cole's help. He's the one who truly showed me, time after time, what I should expect in a partner, what I should demand for myself, and what happiness can be.

"Thank you," I say. I lift up to my toes and press a kiss to his lips, stealing that smile for myself.

"Didn't do anything. That was all you, woman," he answers. But I see the quirk of his lip. He knows what he did.

CHAPTER 26
JANEY

SITTING on the arm of my couch, I stare out the window at the street, watching for a silver Suburban to pull into my driveway.

"Do you think they forgot me?" I call out to Cole.

He's in the kitchen, eating reheated spaghetti from a plastic bowl. "Do you have your Red Bull and trail mix?" he answers, avoiding my question. "No telling how long it'll take with all of you going, and I don't want you to get hangry or decaffeinated."

Distracted by his suggestion, I tap the bag at my side, feeling the cold energy drink and hearing the crinkle of my Ziploc baggie of snacks. "Yeah, I've got them."

"They'll be here," he promises, answering my original question. He types on his phone and then holds it up. "Kayla says they're turning into the neighborhood now."

I smile. Not that they didn't forget me—*okay, maybe that a little*—but mostly because Cole just casually texted his sister. Like it's no big deal. Like they talk all the time. Like they're thick as thieves now.

I hop up from my perch and rush him, my heart suddenly racing. "Really? Okay. They're almost here. Be cool, Janey. It's no big deal. Just a girls' day out. It's a pedicure, not an audition. It'll be fine."

Cole chuckles, bending down to get in my face. "You know

they think you're amazing, right? Kayla calls you a lion tamer, like you're a badass or something."

He smirks, and I remember the night of Paisley's wedding, when Cole overheard my self-pep talk. Then, calling myself a badass was almost ridiculously silly. Now, it doesn't feel as absurd, but it's still a stretch compared to Kayla and Samantha.

"They're badasses. I'm just Janey," I counter.

"You're not *just* anything. You're Janey Williams, lion tamer extraordinaire, monster trainer, asshole whisperer . . . wait, not that last one," he corrects with a horrified shake of his head. "We're not *that* freaky."

I can't help but laugh, which I'm pretty sure was his mission because when a horn honks outside a second later, I'm calmer and definitely not freaking out as much. "They're here! I've gotta go!" I tell him, pressing a quick kiss to his cheek.

He follows me to the door, and once it's open—where his family can see!—he shamelessly pulls me back in for a more thorough kiss. "Have fun, and I'll see you tonight, 'kay?"

"Okay!" I repeat. As excited as I am for a girls' day out with Cole's family, I'm a little nervous about tonight. We're all convening at the Harrington house for a mandatory family dinner. But first things first . . . pedicures!

Cole would usually open the car door for me, but the girls have already rearranged themselves inside, leaving the door open for me. When I climb into the back seat, they all whoop and holler. "*Damn*, girl! Getcha sum!" Samantha says.

"Go on and kiss da girl!" Luna sings in a baritone voice, sounding like Sebastian, the crab from *The Little Mermaid*. I found out at the wedding that she's a total Disney movie addict and likes to sing the songs randomly.

Gracie leans over to her, adding in the harmony, "Sha-la-la-la-la, don't be scared!" The two of them dissolve into giggles, and I'm so happy she's coming with us today.

I blush, but it's more about the attention from them than the kiss from Cole.

"Welcome to the Mom-mobile," Miranda says, meeting my

eyes in the rearview mirror with a friendly smile. "Your house is lovely."

"Thank you," I reply, knowing my small ranch house is nothing compared to the Harrington estate. But it's home, and I'm proud of it. I glance out the window as she pulls out of the drive and see Cole still standing in the doorway. I wave goodbye one more time and squirm around in my seat to face forward.

"Looks like Cole's a fan too," Miranda quips, honking her horn once more as we zoom off.

At the salon, Miranda checks us in, happily telling the receptionist, "Mani-pedis for all my girls."

Being included in the Harrington girls' trip alone is awesome enough, but being grouped in with everyone like that is a whole different level of awesomeness that makes my heart skip a beat. I can't hide the giddy smile on my face. But . . .

"Oh, I'd love to do the pedicure, but I can't have nail polish at work," I say, showing her my short, naked nails that are a requirement at The Ivy.

"No problem, you can leave your nails bare if you want, but enjoy the pampering part." She smiles warmly, and I agree, mostly because I don't want to be the odd woman out because even Gracie is picking out a color from the wall.

"Should I do purple or red?" Gracie asks, holding up two bottles.

Kayla looks over and suggests, "Both? Add a magenta too." She helps her niece find a third color to add to the mix, and then they start discussing which fingers should be which color.

"Ready!" Gracie shouts in excitement when she's got it figured out.

Everyone else chooses their color, and we follow the receptionist to a lineup of massage chairs. Somehow, I end up in the middle, with Samantha and Luna on my left and Miranda, Gracie, and Kayla on my right. It's almost a six-part harmony sigh of comfort as we slip our feet into the bubbling, hot water, and the receptionist pushes buttons on each remote, starting the back massage feature.

Things get busy for a moment as our nail technicians swarm

and we all explain what we want on our fingers and toes. Once everyone's treatments are underway, Miranda says, "Thanks for coming with me today. I love getting to hang out with you all."

We share our appreciation too, and then she asks, "So, what're my boys up to today?"

Luna starts, "Carter's looking at a property with Zack—" She stops and leans forward to look at me. "That's my brother, the one I told you about who does real estate." I nod, appreciating the Spark Notes, and she continues, "And knowing the two of them, they'll probably end up finding three other properties along the way and at least two investment opportunities." She laughs, sounding like that's a perfectly normal Saturday.

Gracie jumps in with her own report. "Daddy's working, of course. He's a *work-ma-holic*. I tried telling him that he should do something fun for a change, but he said work is fun." I don't have to see her to hear the heavy eye roll and know exactly what she thinks of her dad's work habits. "But he said we could make pancakes tomorrow morning if I slept in! I tried negotiating for birthday sprinkle ones and six o'clock, but he said those are for special occasions only and six is still the middle of the night. He agreed to chocolate chips and eight o'clock, though, so I'm putting that one in the win column."

I don't know how she can sound so young and so old all at the same time, but she does, somehow fitting right in like one of the girls.

"Next time, try calling them funfetti pancakes," Miranda suggests. "That's what your dad used to eat when he was about your age."

I swear the girl is taking notes in an invisible notebook inside her brain because she stops, stares off into space for a moment, and then nods. "Got it. Thanks, Mimi!"

We all laugh, feeling like Miranda just ran right over Cameron's attempt at reasonableness, though I'm not sure chocolate chips over sprinkles is a hill to die on when there's pancakes and syrup involved.

"Chance?" Miranda asks Samantha.

"Basketball at the club. We've had quite a few new guys join, and he's trying to get to know them. Apparently, getting sweaty on the court is the best way to do that."

That elicits plenty of laughter, and I wait to see if Kayla is going to say anything but realize they're looking at me, waiting for my report on Cole. "Oh! Cole's playing chess at the center with one of the patients."

"He's doing what?" Miranda asks, almost in awe.

"Uhm, we have a patient, Mr. C, who likes to play chess," I say carefully, keeping Mr. Culderon's anonymity. "And when Cole came to visit me one time, they played a game. It's kinda become their 'thing'. It's been good for them both, I think, especially since Mr. C's son hasn't been able to come as often. Cole's been practicing and reading up on how to be a better player so Mr. C won't have to hold back so much, but honestly, he could probably beat anyone in a handful of moves. They have fun, though, and have even had an audience a couple of times."

Kayla leans forward to see around the other girls and smiles at me. "See, you are magic. Cole, my brother, is playing chess in front of a crowd of people with a guy he met at the nursing home?"

"Well, long term care center," I correct. "And I wouldn't go so far as to say it was a crowd, but there're a few people who watched. I think Mrs. D only watches Cole, though, not the chess game."

It's that last part that made me laugh the first time I saw it. Because of all the people Cole has met at the center, the one person you'd least expect to like him—Mrs. Donald, who hates everyone and everything—*loves* Cole. It's practically a schoolgirl crush. You can virtually watch her orneriness melt away when Cole arrives and it's so cute that I can't be jealous. Not even when she crocheted him a pair of slippers, which he immediately put on after kicking off his boots. I mean, that's too adorable!

It's like my plan to make Cole's family see how awesome he is has worked so well that everyone sees it. I think even Cole himself has started to realize it, which has healed some hurt he's held on to for a long time.

Because these people, his family, love him and have always

loved him. There might've been misunderstandings, and even some hate, but still, they'd do anything for each other. Compared to my family where I always had to pretend that everything was fine when it was damaging me in deep, painful ways, I know what I'd choose if given the chance.

The Harringtons. Real love. Not toxicity.

And today, I feel like they're choosing me back.

Me, Janey Williams.

CHAPTER 27
COLE

FAMILY DINNER AT HOME. For so many years, I avoided them at virtually any cost and made an exit as quickly as I could when I did design to actually attend.

Tonight, that changes.

The night at my place with my siblings was a good first step, but it hasn't fixed everything. Only time will do that, and it'll need a lot of effort on my part. That dinner might have felt huge, but in truth, it was actually pretty small. But it's opened a door that was sealed shut and boarded over. By me.

Which means it's also my responsibility to rip those boards down, even if I catch a few splinters in the process.

Knowing I've got a table full of not only family, but friends, makes tonight's dinner the first I'm excited to attend. Especially with Janey at my side.

She's the one who's given me a life. Not only an existence in the shadows. And I want to share that life with her, starting with a simple dinner at my family home.

I glance at my phone. I didn't put an AirTag on Janey despite our jokes, but we do share our locations—at her request, so she knows where I am during stake-outs. Bonus for me, it means I know where she is too. I see her little dot moving toward my dot.

"They close?" Carter asks.

"Ten minutes." Even knowing she's miles away, I glance out the window of the living room like she might magically appear, and Carter laughs.

"You'd better lock that one down. I think anyone else would've already been done with your shit." He points to my phone and the location app. "Luna would roll her eyes if I tried that, and we can both guess what Samantha would do to Chance."

He's not wrong. But none of them work in a field where they occasionally have to go silent for days at a time while doing potentially risky things. That explains why Janey wants the location service. Me? I'm just stalkerish by nature at this point after seeing and hearing some of the stories I have.

"I know," I admit. "Believe me, I fucking know."

A loud rumbling echoes down the street a moment before Kyle turns into the front drive. He's going too fast but expertly leans into the turn, kicking up dust as he hits the end of the driveway. Thankfully, the gate is open because he blasts past it, parking in front of the house. Rather than turning the motorcycle off, he revs the throttle a few times first, announcing his arrival with roaring growls before shutting off the engine. When he pulls his helmet off and hangs it over the handlebars, his grin is wide and toothy. He's here, early even, but he still had to make an entrance of some sort.

The noise pulls Dad out of his office and the two cross paths in the foyer.

"What're you doing here?" Dad asks, not cruelly, but rather, in surprise at Kyle's timeliness.

"Mandatory family dinner, right?" Kyle says without pausing, walking past Dad and into the living room, plopping into a chair across from Carter and me like he owns the joint. He quirks a brow at me, silently letting me know that he's here because I asked him to be, but he's still gonna do what he can to make Dad mad because that's what he does.

"Yes," Dad answers, his brows furrowed as he looks from Kyle to Carter to me. He's probably trying to figure out just what sort of magic Carter or I used to get Kyle here on time and why he isn't able to do the same thing. Problem is, the answer is in his mirror, and Dad's like me, not willing to look there voluntarily. "Let me wrap things up."

He disappears back down the hall to his office, where he and Cameron are doing fuck-knows-what for the family company.

Kyle leans his head sideways to watch Dad go. "They do know it's Saturday, right? As in, The Weekend. Like, no-worky-days."

"Funny," Carter quips dryly. "Pretty sure that's all they do."

Carter shouldn't throw stones. He used to be just as bad, tangled up in the rat race to the top of cheese mountain, fighting to beat Cameron at every turn. It wasn't until he found a way to escape with Luna that he found some work-life balance, but at least he can see beyond the boardroom these days.

I'm not sure that's the case for Cameron, and it's certainly never been the case for Dad.

My phone vibrates, alerting me that Janey's dot has converged on my dot. "They're here." I'm heading for the garage door as I say the words, going out to meet Janey.

Gracie beats me to it, busting into the house and shouting at the top of her lungs in excitement, "*Dad*!! Come look at my nails!"

As all the women walk in behind Gracie, I only have eyes for Janey. It's only been a few hours, but damn, I missed her. I take her in my arms, wrapping her in a big hug and pressing a solid kiss to her lips, which are smiling. "Did you have fun?"

Her gray eyes are dancing as she nods wildly, making her curls bounce. "We did! Everyone got pedicures and manicures. Even me!" She holds up her unpolished nails like I'm supposed to see something there, so I smile at the difference even though they look the same as they did this morning. "I got this cuticle oil that's gonna be life changing with all the handwashes. And my toes are lavender."

"Your favorite color," I say, and she smiles, pleased that I know that small, basic detail as if her favorite mug, keychain, and toothbrush aren't the same color.

I guess Dad and Cameron really were wrapping it up because

Cameron appears to answer his daughter's call. "Let me see," he tells her with a smile. It's good to see Cam smile.

Gracie holds up her pinkie and ring fingers. "See! These are purple." She switches to her index fingers and thumbs. "And these are red." And then she holds up both middle fingers, innocently flipping her dad off as she proclaims, "And these are magenta. Aunt Kayla helped me pick this color."

Kayla beams proudly like 'yep, I did that.'

Cameron doesn't react, not even a quirk of his brow as he looks thoughtfully at his daughter's nails. "They look really pretty, honey. Why don't you go wash up before dinner?"

As soon as she skips off to do so, he laughs. "Do you think she knew what she was doing?" He shakes his head, answering his own question. "Probably not, right?"

Kyle chuckles and admits, "Pretty sure she's seen me flip someone off before, so yeah, she knows." But in the same breath, she makes an excuse for her too. "How else was she supposed to show you the different colors, though?"

He grins and Cameron sighs.

"Can someone help me get dinner? We stopped and picked up pizzas on the way home," Mom says, cutting off the argument. Like she knew would happen, the four of us dash for the Suburban. "Thank you."

Pizza nights were unusual at the Harrington house when we were growing up, and as such, we were basically feral as we fought to claim the number of slices we wanted. Not that there was a shortage. Mom bought plenty then, and now, there are no fewer than fifteen pizza boxes in the Suburban, plus smaller ones of bread and cheese sticks.

Each of us snatch a few, opening boxes to shove a slice into our respective mouths. "Chance's missing out," Kyle says around his mouthful. "Where's he at?"

As we set our boxes on the kitchen island, Samantha answers. "On his way."

"Sucks to be him," Kyle answers, going for a breadstick now.

"Boys, plates are in the cabinet, and there's different kinds, so don't fill up on pepperoni," Mom says as she grabs wine, beer, and soda from the fridge.

That was another part of the ritual of pizza nights. When we were kids, we'd drink so much soda that we'd nearly get sick. Later, beer and wine became options, which also led to a few upset stomachs, and a lot more fighting, to be honest. Somehow, nobody ever chose to drink water or anything else with pizza, though I don't know why.

I never thought about the traditions we did have or how they came to be. I certainly never considered that tussles for the last slice of pepperoni or the cheesiest cheese stick would be a fond memory, not one that ignited fresh anger at having missed out again. But now, I can see how even those brotherly battles bonded us in ways. Some, more than others. But still, silly things like pizza nights did help us become and stay a family.

We take Mom's hint as Kayla pulls a stack of plates from the cabinet and Cameron helps serve Gracie two slices of cheese pizza. Once she's clear, we dive in to fill our plates and glasses, then make our way to the dining room table.

It's probably strange to have pizza at the formal table, but it's the only table that fits us all, especially with spouses and Gracie.

We dig in, happily munching on our pizza as Mom tells us how much fun she had with everyone today. "I can't wait to do it again," she exclaims right as Chance walks in.

"Shit, did I miss it?" he asks, his eyes jerking to me. I glare at him in answer, and he clacks his mouth shut before saying, "I mean, all that pepperoni . . . It's my favorite."

That's obviously not what he meant, but no one calls him on it.

I wait for him to come back with his plate of pizza and take a swallow of beer. As if she can sense my nerves, Janey puts her hand on my thigh beneath the table. I didn't tell her I was for-sure doing this tonight, but we've talked about it. She's certain it's the right choice. I hope to fuck she's right.

"Mom, Dad? There's something I want to tell you," I start.

I swear a hush falls over the table, nobody even chewing

because they don't want to miss this over a bit of too-crunchy pizza crust.

"Yes, honey. What is it?" Mom asks, dabbing at her mouth with a napkin.

I take a big breath. I should've planned what I was going to say, but I thought words would come to me in the moment. I was wrong. "In case you were wondering, I'm a private investigator."

Yep, that's it. No explanation or context clues or warning. Just a bomb drop of 'here's what I do for a living' as if I'm someone they just met.

A solid two seconds later, which feels like an eternity, Mom gasps with wide eyes. "You're a what? A private investigator? That sounds so dangerous!"

If there were Academy Awards for the Worst Supporting Actress, Mom would win hands-down. Her dramatics are on-par with Gracie telling a story about purple monsters dancing through her school hallway.

Mom looks to Dad for help, but he shrugs. "And?"

I'm good at reading people. It's literally my job, or at least a major part of it. But when I look from Mom to Dad and back, I can't connect what I'm seeing with what I expected.

Confused, I try to clarify, asking blankly, "You know?"

"What do you mean? Of course we do," Dad says. "We've always known. I couldn't have my son out there doing God knows what. I got my guy to look into you years ago."

"We were worried, you know?" Mom explains, looking a bit worried about my reaction now.

Dad investigated me. And I didn't know it. How in the hell did that happen? I try to think back, searching my memory for any time there might've been someone surveilling me, but I can't find any suspicious behavior. Of course, depending on how long ago it was, I might've been too green to notice at the time.

I'm stunned, frozen in place as my mind goes a million miles a second. They know. They've always known. It wasn't some big secret they never cared enough to ask about. In fact, they cared so much they investigated *me* and then never said a word, respecting my silence on the matter much the way my siblings did.

Janey squeezes my thigh beneath the table, quietly supportive and maybe begging me to be okay with this.

"We were relieved when you settled into the new place. Good location, great security, and a fair amount of street footage if you ever want to sell. Shows you've created a solid niche market for yourself and are doing well. I'm proud of you." Dad throws out business talk easily, but what really hits are those four words.

He's proud of me?

What the fuck alternate universe am I living in?

Janey's shaking my leg beneath the table to the point I'm nearly wobbling in my seat. I glance over and find her smiling maniacally. "I told you! I knew they'd be happy for you!"

She did tell me that. Several times, in fact. She saw the silver lining in my family even when all I could see were the storm clouds and lightning.

"Uh, thanks," I tell Dad. Looking around the table at my siblings, they all seem as gobsmacked as I feel.

"So wait," Gracie says, looking up from her pizza. "Are you like Magnum P.I., Uncle Cole? 'Cuz I like Jay Hernandez."

"Who?" Mom asks.

"Jay Hernandez," Gracie repeats. "He's Magnum P.I."

"I think you mean Tom Selleck, honey," Mom says assuredly, and Gracie shakes her head.

"There's been a remake, Mom," Cameron says helpfully. "I watch it sometimes, and apparently, someone's been watching with me when she's supposed to be in bed." Cameron gives his daughter a fatherly look of 'this isn't over', but she doesn't seem to notice because she's looking at me for an answer.

"Not exactly?" I say uncertainly, but when Gracie looks disappointed, I correct myself, "But yeah, kinda, I guess."

Mom takes a sip of her wine and casually asks, "So was this supposed to be one of those big secrets you all have, like Ira leaving the side door open? You know that I know all about that, right?"

"What?" Kayla squawks. "That was supposed to be between me and Ira!"

We look at each other in surprise and then at Mom's innocent grin, realizing that Ira and Mom played us all. We were young and dumb, playing checkers while they were playing chess. I think we all had a 'secret' deal with Ira to sneak out, and meanwhile, he was sending us on our merry way and keeping our parents apprised of our every move.

Mom laughs. "I couldn't believe you never ran into each other trying to get back before Charles's midnight nightcap and my two a.m. potty break."

I replay the countless times I stood outside, watching the clock and waiting for a light to shut off, signaling the coast was clear because Mom and Dad were in bed. Never once did I think they were waiting up for me or even cared that I'd snuck out. It also never occurred to me that I wasn't the only kid sneaking out.

"How did we never run into each other?" Kayla wonders.

"I have no idea what you're talking about. I never snuck out," Chance offers.

"Of course you didn't, Mr. Goody Two-Shoes," Kyle teases. "You were in bed by ten every night to get your eight hours like a good boy. The rest of us had lives."

"Shit!" I hiss, connecting more dots. "I saw Ira at the deli that time. He said he was visiting a friend."

Dad doesn't say anything, but I know that little smirk of a grin. I've made it myself when I feel like I've gotten away with something.

Dad knew about my work and life all these years, and Mom knew what we were up to even back when we were kids. They always knew . . . everything. And maybe they were giving me the space I made it seem like I wanted, letting me keep my 'secrets' and not dismissing me entirely.

This doesn't fix everything, especially with my dad. There's still a lifetime of asshattery on both our sides. But Janey helped fix me and my siblings, and maybe eventually, this revelation will help fix me and my parents.

"Are you talking about secrets?" Gracie asks. "Like buying me the grande java chip *frabb-a-chino* Dad won't let me have?"

"What?" Cameron asks, whirling around to look at his daughter. "Who gives you that?"

Gracie shrugs and smiles innocently. "Everyone but you."

Cameron turns a glare to everyone at the table, one by one, and we all pretend like we don't see it or have any idea what Gracie's talking about.

"Next time, you're getting hot chocolate," Mom threatens Gracie, who seems remarkably unconcerned about the punishment. "No whipped cream."

"Wow, tough love there, Mom," Cameron quips.

Gracie just laughs and chews her pizza contentedly. She knows that of all the Harringtons . . . she's the princess in charge.

CHAPTER 28
JANEY

"THAT WENT SO GOOD!" I shout happily as we walk in the front door of my house. "I knew it would. I don't think I even needed my plan. They already knew."

Cole shuts the door, locking it behind us. "Plan? What plan?"

Oops! Shouldn't have said that part.

"Uhm . . . my plan to, uh . . ."

"Janey." Cole raises his brows expectantly. "Just say it."

"Plan Cole: Recognize the Awesomeness," I admit with a flash of my hands like the plan was on a lit marquee all along. Cole frowns, not getting it, so I explain, "You said they didn't know you, so I wanted them to see how awesome you are. But it turns out, they did know! You just didn't know they knew what they already knew, ya know?"

That makes total sense, I'm almost sure of it. And rather than being mad at my scheming, Cole shakes his head with a smile as he gathers me into his arms. "You're the awesome one. About that . . . can we talk?"

I watch his smile fall and his eyes go dark and serious, and once upon a time, I would've gone into full-blown panic mode, expecting a verbal blindside. Or a hurtful insult, blame, or anger. I was conditioned to anticipate and accept those things, and the only way I could mitigate their damage was by pretending it was something else. Something to get through to get to the sunny day on the other side.

But that Janey's gone. I healed her, with Cole's help, so I'm able to give him the moment he needs to collect his thoughts without worry. Words are hard, especially for him, and I can wait.

"This was easier last time," he grumbles, but I have no idea what he means. He guides me to the couch, and we sit down, facing each other. He reaches to take both my hands in his, takes a big breath like he's preparing for something major, and then blurts out, "I love you."

He exhales heavily like a weight's been lifted off his shoulders with the admission. I can't help but smile, a little confused at the big to-do over something so blatantly obvious. "I know."

"What?"

"I know you love me," I clarify for him. "I love you too."

He smiles, one of the big, almost boyish-looking ones where his eyes light up. "You do?"

"Duh," I say teasingly, dumbfounded by his disbelief. "Of course I do. Have you met you? You're awesome, as evidenced by my fool-proof, guaranteed-to-work, complete success of a plan."

"I have met me. Hence, the surprise at your reaction," he quips. "I didn't say it, so I thought . . ."

He doesn't get it. He's being self-deprecating, but I actually love his grumpy, quiet self and that, of all the people in the world, he chose to let me inside his secretly tender heart. Well, maybe I kinda forced my way in like a stage-five clinger, but he didn't seem to mind. Mostly.

"I don't need the words," I say. "I've been burned by them my entire life, and you've shown me that you love me in a million different ways . . . with actions, every single day. When you think of me, consider me, and strive to behave in a way that will make me happy—that's your love. Your actions are your truth, and I feel them loud and clear."

I press a hand to my heart because that's where I feel him.

The way he looks at me makes tears prick at the corners of my eyes.

His actions are enough for me. But Cole?

I saw his face when his dad said he was proud of him. It put a little spit and bubble gum patch on a crack in his heart that'd been there since he was a child. And his face just now when I said 'I love you too.'

He wants my words.

Nobody ever wanted to hear me, so I talked to myself because I was alone. Cole thought nobody wanted to listen to him, so he basically quit talking. But somehow, what we need and what we provide are perfect for each other.

"Cole, I love you," I repeat. Taking his hands, I say it three more times, squeezing his hands each time for emphasis. "I love you, I love you, I love you."

He smiles again, and I secretly vow to tell him every day, a million times a day, until he's sick and tired of hearing it. After that, I'll whisper it to him when he's sleeping, send text messages, and leave him lipstick notes on the mirror until he knows it deep in his soul.

Mental note: buy some lipstick.

"Well, that'll make this part easier, then," he says.

I'm excited when he stands up, thinking he's about to lead me to the bedroom. But instead, he drops to one knee.

I gasp, my hands covering my open mouth. *Is he . . .* "Cole?"

"Last time I did this, it was fake. To be clear, *this* is for real." He stares at me pointedly, and I nod happily.

"Okay, okay . . . I'm ready . . . go ahead . . . WAIT!" I shriek, holding up my hands. I swipe under my eyes and look up at the ceiling for a second, wanting to make sure I can see clearly. "Get it together, girl. You've been waiting your whole life for this moment and it's only happening once, so don't blink, because this is gonna be *so* good."

I finish off with a little squeal of giddiness to let loose the joy rushing through my bloodstream and then focus on Cole again.

"You ready?" he asks with a patient smile as he takes my hands in his once more.

I nod because if I say anything, I'm going to blurt out an answer before he asks the question.

"Janey Susannah Williams, you are the best and brightest thing in my life. You see good in the world and help me to see it too. You love with abandon, freely giving your whole heart. I vow to be worthy of that gift every single day. Thank you for showing me that love exists."

The words are close to his first proposal, but tweaked for who we've become, to each other and in ourselves. Vaguely, I wonder if he remembered what he said so exactly or if he scouted around and found video online somewhere of Paisley's 'ruined' reception and memorized what he said then so he could repeat it now. That seems more like him, and the effort that would take is endearing and makes my heart warm.

I'm vibrating, the 'yes' on the tip of my tongue, and if he doesn't hurry up and get to the question, I won't be able to hold it back. Actually, when my hair falls into my face, I realize I'm bobbing my head up and down, already silently answering.

Cole grins but doesn't make me wait any longer. "Will you do me the honor of letting me be your husband so I can love, cherish, and worship you all the days of our lives?"

"YES!" I shout as I throw myself at him. He catches me solidly as I wrap my arms around his neck, the two of us tumbling to the carpet. "I love you so much! Like stupid amounts of scary, obsessive, want to hole up and be hermit-y with you kind of love, so don't act like you don't know what you're getting into here later, okay?"

I feel his chuckle against my neck. "Same, woman."

He kisses me, and I can feel the universe click into place for once.

We're not a fairy tale story. He's a little rough, kinda stalkery, and with some damage. I'm no prize either, with more sunshine than sense sometimes. But somehow, our weirdo flags match. And that's what matters.

"Come here, there's something I want to show you," Cole mumbles against my lips.

I let him help me up from the floor and guide me down the hallway to my bedroom, *pretty* sure I know what he's going to show me. I've seen it before . . . but that doesn't mean I don't want to see it again.

And again.

And again.

———

Cole

I'm approximately ninety-nine-point-eight percent sure I got this right. I had Louisa hack into Janey's Pinterest boards, talked to Mason—who was zero help, talked to Kayla—who was some help, and ultimately, went with my gut.

Still, when I dig into the drawer Janey gave me in the dresser, I'm nervous.

I pull out the ring box, and Janey's eyes widen. "Oh!" she says in genuine shock. "A ring!"

I think she forgot entirely that proposals usually come with one, which is adorable. Of course, I want everyone to know she's mine, but most of all, I want Janey to look down at her hand every day and see that symbol of my love, right there with her, all the time.

I open the box and her eyes go glittery again. "Cole!"

"Do you like it?" I ask, staring at the ring I've spent hours already looking at and imagining on Janey's finger. "I researched what the policy was at your work for rings, and what's safest for the diamond, and . . ."

I did do all those things, plus, I shopped for a ridiculous amount of time until I found the one that felt right. Like Janey.

The ring is a thick gold band with an inlaid half-carat baguette diamond, smooth and almost flush-fitting to the gold band so it can be worn under gloves without tearing them, and as I slip it onto her finger, Janey's tears overflow.

"It's beautiful," she whispers. "It's a dream."

"Yes, you are," I answer.

She curls her hand to her chest, holding it protectively. I can tell that unless ordered to, she isn't taking it off, ever. Which is exactly what I wanted. "Thank you," she says, looking up into my eyes.

I smile back at her, chuckling. "Pretty sure I should be thanking you."

"I love you."

I don't think I'll ever get used to hearing that or the way it makes my chest feel tight. I think this feeling is . . . happiness.

I want to tell Janey I love her too, but I heard her earlier. She doesn't want words. She wants action, and I swear I will give her all the action she can handle.

Scooping her up into my arms, her legs wrap around my waist as I walk her the few steps to the bed. I undress her quickly, leaving her nude except for the ring on her finger. This is the first time I'll make love to her wearing nothing but that, but it won't be the last. For the rest of our lives, that ring will be on her finger. And soon, there will be one on mine too. I can't wait.

I lay Janey back on the bed, ready to spend forever showing her how much I love her.

I start at the top, running my fingers into her curls to grip them in my hands, guiding her head back to expose her neck. I lay kisses there, licking and sucking at her sensitive flesh, and when I feel the vibration of her moan, I chase it, taking her mouth in a deep kiss and swallowing the sound greedily.

The connection we have is already building, but I want to take my time with Janey. This time and every time. I want to write my love on her skin, fuck her until she feels empty without me inside her, and stare into her eyes as she shatters for me, and me alone.

Kissing and caressing her body, I show love to her shoulders, her arms, down to her fingertips, placing a gentle kiss to the palm of her right hand and then the ring finger of her left, right next to her new jewelry. Pressing her hands to the bed, I move over her to adore her pearled up nipples with my tongue, and she arches for more, which I willingly give.

As I move down her belly, I release her hands in favor of grabbing her hips. I squeeze her left one firmly, likely leaving pink fingerprints on her skin. I told her once that it grounded me, and that's still true. It always will be. But in my grip, I want her to feel that she is all I want, need, and love.

Janey is the soulmate I never dreamed existed for a man like me. She didn't heal me, and I didn't fix her. Instead, we helped each other find the strength to do it ourselves and come together better for it. At least, I'm better. I think Janey was always full of sunshine. She only needed someone worthy to share it with, and I'm so fucking glad she gave me time to be that man for her.

I blow a hot breath on her pussy but bypass it to continue my worship of her body in its entirety. When I press kisses to her inner thighs, she shakes, nearly clamping me in place, but I push her legs open and grin evilly when I see the evidence of her arousal glistening on her lips.

I glance up her body to find her watching me.

"Please," she pleads.

I run my hands down her legs, not wanting to miss an inch but unable to deny her what she wants. I position myself between her spread legs, placing my shoulders beneath her bent knees, and lick my lips at the beautiful sight before me. As much as I'd like to, I don't attack her with my mouth. Instead, I sip at her, enjoying her sweetness and the way she writhes, her hips unconsciously bucking as she searches for my tongue. I lick over her entrance, up to her clit, circling there slow and easy, driving her higher and higher.

When she's ready, I give us both what we want. I suck at her clit, battering it with my tongue as I slide two fingers inside Janey. She cries out in pleasure, one of her legs falling off my shoulder, which only opens her center for more. She reaches for me, her short nails glancing over my shoulders, where she grabs my shirt in her tiny fists.

I stroke into her hard and fast, adding a third finger, which she takes easily when I tease her clit with my thumb. And she shatters in a powerful orgasm that soaks my hand and has her crying out my name.

I can't wait any longer. I need her. My Janey. A dark desire to have her pussy wrapped around my cock like her hands are wrapped around my heart takes over my mind and body.

I jerk back off the bed, nearly ripping my clothes off. Janey's floating back to Earth and watches me with hazy eyes as I take myself in hand for two tight strokes. But that's all the restraint I have. I climb onto the bed over her, lying in the cradle of her bent legs and aligning with her entrance.

One thrust forward and we're joined again. I groan at the delicious feeling. I'm home, where I belong, inside her. Resting on my elbow, I hold her hip, imagining I can feel the lines of her floral tattoo beneath my fingertips, and she squeezes my waist with her knees. Nose to nose, I stroke into her, trying to stave off the inevitable because I want to stay like this forever.

"I love you," Janey says suddenly, her eyes boring into mine.

"Say it again."

"I love you. I love you," she repeats with every deep plunge I make into her. Her arms wrap around me, hugging all my broken parts together, and I'm gone, lost in her. A tingle starts low in my gut, my whole body going tight.

"Janey," I grunt as I explode, shooting jets of hot cum deep into her pussy.

Her answering cry inspires me to keep going, pumping into her shallowly so that I'm grinding over her clit and keeping my cum deep inside her. "I love you too."

She might not need my words, but she appreciates them, and when she blinks, her eyes look extra shiny like she's on the verge of tears. But the pleasure wins out and a second later, her eyes roll back in her head as she spasms beneath me. I feel the waves of her orgasm as her pussy pulses around me, and I guide her through it, prolonging it as much as I can.

Any other time, I'd spread our combined cum over her clit and demand one more orgasm for her, but I can't break the connection we have right now. I want to stay inside her as long as I can. Forever, if she'll let me.

Gathering her in my arms, I roll us, keeping her impaled on my cock as she drapes over me. But when I check to make sure she's comfortable, I can see the tears starting to fall.

"Janey?" I ask gruffly, not sure what's wrong but already wanting to fix it.

She smiles through her tears and explains, "I'm so happy."

The knot in my chest relaxes, and I smile back, telling her, "Me too."

We lie like that for hours, her head on my chest right over my heart, which beats for her, and my hands tracing over her skin, memorizing every inch. Eventually, she falls asleep in my arms, but I stay awake, listening to her cute little snores.

I'm the luckiest bastard alive. I don't know how or why Janey was able to see beneath my asshole exterior and find a tiny pocket of goodness deep in my soul, but I'm so fucking glad she did. Only now, with her in my arms and in my life, do I realize what a shell of a man I was. But she's filled me up with her sunshine and her love.

And I can't imagine a day without her.

TWENTY-NINE

"FIVE MORE MINUTES," I mumble. My face is smushed into my pillow, and though he's not in bed with me, I smell Cole's cologne on the sheets.

Knock. Knock. Knock.

I frown with my eyes clenched shut, listening as I process what I'm hearing. The shower is on, so that must be Cole. But that other sound? Still half-asleep, it takes me an embarrassingly long time to realize it's someone knocking on my front door.

I sit up in bed, grumpy at the too-early intrusion. Everyone knows I like to sleep in on the weekends, and given my weekday early alarms, it's perfectly reasonable to sleep until nine on the two days a week that I can.

But apparently, not today.

I get up, grabbing my robe and pulling it on as I walk into the living room.

Knock. Knock. Knock.

Whoever's impatiently banging on my door must have a death wish, or a sales quota that they have to meet today. But newsflash, I'm not buying. Unless it's Girl Scout cookies.

Tying my robe, I open the door. And nearly slam it right back closed. But I'm too late.

"Geez, Janey, I thought I was gonna die of old age out there before you opened the door," Mom snipes as she walks into my house uninvited.

I'm not ready for this. I'm half-awake, uncaffeinated, and don't have my guards up. "Well, it's nine in the morning," I answer.

"Exactly. The day's half-gone and you're being lazy. It looks like you've barely gotten out of bed." Her eyes rove over me, and unconsciously, I run a palm over my head to smooth my hair down. I'm sure it's frizzy and wild, especially with the way Cole had his hands in it last night.

"I was asleep and not expecting company."

Mom waves a hand dismissively. "Is that coffee I smell? You should offer guests a drink." She doesn't wait for me to do as instructed but rather follows her nose to the kitchen where Cole has apparently already made coffee for us. "Where are your mugs?" she asks, opening and closing cabinets.

I open the cabinet over the coffee maker, because of course, that's where the mugs are, but opening that one wouldn't have let her snoop in all the other ones. I take out two mugs and fill them with skinny pours of coffee. Mom won't need more because she won't be here that long. Hopefully.

She grabs the milk from the refrigerator, checking the date with a frown on her face, seeming disappointed that it's fine and not expired. "Are you grocery shopping today? You barely have any food in the fridge." Yeah, even with relatively fresh milk, there's still something I'm doing wrong to complain about.

"What do you want, Mom?" I ask curtly. The time for polite manners is long past and this conversation is way overdue.

"That's no way to speak to your mother," she replies with a sharp look as she takes a sip of her coffee. Then she peers down into the depths of the mug, sneering like it's dog water, not freshly-brewed dark roast.

How did I do this for so long? Even her voice sets me on edge, making my flight or fight response kick in. I can feel my heart starting to race and the sleep fog clearing from my brain.

Fine. Let's do this.

I'm not ready, but in a way, I am.

I don't apologize the way she expects. I stare back blankly, giving no reaction, which is what she really wants. I don't think it even matters if it's an emotionless apology, a sniveling beg for forgiveness, or a bitchy comeback. Any reaction keeps the game going, and that's what makes her the winner in her book.

I'm not sure if she even realizes that. I don't think I've ever considered what she thinks or feels, too caught up in my own trauma. But I'm repairing mine, bit by bit, day by day. Mom's damage is her own to deal with. It's no longer mine to soothe, especially at my own expense.

Not sure what to do with the change in play, Mom sighs heavily. "Well, I'm sure you know you completely ruined Paisley's reception. It was her special day, but you had to make it about you the way you always do."

I gawk, in shock at her words.

Make it about me? Nothing, literally nothing, in my family is ever about me.

Mom's on a roll, doing a fair bit of rambling herself. "You've always been such a jealous girl—of Paisley, your other cousins, and even Jessica. But I thought you'd behave for a wedding, for Christ's sake. You owe Paisley an apology. Poor Glenda too. She's been calling nearly every day, crying about how ugly everything got and asking if you're ready to make it up to them. I've had to tell my sister ten times already that you're off sulking the way you always do."

Every word is a knife, sharp and precise. She's had years of practice, after all, and knows right where to stab to cause the most damage.

"I'm sorry—" I start, but she interrupts me.

"Don't tell me. It's Paisley and Glenda you need to tell," she says.

I take a deep breath and start again. "I'm sorry that I wasn't the daughter you wanted. But I was the one you had, and you never let me forget, not for a second, that I wasn't good enough."

She rolls her eyes and mumbles under her breath, "Here we go again. Poor, pitiful Janey."

I don't let her derail me. "Funny thing is, once I got away from you, I still thought I wasn't good enough. And I let that little voice in my head lead me into relationships that weren't right for me. But I've done a lot of thinking, Mom, and I want you to know . . . I do have value. I'm worth loving. Maybe not to you, but to an entire world of people out there, I'm loveable. More importantly, I love myself."

I think about Cole and the way he loves me with his whole heart. I think about the Harringtons, who I'm still getting to know but have welcomed me with open arms in a way my own family never has. And I think about my own sense of self and how it's grown exponentially.

I'm not the same Plainy Janey Williams.

"Okay, great. Glad you're all lovey-dovey. Now, call Paisley and apologize." She's sticking to her script and ignoring anything I say to the contrary. I didn't expect anything different. I've played this game before.

But this time, I'm not giving in.

I've grown too much, gotten too strong to care what Mom wants when she's never cared about what I needed.

"No." I don't shake my head, and I don't get loud. It's a simple refusal of a ridiculous demand.

Mom's brows climb her forehead as she looks at me like I grew a second head. "Excuse me, young lady? You will call your cousin and apologize like the polite, well-behaved woman I raised you to be."

I laugh bitterly. "You raised me to be obedient. You raised me to be a silent target. You raised me to accept abuse, neglect, and loneliness. You raised me to hide myself away. Well, Mom . . ." I take a deep breath and stare right in her eyes. "Fuck that!"

Okay, that maybe wasn't what I meant to say, but now that it's out there . . . *Yeah, fuck that!*

Mom recoils as if I slapped her.

But my mouth is off and running. "Paisley is a horrible person. She has been since we were kids. And everything that happened was karma coming back to kick her in the ass for always being so cruel. I hope Max got a really good look at his future with her as his wife and I hope he runs, far and fast, to get away from her. That's what she deserves."

Mom's jaw drops open.

"And how dare you show up uninvited, demanding this and insisting on that. In case you've forgotten, I got engaged. Not that you care." To me, that's the ultimate show of where her priorities lie. She met Cole, watched him propose to me, and then hasn't said a word about it. Didn't call, didn't text, and jumped right in this morning like that didn't matter.

She doesn't know it was fake then. She doesn't know that it's real now.

She just doesn't care . . . about me.

"What the *fuck* is going on here?" a voice bellows from the doorway.

Mom and I both jerk our eyes over. Cole is standing at the edge of the living room in athletic shorts and nothing else, his chest still damp from his shower. He probably heard me yelling and came running. Actually, I think the water is still on in the bathroom. That's how fast he responded to my distress.

His eyes are hard and cold. Asshole Cole is here now, ready to protect me if need be. But I need to do this myself. I meet his gaze, silently letting him know that I've got this.

Still, he comes to my side, making me feel safe and loved without a single word and glaring openly at Mom, who's ready to play the victim because the last thing she wants is an audience that's on my side. "Cole! I'm glad you're here. Janey's refusing to apologize to Paisley—"

"Why would *she* apologize? Janey should be pressing charges against Paisley for assault."

"Wha—" Mom utters. But then she shakes her head and tries to downplay the bouquet beatdown like it was a simple misunderstanding. "It was nothing. Just an emotional day . . . for everyone." It's the smallest allowance on her part, a teeny-tiny admission that *maybe* Paisley was a tad bit responsible for the fight. And she didn't say it because she thinks it's true or to appease me, but to placate Cole.

"She left a mark on Janey's face," Cole informs her icily.

They stare each other down for a long moment, and I watch, on the outside but seeing clearly from this vantage point for the first time.

"Mom," I say, getting her attention. "I'm done. You need to leave now."

I don't mean with this conversation. I mean with . . . her. With my family.

There's so much bottled up inside me, underneath the silver linings and sunshine, where I hid the dark thoughts about my mom. About my family. But bringing them out for her won't do either of us any good. I'm not going to give her ammunition she'll use against me, spreading gossip around to the family about me, and I'm not going to deal with that pain in front of her. She hasn't earned my trust that way. In fact, she's proven herself untrustworthy with my heart over and over.

And I'm done.

Like a switch.

"Janey—" she says, the condescension obvious in only the two syllables.

I shake my head and look at Cole. It's all the signal he needs.

"You heard her. Get out. Now." His tone brooks no argument, and he takes the coffee cup from in front of Mom, dropping it into the sink with a clatter.

Mom frowns. I think this is the first time she's actually hearing me, and it's because Cole is repeating what I've been saying all along. "Well, I never—"

"Go, Mom." My voice is steady and hard. My hands are shaking and ice cold.

She whirls, heading for the door. "I need to get home, anyway. Jessica has a hair appointment today." She's trying to make it sound like leaving is her choice, but we all know the truth.

Cole beats her there and opens the door for her, not gentlemanly like he does for me, but rather so he can glare at her as she walks past. I get the feeling he could spout off some details Mom would rather keep private, kinda like he did with Samantha's dad, but he doesn't. He doesn't have to fight this battle for me. I've done it on my own this time.

And it feels good.

Still, when Cole closes the door behind Mom and immediately rushes back to me, I fall into his embrace. He holds me, running a soothing hand up and down my back as I let all of the emotions I've held back for years escape. The tears are bitter and hot as they track down my cheeks. But as many bad memories as there are, I also remember the few good times too. They were like beacons of hope during the darkest times. But those exceptions don't change the truth.

"You okay?" Cole asks after a while when my sobs subside. He moved us to the couch some time ago, and I'm sitting sideways in his lap with my head on his shoulder.

I sniffle and nod. "I'm sad, but also, I feel . . . free?"

It's the closest I can come to describing the chaos in my mind and the tornado in my heart.

He's quiet, thinking that over, and then finally says, "I can't imagine how hard it was to stand up to her, but you did it. I'm so proud of you."

I know he loves me, but his being proud of me feels good in a different way.

"I'm proud of me too," I whisper.

And that feels best of all.

CHAPTER 30
JANEY

"YOU SWEAR you're not kidnapping us and taking us to a mass burial plot in the woods so you can be the sole heir of Dad's company?" Kyle questions Cole with one brow lifted high and one brow dropped low. He sounds like he might be serious, but I can see the laughter in his eyes.

"Is that an actual concern?" Gabriella laughs, but she looks at me in alarm.

It's a valid question. We gave everyone less than two weeks' notice, rented a party van for transport, and now, we're bumping along a dirt road with trees scraping the sides of the vehicle. Plus, it's Cole, and while the family knows what he does now, the hitman jokes haven't stopped.

"No, of course not," I reassure my boss-slash-friend. "Just your everyday, run-of-the-mill destination wedding."

That's not exactly true. Cole and I decided we didn't want to wait and didn't want a big fuss. I actually got the idea of where to get married from Samantha and Chance choosing their club as their venue. Which is why we're on the way to the cabin. Not the small one Cole and I shared, but rather the larger, fancier one Mr. Webster rented.

"In the middle of nowhere," Kyle adds, not helping Gabriella feel more comfortable.

Thankfully, the dirt road dead ends into the driveway for the cabin, and I shout, "We're here!"

We climb out of the van and walk up to the front door, waiting while Cole unlocks it and welcomes everyone inside. It looks exactly like it did through the binoculars—warm colors, lots of greenery, and . . . wait a minute . . .

"How'd you do this?" I ask Cole, looking at the charcuterie spread laid out on the oversized kitchen island.

He smirks and drops a big, fake, conspiratorial wink. "I've got people."

A simple answer, but remarkably true now. Cole does have people. An entire family, in fact, who are excited to be here for our special day.

I didn't call my parents to tell them about the wedding. Actually, I haven't talked to them since Mom showed up on my doorstep and probably won't. It hasn't been that long, not really, but being no-contact has been such a relief. I just let go. Which sounds easy and sometimes is. I'll have week after week when I don't think about them at all. And then something will remind me, and I'll have to decide again . . . don't call. And that's hard.

But it's not worth ruining my happiness for, and that's what they'd do. The price to be a part of that family is too high, and I won't trade my joy for theirs.

People who are happy that I'm happy are here, surrounding Cole and me as we take a big step toward forever, and that's what I want.

"Okay, go get ready, you two," Miranda orders as she shoos Cole and me off to separate bedrooms. "Gabriella, can you help me with the champagne?"

Gabriella nods, glad to be put to use, and the two women head to the kitchen. Who needs a wedding coordinator when you've got Miranda Harrington at the reins? I'm glad to have her help, though, and wonder if she's one of the 'people' who helped Cole.

In the primary bedroom, Kayla helps me change into my dress, and when I look in the mirror, I can't believe it's me. My hair and makeup were done this morning before we left and are perfect, my curls bouncing and my eyes subtly made up. The dress I chose is exactly what I wanted for a woodsy, forest-y wedding, with long sleeves, a deep V-neck, and lace flower appliqués on the bodice.

"I look like a bride," I murmur, mostly to myself.

Kayla smiles, amused at my reaction as if this is the first time I've ever seen this dress, but she dabs at her eyes. "You do. You look stunning, and if my brother doesn't tell you so, I'll gouge his eyes out with one of those tiny cocktail forks." She points out toward the kitchen and presumably, the forks, but rather than sounding threatening, she's choked up.

"Oh, my gosh, I'm ready. I'm so excited. Let's do this! I'm getting married!" I gush, hitching up my skirt and beelining for the door.

Kayla stops me. "Whoa there, girl. Let me see if Cole's ready and get everyone to their places. There is a process to this, usually, you know? A method to the madness?"

Oh, yeah. There is supposed to be a sort of timeline to things today.

She leaves me in the bedroom for a few minutes, presumably to get everyone and everything set outside, and then peeks her head back in. "Still ready? Haven't changed your mind? Because no refunds, exchanges, or returns on that model. He'd probably just stalk you, anyway," she teases with a smirk.

I nod, already on the verge of tears. Happy ones, but I don't want to ruin my makeup.

"I'm really excited to have another sister," she says, but before I can answer, she closes the door.

Shit! I'm crying. I always wanted a sister, and now I'm getting three of them. Kayla, Luna, and Samantha have accepted me into their trio with open arms and kind hearts. There's no drama, no backstabbing, no gossip. They're genuinely good people. And they're all different, and awesome because of it. One of my life-long wishes is coming true today with them.

I dab at my eyes with a tissue and take a deep breath, then open the door to the rest of my life.

―――――

Cole

Standing on the back deck overlooking a lush, green forest, surrounded by my family, is not something I ever would've predicted. But more surprising than that is the beautiful woman walking toward me with both tears and a smile on her face.

I've come to learn how to read those tears, and they're good ones. They're tears that say she's right where she wants to be and that she's ready for forever. With me.

She's stunning—her red curls a halo, her gray eyes bright, her hands gripping a small bouquet of white flowers for dear life, and her white dress flowing down to swirl around her ankles.

I'm tempted to go meet her halfway but force my feet to stay in place and let her come to me because that feels important. I want her to have her moment of being the center of attention for everyone, not only for me.

She'll be the center of my universe for the rest of our lives.

In a few more steps, Janey's in front of me. She hands her bouquet to Mason, her man of honor, and I whisper, "You look beautiful."

"You do too!" she whispers back.

Everyone's quiet, so they hear us both and laugh, which makes Janey blush. A year ago, I would have been pissed, but I've learned to read the laughter too. It's the laughter of love.

When Janey looks around, she sees Gabriella holding up an iPad with a whole group of people from The Ivy on the screen. They couldn't come but wanted to be here for us both, so live streaming it was a way to share with them. "Hi, guys!" she says, waving to her coworkers and patients, who wave back. "I'm getting married!"

They laugh, and there's some chatter, and I'm pretty sure I hear Ace's voice in the mix, "Protect the queen, kid."

He doesn't mean on the chess board. He's talking about

Janey, protective of her in a fatherly way even now, and I nod, having every intention of doing just that.

Janey turns back to me and we join hands. We decided to marry ourselves, and luckily, our state allows that, so there's no officiant to make a big speech. It's simple, it's us, and that's enough.

I swallow thickly and start. "I suck at words. And people. And talking to people. But you didn't care. You climbed right into my cold heart and poured your sunshine in, making yourself at home there, fixing it with your love. You became my family and then gave me mine back."

I risk looking away to scan the people around us. Mom is crying quietly, Dad's stoic with his arm wrapped around her, Kayla's smiling through happy tears of her own, and my brothers are tight-jawed. We're such carbon copies of each other, and I don't know how I didn't see that before.

To Janey, I finish, "I vow to love you the way you deserve to be loved—wholly, intensely, with kindness, and my full attention. I will devote my days to your smiles, my nights to your dreams, and my life to your happiness. I love you, Janey."

I exhale, relieved. I did it.

"Wow," she breaths as tears run down her cheeks. I swipe them away gently, placing a kiss to each cheek. "You are good with words."

I can't help but beam at the praise. If only she knew how many scribbled napkins, papers, and deleted notes on my phone it took to write those few sentences for her.

"Okay, my turn." She fans her face, drying her eyes as she blinks. "I should've gone first because I don't know if I can say everything I want to say now. I'm all . . . *whoo!*"

It takes her a few seconds, but she gathers herself and her thoughts. She takes my hands back, holding them tightly as she speaks.

"At one of my lowest points, you picked me up, dusted me off, and propped me up when I couldn't stand on my own. You made me feel special. You showed me I had worth and was valuable, exactly as I was. And when I could finally stand alone, you stood *with* me, not in case I failed but because you wanted a front-row seat to see me rise. Out of all the people in the world, no one has ever chosen me, but you did. You chose me."

She sniffles, and I gaze into her eyes, acutely aware of the healing she's done and the hurts she's let go of.

"You think you're hard to love, but the truth is, loving you is the easiest thing I've ever done because we belong together. You're my home, and I'm yours." She places my hand over her heart, where I can feel the steady thrum of her heartbeat, and lays her palm on my chest. "And I vow to spend forever telling you how much I love you until you have no choice but to believe it, because it's the truth. I love you, Cole. With my whole heart, for my whole life."

She takes a breath, and to be fair, I'm not sure whether she means to say more or not, but I need to kiss her. Right now.

So I do.

Stepping forward, I cup her face in my hands, feeling her cheeks puff up in my palms as she smiles, and we seal our vows with a kiss.

"Whoo-hoo!" Kyle shouts, the echo reverberating through the woods.

"Congratulations!" someone else says.

Of course, there's a lot of clapping from our family. Because these people, all of them, are our family now. Janey is a Harrington, and as complicated as our family may be, we're going to be the best family she's ever had.

EPILOGUE

COLE

"THIS SEEMS LIKE A REALLY BAD IDEA," Mom warns, sounding exactly like a worried mother should.

But I'm sure about this.

I take Janey's hand, and we walk down the steps off the back deck of the cabin and into the surrounding woods together. I told her to let me figure out the honeymoon, and I knew exactly what to do, especially when we decided to get married in the larger cabin next door. So our family and friends are getting back in the van to return to the city, but Janey and I are going back to the place it all began.

The little cabin with a loft bed, a hot tub on the deck, and a surprise waiting for Janey.

"Watch out for poison ivy!" Kayla shouts after us, and Janey laughs as she throws her a thumbs-up.

Far out from the cabin, where we can still see our family watching us, I pause and wrap my arms around Janey.

"This spot is when I knew," I tell her as I look around, smiling. "You sought me out and came to check on me. Nobody'd ever done that before. But you did, with your smiles and sunshine. Right here is when I knew I loved you."

"You did not," she argues, laughing. "You thought I was an annoying nutjob who wouldn't shut up when you were trying to work."

I tilt my head and grin. "Okay, that too. But deep down . . . *way deep* . . . I knew."

She looks overhead like she's searching for the owl we saw that first day, but it's nowhere to be seen. "I didn't know here. I thought you were handsome but stupid, going out without bear spray." She shrugs like she's embarrassed by the truth. "I figured it out at the cabin on the porch. You didn't kick me when I was down. You fed me. That's when I knew."

Such a small gesture, but to Janey, it meant everything.

I place a kiss to her lips, both of us smiling. "Come on, I've got something to show you."

She thinks I mean my dick, and yeah, we'll definitely get to that. I can't wait to be with her as husband and wife for the first time. But I really do have a surprise for her.

We walk up the back stairs of the little cabin to the deck Janey was talking about, and she makes eyes at the hot tub, pointing at it. "I've got plans for you," she tells the water. "Lots of plans."

I lead her inside to the living room and place her directly in front of the fireplace where she can see the new, huge photograph hanging there.

"It's our owl!" she exclaims as she whirls to face me. "Is that the picture you took?"

I nod as I glance up at it. "I'm no nature photographer, but I thought it was pretty good."

It wouldn't matter if it was blurry as fuck. I think Janey'd still love it. And because she does, I do too.

"Does Anderson know you changed out his artwork?" The devil in her eyes says she doesn't care what Anderson does or doesn't know.

But I shake my head and pull her closer. "No, because it's ours."

She looks at me, tilting her head in confusion. "What is?"

"The cabin," I explain, lifting one hand to gesture to the space around us. "It's ours. I bought it. Happy Wedding Day."

I sound a bit gruff, even to my own ears, but it's because this place is our escape now. When life gets busy or our family gets too needy with all the mandatory dinners, we can come here and it'll just be us. Janey and me.

Forever.

And there won't be a single bear in sight. Other than my grumpy self. But even that bear is a rare sight now that I have Janey.

My sunshine.

EXTENDED EPILOGUE

JANEY

Six Months Later

"Are you sure all that's necessary?" I ask even though I already know Cole's answer.

He quits tapping on his phone long enough to shoot me a glare with a bonus one-brow lift. "Yes."

Yeah, that's what I thought he was going to say, but still… "It's a safe neighborhood. You've checked out all the neighbors, the crime stats, and even the police and ambulance response times. All of which passed your requirements with glowing approvals. The regular security system was fine."

He sets his phone on the coffee table, the one where he's comfortably resting his feet because we decided to make my little ranch house our home. "It was fine, when it was the two of us. But with a baby on the way, fuck that. This place is gonna be locked down like supermax so I can keep you and him safe at all times."

Yeah, the reason why we chose to settle here is because we want our son to grow up in a neighborhood with sidewalks, yards, and friends. Cole's building – well, our building now – is great for work, but it's not exactly family friendly like this home is.

I can't fight the smile that steals across my face. I'm four months along, but every time I think about Cole and me having a baby, I smile. Well, sometimes I cry, but they're happy tears.

"Fine. Do I need to download the app too?" I say, giving in.

He smirks, picking up his phone again. "Already downloaded it for you and set up your account. You're logged in as L-O-M-L, wife. All one word, capital LOML and W."

Of course he did it for me. And called me "love of my life wife". And will probably do a quick show-me session later so I know how to work everything. Because that's how Cole is – sweet, protective, and likes taking care of me.

I look at my phone, finding the app easily. For such a high-grade system, with *alllll* the bells and whistles Cole wanted, the app is pretty user-friendly. I click around a little and then see something unexpected. "Cole? What's this?"

I spin my phone around, showing him the camera feed for the spare bedroom. It's going to be the baby's nursery. Or well, it was going to be, but apparently, it already is. He looks at me, his eyes sparkling with glee. "Go see."

I'm up, running for the nursery, and when I burst through the closed door, I stop in my tracks.

It's perfect. Everything I've talked about, shopped for, and pinned to my newly made 'Baby Board' on Pinterest... it's all here. The navy crib with the blue, white, and brown plaid sheets, the tan rocking chair, and even the bear watercolor painting on the wall to commemorate how we met.

"When? How?" I mumble, my eyes finding new details everywhere.

Cole comes up behind me and wraps his arms around my waist, his hands resting on my mostly-still-flat belly. "When you were at work yesterday. Kyle came over to help with the crib. I nearly killed him because he didn't want to read the directions, but if there's one thing you read the fucking directions on, it's the place where your baby's gonna sleep."

I'm crying. A lot. Happy tears stream down my cheeks and I whirl, burrowing my face in Cole's chest. "Thank you. I love you," I manage to say. Well, it sounds more like '-ank fu, ah wub u' but I think he understands because he holds me tight, running his hands up and down my back.

"I love you too, Janey."

I nod because I know.

———

Cole

I'm on my way home.

Home. I never had one of those. Not really. I had places I lived of course. Some of them were even fancy, but none of them were *home*. Until Janey.

The drive from the city to the suburbs is part of my day now, and I like it. It lets me leave the ugliness of my work behind so I don't bring it into our sanctuary. Our home.

When my phone dings with an alert, I'm not surprised. Janey said Mason was coming by to deliver some cookies she bought from his new girlfriend's daughter, who's a Girl Scout. But when I open the security system app, it's not Mason with a cute little kid cookie bearer. It's Mason plus another man, who admittedly are holding an insane number of boxes, but that's nothing I'd say to my pregnant wife. I have a life-wish, not a death-wish, and she can have as many cookies as she wants. I'll even dunk them in milk and feed them to her if she wants.

The stop light turns green, and I press the gas pedal, along with the sound on the house's camera. I trust Mason implicitly. Hell, he's kept an eye on Janey for me when I had to leave for an overnight stake-out, but the guy with him? I don't know him from Adam, which means I don't want him in my house, especially not with Janey.

"Hey Mason! Come on in," I hear Janey's voice. I'm eavesdropping and I know it, but I don't give a shit. It's my house too now. And she's my wife.

"Thanks. Janey, this is Ben. Ben, Janey," Mason says.

"Nice to meet you," she answers. I don't glance at the video feed, keeping my eyes on the road, but I assume she's shaking his hand.

"Wow! Mason said his friend was pretty, but he should've said gorgeous. Damn man, you holding out on me?" a male voice says.

That draws my eyes instantly. A quick scan of the full-color image shows that Ben is six-foot, dark hair, dark eyes, and smiling at Janey like he sees something he likes.

Janey takes her hand back and steps away, into the living room, where she glances up at the camera. I see her eyes. She doesn't like Ben any more than I do, and she's wondering if I'm watching.

Of course, I'm fucking watching. Just because we're married doesn't mean I don't still stalk her. Only now, she knows. And she likes it. Hell, I stalk her around the house sometimes. She calls it hide and seek. I call it find and fuck. Either way, it works for us.

Mason and Ben follow Janey. I watch as Mason sends Ben a 'what the fuck' look. He didn't say shit to Ben, who probably thinks he's a charmer.

"You can put the cookies right here," Janey tells the men.

They drop them to the coffee table and Mason says, "Thanks for supporting Troop 1204." He sounds ready to go, or at the least, ready to get Ben out of there.

"What's your favorite?" Ben inquires, not asking Mason. "Me, personally, I like the peanut butter sandwich cookies. They're so rich and thick, but still have that creamy center."

Why the fuck is this asshole making cookies sound like dirty talk?

Mason chuckles, "Man, you need to shut up. Now." He's trying. Gotta give him some credit for trying to save his friend.

But I'm close. One stop sign and I'll be home.

"I like Thin Mints," Janey answers, polite but cold in her work-professional 'this family member is annoying' voice. "Mason, I know you're busy today so I won't keep you. Thanks again for the cookies."

She's trying too. But she's too late.

I screech into the driveway, my phone dinging again as our dots converge at home.

I hear Mason say, "You fucked up, bro. You don't even realize what you're fucking with or how bad you fucked up."

"What?" Ben says.

And then I'm through the door. "Janey!" I shout.

She holds up her hand, waving her fingers at me in the cutest 'hi, honey, you're home' move with a happy-to-see-me grin on her face. She knew I was flying, breaking land speed records to get to her.

I scan her even though I saw her a second ago on the screen. She looks okay. Hell, she looks beautiful as always, but mostly, she looks uninjured and unbothered by Ben's inappropriateness.

I'm not.

I pin Ben with cold, dead eyes. "Get the fuck away from my wife."

He chuckles like I'm joking. I'm absolutely not.

He came into my home, with my wife, who's carrying my son, and made her uncomfortable by saying inappropriate things. And now he's going to try to play it off like he was really talking about cookies and I'm overreacting. Fuck that.

"Dude, chill," he tells me with a shit-eating grin. Ben has a death wish. It's the only explanation.

Mason steps in front of his friend, his hands up in surrender. "He didn't know. I didn't think I needed to explain that my friend is very happily married to a psychopath when we were only stopping by to drop off some cookies. My bad."

Janey comes to my side, curling up against me like a kitten. "You say psychopath. I say sweetie. To-may-to, to-mah-to." She's answering Mason, but I can feel her eyes on me and hear her smile.

I wrap an arm around Janey, squeezing her hip instead of killing Ben where he stands. "Get out. Now," I tell Ben harshly. To Mason, I add, "Take the peanut butter ones with you. Take them to work or something."

"Oh, that's a good idea," Janey offers. "Jackie and Pam would love those."

"Yep, on it," Mason says with a nod. He picks up a few boxes and shoves them into Ben's arms, who's looking from me to

Mason to Janey in confusion. Mason shakes my hand as he passes, silently apologizing for his friend, and then basically shoves Ben out the front door as he says, "See at work, Janey."

I kick the door closed and lock it behind them.

To Janey, I ask, "You okay? Really?"

She nods, "Yeah. He was flirty, but I'm yours. You know that." She looks at me with eyes full of love. I'm an asshole - a possessive, obsessive one - but I'm hers and she loves me just as I am.

I press a sweet, gentle kiss to her lips. Then, I growl, "Run."

She blinks once, then twice, and with a whoop of excitement, she runs straight for the bedroom. She knows what I want. Her. I want to fuck her, love her, brand her all over with my touch, and though she already knows it completely, I want to remind her whose she is.

She's mine. My wife, the mother of my child, and the love of my life.

So I chase her, catching her easily because she wants me to. Stripping both of us quickly because she helps me. Folding her over the bed where she sways that sexy ass to entice me, like I'm not already rock hard for her.

I trace my fingertips down her spine and she arches into my touch, lifting her hips. I bend down, licking through her folds and circling her clit with my tongue as I test her entrance. She's wet and despite Ben's hapless flirting, I know every drop of this is for me and me alone. I slip two fingers inside her, fucking her slowly while I watch with my cheek resting on her ass. She takes me so good that I add a third finger and go a little harder.

The doctor reassured me there was nothing to worry about, but I'm careful with Janey. She's carrying precious cargo. Our son.

I'm impatient to meet him, but I'm also excited to watch Janey grow big and round with every passing day. She's so sexy already, but that's only going to be sexier. The thought alone has me leaking pre-cum and needing to be inside her. Now.

But she needs to come first.

I tease over her clit with my thumb while fucking her with

my fingers, and the wet sounds of her pussy harmonize with the song of her moans. "Say my name when you come," I order.

A second later, she gasps, "Cole!" and shatters into a quivering, panting mess while looking back over her shoulder at me.

I'm behind her, notched at her entrance in the span of a heartbeat, and thrust into her. Finally home, where I belong. With Janey impaled on my cock.

I stroke slow and deep a few times, and then I'm can't hold back any more. I grip her hips, right over her tattoo, and fuck her. And when I explode inside her minutes later, I say her name too.

"Janey," I growl.

My wife. My life. My love.

Thank you for reading!

If you enjoyed Cole & Janey's story, make sure to read Carter/Luna's book, and Chance/Samantha's book!

ABOUT THE AUTHOR

Big Fat Fake Series:
My Big Fat Fake Wedding || My Big Fat Fake Engagement || My Big Fat Fake Honeymoon

Standalones:
The French Kiss || One Day Fiance || Drop Dead Gorgeous || The Blind Date || Risky Business

Truth Or Dare:
The Dare || The Truth

Bennett Boys Ranch:
Buck Wild || Riding Hard || Racing Hearts

The Tannen Boys:
Rough Love || Rough Edge || Rough Country

Dirty Fairy Tales:
Beauty and the Billionaire || Not So Prince Charming || Happily Never After

Pushing Boundaries:
Dirty Talk || Dirty Laundry || Dirty Deeds || Dirty Secrets

.

Printed in Great Britain
by Amazon